Praise for Robert Thorogood

'Very funny and dark with great pace.
I love Robert Thorogood's writing'
Peter James

'This second DEATH IN PARADISE novel is a gem'
Daily Express

'Deftly entertaining … satisfyingly pushes all
the requisite Agatha Christie-style buttons'
Barry Forshaw, *The Independent*

'A treat'
Radio Times

'Fans of the Agatha Christie-style BBC drama
DEATH IN PARADISE will enjoy this
book from the show's creator'
Mail on Sunday

'This brilliantly crafted, hugely enjoyable
and suitably goosebump-inducing novel
is an utter delight from start to finish'
Heat

'A brilliant whodunnit'
Woman

Robert Thorogood is the creator of the hit BBC One TV series, *Death in Paradise*.

He was born in Colchester, Essex, in 1972. When he was 10 years old, he read his first proper novel – Agatha Christie's *Peril at End House* – and he's been in love with the genre ever since.

He now lives in Marlow in Buckinghamshire with his wife, children and an increasingly cranky Bengal cat called Daniel.

Follow Robert on Twitter @robthor

The Killing of

Polly Carter

Robert Thorogood

ONE PLACE. MANY STORIES

HQ
An imprint of HarperCollins*Publishers* Ltd
1 London Bridge Street
London SE1 9GF

www.harpercollins.co.uk

HarperCollins*Publishers*
Macken House, 39/40 Mayor Street Upper
Dublin 1
D01 C9W8 Ireland

This edition 2022

2

First published in Great Britain by
HQ, an imprint of HarperCollins*Publishers* Ltd 2015

Copyright © Robert Thorogood and Red Planet Pictures Limited 2015

Robert Thorogood asserts the moral right to be
identified as the author of this work.
A catalogue record for this book is
available from the British Library.

ISBN: 978-1-84845-926-7

MIX
Paper | Supporting
responsible forestry
FSC™ C007454

This book is produced from independently certified FSC™ paper
to ensure responsible forest management.

For more information visit: www.harpercollins.co.uk/green

Printed and Bound in the UK using 100% Renewable Electricity at
CPI Group (UK) Ltd, Croydon, CR0 4YY

For Charlie and James

Prologue

Detective Inspector Richard Poole sat on the verandah of his beachside shack looking up at the cloudless Caribbean sky in inarticulate outrage.

A passing parrot had just crapped in his cup of tea.

It didn't seem possible, but Richard had watched the little bugger fly in over the sea and defecate in mid-air, the little ball of released guano flying in a perfect parabola only to land in his English Breakfast Tea with an accuracy, Richard realised, that Barnes Wallis could only have dreamed of.

In a spasm of disgust, Richard sloshed the contents of his china cup over the balustrade and tried to return his attention to the book he'd been reading. It was an old hardback he'd found at the back of the police station called *A Field Guide to the Insects of the Caribbean*, and he'd been fascinated by what he'd so far been able to learn from it. For example, he'd had no idea that the brightest bioluminescent insect in the world wasn't in fact the firefly, but was a species of click beetle that lived in the Caribbean called the Fire Beetle.

But it was no good, Richard couldn't settle back into his book, and instead he found himself glancing nervously back up at the sky every few seconds. After all, what if another parrot came for him out of the sun? Richard sighed heavily to himself. Honestly, when you got down to it, the Caribbean was a bloody nightmare from start to finish.

It didn't help that he had already been in a bad mood that morning, even before the aerial bombardment. This was because Richard had a secret. A deep and dark secret he'd not even dared mention to his team yet. In fact, as he went through to the little galley kitchen at the back of his shack to wash up his tea things, Richard decided that there surely couldn't have been another person on the whole island of Saint-Marie who was having as miserable a morning as him.

But he was wrong. There was someone.

This was because, just a few miles further along the coastline, a woman called Polly Carter was sitting in her kitchen wearing a bright yellow summer dress, drinking a freshly pressed glass of mango juice, and smoking a cigarette—and although she didn't know it yet, she only had a few minutes left to live.

Polly was forty years old and a fashion model famous the world over for a look that in person could come across as gawky inelegance, but, in photographs, translated into a gap-toothed beauty. Her face had adorned billboards, magazine covers, and a rock group had once written a chart-topping record lionising her looks. Not that Polly took much notice of the hubbub that surrounded her life any more. She'd been trawling up and down catwalks since she was twenty-two years old, she'd earned more money than she'd ever dreamed—had spent even more—and all she wanted now was a break from it all. Which, ironically, she was about to get.

The door to the kitchen banged open, and Polly's wheelchair-bound sister Claire was pushed into the room by her nurse, Sophie.

Claire and Polly were twins, although Claire was the older of the two by a few minutes. This should have created a special bond between the two sisters, but Claire was one of those older siblings who felt that it was her seniority that defined her entire relationship with her sister. So, because Polly was naturally impetuous, irresponsible, and had a wicked sense of humour, Claire was superior, overly responsible and felt that life was nothing to laugh about. This outlook was sharpened further by the fact that, following a riding accident ten years ago, Claire no longer had the use of her legs. It was no consolation to Claire that although she and her sister were non-identical, she was blessed with an uncanny beauty very similar to her famous sister's. But then, as Claire would remark to anyone who cared to listen, her and her sister Polly's supposed good looks only ever seemed to become apparent in fashion photographs, and who ever took fashion photographs of a cripple?

'Well this is a first, you're already up,' Claire said to Polly as Sophie finished pushing her over to the breakfast bar.

'Is that so surprising?' Polly asked, briefly thrown by her sister's tone.

'Well, you don't normally get up before lunchtime, so yes, I'd say it was a surprise.'

Polly was affronted.

'I don't just laze about all day, you know.'

'Oh you don't, do you?' Claire said with a disdainful laugh, and Polly looked at her sister a long moment before—very slowly—plucking another cigarette from the battered pack on the table and lighting it.

Once she'd taken a long, rasping drag from her cigarette, Polly said, 'Look, if you must know, I only got up this morning so I could spend some time with you.'

'Ha! Well, that's a first,' Claire said, still unable to take her sister at all seriously.

Claire's nurse, Sophie Wessel, was used to how Claire bickered with her sister Polly—and vice versa—so she tuned the two women out while she made some coffee for herself and Claire. It wasn't in her job description to make drinks for her client, but Sophie had soon learnt that Claire was one of those people who not only expected her nurse to push her wheelchair and help with all of the tasks she wasn't capable of doing herself, but she also felt that Sophie should act as her personal assistant and lackey.

Once Sophie had pushed the plunger down on the cafetière, she turned back to the room only to see Polly wheeling Claire out of the kitchen door and into the garden.

'Would you like a coffee?' Sophie asked the sisters before they left the room.

'No thanks,' Claire said. 'Polly says she wants to take me for a walk in the garden.'

'You do?' Sophie said, surprised. She and Claire had been house guests of Polly's for the last ten days, and Polly hadn't once offered to push her sister's wheelchair in all that time.

'I do,' Polly said with a tone that made it clear she expected Sophie to back off.

Sophie didn't want to get in between the two sisters, but pushing a wheelchair wasn't easy.

'No, really,' she said. 'Let me push Claire for you.'

'I said I'd be fine,' Polly said, irritation flashing in her eyes.

Sophie looked at Claire for guidance, but Claire just shrugged. She didn't seem to care one way or another. So Sophie kept silent as Polly pushed her sister out into the garden.

Once she'd been left on her own, Sophie finished pouring herself a cup of coffee, left the kitchen and went into the main hallway of the house. It was a large space with a wide wooden staircase that swept up to a minstrel's gallery that went around all four walls of the house, and led onto the various bedrooms, bathrooms and private suites upstairs.

But as she entered the hallway, Sophie hung back in the shadows because Polly's agent, Max Brandon, was already heading up the stairs, a bunch of files and papers clutched in his hands. Max was a thin man in his early fifties who was wearing round sunglasses with yellow lenses, a midnight-blue velvet jacket and burgundy cord trousers, and Sophie suspected he dyed his hair to keep it so lustrously black.

Sophie didn't much like him, but she made herself say, 'Good morning, Max,' to his retreating back. Fortunately for Sophie, Max didn't hear her—or pretended that he didn't hear her—and she watched him head up to the top of the stairs and disappear, she presumed, to his bedroom. Sophie was about to head for the stairs herself when she heard a shout from outside.

It sounded like a woman's voice.

Sophie looked through the large picture windows that overlooked the garden and saw Polly standing at the far end of the lawn shouting at Claire in her wheelchair. Sophie couldn't hear exactly what was being said, but it was clear that Polly was angry with her sister about something.

Sophie knew that while it was one thing for the sisters to be irritable in each other's company, it was quite another for the able-bodied Polly to take her wheelchair-bound sister into the garden and then start shouting at her.

There was a doorway in the corner of the hall that led straight onto the garden and Sophie went through it to see if she could intervene, but as soon as she crunched out onto the gravel path outside, Polly looked over at her. She then grabbed hold of the handles of Claire's wheelchair and pushed her further into the garden, soon disappearing beyond a large clump of bushes.

Sophie briefly hesitated. Polly's house—mansion, really—was built high on a bluff above the ocean, and

Sophie knew that the direction that Polly had taken Claire led to a sheer cliff face that protected a horseshoe-shaped bay and private beach far below. Sophie started across the lawn, but before she'd even gone half a dozen steps she very distinctly heard Claire shout 'Stop it!' from beyond the bushes.

Sophie looked back at the house. Had no one else heard or seen anything? It was hard to see if anyone was even looking out, such was the glare of reflected sunshine from the windows, but Sophie caught a movement at one of the upstairs windows. *Someone* was looking out at the garden, even though this person was in shadow, and she couldn't quite tell who it was.

A woman's scream pierced the air. Sophie's head whipped round. The scream had come from beyond the bushes in the direction of the cliff.

Sophie then very distinctly heard Claire shout, 'Oh dear God, someone help!'

Sophie broke into a run, and, as she got past the bushes, she could see Claire sitting in her wheelchair over by the top of the cliff where steps led down the cliff face to the beach below.

As for Polly, she was nowhere to be seen.

'Help me!' Claire screamed as Sophie approached. 'She just jumped!'

Claire turned her wheelchair away from Sophie and started racing off along the curve of the cliff's edge as it swept around the bay.

'What's going on?' Sophie asked as soon as she caught up with Claire.

'I couldn't follow her, she ran down the steps!'

As Sophie looked down to the beach far below, she finally understood why Claire had been pushing herself so desperately along. It was only this far around the curve of the cliff top that it was possible to look back and see the stone steps that ran in loose zig-zagging flights from the top of the cliff all the way down to the private beach a hundred or so feet below.

There was a body lying in the sand at the base of the cliff.

A body that was wearing the same bright yellow dress that Polly Carter had been wearing only moments earlier.

Sophie turned to look at Claire and saw that she was physically shaking, and her eyes were wide and staring as she replied, 'She said I was evil, she said I'd ruined her life…' Claire took a sharp intake of breath to allow herself to finish her sentence. 'She said she was going to end her life.'

'What?'

'She said it was all my fault. That she was going to end her life. And then she ran down the steps and jumped!'

Sophie knew that Claire could wait. As a trained nurse, she was needed elsewhere.

'Don't move,' she said, before starting to sprint back along the cliff top, her breath loud in her ears as she pumped her arms hard, knowing that every second of delay could be critical. She had to get to Polly.

Reaching the stairs that led down to the beach, Sophie didn't stop to think, she just barrelled down them—taking the uneven stone steps two at a time as she careened down the cliff, her arms out wide for balance, until her flip-flopped feet finally slapped onto the hard white sand far below.

Sophie took a moment to recover her breath. She then looked around to see if there was anyone nearby who could help, but the beach was entirely empty, perhaps unsurprisingly so. At this time in the morning, everyone else was almost certainly back at the house.

But Sophie could see that the body in the yellow dress was lying near the base of the cliff about thirty feet away.

It was Polly. And she wasn't moving.

Sophie strode across the sand as quickly as she could, but even as she approached the body, she could see that Polly's legs were splayed at an almost unnatural angle—she had an arm jammed under her body—and her eyes were closed.

Sophie bent down, put two fingers to Polly's neck and tried to find a pulse.

There wasn't one.

Sophie gulped.

She stepped back, looked back up to the top of the cliff and saw the tiny figure of Claire still looking down from her wheelchair.

Sophie cupped her hands to her mouth and shouted up, 'We need an ambulance! At once!'

★★★

At the same time that Claire pushed herself back to the house and Sophie turned the body of Polly Carter over to see if she could begin to administer CPR, Richard Poole was inside his shack having a shower. Or rather, in a world where the shower mixer provided him with periods of cold water interspersed with impossible-to-judge periods of water so hot it could sear skin, he was trying to time his dips into the shower so that he could wash his hair without getting third-degree burns. And it was just as he was waiting for the next pulse of boiling water to hit him—with his eyes scrunched up against the shampoo already dripping down his face—that Richard felt something skitter up his leg and then stop at his knee.

Richard froze.

There was a creature on his leg. And he was completely naked. His hand reached ever-so-slowly for his towel so he could wipe the soap from his eyes and finally see what stinging scorpion or venomous spider had just run up his leg. But before he could reach his towel, the creature started running upwards again and Richard opened his eyes against the screaming pain of soap, saw a bright green lizard racing up his thigh—a lizard that Richard had been sharing his shack with ever since he'd first arrived on the island, and who, in more innocent times, he'd thought it would be amusing to name Harry—but before the creature could reach the danger area of Richard's groin, he grabbed up his towel, swiped, missed, slipped on some soap, and fell arse over tip to the floor.

As Richard lay bruised and panting on the floor of his shower room under a stream of water that was sometimes freezing cold and at other times boiling hot, the sting of soap still in his eyes, and with a crushing sense of defeat from being once again outwitted by a reptile only eight inches long, he decided that yes, now he was surely the unluckiest person on the whole island of Saint-Marie that day.

And he was still wrong. Because that honour belonged to the world-famous supermodel, Polly Carter.

Because it was the day she was pushed from the top of a cliff, fell nearly a hundred feet to the hard sand below, and broke her spine and neck on impact, dying instantly.

It was the day Polly Carter was murdered.

Chapter 1

Richard Poole's dark secret was that his mother Jennifer was about to arrive on the island. Why on earth she'd chosen to visit on her own, Richard had no idea, but he also had no idea how he was going to get through two weeks of keeping her company, and that seemed the more pressing problem.

It's not that Richard didn't like his mother. In fact, if he interrogated his feelings, he knew that he must even love her, it's just that she was so perfect that he found her company exhausting. Her clothes were perfect, her friends were perfect, her whole life was perfect. She didn't complain, she didn't even express her feelings as far as Richard could tell, she just got up before everyone else, did more than everyone else, and then retired to bed once she'd done all the cleaning and tidying up and made sure that everyone else had turned in first.

If even a single thread stuck up from any of the immaculate plush carpets in her home, Jennifer would get down on her hands and knees and use nail scissors to give the individual thread a haircut. And after she did the washing up—always wearing washing-up gloves, of course—she'd then put on a second pair of washing-up gloves so that she could wash up the first set of washing-up gloves—unaware, Richard thought, that she risked falling into a logical feedback loop where she spent the rest of her life washing up the gloves she'd just used to wash up in. When Richard had tried to explain this to his mother, she'd smiled delightedly— 'You've always been so clever, darling'—and then gone off to plump up sofa cushions with her bare fists.

It was fair to say that Richard had a complicated relationship with his mother.

Far more so, in fact, than he did with his father. After all, his father, Graham—a one-time Superintendent in the Leicestershire Police Force—was entirely consistent in how he handled his son. No matter what Richard did, it always left his father disappointed. What was more, Graham was always the first to point that he'd done the same thing as Richard, but much better—or at an earlier age—or he'd chosen to go down a different path entirely.

So, when Richard was the first member of his family to be sent to private school, his father had managed to give the impression that it was only because no one thought Richard was clever enough to get into the local state-funded grammar school, where Graham had himself gone.

And as top scholar—a fact Graham managed to mention nearly every time he was alone with his son, which, if truth being told, wasn't that often.

Seven years later, when Richard got a place at Cambridge University, he finally felt that he'd proven to his father that he did indeed have a brain, but on the one occasion that Graham Poole visited his son in the three years he was there, Graham spent the day pronouncing that he himself had of course gone to the 'University of Life' where he'd learnt the real lessons in life, got the rough edges knocked off him quicker, and he'd not turned out too badly, had he?

When Richard announced that he was going to join the police force—as his father had done—Graham had sucked air in through his teeth as though Richard was making a very brave choice indeed. And then, when Richard threw a party to celebrate his promotion to Detective, his father was too busy at a local Rotary event to attend. His mother came, though, and did the buffet beforehand and hoovering afterwards.

In short, Richard would have been hard pressed to know which of his two parents he'd have more difficulty spending two weeks with: his dad, who always looked at him with such disappointment; or his mum, who always looked at him with such hope.

There was a loud honk from outside his shack and Richard snapped out of his reverie. His mother wasn't due to arrive on the island until later that afternoon, so who was that outside trying to get his attention? The car horn honked again. And, before Richard could even get up, it honked again another two times.

Richard's shoulders sagged. There was only one person on the whole island who'd so rudely interrupt his peace like this, so he went through his galley kitchen and opened the back door. Or rather, he tried to open the back door, but, as was typical, it was jammed shut by a build-up of sand on the other side. This was merely one of the almost infinite number of ways that the Caribbean tried to spoil his entire existence, Richard knew. All it took was a light breeze and a sunny day to loosen the individual grains of sand on the beach—and it was *always* a bloody sunny day—and whole dunes would start to build up against the walls of his shack.

Giving the door a proper shove with his shoulder, Richard finally got the door moving, the whole lean-to annexe to his shack shuddering as he finally managed to scrape the door open.

Richard briefly flinched at the sudden burst of sunlight—he never got used to how much sunshine there was in the Caribbean—but he saw that his initial suspicions had been correct. Detective Sergeant Camille Bordey was waving a happy hello to him from the driver's seat of the battered police Land Rover.

Camille's skin glowed in the sunshine, her hair was glossy and untamed, and she wore an electric-blue vest top, but Richard didn't much notice any of this, if only because he knew that the staff rota had Camille down as having a day off, so why had she turned up at his shack?

'Careful of that sand, sir!' Camille said with mock seriousness as he awkwardly picked his way across it. 'It might get into your socks.'

Richard knew that Camille found it incomprehensible that he insisted on wearing a dark woollen suit, polished shoes, a white shirt and a tie in the tropics, but, for him, the matter was a simple one. A policeman wore a dark suit, and Richard didn't see why he should have to lower his standards just because he'd been posted to the Caribbean.

'What are you doing here?' Richard asked.

'Oh, and a good morning to you, too,' Camille said, now a lot less jauntily.

'But it's your day off,' Richard said, unable to stop himself from glancing at his wristwatch to make sure his mother hadn't in fact landed on the island yet.

'What's up?' Camille asked, sharp as a knife, and Richard cursed silently to himself. His subordinate never missed a thing.

'Oh, nothing,' he said with what he hoped was insouciance.

'Why are you looking so guilty?'

'I'm not looking guilty.'

'You are.'

'I'm not.'

'You are.'

There was a long pause while both of them realised that the conversation wasn't going anywhere.

'I'm not,' Richard said.

'You are.'

'Look,' Richard said. 'Much as I'd love to continue this game of "You are, I'm not", can you please tell me what on earth you're doing at my house on your day off?'

Camille's jaw set in instant irritation, and Richard wondered what he'd done wrong this time. As ever, he found Camille's inner thoughts impossible to divine. On the one hand this was because she was female, spontaneous, passionate and always wanted to think the best of people, and—on the other hand—it was because she was French, which, Richard felt, was what military analysts would very much call a 'force multiplier'. So, as Richard stood sweating on the white sand in his Marks & Spencer suit, he genuinely didn't know how he'd managed to cause offence, and had even less of an idea about how to mend the situation.

'Okay,' Camille eventually said. 'I'll tell you what I'm doing here, but on the condition you tell me what that book is.'

Camille indicated the book in Richard's hand. He'd picked it up just before he'd left his shack. It was his intended lunchtime reading.

'Oh this?' Richard said, only now realising that the book wouldn't be that easy to explain. 'It's just a…you know, a field guide to the insects of the Caribbean.'

Camille's eyebrows rose at this news. 'I'm sorry?'

'I, um, I found it at the station, and I thought it would be fun to learn about the insects of the Caribbean.'

'You thought it would be fun?'

'Yes.'

'Learning about the insects of the Caribbean?'

'Anyway, I've told you what I'm reading. You've now got to tell me why you're here.'

'Oh,' Camille said, as though it were of no consequence. 'There's been a suspicious death.'

'*What?*' Richard blurted.

Camille grinned, and said, 'Sorry. Should I have said sooner?'

Richard dashed round to the passenger side of the police jeep, opened the door and climbed in.

'Yes you bloody well should have said sooner!' he huffed, belting himself into the passenger seat as fast as he could.

Camille watched her boss make sure that his buckle was properly clicked into its housing, then check there were no twists in the belt itself as it went over his shoulder, before then giving two tugs on the strap to confirm that the auto-lock mechanism was indeed working satisfactorily.

'Come on,' he said impatiently. 'What are you waiting for?'

Camille couldn't help but smile to herself as she put the jeep into a low gear and drove off across the bumpy sand in the direction of the main road.

★★★

As Richard walked into Polly Carter's house for the first time, he sneezed. This was because it may have been a grand villa in a stunning jungle setting—with orange-painted shutters to the windows, a bright blue front door and a red-tiled roof—but it was as messy as hell on the inside, and *everything* was covered in dust. Artefacts from Polly's world travels, random pieces of furniture, local artworks and stacks of old magazines, books and photos were piled pell-mell so that sharp-edged Perspex awards sat next to ancient tribal masks, the antique dining table had modernist chrome chairs arranged around it, and the walls were just as crammed with modern collages as they were with faded oil paintings.

But it was only when Camille showed Richard the garden that he knew the meaning of true horror, because he discovered that the house was built near a cliff, and he was now expected to walk down the stone steps that had been carved into it so he could reach the body on the beach below.

'But there's no safety rail!' he said as he stood looking at the Health and Safety nightmare that lay ahead of him.

'Come on,' Camille said. 'We need to get to the body. And it's not as bad as it looks.'

Richard looked at the stone steps again and saw that maybe Camille had a point. They were roughly hewn, but they were a good four or five feet wide. What's more, although there was a vertical drop to almost certain death if you fell over the edge, there was actually a little escarpment of dirt and scrubby bushes and thorns running along the edge of the stairs to give the appearance of safety. And to divide the challenge into more manageable chunks, Richard could see that the whole staircase doubled back on itself four or five times as it wound its way down the cliff face. In fact, Richard realised, even if he fell over the edge, there'd be a chance he'd perhaps have his fall broken by the stone steps on the flight of stairs directly beneath.

In conclusion, Richard decided, it was scary, but he could do it. It helped, of course, that he was wearing such sensible shoes, he kept telling himself in a repeated mantra as, arms wide, he took six or seven minutes to pick his way down to the beach far below.

Once there, Richard could see, with relief, that Sergeant Fidel Best and Police Officer Dwayne Myers were already working the scene. Or rather, he was relieved to see that Fidel was working the scene. Richard's feelings towards Dwayne were a little more nuanced. This was because, whereas Fidel was young, fresh-faced and lived and breathed correct police procedure, Dwayne had been on the force a number of decades, had refused every offer of promotion in all that time, and felt that following correct procedure was for 'other people'. For Dwayne, in fact, his work was only partly about catching criminals, because it was also about making sure he knocked off on time so he could take one of his many and apparently concurrent girlfriends out partying every night. And the problem for Richard was, much as he'd like to chastise Dwayne for his lax attitudes, on an island like Saint-Marie, it was often Dwayne who got the results, if only because he drank in the same bars as the island's dealers, grifters and general ne'er-do-wells. And, more improbably, he was accepted by them, to Richard's eternal frustration.

Richard saw that there was a churn of footprints in the sand that led from the bottom of the stone steps to the body—and a similar mess of footprints around the body where Fidel and Dwayne were working the scene—but there weren't any other footprints on the beach leading to or from the body. In fact, Richard could see, there weren't *any* footprints anywhere else on the beach. In particular, there weren't any footprints leading to or from the gently lapping sea in any way.

Having noted this, Richard said his hellos to Dwayne and Fidel and got down on his haunches to inspect the body. There was white sand stuck to the dead woman's cheek and hair, but he also noticed that, apart from that, her face seemed almost entirely undamaged.

'Sir,' Fidel said. 'You *do* recognise her, don't you?'

'The victim?' Richard asked.

'Told you,' Dwayne said with a deep chuckle.

'What on earth are you talking about?'

'Well, sir,' Fidel said, 'I know it's a bit disrespectful, but Dwayne here said he didn't think you'd recognise the victim, and I said that you would.'

Richard looked at his team and once again marvelled at how often he seemed to operate in an alternate universe to them all.

'What on earth are you both talking about?' he asked.

'You *really* don't recognise her?' Camille asked, just as surprised.

'No I don't,' Richard snapped. 'Because if I did recognise her, I'd have said that I did, wouldn't I? But I didn't, so I didn't.'

'It's Polly Carter,' Camille said.

'Right. Good. And who's she?'

'You really don't know who Polly Carter is?'

Richard jutted his jaw out. He didn't want to have to say it again.

'Okay,' Dwayne said, happy to act as peacemaker. 'She's one of the most famous supermodels in the world. And you've not heard of her?'

Richard looked at the body. He looked up again.

'Can't say that I have. Now,' he said, suddenly wanting to move the conversation on, 'could someone please tell me what we've got so far?'

Dwayne was grinning as Fidel flipped his notebook open.

'Well, sir, so the victim's name is Polly Carter. She's a top model. Or was. She's British by birth, and she's in the papers the whole time. She parties hard, gets into fights, and she's got houses around the world, but lives on Saint-Marie most of the year. There are a number of guests staying with her at the moment, but I've only managed to speak to a woman called Sophie Wessel so far. She's a nurse for Polly's twin sister.'

'Polly's got a twin sister?' Richard asked.

'That's right. Her name's Claire Carter. And her nurse, Sophie, said that Claire and Polly were in the garden together at about ten o'clock this morning when the two sisters started having an argument. Sophie doesn't know what it was about. But when she heard a scream, she went to find out what was going on and found Claire— upset—at the top of the cliffs, and Polly Carter dead—just here—on the sand below.'

'Any suggestion that Claire maybe pushed her sister off the cliff?'

'That's unlikely,' Fidel said. 'Claire's in a wheelchair. I don't see how she could overcome an able-bodied person.

And, according to Sophie, Claire's saying Polly had just announced that she was going to commit suicide before she ran down the cliff steps and threw herself to her death.'

'She did?'

'Apparently so.'

'I see,' Richard said, looking down at the body of Polly Carter as she lay twisted in death on the sand. Richard couldn't help but notice how at peace her face looked. Almost as if she were only sleeping. Richard looked up at the cliff that loomed above the body and tried to guess at the state of mind someone would have to be in before they could jump to their death like this. Despite the heat, Richard shivered.

'And were there any other witnesses to this suicide?'

'I don't believe any of the other house guests were nearby at the time, sir.'

'Then can you tell me who the other house guests are?'

'Of course,' Fidel said, turning to another page in his notebook. 'There's Polly's twin sister Claire Carter, I've mentioned her. Sophie Wessel is her nurse. She's been hired from an agency in London for the duration of the holiday. Then there's Max Brandon, Polly's agent and manager. And the film director, Phil Adams.'

'Phil Adams?' Richard had seen a few Phil Adams films before now and hadn't liked any of them.

'That's right, sir. Polly also employs a husband and wife team who live in a cottage in the grounds and look after the house when she's not here. Name of Juliette and Alain Moreau. But they were off at church this morning and have yet to return.'

'I see,' Richard said. 'So what have we been able to discover about the body?'

'Well, sir,' Fidel said, 'with a death from a height like this, it's hard to know what injuries were pre- or post-mortem until we get the results back from the autopsy. However, there is something we noticed.' Fidel got down on his knees and carefully turned Polly's right arm so that Richard and Camille could see the inside of her forearm.

There was a deep gash running five or six inches along the inside of her forearm—from just below her elbow to just above her wrist. But what got Richard's attention was the dirty tinge of green that seemed to smear around the edges of the cut.

'What's this?' Richard asked, indicating the green tinge to the wound.

'She's got green marks on her hands, as well, Chief,' Dwayne said.

Fidel opened the fingers on the victim's right hand and Richard could see similar green smudgy marks on her palm and fingers.

'Looks like she tried to grab hold of a bush or something on the way down,' Camille said.

Richard opened the victim's left hand and saw the same mossy markings on her left hand as well. Maybe Camille was right. The green marks on the victim's two hands and inside forearm—and the deep cut down her right forearm—were consistent with the victim having tried to grab hold of something woody before she fell.

Richard looked back up the cliff and didn't immediately see any kind of bush directly above the body that the victim could have clung to on the way down. However, with a cut as deep as that, Richard knew it would be easy to identify whatever it was she'd clung to. It would almost certainly have a good smear of the victim's blood on it.

'Fidel,' Richard said, 'I want you to work out what on the cliff face the victim grabbed onto before she fell.'

'Yes, sir,' Fidel said, seemingly unbothered by the fact that his boss had effectively just asked him to search a vertical cliff face.

For his part, Richard strode off to the base of the cliff, now interested in the horizontal distance the body had fallen on its way down.

Camille stood up from the body as well. 'So, what are you thinking?'

'That suicides don't leap,' Richard said, but Camille already guessed where her boss was going with this as Richard started to put one foot in front of the other to measure the distance the body had fallen from the cliff. It was a well-known fact that jump suicides tended to drop from whatever height they'd chosen to commit suicide from. They didn't leap out to their death. Although, Camille found herself thinking, if the victim had announced her suicide in a heated argument, maybe she'd run for the cliff edge and then jumped.

'Seventeen feet,' Richard announced as he reached the body, which gave him pause.

'Much further than you'd expect,' Camille agreed.

'Yes.'

'Maybe it wasn't suicide?'

'Indeed,' Richard said, once again checking his wrist-watch. It was still long before his mother was due to arrive on the island. There was every chance he'd be able to finish up here and still have time to meet her at the airport.

'Fidel, keep working the scene and supervise the removal of the body with the paramedics. Dwayne, I want you to search the victim's house. See if you can find any kind of suicide note. As for you and me, Camille, I think we need to talk to the witnesses, don't you?'

A few minutes later, Richard and Camille were in the sitting room of Polly's house and Richard was trying hard not to cough, because if the rest of the house was dusty, this room seemed to be where all the dust in the rest of the world came to when it wanted to die. The curtains, old sofas, stacks of books and piles of nick-nacks were all covered in a worn-in grime of ancient dirt, and Richard had noticed that when he shut the door, dust had fallen in a great cloud from the filthy crystal chandelier that hung in the centre of the ceiling and which was missing a good third of its pendants.

As Camille made the introductions and explained to the four assembled witnesses that the police had a duty to investigate all suspicious deaths on the island, Richard took the opportunity to give them all a once-over.

He could see that the victim's sister, Claire Carter, was sitting in her metal-framed wheelchair wearing beige cotton trousers, simple slip-on shoes, and a light blue cotton top. She had a similar slender build to her sister, similar high cheekbones, but Richard could see that they had very different hair styles. While Polly's hair was dark, long and unruly, Claire's was similarly dark, but it was cut into a tight and tidy bob that fell just below her ears. As for her demeanour, Richard could see that Claire had turned entirely in on herself, her shoulders hunched in grief, her head bowed as tears rolled down her cheeks that she dashed away with the back of her hands. It was a sight that Richard felt he'd had to see too often in his career. The grief of the family member who was left behind.

As for Claire's nurse, Sophie Wessel, she was a plump woman who Richard guessed was in her mid-to-late forties. She had a friendly face, wide, trusting eyes, and dark hair streaked with plenty of grey that was tied behind her head in a loose ponytail. She was wearing a long dark green dress, simple leather shoes, and she even had a watch pinned upside down on her dress just below her left shoulder. Richard could see that Sophie was holding one of Claire's hands while also not seeming to be that engaged with the situation, either. As a person who was paid to care for others, Richard felt he recognised the type. Sophie was caring and uncaring both at the same time. Like 'Matey'—the matron of Richard's boarding house at school—he thought to himself. Kind when she had to be, but only because it was her professional duty.

Then there was Max Brandon, Polly's agent. Richard could see that he was a thin man in his fifties who had an angular face under neatly parted jet-black hair—and he hid his eyes behind yellow-lensed sunglasses. A ratty looking man, Richard thought to himself. But what Richard found most interesting about Max was the way he was using the forefinger on his right hand to pick at the skin around the nail of his thumb. In fact, Richard could see that the skin around both of Max's thumbnails had been picked raw and Richard found himself wondering what it was that was making Max so tense?

As for Phil Adams, Richard guessed that he was also, like Max, in his fifties, but that's where all similarities ended. Phil was tall, broad-shouldered, and he looked entirely at ease. His hair was blond and glossy—swept back from his handsome face—and his eyes were crinkled with laughter lines. He wore a collarless white cotton shirt that Richard guessed came from a Jermyn Street tailor, knee-length khaki shorts—that Richard noted, with irritation, Phil was able to make look good—and an old pair of flip-flops.

Once Camille had finished the introductions, Richard said, 'Thank you all for waiting for us. Detective Sergeant Bordey will be taking your formal statements shortly, but first I just wanted to get a sense of what happened this morning. For example, I understand that you, Claire, were with your twin sister when she died. Is that right?'

Claire looked up at Richard, her eyes red-rimmed with grief.

'That's right,' she eventually said, still disbelieving the words she was having to say.

'Then perhaps you could take us through what happened?' Camille asked gently.

Claire thought for a moment and then slowly nodded.

'Of course. Well…I'd gone to the kitchen for breakfast this morning and Polly was already there.'

'What time was that?' Richard asked.

'I don't know. Just before ten, I suppose.'

'Thank you. And was that the first you saw of your sister today?'

'It was.'

'And how would you describe her mood when you saw her?'

'I don't know. She was her usual self. Somewhat snappy. Slightly irritating. But nothing out of the ordinary.'

'You didn't get on with her?'

'Not always. Although I think it's fairer to say that it was Polly who didn't get on with me.'

'And why was that?'

'We didn't have much in common,' Claire said sadly. 'Anyway, she said she wanted to take me for a walk in the gardens, so that's what we did.'

'And did you and your sister often go for walks together?'

Claire hesitated a moment before answering. 'Not really.'

'Had your sister in fact gone for a walk with you before?'

'Actually, no. We'd been out together of course, but only as part of a group. And always with Sophie in attendance.'

'Is that right?' Richard turned to ask Sophie.

'Yes,' Sophie said. 'Agency rules say I should be available to assist my client at all times, but Polly insisted that she go out with Claire this morning on her own.'

Richard and Camille exchanged a glance.

'In fact,' Claire said, equally puzzled, 'Polly was insistent she didn't want Sophie to come with us.'

'And do you know why she wanted it to be just you and her on this walk?' Richard asked Claire.

'I have no idea,' Claire said, 'but almost as soon as we got out into the garden, Polly started shouting at me. I've no idea where it came from. She just seemed to explode. Telling me how unhappy she was, and how her unhappiness was all my fault. I was shocked. I had no idea what she was talking about.'

'You didn't?'

'No. You see, we weren't that close. In fact, I haven't even seen Polly since last year.'

'I see.'

Camille turned to Sophie. 'So, if you were around at the time, did you witness this argument, Sophie?' she asked.

Sophie nodded. 'I did. I was about to go upstairs when I heard raised voices coming from the garden. It was Polly shouting at Claire.'

'Did you hear what was being said?'

'I'm sorry, I didn't. They were too far away. And when I went into the garden to see if I could help—or intervene—that's when Polly started pushing Claire towards the cliffs.'

'That's right,' Claire agreed. 'I saw Sophie come out of the house, and that's when Polly said something like "you're coming with me"—and she grabbed my chair and started pushing me really fast towards the cliff. And I can tell you, I was frightened. I was shouting at her to stop, but she wouldn't listen to me.'

'And I followed a bit,' Sophie said. 'You see, I still couldn't work out if I should intervene or not. And when I lost sight of Claire and Polly, I stopped altogether.'

'Why did you lose sight of them both?' Richard asked.

Sophie seemed surprised by the question.

'Well, there's a large bed of shrubs across that end of the garden. The steps down the cliff are just beyond it.'

'I see,' Richard said, looking at the room, and once again he noticed how Max was looking down at his hands and picking at the skin around his nails.

Phil cleared his throat to announce that he had a contribution to make.

'I can second all that Sophie and Claire are saying,' he said, entirely comfortable as he took the floor. 'You see, I was upstairs in my bedroom at the time. Working on my latest screenplay. And I heard a ruckus coming from the garden, so I went to the window and saw Polly shouting at Claire in the garden. And then, when Polly pushed Claire off to the bottom of the garden and disappeared behind the bushes there, I saw Sophie follow a little way and then stop in the middle of the lawn.'

'That's right,' Sophie said, remembering. 'I didn't know if anyone else was around to help, so I looked back at the house and I saw someone standing at one of the upstairs windows.'

'Well that's easy to explain,' Phil said with a tolerant smile. 'That was me.'

'What's that, Phil?' Max asked, speaking for the first time.

'It's not hard to understand,' Phil said in a condescending manner. Richard could tell that there was little love lost between Phil and Max.

'I was looking out of my bedroom window,' Phil continued, 'so if Sophie saw someone at an upstairs window, it must have been me.'

'But hang on,' Max said, licking his lips before he carried on. 'That would have been me she saw, because I was at the upstairs landing window and looking down on Sophie when Polly died.'

'You were?' Camille asked.

'That's right,' Max said. 'I'd just seen Sophie in the downstairs hallway.' Here, Max turned to address Sophie. 'And I'm sorry I didn't say hello back to you when you wished me good morning.' Max knew that this was an inadequate thing to say, but he turned back to address Camille. 'But Sophie can confirm that she saw me inside the house just before Polly died.'

Richard was intrigued. Why was Max trying to establish an alibi for the time of death?

'Is that right?' Camille asked Sophie.

'Yes,' Sophie said, not entirely sure where Max was going with his story. 'I definitely saw Max head upstairs just before I went out into the garden. And I said hello to him, but he didn't say hello back.'

'But the point is,' Max said, picking up the story, 'I was looking out of the upstairs landing window at the time of death. I saw Sophie in the middle of the garden. She was looking straight back at me.'

Richard could see that Sophie was frowning.

'Tell me, Sophie, was it Max you saw at the upstairs window? Or was it Phil?'

'I don't know,' she said. 'The sun was shining on the windows. And I can't remember precisely which upstairs window I was looking at. But I know I only saw one person.'

'Who must have been me,' Max said insistently.

'Rubbish,' Phil said. 'It was me Sophie could see.'

Sophie looked in confusion at Richard, hoping for a steer.

'Either way,' Richard said, not wanting his witnesses to get bogged down, 'tell me, Sophie, once you'd looked back at the house and seen someone at the upstairs window, what happened next?'

'Well, that's when I heard a scream,' Sophie said. 'An awful scream. And then, a few moments later, I heard Claire shout for help.'

'And did you see any of this?' Camille asked.

'Well, no. It was all behind the bed of shrubs. But I heard it.'

'And did you, Phil, see what was going on at the cliff top?'

'I didn't,' Phil said. 'Because it's like Sophie's saying. You can see the lawn from the house, but you can't see the cliff top. There's a bed of shrubs and bushes in the way.'

'And I couldn't see anything, either,' Max said, reminding everyone that he'd also been at an upstairs window at the time.

'But it doesn't matter who else saw what,' Claire said, and Richard could see from the look in her eyes that she'd just worked out that she was the only person who'd witnessed the death—and therefore the police were treating her testimony with suspicion. 'Because the thing is, I saw what Polly did once we were both at the cliff.'

'Yes,' Camille said, kindly. 'Then could you tell us in your own words what that was?'

Claire blinked back tears before continuing her story.

'Well, it was like she was possessed just before she jumped. I mean, she was angry with me when we first went into the garden, but by the time we got to the cliff top, she was going crazy. Saying how selfish I was. How I'd let her down. How I'd never understood the pain she was in. That sort of thing. And then she said she was going to kill herself—it was all my fault—and there was nothing I could do to stop her!'

Claire choked back a sob as she finished speaking.

'Then what happened?' Camille asked.

'Well, she…she ran down the steps a little way, and then, once she was around the corner, she screamed as she jumped.'

'What's that?' Richard asked.

'I'm sorry?' Claire said, looking at Richard, confused.

'You said that once Polly was around the corner, it was only then that she screamed and jumped.'

'That's right.'

'So she didn't jump from the very top of the cliff?'

'No. She went down the first flight of steps, and it was only when she'd turned around the corner that I heard her scream as she jumped.'

'So you didn't actually see the moment it happened?'

Claire seemed surprised by the question.

'Well, no. I suppose not. If you put it like that. But then, I couldn't follow her down the steps in my wheelchair, could I? So, no, I didn't see the exact moment my sister jumped to her death. Thank God for small mercies.'

Richard wrote this fact into his notebook and very carefully underlined it three times.

Richard next turned to Sophie. 'And you didn't see what happened, either, did you?'

'I'm sorry. No.'

'Which is interesting. Because it means we've only got one witness to what happened. You, Claire. And even you didn't see exactly what happened.'

Claire was quietly affronted. 'But I didn't need to see it. My sister said she was going to end her life. She then ran down the steps and I heard her scream as she fell. I didn't need to see it to know what happened.'

Richard turned from Claire to Sophie.

'So tell me, Sophie, how soon after you heard Polly's scream did you arrive at the cliff?'

'Oh, not long,' Sophie said. 'Thirty seconds? Something like that?'

At this, Claire turned her wheelchair around so she was looking directly at Richard, and he saw a look in her eyes he couldn't quite place. Was it defiance? Or even desperation? Why did she look so on edge so suddenly?

'But since you're so interested in what I saw,' Claire said, 'you should know that there was someone else on the cliff steps just before Polly went down them.'

This got everyone's attention.

'There was?' Camille asked.

'That's right.'

'And you didn't think to mention this before now?' Richard asked.

'You didn't ask,' Claire said.

'I see,' Richard said. 'So who was this person you saw beforehand?'

'Well, I think it was a man.'

'You *think* it was a man?'

'It might have been a woman. You see, I only caught a glimpse of the person as Polly was pushing me towards the cliff. But as we got to the top of the steps, I saw this flash of yellow as whoever it was went down the steps and disappeared around the first bend.'

'A flash of yellow?' Richard asked.

'That's right,' Claire said, finally warming to her theme. 'Because, whoever it was was wearing a bright yellow raincoat. You know, like a plastic cagoule. And the thing is, they had the hood up over their head so I couldn't see their face.'

'So you're saying that this person—whether it was a man or woman—was wearing a plastic yellow raincoat with the hood up, and was on the cliff steps just before your sister jumped to her death?'

'That's right.'

Richard knew what he had to do next.

'Would anyone here mind if Detective Sergeant Bordey now did a search of all your rooms to look for a yellow raincoat?' Before anyone could answer, Richard continued, 'Good. Camille, if you would?'

With a nod to her boss, Camille left the room, but Richard only had eyes for the four witnesses. Did any of them look particularly worried at the prospect of their rooms being searched? He had to admit that they didn't, so Richard turned back to Claire.

'You see, it strikes me as odd that someone would be wearing a raincoat with the hood up on a boiling hot day when there wasn't a single cloud in the sky.'

'Yes, when you put it like that,' Claire said. 'It does seem strange. But it's what I saw.'

'Then can I ask, if there was a person in a yellow coat on the cliff steps before your sister went down them, who was the next person to go down the steps after Polly?'

'That was me,' Sophie said.

'And how soon afterwards did you follow her?'

'I don't know, but it could only have been a minute or two later. When I got to the cliff, Claire was upset, and it was only when we saw the body on the beach that I realised what might have happened.'

'So you'd already seen Polly's body on the beach before you went down the cliff?'

'That's right. Claire had gone a little way along the cliff's edge. We were both able to look back at the beach from there.'

'Then did you see a person in a yellow raincoat anywhere on the beach when you looked down at Polly's body from the top of the cliff?'

Sophie thought for a moment before answering, 'I'm sorry, no.'

'Then perhaps you saw this person in the yellow coat on your way down to the beach?'

'I'm sorry. I didn't see anyone else on the steps. Or on the beach below. In a yellow raincoat or otherwise. When I got down there, there was just Polly's body. There wasn't anyone else.'

'But that's not possible,' Claire said. 'Because I'm telling you I saw a person in a yellow raincoat go down the steps just beforehand, you must have seen them, Sophie! Did you not see a flash of yellow at all? Maybe only after you got down to the beach?'

'It's unlikely,' Richard said. 'Even by the time my officers arrived at the scene, the only footprints we could find in the sand led from the steps to the body and nowhere else. So, if there was a "Man in Yellow" who went down the steps beforehand, he didn't go off and hide anywhere else on the beach.'

'Then perhaps they managed to hide on the steps themselves, Sophie,' Claire said.

Richard could see that Sophie was briefly conflicted. But only briefly.

'I'm sorry,' she said to Claire. 'I'm pretty sure there wasn't anyone hiding on the cliff steps, either. And definitely no one in a yellow coat.'

'But they must have been,' Claire said with shrill insistence. 'I know what I saw!'

Richard made a note that whoever Claire saw on the cliff steps before Polly's death—assuming, of course, she saw anyone—had somehow managed to vanish into thin air afterwards.

'Very well,' Richard said. 'Then can you tell me, Claire, did Polly have a cut in her forearm at all before she went down the cliff steps?'

The question threw Claire. 'A cut?'

'That's right. A deep cut about six inches long, running from the inside of her elbow down to just above her wrist,' Richard clarified, indicating on the sleeve of his right arm. 'It would have been bleeding quite heavily.'

'No,' Claire said. 'She wasn't bleeding at all. And her dress was sleeveless, I'm sure I'd have seen if she'd cut herself in any way.'

'Then what about you, Sophie?' Richard asked, turning to the nurse. 'You must have seen the cut on Polly's forearm when you found her on the beach?'

Sophie thought for a moment before answering. 'No... I'm sorry. I didn't notice any cut on her arm, either.'

Richard made a note. So there was no independent corroboration that the cut on Polly's arm had been inflicted before she fell. So when exactly had she cut herself? It couldn't have been *post-mortem*, could it?

Richard looked back at Sophie. 'Okay, so once you'd gone to Polly on the beach, what did you do next?'

'I established that there was no pulse in Polly's neck and then I called back up to Claire to phone for an ambulance.'

'That's right,' Claire said, 'but I didn't have my mobile phone on me, so I had to go back to the house.'

'I'm sorry?' Richard said, surprised.

'I...I didn't have my mobile on me, so I pushed myself back to the house and used the landline to call for an ambulance. That's when I saw Max coming down from upstairs and I told him what had happened.'

'That's right,' Max agreed eagerly. 'I saw Claire heading back across the garden, so I went down to meet her in the hallway. After she'd explained to me what had happened and was phoning for an ambulance, I went down to the beach and waited with Sophie until the ambulance arrived.'

'Then how about you, Phil?' Richard asked. 'When did you discover that Polly had died?'

'Well that's the thing,' Phil said. 'After I saw the argument in the garden, I went back to my work. I didn't want whatever was going on between Claire and Polly to distract me. And I carried on working in my room until I saw an ambulance arrive at the front of the house about half an hour later. That's when I came downstairs and finally heard the terrible news.'

'I see,' Richard said, realising that, putting aside which of the two men Sophie saw at the window when she looked back at the house, Max now had a definite alibi for just before the time of death—when he was seen going up the stairs by Sophie—and just afterwards as well—when he was seen coming down the stairs by Claire. As for Phil, seeing as Sophie's view of the person at the window just beforehand had been so vague, he didn't seem to have a definite alibi for before the time of death, or for the minutes immediately afterwards.

'But I don't understand why you're asking where we all were,' Max said nervously. 'Or wondering who this man in the yellow coat was. None of it's relevant, because we know what happened. Polly said she'd end her life, she went down the steps and then she threw herself to her death.'

'Indeed,' Richard said. 'And you raise an important point, so can I ask, how surprised are you all that Polly would end her life like this?'

Richard could see the witnesses exchange glances. He'd struck a nerve.

'If someone could answer the question,' Richard asked again.

'Well maybe I should take this,' Max said. 'As her agent. Because, if we're being honest, Polly's been depressed for some time. So one minute she was up, up, up, and the next, everything had crashed around her and she'd get destructive. She'd want to hurt you until she felt better.'

'That's what I meant when I said it was more that she didn't get on with me,' Claire said. 'She was difficult and wilful at the best of times.'

'But she didn't do herself any favours, either,' Max said. 'Because you should know, Polly was also a recovering drug addict, and that caused terrible mood swings as well.'

'And when you say drugs?' Richard asked.

'Heroin,' Claire said. 'She'd been using for years.'

'Your sister was a heroin addict?'

'But she checked herself into rehab earlier this year,' Phil said loyally. 'She's been clean since then.'

'And when was she in rehab?'

'It was six months ago,' Max said. 'Just after Christmas. She spent three months in a clinic in Los Angeles. And since she came out, she's been clean. I'm sure we'd have known if she wasn't.'

Max looked around the room, and no one disagreed with him.

'The point is,' Phil said, speaking for all of them, 'we can all imagine that if Polly wanted to end her life, this is the sort of crazy mad-arse way she might go about doing it. She always loved melodrama.'

Richard looked at the witnesses and realised he'd probably got enough from them for the moment. Although there was one loose end he needed to tie up before he could leave.

'Then thank you all for your time,' he said to the room, closing down the topic of Polly's drug addiction for the moment. 'But one last question. If you don't mind? Claire, are you really saying you didn't have your mobile on you when your sister died?'

'I'm sorry?' Claire said.

'Only, in my experience, people who have issues with mobility *always* have their mobile phones on them. Or some other form of emergency communication or panic button.'

'Well…that's true,' she conceded. 'I do normally have my mobile with me. I keep it in here.'

Claire indicated a fabric pouch that hung from the armrest of her wheelchair.

'But your phone wasn't in your pouch this morning?'

'I thought it was,' Claire said, increasingly confused that Richard was following this line of questioning. 'But when I looked for it on the cliff top, it wasn't there. It's why I had to go back to the house to phone for an ambulance. Like I said.'

'Can you tell me, where is your mobile phone right now?'

'Really?'

'If you could just answer the question?'

Claire huffed. 'Well, as it happens, I've not been able to find my mobile since then. To be honest, it's not been a top priority.'

'You're saying it's still missing?' Richard asked, unable to keep the eagerness out of his voice.

'That's right. I can't find it.'

'Then could someone phone Claire's phone at once,' Richard asked the room urgently. 'Then, if we can hear it ringing in the house, I want to locate exactly where it is.'

No one could quite see why this was important to Richard, but Phil pulled his smartphone from his pocket with a sigh.

'Very well,' he said sceptically, as he scrolled through his list of contacts. 'I'll ring it.' After pressing the screen, he waited a few seconds, and he then said, 'Right, then. It's connecting.'

After a moment, everyone could hear a phone ringing.

It was somewhere in the room.

And then, they all realised where the noise was coming from and looked up at the ceiling.

The chandelier in the middle of the ceiling was ringing.

Claire's phone was hidden in the chandelier above their heads.

What the hell was it doing there?

Chapter 2

It took a few minutes to liberate Claire's mobile from the chandelier. In the end, it involved Richard scraping a coffee table over to the middle of the room so that he could stand on it and fish into the chandelier with one hand, his other hand clamping his hankie over his nose against the clouds of dust he was creating in the process.

Once he had Claire's phone in his hand, Richard asked the assembled witnesses if they knew how it had got into the chandelier, but they were just as flummoxed as he was. It didn't even begin to make sense.

As Richard put the phone into an evidence bag for processing back at the station, he saw an old Citroën estate car pull up in the driveway with a crunch of wheels on gravel. He then saw a man and a woman get out.

'Who's that?' he asked the room.

'That's Juliette and Alain,' Phil replied. 'Polly's staff. I think they've been at church.'

Going to the windows, Richard could see that Alain was perhaps in his forties, was of average height, and had short-cropped hair. He was wearing khaki trousers, smart black shoes, a long-sleeved white shirt—and, as he carefully closed the door to his car, Richard got the impression that he was a man who liked everything to be precise and neat. As for Juliette, Richard could see that she was of a similar age to her husband, had a cascade of dark hair that was constrained by a pink bandana, and she was wearing figure-hugging grey Lycra running clothes with bright lime green flashes down the side. It was pretty clear that if Alain had just returned from church, Juliette had been out doing exercise of some sort.

Richard told the witnesses that Camille would take their formal statements in due course, but first he had to break the sad news of Polly's death to Mr and Mrs Moreau. If they hadn't already heard.

Once in the hallway, Richard bumped into Camille as she was coming down the main staircase. She told her boss she hadn't been able to find a yellow plastic coat in any of the bedrooms upstairs, or anywhere else obvious she'd been able to look. What was more, she hadn't found anything else of note, either. Although they'd have to do a proper search of the house later on.

'But you should see Polly's bedroom,' she said.

'Why?' Richard asked, puzzled.

'Because it's nothing like the rest of the house. It's tidy and clean.'

'It is?'

'You should take a look at it. You'll like it,' she said, with a twinkle.

'Unfortunately, we've got a more pressing job on our hands,' Richard said, and he explained how Juliette and Alain had just returned.

When Richard and Camille stepped out of the house into the blinding Caribbean sunlight, they could see that Juliette and Alain hadn't gone into their cottage yet and were instead looking at the police jeep that was parked in the driveway.

'I'll take this,' Richard announced, before striding off.

'Are you sure that's a good idea?' Camille said, knowing that her boss wasn't exactly the most sensitive when it came to breaking bad news.

But it was too late. Richard had called out 'One moment, if you please!' in his most hail-fellow-well-met voice and was already approaching the witnesses.

Camille caught up with Richard after he'd already made the introductions.

'But what are the police doing here?' Juliette asked bluntly, her hand on her hip.

Richard could see that Juliette was the sort of woman who was used to getting her own way. As for Alain, Richard was unsurprised to see only meek obedience in the man's eyes.

'Just before I answer that,' Richard said, 'can I ask where you both were this morning at about 10am?'

'Why on earth do you need to know?' Juliette said.

'If you could just answer the question,' Richard said in his 'police' voice, and Camille's heart sank because, while it was always useful to get someone's alibi before they knew why they needed one, it was hardly the kindest way of breaking the news that a friend had just died.

'Well,' Alain said, stepping into the conversation bravely. 'At ten this morning, I was at church.'

'And you, Mrs Moreau?' Richard asked. 'Were you also at church?'

'Dressed like this?' Juliette said dismissively, indicating her exercise clothes. 'No, I was in the middle of my run then. I'm training for a triathlon,' she said proudly. 'I then met up with Alain after the church service finished at about 10.30 and we went for a coffee together at a place called Catherine's bar. I'm sure you know it.'

Richard did indeed know it. It was run by Camille's mother—and his sometime nemesis—Catherine Bordey.

'But why do you want to know where we were?' Alain asked, his forehead furrowed with concern.

'Forgive us for not saying sooner,' Camille said. 'But I'm sorry to say that Polly Carter died at about ten o'clock this morning.'

Neither Juliette nor Alain spoke for a moment.

'*What?*' Juliette eventually asked.

'I'm sorry. She fell from the cliff at the end of the garden. Her death would have been instantaneous.'

Alain's legs briefly went, and he put his hand out to steady himself against the car.

'I'm sorry,' he said, still unable to process what he'd just been told. 'She's…?'

Richard and Camille steered Alain and Juliette into their cottage so they could recover from the shock in private. It also allowed Richard to check out the Moreaus' home.

He was pleased to see that Juliette and Alain clearly lived neat and ordered lives. The furniture in the room was simple, the floor was tiled and the walls were white-painted. Little shelves with books on them were arranged by height, a piano sat in the corner with hymn books on—and there were a clutch of colourful pictures of saints on the walls. There were also white cotton curtains that covered French windows looking out over a little yard that contained a washing line, pot plants in a row, and a couple of chairs for sitting out in the sunshine.

It was a modest home, but it was comfortable, Richard decided. Perhaps like its owners.

'I don't understand,' Alain said, still uncomprehending. Polly's death had hit him hard. 'You're saying she *jumped*?'

'It's what it looks like,' Richard said, not wanting to explain that he still wasn't one hundred per cent convinced that Polly's death had been suicide. After all, her body had been found too far from the cliff for a normal suicide. And there were plenty of aspects to the witnesses' statements that suggested there was more to Polly's death than first met the eye—not least the fact that the only witness to her death only heard the sound of her commit suicide, rather than saw it.

'Does that surprise you?' Camille asked.

'Yes. She had everything to live for. Why would she want to kill herself?'

'Well,' Richard said, 'I understand Polly could suffer from mood swings.'

'You're damned right about her mood swings,' Juliette said. 'She'd be happy one minute and snappy as hell the next. Isn't that right, Alain?'

Juliette looked at her husband for confirmation, but Richard could see that Alain was a lot less comfortable speaking ill of the dead than his wife.

'She could also be capable of great kindness,' he said, wanting to defend his former boss. 'Like the way she always brought gifts back for us whenever she went abroad. Or still paid you your salary even when you broke your foot the year before last. That was kind of her.'

'It was the least she could do,' Juliette said, more for her husband's benefit than for the police. 'And all those drugs she took didn't help with her moods, I can tell you that much.'

'So you knew about her drugs?'

'It was impossible not to.'

'But she'd stopped,' Alain said, still trying hard to remain loyal. 'All that was in the past.'

'And how would you know?' Camille asked politely.

Alain frowned. 'Because she never hid her drugs from us. You'd be cleaning the pool, or tidying away after breakfast and she'd just get out her…you know, all that terrible paraphernalia in front of you. The foil, the filthy spoon, the whole thing, it was disgusting.'

'She'd inject herself in front of you?'

'She never injected. As far as I know. She used to smoke her heroin. She called it "chasing the dragon". But that's the thing. I'd not seen her do any drugs since she got back from rehab a few months ago.'

'Yes, we understand she was in rehab in the States. Was that right?'

'That's right,' Alain agreed. 'And when she got back, I'm pretty sure she'd kicked the habit.'

Juliette snorted, and Richard looked at her.

'A leopard doesn't change its spots,' she said. 'And if we didn't see Polly taking her heroin, that just means she'd found somewhere secret to do it, if you ask me.'

Richard looked at Juliette and couldn't work out if he was grateful for her lack of sympathy for the deceased, or if he should consider it deeply suspicious.

'Then can you help with something else?' Richard asked. 'Only, it's possible that there was someone already on the cliff steps before Polly died. Someone who was wearing a yellow raincoat.'

'There was?' Juliette asked, sharply.

'Apparently so,' Richard said, trying to keep the interest out of his voice. It was clear that what he'd said had chimed with Juliette.

'What sort of yellow coat?' Juliette asked.

'A bright yellow raincoat.'

'With a hood?'

'Do you know someone who owns a coat like that?'

'I don't. But a few days ago, I saw someone down at the bottom of the garden—you know, over by the cliff's edge—wearing a shiny yellow raincoat with a hood, and I couldn't work out who it was. I just presumed it was someone from the house.'

'Did you see if this person was a man or a woman?' Richard asked.

'I don't know. I was too far away.'

'Then what about the person's build? Or hair, even? Think. It could be important. What can you describe of this person?'

Juliette thought for a long time before answering.

'I'm sorry. Whoever it was, I couldn't see, but I remembered it because they had their hood up.'

'This person had the hood up on their raincoat so you couldn't see their face?'

'That's right.'

Richard frowned. This was the second time someone in the house had seen a mystery person wearing a yellow raincoat over by the top of the cliff. It couldn't be a coincidence, could it?

'But if you had to guess, who in the house could it have been?' Richard asked.

'I'm sorry. It could have been anyone.'

'Maybe the person wasn't from the house,' Alain offered. 'Is that possible?'

'It might be. There's an old smugglers' path that goes around the headland up here. People sometimes use it as a shortcut to get around the coast even though they're not supposed to.'

'There's a smugglers' path up here?' Richard asked, surprised.

'That's right,' Juliette said, taking control of the conversation back from her husband. 'This used to be a smuggler's house. Because of its access to the hidden bay. Back in the day, illegal shipments would come in by boat and get unloaded on the beach at the bottom of the cliffs where the British customs officials couldn't see. You know?'

'So the general public have access to Polly's garden?'

'They aren't supposed to, but there's plenty of people who know about the paths. There are old smugglers' paths all over the island.'

Richard was disappointed. As long as the mythical yellow-coat wearer was one of the people from the house, then proving that person's identity might have been an achievable aim. But if it could have been anyone on the island who went down the steps wearing a yellow coat just before Polly died…?

'I see. Then would you mind if we search your house for a yellow coat?' Richard said and he noticed Juliette's eyes narrow at once.

'Why would you want to do that?' she said, and both Richard and Camille could see the intelligence in her eyes as she asked the question.

'Because it's possible that Polly interacted with this person in the yellow coat just before she fell to her death. And we're trying to find the coat.'

'What?' Juliette said. 'Are you saying the guy in the yellow coat pushed Polly to her death?'

'We're very specifically not saying that,' Richard clarified. 'However, we're not ruling anything out for the moment, either.'

Juliette looked at the police and Richard wondered if there was a hint of triumph in her voice as she said, 'Search wherever you like.'

As the cottage was small, it didn't take Richard and Camille long to discover that there wasn't any kind of yellow raincoat anywhere—and nothing much else of interest, either. Once Richard and Camille had thanked the Moreaus for their time, they went back outside.

'So what did you think?' Richard asked.

'I don't know,' Camille said. 'He seemed shocked. Decent. But there was something about her, wasn't there?'

'She was happy enough to stick the knife into the deceased,' Richard agreed.

Before Richard could say anything more, the alarm went off on his mobile phone—which he was quick to pull out of his pocket and silence.

'What's that?' Camille asked.

Richard knew that it was a reminder he'd set earlier to tell him his mother would be touching down on Saint-Marie in an hour's time.

'Oh, nothing,' he lied.

'No, I don't buy it,' Camille said. 'You've been checking your watch all day, and I've never known you set an alarm before. Something's up.'

Richard looked at his subordinate and knew that he had no quick answer, so he decided that his best course of action would be to pretend that she hadn't spoken at all. He started walking away from her.

'Hey!' Camille called out after her boss, before setting off to catch up with him.

'I want to see this old smugglers' path,' Richard said, as though he weren't sidestepping Camille's question.

'Okay, if you want to be like that,' Camille said, 'but I'll find out what's going on. You know I will.'

'Nothing's going on,' Richard lied again. 'But where's this path?'

'Don't worry, it'll be over by the cliff's edge, I reckon. If it's an old smugglers' path.'

Once they'd passed the border of shrubs and plants that separated the main garden from the cliff top, Camille looked at where the garden stopped and the jungle began.

'Yes, you can see it there,' she said, pointing at an old dirt path that was set ten or so feet back from the cliff's edge—and which started at the edge of the lawn and disappeared into the thick jungle that swept down the headland.

Now that he knew what he was looking for, Richard could see the old path as well.

'And where do you think the path leads?' he asked

'All the old coastal paths around here lead back to Honoré.'

As Camille was saying this, Fidel appeared over by the cliff's steps.

'Sir, sir, I think I've found it!'

Richard and Camille went over to Fidel, and, as the three police officers descended the steps that were carved into the cliff face, Fidel explained how the paramedics had removed the body, and since then he had been trying to identify the place on the stairs from where Polly had jumped.

'And I think I've found it, sir.'

As Fidel said this, he led around the first bend in the stairs, and, just a few steps further on, he pointed at the edge of the step. Richard could see there was a gap in the stubby thorn bushes that ran along the edge of the steps, and the escarpment of red dirt had given away a bit. Edging as close to the vertiginous drop as he dared, Richard looked over and could see that the gap in the thorns was directly above where Polly's body had been found on the beach below.

Richard looked about himself and saw that this spot on the stairs was, as Claire had said had been the case, just beyond the first turn in the steps as they led down the cliff face. As such, this was pretty much the first place on the whole staircase where a person would have been invisible to anyone standing at the top of the stairs. Or sitting in a wheelchair.

This troubled Richard. After all, why didn't Polly just jump to her death from the top of the cliff? Or from the first flight of steps? Why did she wait until she'd gone around the first bend and started down the second flight of steps before she jumped?

Putting the thought to one side, Richard looked again at how the gap in the thorns was directly above where Polly's body had been found on the sand far below, and decided that Fidel was almost certainly right. This was where Polly had fallen to her death. In which case, what had Polly cut her arm on? Richard couldn't immediately see any blood on the steps or anything obviously woody that might have imparted the green tinge they found on her hands and around the cut in her arm.

Fidel already had the crime scene kit to hand, so Richard got out a spray bottle of Luminol and the portable ultraviolet lamp. If Polly had already been bleeding when she went over the edge—as seemed likely—then there should be evidence of blood spatter on the red earth where she'd gone over.

Richard sprayed a fine mist of liquid Luminol over the dirt where he thought Polly's blood might have dropped. He then shone the ultraviolet light over the same ground immediately afterwards. Blotches of blood immediately started to fluoresce a purplish silver under the UV light.

'Okay, so there are drops of blood here,' Richard said. 'Good work, Fidel. This is now a secondary crime scene. Please secure and process it. In particular, I want you to check if there's any trail of blood spots that leads to here, or whether the blood is in fact confined to this one site.'

'Yes, sir.'

Richard creaked back to a standing position, pulled his hankie from his jacket pocket and tried to wipe the sweat from his face and back of his neck.

Camille could see that her boss was troubled.

'What is it?' she asked.

'Well, don't those spots of blood strike you as odd?'

Camille had played this game often enough to know that it was quicker if she just pleaded ignorance. 'No, sir. Not odd in any way. So why don't you tell me why they're odd.'

'Because,' Richard said, 'if this blood came from Polly's wound in her arm—which seems to be a fair working assumption—then where's the object that caused the cut?'

Camille thought for a moment. 'Maybe she cut herself elsewhere and that's where the object still is.'

'But you've seen the blood spatter. It looks as though it's localised to this one step here.' Richard looked about himself, nonplussed. 'Okay, let's work this through. I think the moss on her arm means that she was cut by a branch or bit of wood.'

'That seems reasonable.'

'And it will have to have been of decent size to cause such a deep wound.'

'That also seems reasonable.'

'So where is it?'

'Oh, I see what you mean. Good point.'

Richard and Camille started looking for any kind of loose piece of wood in the scrubby bushes that ran up and down the seaward side of the stone staircase. For Richard, this task required nerves of steel, if only because it involved going right up to the edge of the staircase—a vertical drop to almost certain death only inches beyond—and then reaching in to the bush to see if there was any loose branch hidden inside. And it *really* didn't help that the bushes were all thorn bushes.

Richard called out a sudden 'Ow!' for the hundredth time as he removed his right hand from one of the thorn bushes, and Camille found herself having to suppress a smile. Watching her boss in his woollen suit pull thorns from his hand while halfway up a cliff face in the searing Caribbean heat, she couldn't help but conclude that he was one of the most extraordinary men she'd ever met. And even though she mostly found him stubborn, arrogant and lacking in any kind of human warmth, there was no denying that, as a policeman, he got results. And for that, Camille could almost forgive him all his other personal failings. *Almost* forgive him.

'Aha!' Richard called out from further down the steps.

'What is it?'

Camille headed down to join her boss, who she could see was standing at the next bend in the steps as they zig-zagged down the cliff face. Here—where the steps turned down for the next flight—some proper bushes had been allowed to grow up to about shoulder height in the red dirt, and Richard was on his hands and knees lifting the lower branches on a particularly vicious-looking thorn bush.

As Camille arrived, Richard called back to her, 'Don't come any closer.'

He then reached into the bush and carefully pulled an object out.

It was an old bit of driftwood about four feet long. And it was covered top to bottom in a green moss from being in the sea for so long.

'Now, can you tell me what a piece of driftwood is doing hidden in a bush halfway up a cliff?'

Richard turned the branch over in his hands. At one end, there was still a bit of wood sticking out at a sharp angle where another section of branch had snapped off. This snapped-off bit of branch was only an inch or so long, but Richard and Camille could both see that there were dark stains on it—and around that end of the branch as well.

As the UV lamp and bottle of Luminol were soon able to confirm, the dark patches around the stubby bit of broken-off branch were blood. And the smears on the rest of the driftwood were also blood.

If this was Polly's blood, then Richard realised that someone else must have hidden the branch *after* she'd fallen to her death.

In fact, Richard realised, the find was even more significant than that. His suspicions about Polly's death had been right all along.

'You know what?' he said. 'Polly Carter didn't jump. She was murdered.'

Chapter 3

Giving the branch to Fidel so he could bag it for processing, Richard explained his theory.

'Putting aside the question of how a piece of driftwood ended up near the top of a cliff, let's see what this means. Polly argued with her sister in the garden, all the witnesses agree on that. And Polly then said she was going to commit suicide. Well, we only have her sister Claire's word for that, but we've got no reason to disbelieve her for the moment, so let's say that that's what happened. In a wild fury, Polly turned to Claire and said she was going to kill herself.

'Then, rather than just jump to her death from the top of the cliff, she made sure she came down the first flight of stairs and turned the corner so she was now out of sight of her sister. Which brings us to the cut in her arm.

'Because we've almost certainly found the piece of wood that cut her—I'm sure we can all agree on that. So, if this were suicide, Polly must have found the piece of driftwood lying here. She must then have picked it up, and then, for reasons known only to herself, she must have stabbed that sharp bit of the branch into her skin and ripped a vicious cut down her forearm. Which doesn't seem likely, does it?'

'It doesn't, sir,' Fidel agreed.

Richard indicated the break in the bushes where Polly had fallen to her death.

'And we know that Polly was bleeding quite heavily when she went over the edge. There's blood in the dust here where she fell.' Richard then pointed a good twenty or thirty steps further down the staircase at the bush where they'd found the bloody piece of driftwood. 'So how did she manage to get to that bush all that way down there, hide the branch in the bushes, and then get back up here without leaving a single drop of blood on the steps in between? And if *that's* impossible—which frankly it is, if you ask me—just why would she self-harm herself with a branch, go down the steps, hide the branch, then come back up to here, and only *then* jump to her death?'

Fidel and Camille could see the logic of what Richard was saying.

'Which means we've got a problem.'

'It does, sir?' Fidel said.

'Because the scene only makes sense if there was someone already waiting here *before* Polly came down the steps.'

'You mean the man in the yellow raincoat?' Camille asked.

'It's a possibility, isn't it?' Richard said. 'But whoever it was, they were not only waiting here, but they also had that branch with them. Ready to knock Polly to her death the moment she came round the corner.'

'Which is why her body fell so far from the cliff's edge.'

'Indeed. A whole seventeen feet. She didn't jump. She was knocked off the steps with considerable force.'

'And the thing is, sir,' Camille said, realising the implications of what Richard was saying, 'I can see why you'd use an old branch to commit the murder. You'd want to keep your distance so the victim couldn't grab at you and pull you over the edge when she went over.'

'Good point,' Richard said.

'And you'd also want to ensure that none of your DNA or fibres from your clothes got caught under the victim's fingernails if she fought back.'

'Yes. That's true as well,' Richard said, unable to stop a hint of irritation from slipping into his voice. This was supposed to be his revelation, not Camille's.

'But that's exactly what happened, isn't it?' Camille continued. 'Polly grabbed hold of the branch and cut her arm on it just before she fell.'

'Yes, very good,' Richard said, finally interrupting Camille's flow before she could steal all of his thunder. 'Because, in any tussle to the death, our killer wouldn't necessarily have noticed that Polly had cut herself just before she went over the edge. And he or she would then have hidden the piece of driftwood in the bush perhaps without realising that it was now covered in Polly's blood.'

'But if the killer didn't notice the blood on the branch,' Fidel said, 'then that suggests that he or she was in a serious rush after the murder.'

'But that's not surprising,' Camille said. 'The killer must have guessed that someone would have heard the scream as Polly fell to her death. And would come to investigate.'

'Precisely,' Richard agreed. 'Which is exactly what happened, isn't it? Sophie came down these steps only a minute or so later. Which is why we have a problem. Or rather, four problems. Because, firstly, if there was someone already on the steps here—whether it was our man in yellow or someone else—then how on earth did he or she know that Polly would come down these steps at that precise moment? And secondly, what are the chances that Polly would announce that she was going to commit suicide at the precise moment that the killer was planning to commit murder? The whole thing is the most incredible coincidence, don't you think? And thirdly, and even more impossibly, seeing as we know our killer was on these steps beforehand, how on earth did this man in yellow—or whoever-it-was—then manage to vanish from the cliffs before Sophie got here only a minute or so later?'

Richard looked at Fidel and Camille and knew that they agreed with him. It didn't seem possible.

'But, sir, that was only three things,' Fidel said.

'I know,' Richard said, delighted that one of his team had fallen into his trap. 'Because the last question I'd ask is:

why on earth did we find Claire's phone in a chandelier back at the house?'

There was a moment before either Fidel or Camille responded.

'You'd ask that as your fourth question, would you, sir?' Fidel asked tentatively.

'Of course!' Camille told him in well-worn exasperation. 'We've got a killer committing murder here, but let's make sure we work out how a phone got into a light fitting.'

'Indeed,' Richard said, entirely delighted. 'I'm telling you, it doesn't make sense, and I don't like things that don't make sense.'

There was a clattering of footsteps from above them and Dwayne appeared around the corner of the stone steps.

'Oh okay, Chief,' he said, once he'd regathered his breath. 'I think this could be murder.'

'You do?' Richard said. 'How gratifying. We've just come to the same conclusion. But what have you found?'

Dwayne wanted to show them, so Richard and Camille followed Dwayne back to the house and into a room that Dwayne explained was Polly's study.

On entering the room, Richard could see that it was identical in shape and size to the sitting room they'd interviewed the witnesses in, with exactly the same floor-to-ceiling windows and curtains overlooking the garden and sea beyond. And with a similarly dusty chandelier in the centre of the ceiling. In fact, the only architectural difference between the two rooms as far as Richard could tell was the fact that one wall of this room had a floor-to-ceiling bookcase running down its side that was stuffed with old books, junk and Polly's mementoes in pretty much any order.

But seeing as it was Polly's study, there was also an old metal filing cabinet, a desk made from what looked like an old door balanced on trestle tables, a battered old laptop sitting on it among a slew of old bills and unopened post, and various odds and sods of furniture sitting any old way around the room.

'Okay, so you should know,' Dwayne told Richard and Camille, 'I've had a good look through the rest of the study, and I can't find any kind of suicide note anywhere.'

'Have you looked on her laptop?' Camille asked.

'Just quickly,' Dwayne said. 'And there's no emails in her sent folder, or recently written documents at all.'

'So what makes you think it was murder?' Richard asked.

Dwayne indicated the battered filing cabinet, and Richard could see that there was a metal clasp attached to the top drawer, with a combination padlock keeping it shut. Or rather, the lock would have been keeping the drawer locked, but somebody had jemmied the whole clasp from the drawer, and now it hung limply.

'Someone's broken into her filing cabinet!' Richard said.

'Yeah,' Dwayne said before coughing a couple of times. 'That was me.'

'What?' Richard said, incredulous.

'Hey,' Dwayne said defensively. 'We've got a dead body. I wanted to see what was worth keeping behind lock and key.'

'But that's criminal damage!'

Camille wanted to get on, so interrupted. 'What did you find?'

With a grateful smile to Camille, Dwayne opened the top drawer.

'Well, for starters, this is where Polly once kept her stash of drugs.'

Richard and Camille were both hit by a pungent smell as they looked inside the drawer and saw a tiny set of brass scales, old spoons that had been blackened from heroin use, cigarette papers, smoke-discoloured bongs, a mirrored tile, and crumbs of hash, brown heroin and white powder dusted everywhere. In a flash of recognition, Richard realised that the mess and fetid stink of the drawer reminded him of his Great Uncle Harold's pipe cupboard, with its various bits of paraphernalia—from pipe cleaners, to penknives, to old broken pipes and boxes of Swan Vestas matches—but then, it occurred to him, both pipe smoking and heroin abuse were essentially the same thing: drug addiction. It's just that one of the addictions required considerably more wearing of slippers than the other.

Richard also saw a rusty mortice key sitting on top of a pile of old papers. He fished the key out and saw that it was about as long as his forefinger, had three worn teeth, and was obviously quite old.

'Now this is interesting,' Richard said. 'Who keeps a key locked inside a locked drawer?'

'Someone who wants to keep a key inside a locked drawer,' Camille offered, a lot less impressed with the find than her boss.

Before Richard sidetracked them with the key, Dwayne pulled out the pile of papers that were at the bottom of the drawer.

'But this is what makes me think somebody wanted Polly Carter dead, Chief.'

Dwayne took the papers to the desk and laid them out one by one.

They were each A4 in size and there were six of them. And on each of them was a message that had been made from cutting individual letters out of a newspaper headline and then gluing them to the sheet of A4.

The first patchwork message of cut-out newspaper letters read: y**O**u A**R**e g**O**in**G** tO **PA**y

The second: **I KN**o**W** w**HA**t yo**U** Di**D**
The third: I c**AN** r**U**In y**OU**
The fourth: **Y**o**U** deS**e**R**V**e to die
The fifth: I hat**E** y**OU**
And the sixth: B**Et**T**er **YO**U** d**IE**

The three police officers looked at each other. Dwayne was right. Someone out there had wanted Polly Carter dead. And now she was.

'Did you find any envelopes with these notes?' Richard asked, knowing that with anonymous letters, the most useful clue was often the envelope itself, which could sometimes be handwritten, but was almost always dated and franked with a posting location at least.

'I looked and couldn't find any,' Dwayne said.

'Then are there any other indicators on the letters themselves as to who sent them?'

'Not to the naked eye. But this is important, isn't it?' Dwayne said. 'Because, if you ask me, someone who's prepared to create anonymous messages from newspaper headlines is pretty desperate. And desperate people can end up doing desperate things like committing murder.'

'I agree,' Richard said.

There was a sharp ringing from Richard's inside jacket and he realised that someone was calling his mobile phone. He pulled it out from his jacket pocket and looked at the screen. It was his mother. He checked his watch. Of course. She'd have just landed at the airport.

'One moment,' Richard said to Camille and Dwayne, and, trying not to look too guilty—which only made him look guilty as hell—Richard moved off to one side to take the call as quietly as possible.

'Hello,' he whispered into his mobile.

Richard listened a moment before replying, 'Yes, okay. I can be at the airport in half an hour. Yes, okay. Of course. Then I'll take you to your hotel. Good. Right. Well, I'll see you then, then. Yes, of course. Half an hour. I'll see you then.'

Richard hung up his phone and returned to the table so he could look at the anonymous letters, hoping he'd got away with it.

'Okay, now you're going to have to tell me,' Camille said.

'Tell you what?'

'Who that was on the phone?'

'That phone call?'

'Yes, that phone call.'

'Oh, no one of note,' Richard said, looking back down at the threatening letters as though the conversation was now closed.

'All right,' Camille said, with a deadly smile. 'But if you don't tell me what's going on, then I'm going to reach into your jacket pocket, pull out your phone and find out for myself.'

Richard looked up from the notes in a panic.

'I'm sorry? You'd reach into my pocket?'

'Yes.'

'And pull out my phone?'

'Yes.'

Camille just kept on looking at her boss. She knew how this would go.

She wasn't wrong.

'Oh all right,' Richard eventually said. 'If you must know, my mother's just arrived at Saint-Marie airport.'

'I'm sorry?' Dwayne said.

'My mother's come to visit me.'

'Your mother's on the island?'

'Yes. What's so strange about that?'

Camille clapped her hands together in delight. 'How long is she over for?'

'Two weeks.'

'And she's here now?'

'She should be.'

'But you've got to tell us, what's she like?'

Richard frowned. 'What do you mean?'

'You know, your mother! I mean, is she like you at all, sir?'

'Like me?' Richard was appalled by the question. 'Of course not.'

'Then what's she like?'

Richard didn't even know where to begin. After a moment of further reflection, he said, 'Well, for starters, she's very neat and precise.'

'Which isn't like you at all, sir,' Dwayne said.

'And on top of that, she's a terrible worry-wort.'

Dwayne and Camille frowned.

'A what?' Camille asked.

'You know, she worries about everything.'

'Which is *also* unlike you, is it, Chief?' Dwayne eventually asked as diplomatically as he could.

'And she's a fusspot.'

'She's a worry-wort *and* a fusspot?' Camille asked, unable to keep the laugh out of her voice.

'Yes. That's what I said.'

As for Dwayne, he also felt as though he needed further clarification from his boss. 'Again, sir...so you're saying these are traits that are *unlike* you?'

'Of course they're unlike me!' Richard exploded. 'I mean, don't get me wrong, I believe everything has a place, and there's a place for everything—and I definitely believe that there are certain standards you have to keep up—but you have to believe me, I'm *nothing* compared to my mother.'

'Wow,' Dwayne said, summing up both his and Camille's feelings on the subject.

'So when do we get to meet her?' Camille asked.

'Ah, well that's the thing,' Richard said, finally glad to be getting back control of the conversation. 'While I'm picking her up, I want you, Camille, to get all this evidence logged and into bags. And, Dwayne, I want you to search the house properly from top to bottom. Keep looking for a yellow raincoat, but I also want you to try and find out what this key opens.' As Richard said this, he went over to the filing cabinet and pulled out the old mortice key. 'Because it may be connected. But someone killed Polly Carter. I suggest we find out who it was, and why Polly had to die.'

Before either of his subordinates could stop him, Richard made his excuses and drove off in the police jeep, bound for Saint-Marie airport.

Once there—and while he waited for his mother to clear Customs—Richard stood beside a palm tree a little way off from the white-washed building that acted as both the island's Arrivals and Departures lounge. The building was only small because Saint-Marie didn't have a runway long enough for international flights, so tourists first had to fly to the neighbouring island of Guadeloupe and then change onto a little propeller plane that the locals called 'the grasshopper'. Richard had only taken this plane a handful of times, but it was aptly named. By the time it had ascended vertiginously to its cruising height, it immediately fell out of the sky to land on Saint-Marie.

Richard straightened his tie as he waited, and then realised it had come a little loose. But it would be okay, he was sure.

In a sudden loss of sartorial confidence, Richard ducked behind the palm tree, undid the knot of his tie, yanked the whole thing from his neck, flicked the collars up on his sweat-sodden shirt, and made himself tie a better knot at speed. He then flipped the collar of his shirt back down, stepped back out into the sunshine and exhaled in relief. He'd got away with it. His mother still hadn't emerged.

Richard felt a trickle of hot sweat roll from his cheek, down his neck and into his shirt collar, and suddenly every inch of his skin under his suit seemed to prickle from the blistering heat.

And then there she was.

A slender woman in her late sixties, wearing a pink floral dress and an immaculate straw hat with a hatband in the same pink floral fabric as her dress, Jennifer Poole stepped out into the sunshine, a black suitcase-on-wheels at her side.

Richard took half a step forward and raised his hand in a nearly-but-not-quite wave.

'Hello, Mother,' he said.

'Oh, Richard, what a terrifying journey!' Jennifer said, as she wheeled her suitcase over to her son. 'I mean, they call it economy, and they really mean it, don't they? Before we'd even left London, I was trying to get the dust out of my seat, and do you know what? The woman sitting next to me told me I should just put up with it. Can you imagine? And when I started using my wipes on the fold-down tray in front of me—and on her fold-down tray—she called a flight attendant over and point blank complained. Which made for a frosty silence between her and me for the next eight hours, I can tell you. But by the time we landed at Guadeloupe, she was sneezing, so for all she gave me funny looks whenever I used the antibacterial gel on my hands, I'm not the one who's going to come down with Legionnaires' Disease.'

Even Richard was pretty sure that no one caught Legionnaires' Disease from aeroplane air conditioning systems. But before he could tell his mother this, she was off again.

'And when we landed in Guadeloupe, I couldn't believe how hot it was. I mean, I expected the tropics to be hot, but I wasn't expecting heat like this, and I remember the heatwave of 1976. But I'd decided I'd just have to cope with it when they took us to the plane they told us we were transferring to Saint-Marie on. Well! I could see rust around the rivets on the wings. And you know how your great uncle was in the Fleet Air Arm, and he always said you should never get in a machine that didn't look as though it was looked after with pride?'

Richard noted the pause, and gave the correct response. 'Yes, Mother.'

'Well, I very nearly didn't get on it, and then—when I did—I discovered that I was sitting next to a man who had a chicken on his lap in a crate. I mean, it was a very fine-looking chicken, but you don't expect to see a chicken on a commercial flight, do you?'

Again, Richard gave the correct response. 'No, Mother.'

'But I'm here now, I suppose, and it really is wonderful to see you.'

Jennifer stopped talking long enough to look at her son.

'And I must say, you look *very* smart.'

Richard couldn't help but feel a little burst of pride at this compliment.

'So where's Dad?' he asked, and recognised the maternal frown at once.

'Do I need to go everywhere with him? I am my own person, you know,' she said.

'No, of course you are,' Richard quickly agreed. 'It's just, I've only really got time to drop you off at your hotel, I'm afraid. There's been a murder.'

Jennifer looked at her son and sighed.

'Oh well,' she said. 'I've been putting up with your father's murders my whole life, I'm sure I can put up with yours.'

As Jennifer said this, Richard saw a pair of passing nuns in wimples look over in shock and then skitter off in a panic.

'But you should know,' Jennifer finished, 'I'm here to have a holiday whether you're free to be a part of it or not.'

'No. Of course. What hotel are you staying in, and I'll take you there,' Richard said.

On the drive to the hotel, Richard and his mother exchanged pleasantries. He heard about Beth from number seven and the problems she was having with her son-in-law. He then heard the story of Professor Brodowski's cat. *You remember Professor Brodowski? Lives in number eleven? Has the daughter with the lazy eye?* It was the typical flotsam and jetsam of life in his mother's close, and Richard was able to keep up his end of the conversation without having to engage his brain too much. This allowed him to become enveloped by an increasing sense of unease as the journey progressed, if only because in all of his forty-four years, he'd never known his mother spend a single night away from his father. And now she'd booked a whole holiday on her own, and on the other side of the world at that. What was going on?

Once Richard made sure that his mother was comfortable in what had turned out to be a far more top-end hotel than he was expecting, he made his apologies and returned to the police station.

'So what have you got?' Richard shot at his team as he strode back into the swelteringly hot station.

Dwayne, he saw, was on the phone, Fidel was dusting Claire's mobile phone for fingerprints, but Camille was at the whiteboard writing up the details of the case.

'So how's your mother?' she asked him. 'Safe flight?'

'Yes, thank you,' Richard said as brusquely as he could. He was not going to be sidelined by familial chit chat. 'So did you manage to process the anonymous letters we found in the victim's filing cabinet?'

Camille looked at her boss tolerantly, accepting that he was refusing to play ball.

'I took digital photographs of the front and back of all six letters for our records, but have sent the originals to the labs on Guadeloupe for analysis. We've also bagged and sent over the branch we found at the scene and which was covered in blood. And Fidel has also sent samples of the blood spatter he found in the dirt at the jump point.'

Richard smiled tightly, as ever, deeply frustrated that Saint-Marie was too small an island to have any crime scene labs of its own.

'Thank you. Then how about you, Fidel? How are you getting on?'

'Well, sir,' Fidel said, looking up from where he'd been dusting Claire's mobile phone on his desk. 'First I tried dusting the key you found in the victim's filing cabinet, but it's so rusty and old, it's not possible to raise a single print.'

'It isn't?'

'No, sir.'

'Then could I have it, please?'

Fidel reached over to a small plastic tray where the key was sitting. He picked it up and handed it to Richard. Richard looked at it again, trying to divine its meaning, and then, with a disappointed tut to himself, he slipped the key into his trouser pocket.

'But since then, I've been lifting fingerprints from Claire's mobile phone that you found in the chandelier, and matching them with the exclusion prints we took from the witnesses.'

'So whose prints are on the phone?'

'I've only been able to raise twelve clear fingerprints. The rest of the phone is just a smear. And while eight of the fingerprints belong to Claire Carter, the remaining four fingerprints belong to her sister, Polly.'

'I see,' Richard said, working through the logic of what this might mean. 'So, as there's no way Claire could have put the phone in the chandelier herself—seeing as she's confined to a wheelchair—that either means that it was put there by Polly, or her fingerprints just happened to be on the phone anyway, and it was put there by someone else who was wearing gloves so they didn't leave their prints on the phone.'

'Exactly, sir,' Fidel said.

Richard considered what Fidel had just told him, and then decided it was time to get on.

'So, Polly Carter!' he said, indicating the notes Camille had written up on the whiteboard. 'A world-famous super-model is at home with her sister, Claire Carter; Claire's nurse, Sophie Wessel; her manager, Max Brandon; her friend and film director, Phil Adams. Oh, and her live-in home help Juliette and Alain Moreau are also in the picture, although they say they were both elsewhere at the time of the murder.'

'Assuming they're telling the truth,' Camille pointed out.

'Indeed. Anyway, we know that Polly was a tricky woman to work for—according to Juliette, her home help. Although she could also be generous, according to her husband, Alain.'

'And she could be hyper one minute and depressed the next,' Camille added. 'According to Max, her agent.'

'And way too trusting, according to her good friend, Phil.'

'She just sounds like your typical self-centred celebrity,' Dwayne summed up for them all.

Richard looked at Dwayne in mock surprise. 'You know about the world of celebrities, do you, Dwayne?'

'I know it's not healthy,' Dwayne said. 'And if Polly's been famous since her early twenties, she's going to have a pretty warped view of the world, I can tell you that much, Chief.'

'Very well. So that's our victim. And this morning, she went for a walk with her sister, Claire.'

'Even though this was the first time she'd been out for a walk with her sister on her own,' Camille offered.

'Quite so,' Richard agreed. 'And, according to Claire, once they were in the garden, Polly started losing her temper with her. And then—again, according to Claire—Polly took Claire to the top of the cliffs and threatened to kill herself before then going down some of the steps and throwing herself to her death. However, the wooden branch we later found covered in blood at the scene suggests that that's not quite what happened. In fact, what the branch suggests is that someone was already waiting on the steps before Polly had arrived.'

'The man in the yellow raincoat,' Dwayne offered.

'Precisely,' Richard agreed. 'But whoever this person was, they attacked Polly with the branch, knocked her to her death, and then hid the branch before making their escape. Somehow. But the point is, we already know from the anonymous letters that there's already one person out there who wanted Polly Carter dead, so I want background checks run on Polly Carter and everyone who was up at the house. Who benefits from her murder? Who'd want her dead? I also want us chasing the autopsy on her body. If she was attacked by someone wielding that branch, I bet there'll be further evidence on her body.'

'And there are your questions from earlier,' Fidel offered.

'Indeed, but I think I've got a slightly different set of four questions now,' Richard said, turning back to the board and writing up a list in his neat handwriting.

Once he'd done so, he stepped away from the board so his team could see what he'd written.

The Key Questions

1. *How did the killer know to be on the cliff at that precise moment?*

2. *How did the killer vanish into thin air afterwards?*

3. *Why was Claire's mobile phone found in a chandelier?*

4. *Who sent the anonymous letters?*

'And you know what?' Richard said, putting the lid back on his whiteboard marker with a satisfying pop. 'I think that if we can answer those four questions, we'll stand a good chance of identifying who killed Polly Carter, knowing just why she had to die, and—above all else—just *how* the killer escaped afterwards without being seen. Now then, team, let's get to work.'

Chapter 4

The following day, Richard was sitting at his desk trying to focus on work, but his mind kept drifting back to the dinner he'd had with his mother the night before. It's not that she'd been difficult in any way—if anything, she'd wanted only to talk about Richard's life on the island—but, as an experienced copper, Richard got the impression that his mother was being evasive somehow. There'd been a reserve in her eyes he couldn't place. And Richard's disquiet was stirred further by the way his mother seemed to deflect any questions he asked about his father. 'Oh you know what he's like,' she'd just said brightly, without any real meaning to her words at all.

But perhaps most unsettling of all, Richard had discovered that his mother didn't have any set plans for her visit, and he'd never known her travel anywhere without detailed notes and pre-planned itineraries. Instead, she told him that there was a lovely boy she'd met on reception called Karl who was putting together an itinerary for her, starting with a tour of a local rum distillery the following morning.

In short, the whole evening had been quite peculiar for Richard, and as he'd pecked his mother on each cheek to bid her goodnight, he couldn't shake the feeling that he'd been 'played' somehow.

However, Richard knew he was supposed to be researching Polly's life before her death—not thinking about his mother—so he made himself look at the news article he'd got up on the computer monitor. And then he realised what the article said.

'Good grief!' he said in amazement.

Camille sighed heavily. 'What is it this time?'

Richard indicated the webpage on his screen. 'It says here that, back in 2005, Polly attended an orgy in Cheam.'

'I told you, sir, they'll print anything,' Camille said, not even remotely for the first time.

'But how do they know?' Richard asked in awe. 'Do you think a reporter was actually there?'

There was a warm chuckle from behind Dwayne's monitor. And then his face appeared, his eyes sparkling. 'You'd be surprised, Chief.'

'I certainly would be surprised if I found myself at an orgy in Cheam.'

Richard made a note of this latest impossible-to-believe fact on his ever-expanding list of lies, truths, half-truths and PR puff he'd so far been able to uncover about Polly. He'd learnt that she'd at one time been the highest paid model in the world; that she was patron of a hedgehog sanctuary in Cornwall; that she was a well-known heroin addict who'd spent her life battling addiction; that she'd designed a range of clothes for toddlers; that there was still an active warrant for her arrest in Portugal for assaulting a press photographer; that she'd done the Duke of Edinburgh Outward Bound courses as a teenager and had a Gold Medal; and that she'd dated a famous rock star for many years, even though, as far as Richard could tell, the man in question didn't look so much like a rock star as a bin man.

The only useful facts Richard had so far been able to glean from the internet were that the previous September Polly had suffered a massive drugs overdose and nearly died. She'd been rushed to hospital, had her stomach pumped and had a blood transfusion, and had only just survived. There were photos all over the web that Richard had been able to find of a stick-thin Polly leaving the hospital on Saint-Marie wearing dark shades and using a walking stick twelve days after she was admitted.

But if she'd nearly died from a drugs overdose in September, he'd also discovered that, after Christmas, just as the witnesses had said in the first interviews, she'd checked herself into a rehab clinic just outside Los Angeles and had spent ten weeks there. Richard knew all this because he'd found a press release online that had been issued by Polly's manager Max back in March when Polly had got out. In his statement, Max said that Polly had finally won her lifelong battle with addiction and was now eager to return to her work as one of the most in-demand models in the world.

Richard realised that his thoughts kept slipping back to what an orgy in Cheam would look like, so, before he got too confused, he jumped out of his chair and clapped his hands together in a way—far too late—he realised, probably made him look like a newly qualified Geography teacher.

'Right, then, team,' he said. 'What have we got so far?'

'Well, sir,' Fidel said, picking up his notes eager to report to his boss. 'I've been looking into Phil Adams, and he's from quite an impressive family. Before he retired, his dad was a teacher at Eton College, and his mum is a senior civil servant at the Foreign Office. As for siblings, he's got an older brother and a younger sister. The brother's a banker who owns his own hedge fund company—so he's worth a fair bit—and his sister's the British Ambassador to Slovenia.'

'I see,' Richard said, unable to stop himself from being impressed. Phil came from a super-successful family.

'As for Mr Adams himself,' Fidel continued, 'he made his name with a string of violent gangster films back in the 1990s, but he's not made much since then. And the main thing I've been able to dig up about him is, he was also in rehab in Los Angeles earlier this year.'

'He was?' Richard asked, thrown. 'Was everyone in Polly's house in rehab?'

'No, sir, just Phil Adams and Polly Carter as far as I can tell. But I don't know what clinic he was booked into, or why he was booked into it. It was just a few references in the gossip columns of a couple of UK newspapers. That following the failure of his latest feature film last year, he'd booked himself into rehab.'

'So his last film wasn't successful?' Richard asked.

'Apparently not,' Fidel said.

'Interesting. Good work, Fidel. Then what about you, Dwayne? What have you got?'

'Well, Chief,' Dwayne said, 'I've not been able to get much on Max Brandon. But he was a top agent at a talent agency in London back in the day. He then decided to go it alone when he took on Polly, and she's been his only client since then. And it's no surprise he doesn't represent anyone else. Looking after her career is a full-time job. He spends most of his time trying to stop the press from running stories about her latest sex scandal or drugs bust. It's even rumoured he tells her who she has to go out with to promote her career. But the thing is, Chief, because Polly's his only client, Max is unlikely to be our killer. With her dead, he's now lost his one source of income.'

'I see,' Richard said. 'Good point.'

'But things get more tasty when we look at Claire's nurse, Sophie Wessel.'

'They do?'

'Sure do,' Dwayne said. 'I rang the agency Sophie works for back in the UK. And it turns out she stopped working for them a few months back. But when Claire wanted a nurse to accompany her to Saint-Marie, she asked for Sophie by name because—get this—it turns out Claire came to Saint-Marie last year just before her sister Polly had her massive overdose—and Sophie came with her last time as well.'

'Really?' Richard said. 'And how long was Claire here for last year?'

'According to Sophie's agency, it was a five week booking starting at the beginning of last August.'

'So,' Richard said, working through the timings, 'Claire and Sophie were here last year for five weeks just before Polly took an overdose that nearly killed her…and they were both here again this year, and this time Polly did die.'

'Got it in one, Chief!' Dwayne said, leaning back in his chair, satisfied.

'Then good work, Dwayne. We need to look into that. Why did Claire come out here last year? And was it connected in any way with Polly's overdose?'

Richard turned to Camille. 'What about you, Camille? How are you getting on with Alain and Juliette Moreau?'

Camille looked at Richard and then shrugged as if to say she had no idea, which was a physical tic that Richard always found puzzling in his subordinate. After all, the stereotype of a French person was that they shrugged the whole time, so—he thought to himself, as he stood sweltering in the midday heat wearing polished brogues, a woollen suit and old school tie—why would she be so foolish as to conform to the national stereotype?

'Well, sir,' Camille said, and this was another thing about Camille that got under Richard's skin: she never called him 'Chief' like Dwayne did. Or Fidel did. Or Catherine, for that matter. And now that Richard was thinking about it, even Selwyn Patterson, the island's Commissioner of Police, would sometimes call him 'Chief'—even if only ironically. So if all these people were prepared to give him the affectionate soubriquet of 'Chief', then why couldn't Camille call him 'Chief'? Even once? Frankly, it rankled.

'Are you even listening to me, sir?' Camille asked as she shifted her weight onto a hip. Richard realised too late that he hadn't been.

'Sorry. Yes. Of course. Go on.'

'Only, there's next to nothing on Juliette or Alain— although Alain is Juliette's third husband. She married her first husband when she was nineteen years old. It lasted two years. She then married her next husband—a Frenchman over here on holiday—when she was twenty-nine. And this time the marriage lasted four years before he left her and returned to France. As for Alain, he and Juliette got married seven years ago—just before they took the job at the house.'

'I see. Interesting. Thank you, Camille.'

'And sir,' Fidel chipped in. 'I know Alain and Juliette a bit. We go to the same church.'

'You do?' Richard said.

'Although Juliette doesn't attend as often as Alain.'

'Then what would you say they were like?'

'Oh they're nice enough, I suppose,' Fidel said. 'Especially him. He's one of those people who's quietly impressive, if you ask me. You don't really notice him, and then you realise he's the guy who's helping out with Sunday school every weekend. Or taking food to some of the older people on the island who are living on their own.'

'He visits old people?'

'He does, sir.'

Richard thought for a moment.

'Yes. Doing Meals on Wheels isn't exactly the M.O. of your typical killer, is it?'

'That's my thinking, sir.'

'And as for his wife, Juliette?'

Fidel looked briefly uncomfortable. 'Well, sir, I don't know her so well, so I wouldn't like to say.'

Richard exhaled in exasperation.

'Fidel,' he said, 'this is a murder inquiry. If you know anything negative about any of our suspects, that's very much the territory I want you to be in.'

'Well, sir, it's not that I know anything about Juliette that's definitely negative, it's just that I don't think I much like her. You know? She doesn't come to church that often, and she isn't that nice when she does. She's one of those people who seems hard, if you ask me. Hard and cold.'

'Yes,' Richard said. 'And she seemed particularly unmoved when she found out about Polly's death. So we've got a tough woman who's on her third husband who's married to a softie? Is that what we're saying?'

'That seems to be about it, sir,' Fidel agreed.

'Then tell me, Fidel, seeing as Alain said he was at church last Sunday when Polly was killed, you don't happen to remember seeing him there, do you?'

'I'm sorry, sir. I wasn't at church last Sunday. But I can ask around. See who remembers seeing him.'

'Thank you. Please do.'

'Oh,' Camille said, 'and I've also spoken to my mother and she's confirmed that Juliette and Alain were at her bar having a coffee at about 10.30am on the morning of the murder. So that's their alibi.'

'And yet,' Richard said, 'is it that much of an alibi? Because even if Juliette and Alain were having coffee at your mother's bar by 10.30, it's still possible that one of them was committing murder back at the cliffs at 10am. Isn't it?'

As Richard said this, he turned to look at the notes he and Camille had been able to write up on the office whiteboard, and once again he found himself with an almost physical yearning to be back in the UK. Back in the UK there were climate-controlled incident rooms; here, the climate was controlled only in the sense that it was always boiling hot. Back in the UK they had AV suites and wall-mounted touchscreens; here they had an old whiteboard with three bent legs. And there, they had access to a nationwide network of thousands of Law Enforcement officers; whereas on Saint-Marie, Richard always felt that it was just the four of them solving each case on their own. This was mainly because it was just four of them solving each case on their own.

Richard sighed, and made himself look at the meagre facts they'd been able to collect on the whiteboard.

Polly Carter. **The victim. A model. One-time heroin addict. Said she'd commit suicide just before she was murdered.**

Claire Carter. **The twin sister. In a wheelchair. Last to see the deceased alive.**

Sophie Wessel. **Claire's nurse. Didn't see the**

moment of death, only heard it, but was second to the scene.

Max Brandon. Polly's agent. Sophie saw him go upstairs before the murder and Claire saw him in the house afterwards as well. At an upstairs window at the time of death?

Phil Adams. Film director. At an upstairs window at time of death?

Juliette Moreau. Was on a 10k run at the time?

Alain Moreau. Was at church at the time?

And, as Richard considered the names, he realised that there was one more name he needed to add at the bottom.

The Man in Yellow?? Was seen going down the cliff steps by Claire just before the murder...?

'Okay, team,' Richard said. 'Whether or not there was a man in a yellow raincoat on the cliff steps before Polly Carter was killed, clearly there was *someone* waiting there. So who of our witnesses might it have been?'

Camille joined Richard at the whiteboard.

'Well, sir,' she said. 'It can't have been Claire. If she's the person who saw the man in yellow.'

'Agreed,' Richard said.

'And Sophie was in the garden at the time,' Dwayne said, joining Richard and Camille at the board.

'Indeed. So she couldn't have also been on the cliff steps at the same time.'

Fidel joined the others at the board. 'But Sophie did tell us something important, sir, didn't she? She said that when Polly was killed, she looked back at the house and saw someone looking out of an upstairs window.'

'That's right,' Richard agreed. 'Even though both Max and Phil say that they were the person she saw.'

'So one of Max or Phil is lying?' Dwayne asked.

'It's possible,' Richard said. 'Or perhaps they were both looking out, but Sophie wasn't looking back at the house that carefully. Either way, seeing as Sophie said she definitely saw Max in the house *before* she'd even gone into the garden—and Claire saw Max in the house immediately afterwards—it's hard to see how Max could have got past Sophie and Claire to be on the steps before Polly got there. Or got back to the house afterwards without being seen as well.'

'So maybe it was Max who Sophie saw at the upstairs window,' Dwayne said. 'Which would mean that Phil doesn't have an alibi for the time of the murder. He could have been on the cliff steps before Polly got there.'

'Yes,' Richard agreed. 'And I definitely think it's a touch suspicious that Phil says he saw an argument between Claire and Polly from his bedroom window and then calmly went back to work for half an hour or so before he—rather conveniently—emerged from his bedroom only long after the murder had taken place. Although he's not the only one without a watertight alibi for the time of the murder, because Juliette and Alain don't have one, either.'

'Then what if Juliette's our killer?' Camille said.

'Okay. What makes you say that?'

'Well, it's just, she says she was out running—which she may have been, of course—but it occurs to me, don't runners sometimes wear high visibility running tops?'

'Why's that important?' Fidel asked.

'High visibility *yellow* running tops,' she clarified. 'Because, remember, Claire couldn't categorically say whether the person she saw go down the cliff steps beforehand was a man or a woman. Could she? So what if it wasn't a raincoat at all but was actually a high-vis running top that Juliette was wearing?'

'But it was Juliette who told us she'd also seen a man in yellow in the garden a few days before,' Richard said.

'Maybe she was trying to throw us off the scent,' Camille countered. 'After all, if she tells us about there being someone else in the garden a few days before, we're not going to be looking too closely at her, are we?'

Richard could see the logic of what Camille was suggesting, but he also remembered the old smugglers' path that led through the jungle to the cliff where Polly was thrown to her death. It was still possible that there was someone else out there—not directly from the house—who was their killer.

'That's true,' Richard said. 'But even if Phil, Juliette and Alain don't have decent alibis, we also can't rule out the killer being someone else entirely who went up to the house via the old smugglers' path from Honoré. So, Dwayne, I'd like you to walk the old smugglers' path from Polly's house back to Honoré, making sure you inspect the path as much as possible. See if you can find any cigarette butts, old Coke cans—anything that might have been left by our killer on his or her journey up to Polly's house.'

Dwayne's eyes widened.

'You want me checking the path all the way from Polly's house back to Honoré?'

'That's right. I just said.'

'Oh okay,' Dwayne suggested in his most hopeful voice, 'although how about I just check the first fifty yards of path? Something like that?'

'No, I'd like as close as possible to a fingertip search of the whole path from Polly's house down to Honoré, please.'

Dwayne thought for a moment, and then he clicked his fingers together as he had an idea.

'I know! I mean, Chief, it's a great idea—we need to search that path, that goes without saying—but what if I miss a crucial clue? After all, my eyes aren't what they once were. So what I'm thinking is, what if we maybe get a younger pair of eyes for the job?'

Dwayne looked at Fidel as he said this.

'Very well,' Richard said. 'Fidel, can you search the path? Dwayne, I'll give you the job I was going to give to Fidel.'

Dwayne beamed, happy to have dodged the bullet.

'So, Dwayne,' Richard said, 'Juliette says she went on a ten-kilometre training run on Sunday morning. Can you get the route from her, run it yourself, and stop at every house you pass to see if you can find a witness who will alibi her for the time of death.'

'*What?*'

'It wasn't that hard to understand, was it?'

'You want me to run a 10k?' Dwayne said, dismayed. 'With *my* knees?'

'Don't worry,' Fidel said, jumping in, ever the peacemaker. 'I'll do the 10k. You can do the cliff path, Dwayne.'

Dwayne exhaled in relief.

'Thanks, partner,' he said, and offered up a fist bump for Fidel.

'Good, glad that's all sorted,' Richard said. 'But from this moment on, I want us to all keep thinking. If we're ever going to discover who killed Polly Carter, we first need to uncover the how and the why of it. Just *how* did the killer push Polly to her death and then vanish into thin air afterwards? And why did Polly have to die in the first place? Who benefits from her murder?'

'I think I might have an idea,' a woman's voice said from the doorway.

Everyone turned and saw a nice-looking Englishwoman in her late sixties standing at the entrance to the police station wearing a floral summer frock and a cream cardigan.

'Can we help you?' Fidel asked, a touch confused.

'It's just that I think I might know who benefits from Polly Carter's death.'

Fidel, Dwayne and Camille looked at Richard, expecting him to get rid of this strange Englishwoman, but, instead, they saw that their boss was standing in silent mortification.

'Aren't you going to introduce me?' the woman said to her son.

'Are you…?' Camille managed to get out as Richard mumbled, 'Everyone, this is my mother. Jennifer Poole.'

There was a moment while his team looked at mother and son as they stood side by side. So different, of course. And yet, so similar. Camille was the first to recover.

'How wonderful to meet you, Jennifer! I'm Camille, and welcome to Saint-Marie!'

Camille went up to Jennifer and kissed her on each cheek—which initially made Jennifer recoil like a startled bird—but she was just about able to hide her confusion as Camille then introduced her to Dwayne and Fidel. And within moments, Richard's team were telling Jennifer all the must-see tourist sights she had to visit while she was on Saint-Marie. Unfortunately, as Jennifer kept having to point out, everything the team were suggesting either involved a considerable increase in her chance of catching dengue fever, or getting seasick—which she was a martyr to—or eating spicy food, and she really didn't like spicy food, she was afraid—but she was ever so grateful for their every suggestion. So, after a few minutes, they all agreed that perhaps Jennifer should just spend the morning wandering around the shops and harbour of Honoré.

And during the whole conversation, Richard stood a little way off in his dark suit, sweating. The truth was, seeing his mother talking to his team, Richard found that he was frozen to the spot. Every now and again, he'd begin to lift his arms up from his side as though he was about to join in with the conversation, but he found he had nothing to say, so his arms would drift back to his side again.

'Good morning, Mother,' Richard eventually managed to blurt, which hadn't been what he'd meant to say at all, but the words had seemed to rise unbidden to his mouth, as though his entire existence as an Englishman was no more than Pavlovian conditioning, which—perhaps—it was.

Jennifer looked at her son, puzzled by his awkwardness.

'Anyway,' she said. 'The whole island's abuzz with Polly Carter's death, but are you really saying it was *murder*?'

'It was,' Dwayne said, as though he could personally take credit for this deduction.

'And is it really true that the film director Phil Adams was staying with her when she died?'

'He was,' Dwayne said, once again as though he were personally responsible for this breakthrough in the case.

Richard despaired. It was no wonder people had found out about the case when his own team were so happy to talk about it.

'Then, if you're asking who benefits from Polly Carter's death,' Jennifer said, 'I suggest you focus your investigation on Phil Adams.'

This got Richard's attention.

'Really?' he asked.

'Oh yes,' Jennifer said. 'Because I'm pretty sure Phil Adams benefits from Polly Carter's death.'

'But how does he benefit?' Camille asked.

'Well! I was at the hairdresser's a few years ago, and I remember reading in a magazine that Phil Adams and Polly

Carter had gone to Las Vegas. For a holiday. But anyway, I remember this article saying that Phil and Polly had gone out partying in Vegas, and ended the evening in the Chapel of Love getting married. So, what I'm thinking is, now she's dead, Phil Adams would inherit all her money. Wouldn't he? Seeing as he's her husband.'

'You know all that?' Richard asked, amazed.

'But if you're saying she was murdered, then you should start with the husband. After all, in relationships, it's always the man who's to blame.'

Jennifer said this brightly enough, but everyone—even Richard—noticed that it was a somewhat cryptic statement to make. Before his mother could say any more, though, Richard made sure that he stepped into the breach.

'Very good, Mother. Thank you. But I suppose the question is, is Phil Adams really married to Polly Carter?'

'Apparently, he is,' Fidel said, having spent the last few moments back at his desk checking his computer. 'Because I'm getting loads of hits for Phil Adams and Polly Carter getting married seven years ago in Las Vegas.'

Jennifer clapped her hands together in delight, but, as Camille looked at her boss, she could see that, for some reason, Richard was the only person in the room who didn't seem impressed with his mother's contribution. In fact, Camille could see that Richard was now in a glowering funk, and she decided that she'd make sure she used the car journey to interview Phil Adams to discover all she could about Richard's relationship with his mother.

Chapter 5

By the time Camille arrived at Polly's mansion, she was ready to kill. She'd tried asking Richard obliquely, she'd tried being direct—she'd even tried cajoling him, bullying him, and, most demeaning of all for her, being polite—but he'd point blank refused to talk about his mother. All he was prepared to say on the subject was, 'I'd rather not talk about it, thank you.'

When they left the police jeep, Camille slammed her door shut in a fury, but Richard just ignored that as easily as he'd ignored her questions.

They found Phil in the sitting room with his laptop open and pages of drawings spread out in a mess around him. But he was staring out of the window.

'Good morning, Mr Adams,' Richard said.

Phil looked at the police. He then indicated the paper in front of him.

'Sorry. I thought I could maybe distract myself by doing some work.'

Camille picked up one of the drawings. It was of a rectangle with a cartoon of two people walking along a path, and there was a big swishing arrow pointing upwards with the word 'Tilt!' written through it.

'What's this?'

'The storyboard for my new film,' Phil said. 'Or what will be my new film.'

'The storyboard?'

Phil sighed, although it was clear that he was happy to be focusing on something other than the death of his friend.

'Well,' he said, 'when we shoot a movie, we plan all the shots in advance by drawing them out on hundreds of pieces of paper. So that's what I was trying to do here.'

'And what's the film about?' Camille asked.

'It's about a group of retired crooks who decide to get together to rob a bank.'

'Ha!' Richard said in an involuntary spasm.

Camille and Phil looked at him, and Richard realised he had some explaining to do.

'Well, it's just… I mean, hasn't that been done before?'

'This is a new take on the genre,' Phil said.

Richard could see a brittleness in Phil's eyes as he said this, and Richard realised he knew the confident-but-insecure look well. After all, Phil came from a successful family and hadn't maybe achieved as much in his career as he might have done. Richard could identify with that.

'Anyway,' Phil said, 'that's what I'm doing here, so how about you tell me what you're doing here?'

Richard gave a parched smile. 'We just want to know why you didn't mention to us before that you're Polly Carter's husband.'

It took a moment for Phil to register the question.

'I'm sorry?'

'Why didn't you tell us that you're the deceased's husband?'

'Why should I have done?'

'Because, depending on her will, it's possible that you now inherit all her money.'

'Oh dear. You don't know, do you?'

'Do you admit that you're Polly's husband?' Richard pressed.

'Sure,' Phil said. 'We went to Vegas a few years back. Got wasted over a weekend, the weekend turned into a week, and at the end of it all we got married in the Chapel of Love. And if you're really interested, I'm happy to admit to it. It was about the best week of my life. Just booze, drugs and sex with the most famous model in the world for a whole week. It's every man's dream come true.'

This wouldn't in fact have been Richard's dream come true, but he nonetheless found himself sticking his finger into his shirt collar to let some of the heat out.

'But after that,' Phil said 'we kind of went our separate ways. It wasn't serious.'

Richard cleared his throat. He really had to step in now. 'You got married but it *wasn't* serious?'

'Sure. But we still managed to meet up every now and again after that. If we were looking for a good time. Although, we always said if one of us wanted to get married for proper—you know, to someone we actually wanted to spend the rest of our lives with—we'd get divorced.'

'I don't understand,' Richard said. The idea that someone could get married so thoughtlessly—and then divorced just as thoughtlessly—offended every sense of propriety he had. In truth, Richard's ideas of romance, fidelity and love were most closely aligned to a form of chivalry that had become outdated even before the turn of the fourteenth century, but he couldn't help himself. He felt that there was a nobility to love—and to the union of a man and woman—and the fact that no one else took these ideals as seriously as he did was just one of the many burdens he had to shoulder in his life.

Phil smiled sadly again. 'I wouldn't expect you to understand, but it was fun being married, you know? It was such a boring thing to do. So conventional.'

'And were you in a sexual relationship with the deceased when she died?' Richard asked, before coughing.

'Well, as it happens,' Phil answered, 'we weren't. And it wasn't for lack of trying on my part. We met up earlier this year, but it turns out she didn't seem interested in rekindling that side of our relationship.'

'Was that when you were in rehab with her?' Camille asked, and Phil looked at Camille, impressed.

'You know we were in rehab together?'

'Actually,' Richard said, 'we only knew you were in rehab in Los Angeles at the same time as Polly. We didn't know you were both in the same place until just now, so thanks for telling us that.'

Phil considered Richard before replying.

'I really don't mind telling you anything, I've got nothing to hide. And anyway, in Hollywood, if you don't have at least one spell in rehab, you aren't really taken seriously as an artist.'

'So what were you in rehab for?'

'Anxiety,' Phil said, as though it were the most natural thing in the world to admit.

'You can go to rehab for being anxious?' Richard asked.

'Sure can. Sure did.'

'You don't seem very anxious now.'

'That's because the therapy worked,' Phil said, and Richard was briefly irritated to see Phil's quip raise a smile from Camille. 'But back at the turn of the year, I was a bit of a mess. My last film hadn't done so well, I was getting these horrendous panic attacks, and I knew I needed a complete detox of my psyche before I could even begin to start writing my next movie.'

'I see,' Richard said. 'So you weren't in rehab for drugs like Polly?'

'No way,' Phil said. 'And I never did hard drugs like Polly anyway. If I'm honest, her heroin use was one of the least attractive aspects of her.'

'Then can you tell me how you got on with Polly when you were in rehab with her?'

'We always got on well. It's why she invited me out here. She told me I could have a room to write my next movie in, and that's what I've been doing here ever since. Writing my movie. I've been here about six weeks.'

'And now she's dead, you inherit her money?' Richard asked.

'You really don't know, do you?'

'Know what?'

'She didn't have any money.'

'I'm sorry?'

'The thing about Polly—why we all loved her—was because she was crazy. Impetuous. And one hundred per cent trusting. In her own way. But because of that she was a terrible judge of character and one of the easiest people in the world to manipulate. She was like a child when it came to money, so she'd give it away to any and every sob story that came along. But more than anything, she was extravagant. I mean, look at this place. I know it's tatty, but that's because Polly bought it without having the money to keep it up.'

'But she was a world-famous model.'

'Who's not done any work since her overdose last September. And, in that time, she's continued to spend, continued to keep up the houses, but that's nearly a year without any kind of income at all. And, if you ask me, you should look at Max, her agent. Even when she was earning, she never seemed to have as much money as she should if you ask me. I think he's been rooking her for years.'

'You think Max Brandon is a crook?' Richard asked.

'I'm not saying that, but I know I don't trust him. And you know what? Only last week, I was in this very room with Polly. She was sitting there.' Phil pointed at a dusty old wingback. 'It was just before midnight. And she told me she was so skint she was going to have to put this house up for sale. And her flat in Los Angeles. And her apartment in London. It's why I think she flipped at the end and killed herself. She had no work, no money, and she decided to end it all.'

'The thing is,' Richard said, leaning forwards in his chair as he spoke, 'she didn't commit suicide. She was murdered.'

Phil blinked once. Twice.

'What?'

'She was killed.'

'You're kidding me?'

'It looks as though Claire was right,' Richard explained. 'There was someone already on the cliff steps before Polly went down them—very possibly this person in the yellow raincoat—who then pushed her to her death.'

'She was pushed to her death...?'

'I'm sorry,' Camille said, 'but the evidence is conclusive.'

'It's just not possible.'

'And why's that?' Richard asked.

'Because, well, she was infuriating, don't get me wrong, but murder? Who'd want to kill her?'

'That's very much what we're trying to find out.'

Richard and Camille saw Phil frown as a thought occurred to him. After a few further moments of introspection, he looked back at Richard. 'But you're saying she was pushed from some way down the steps?' he asked.

'Why do you ask?'

'Because, I suppose if you're looking for someone who might have wanted to kill Polly, Claire wasn't joking when she told you she and Polly didn't get on. In fact, I can well imagine Claire wanting Polly dead. But seeing as she's in a wheelchair, there's no way she could have got down the steps, if that's where she was killed.'

'But you think Claire might have wanted to kill Polly?'

'Hell yes. Of course.'

'Why do you say, "of course"?'

Phil looked at the police, puzzled.

'Don't you know how Claire lost the use of her legs?'

'No.'

'Well,' Phil said after only a moment's hesitation. 'If I do one thing for Polly, I'll do this. I'll tell you the story before you hear it from anyone else. So, Polly and Claire are twins. As you know. But the key thing about their relationship is that Claire was born a few seconds before Polly. She's the older sibling. And in her family, that meant that about from the moment she could understand English, Claire was told that she was going to inherit everything. The everything in this case being a mansion in Lincolnshire, a dairy farm, a fishing lake, and hundreds of acres of prime arable land. It's worth millions. And Claire would get it all while Polly wouldn't get a penny.'

'Because Polly was the second born.'

'And the way Polly told it, when they were growing up, Claire made Polly's life a misery, always treating her as inferior. The poor relation—which, in fact, she was. And her parents were just as bad. Claire was the "heir", and Polly the "spare". If you ask me, it's why Polly ended up like she did. She spent her life looking for approval in others because she never got any at home. Anyway, when Polly was old enough to escape her crazy family, she did, and moved to London. And it was there where she was talent-spotted at a party and started her life as a fashion model. And before too long, she'd earned a shedload of money, spent more, and travelled the world working and partying. But—and there's always a "but" when you're talking about Polly—she had to go back to Lincolnshire from time to time. She couldn't cut the ties with her family completely.

'About ten years ago, her dad was ill—dying, as it turned out—and Polly was summoned home for a family Christmas because everyone thought it was going to be his last. Anyway, in that part of Lincolnshire, the Boxing Day foxhunt meets at their house every year. So, the way Polly told it was, she'd had to endure a terrible Christmas—with Claire and her parents belittling her at every turn—and then, on the day of the hunt, she woke up to find hundreds of beagles barking like crazy and a load of posh arseholes wearing red tailcoats and black top hats outside the house while hundreds of locals watched on as though it was a privilege to see rich people sit on a horse. Polly hated the whole lot of them, so before the hunt set off, she tried to join up with the hunt saboteurs. And she said it wasn't hard to find the sabs, they were at the end of the driveway holding placards.

'I don't think any of them knew who she was, actually. But the sabs' plans were always to try and get in the way of the hunt, so Polly took a few of them off to a back lane she knew would probably be used at some point that day, and she was right. An hour or so later, they saw a rider coming along it. I reckon Polly knew it was her sister at once, and she told her gang that they should give this rider a special surprise. So they hid behind a hedge and, when Claire came riding past, they jumped out and shouted.

'Polly said it was only supposed to be a stupid joke, but Claire's horse startled, reared and threw her to the road. The other hunt sabs scarpered, but Polly ran to her sister to offer her help—of course she did—you can see what I mean about Polly having terrible judgement. If you're going to injure your sister, you don't go to her aid. Or maybe that's just me. Anyway, it turned out that Claire had broken bones in her legs, her pelvis and she'd also broken her back. She was airlifted to hospital and spent the next six months in traction. By the time she got out, the doctors had been able to patch up her back and pelvis, but she's not been able to walk since then.'

'And it was all Polly's fault?' Camille asked.

'It was. Which was why Claire always hated Polly— although I never agreed with Polly that she was now using her wheelchair to spite her.'

Richard looked up sharply from where he'd been writing in his notebook. 'What's that?'

'Well, Polly used to think that Claire's disability wasn't quite as bad or as permanent as she made out.'

'Really?'

'But this was just a typical Polly flight of fancy if you ask me.'

'But how could Claire's injury not be permanent?'

Phil sighed before going on. 'Look. I don't believe any of this, but Polly suspected that Claire was only pretending to remain injured. It's called "conversion disorder", she told me. It's a condition where someone is physically capable of walking but, for some crazy psychological reason or other, they can't. But to be clear: I've spent the last week with Claire. There's no question she needs that wheelchair. And think about it. Even though I'm sure Claire hated Polly with every fibre of her being, it's pretty delusional for Polly to think that Claire would then pretend to be disabled just to spite her.'

Richard considered what Phil had just said.

'Is it possible that it's Claire who's been sending the anonymous letters to Polly over the last few months?'

Phil looked puzzled. 'I don't know anything about that. What anonymous letters?'

'They've been made from the cut-out letters of newspaper headlines. And they're of a very threatening nature.'

'And they were addressed to Polly?'

'We assume so. We found them in the filing cabinet in her study.'

'Then I'm sorry, that's the first I've heard of any threatening letters.'

Once Richard had thanked Phil for his answers, he led Camille out of the sitting room, where he briefly paused at the bottom of the staircase.

'I think we need to talk to Claire, don't you? We need to find out if she hated her sister as much as Phil says.' As Richard said this, he headed up the wide wooden staircase to the landing above, Camille falling in step with him.

Once on the landing, Richard looked out of the windows that overlooked the gardens and the Caribbean sea beyond.

'It's interesting, isn't it,' he said to himself as much as to Camille. 'You really can't see the steps down the cliff from here, can you?'

It was true. The wide lawn outside swept down and to the right, and then it disappeared behind a thick border of bushes, shrubs and trees that blocked any kind of view of the cliff top.

A door opened further along the landing, and Richard and Camille saw Sophie emerge from a bedroom holding an old fashion magazine in her hand. She stopped, surprise on her face as she saw the police.

'Oh, sorry. Hope I'm not interrupting,' she said.

'Far from it,' Richard said. 'In fact, I think you can help us.'

'I can?' Sophie said as she approached.

'It's quite a simple thing,' Richard said. 'It's just, when you were out on the lawn before Polly died, and you saw someone up here looking out of the window, can you really not remember which window you were looking at?'

'I'm sorry,' Sophie said. 'I've been trying to think about it since then, but the truth is, I was in a bit of a panic at the time. It really could have been Max if he was standing here. But Phil's room is just there.' Here, Sophie indicated the first door that led from the landing. 'It could just as easily have been Phil I saw at his window. I just don't know.'

'Very well,' Richard said, unable to hide his disappointment. 'Then can we ask, do you know where Claire is? We'd like a word with her.'

'Yes. She's in the bath. She'll be there a while and then I'll be helping her out.'

'Of course. Because she can't walk,' Richard said.

'That's right,' Sophie said, quietly offended at Richard's lack of sensitivity.

'It's just, we were wondering if Claire was quite as disabled as she lets on,' Richard asked.

'I'm a trained nurse, and I can tell you categorically that my client has absolutely no use of her legs,' Sophie said, appalled that the police would doubt this fact.

'I see,' Richard said, not really appreciating the offence he'd just caused. 'Then can you tell me, you mentioned earlier that Claire and Polly didn't get on—were always sniping at each other—is it possible that Claire might have wanted to kill her sister?'

Sophie was now aghast.

'I'm sorry?'

Richard explained to Sophie how they now considered the death to be murder, and all the colour drained from Sophie's face.

'No…it's not possible,' she said.

'I'd agree it's not *probable*,' Richard demurred, 'but it is unfortunately what happened. So I repeat the question: in your opinion, is it possible Claire might have wanted her sister dead?'

'No, there's no way,' Sophie said loyally. 'I mean, they didn't get on that well, that's true, but there are lots of siblings who don't get on. And anyway, I ran straight for the cliff top the moment I heard Polly scream. And when I got there Claire was still in her wheelchair at the top of it. There's no way she could have been the killer—if you're saying Polly was already down the steps when she fell. Claire couldn't have got down those steps in her wheelchair, let alone back up again without me seeing her.'

'Then can you tell me, if Claire couldn't be the killer, do you by any chance have any insights into who in the household might have wanted to do harm to Polly Carter?'

Sophie thought carefully before answering. 'I don't think anyone would.'

'But if you had to guess?'

'I'm sorry, but I don't get to spend much time with the other house guests, so I don't know them that well. To be honest, they mostly treat me like I'm staff.'

Camille could hear the note of bitterness in Sophie's words, and she remembered that Dwayne had said that Sophie had recently left her agency.

'Yes, that's right. You've been with your agency a long time, haven't you?'

'That's right. Since I qualified as a nurse and chose to go into the private sector.'

'But I understand you no longer work for them?'

There was a look of slow surprise in Sophie's eyes.

'Perhaps you could tell us why that is?' Richard asked.

'You want to know why I left the agency?'

'That's why I asked.'

'Okay. I left the agency because they sacked me.'

This got Richard and Camille's attention.

'And why was that?'

Sophie flushed bright red as she said, 'Well, if you must know, I was…I was caught thieving.'

'You were?' Camille said, surprised. 'What did you steal?'

'Look,' Sophie said, launching into a speech Richard could see she'd rehearsed many times to herself. 'I know it sounds bad, but the thing is, you don't know what it's like working for rich people. They've got so much money, I don't know…it's like they don't feel they need to have manners. You get the wrong client, and you're less than human sometimes to them. And it wears you down, particularly when they show off about how much money they've got while also refusing to let you claim expenses.

That's what happened on the last job I had with the agency. I was working for this guy who hadn't even earned his money. He'd inherited it all from his dad, this big banker. And it was the dad I was there to help look after. He'd had a stroke and was a lovely man. With such kind eyes. So he was all right. It was just his son I had a problem with. Mainly because he was mean. Mean to me, mean to his dad—and he also left these piles of fifty pound notes around the house as though it was all so much small change to him. Which, it has to be said, it was. And, one day, he'd been really nasty to me, making me go and pick up his dry cleaning, which wasn't in my job description at all, and I saw four fifty pound notes folded up on the mantelpiece…and I couldn't help myself. I took them.'

Richard asked, 'But you were caught?'

Sophie sighed deeply. This was her shame. 'It turns out one of the other staff members in the house had already been stealing, and my employer had left these notes out to trap them. They were covered in that blue police dye. I was so ashamed when the police arrived and got out the UV light. But I was lucky, too. My boss's dad—the guy who I'd been caring for—convinced his son not to press charges. I of course had to leave the agency. But, if I'm honest, by then I was happy to go. I'd been getting more and more fed up with the people I'd been working for over the years. I got a job in a local hospice soon after. It's been far more rewarding being back in the real world. Dealing with real people. With real problems. It's why I became a nurse.'

'But if you've got a new job at a hospice, how did you end up working for Claire?'

'Because I'm a good nurse,' Sophie said, her chin rising with a touch of pride as she said this. 'So when the agency rang and said Claire had asked for me by name, I was happy to take some of my annual holiday allowance to come to Saint-Marie and earn a bit of extra cash in the Caribbean sunshine. Although I don't think that now, of course.'

An alarm went off on Sophie's phone. She pulled it from her pocket and swiped to turn it off.

'I'm sorry, but that's my timer. I need to get Claire out of her bath. Would that be okay?'

'Yes, that's fine,' Camille said.

'But can you be sure to tell her we need to talk to her?'

'Of course.'

As Sophie left to get Claire out of her bath, Richard considered what he'd just learnt. He could certainly believe that Sophie was treated as a lowly member of staff by

Claire and the others in the house—which would cause resentment with Sophie—but he didn't quite see how this would necessarily escalate into murder. After all, as Sophie had just told them, she must have learnt long ago how irritating wealthy people could be. Unless, of course, Polly's death was somehow connected to Sophie's previous history of stealing money. But then, if Polly had no money to her name—as Phil was now claiming—then it was hard to see what money Sophie might have stolen that would then have been worth killing over. They had to get to the bottom of Polly's finances as soon as possible, Richard decided.

But with Sophie gone, Richard realised he was at a bit of a loose end—until he remembered how Camille had said that he'd find Polly's bedroom interesting, so he suggested they both go and give it the once-over.

When they entered Polly's bedroom, Richard saw that Camille had been right. It was fascinating—if only because it was the one room in the whole house that seemed to be spotlessly clean. A glorious old brass bed had a freshly laundered duvet on it, and the pillows were soft and damask, Richard noted, impressed. As for the wardrobe and dresser in the room, they were polished antiques without a speck of dust on them anywhere. And best of all to Richard's mind, there was even a cream-coloured wall-to-wall carpet.

Richard had reverently taken his shoes off before he'd even entered the room, and while he searched through the tidy rack of clothes inside the wardrobe, he found himself musing that there really was nothing finer in life than that feeling of wiggling your toes into the plush pile of a deep and expensive carpet. As for the rows of smart clothes and shoes he found neatly lined up inside the wardrobe, Richard's thoughts returned to the woman who'd owned them. After all, just what sort of person would live in such a mess of a house and yet have an entirely pristine bedroom?

Once he'd finished looking through the wardrobe, Richard turned to Camille. 'You're right. This isn't how I'd imagine Polly's bedroom to be.'

'I know. So how come it's so tidy in here when it's so messy elsewhere?'

'Maybe someone tidied it up before she died? Or afterwards?'

'Why would anyone want to do that?'

Richard didn't have an answer. But he could see that there was nothing here that suggested a personality that was in any way impetuous, slapdash or irresponsible—as Phil had said Polly had been. So had Phil misled them and the room was the 'real' Polly, or was it the other way round, and the rest of the house—in all its dusty disorder—was the real Polly, and the bedroom was a stage-managed fiction? Either way, it was a puzzle, Richard felt. People with spotless bedrooms didn't live in messy houses, and vice versa.

Camille went into the en suite bathroom and saw that it was just as smart as the rest of the bedroom. There was a brand new walk-in shower, and clean mirrors sparkling above the white porcelain sink. Camille opened a medicine cabinet and saw only neat piles of vitamins. And still no evidence of drugs use.

'And I can't find any evidence of Polly still using drugs. Can you?' Camille asked her boss as she returned to the bedroom.

But Richard was nowhere to be seen.

'Sir?'

'Hold on,' she heard Richard say from the floor just beyond the bed.

Camille went round to see that Richard was on his hands and knees and had pulled up the corner of the cream carpet.

'What on earth are you doing?' she asked.

'Following a lead,' Richard said, indicating a thin electric cable that was running under the carpet.

'What I mean,' he then said, knowing that he hadn't been entirely clear, 'is that I'm following a lead both figuratively and literally.'

'I understood you the first time,' Camille said, joining her boss on the carpet. 'You've got a cable.'

Richard indicated the thin white electric cable.

'You see, when I looked behind the chest of drawers, I saw a plug in a socket, with the cable running down to the carpet.'

'So you're now pulling up the carpet?' Camille asked, surprised.

'Of course. The only electrical device in the whole room is the lamp on the bedside table, and, as I'm sure you've already noticed, it's plugged in by the wall just underneath it.'

Camille looked over and saw that what Richard had said was true. There was only one electrical device in the room—which was clearly plugged in—so what was the cable under the carpet powering?

With a loud rip, Richard pulled up another half foot of carpet up in between the wall and the bed and saw that the little electric cable was still heading towards the bed. However, it was now near enough that Richard could pull on the cable alone, and it ripped up through the gap between the carpet and the wall.

The cable went up the back leg of the bed and seemed to go into the underside of the bedframe.

'Hold on, I'll get this,' Richard said.

Richard lay down, so he could gain access to the underside of the bed. The clearance was only a foot or so, but it was just enough for him to slip underneath.

Once his eyes had adjusted to the darkness, Richard followed the cable up and saw that it went into a grey plastic box no bigger than a pack of cards that had been gaffer-taped to the underside of the bed. But the grey box had a pattern of what looked like dozens of air holes on its underside and a tiny green LED light on its side.

It was a surveillance bug.

Someone was listening in to everything that went on in Polly's bedroom.

Chapter 6

At the same time that Richard and Camille were finding the surveillance bug under Polly's bed, Fidel was in his running gear jogging around the byways of the island trying to follow the route Juliette had taken on the morning of the murder. It was hot and exhausting work if only because Fidel—diligent as ever—felt he had to stop and ask everyone he could find if they remembered seeing Juliette out on her run the previous Sunday morning. So far, over an hour into his task, he'd barely covered a tenth of the distance and he hadn't found a single person who'd seen Juliette. It didn't mean she hadn't been on her run, of course, but Fidel already found it interesting that he couldn't find anyone who remembered seeing her.

As for Dwayne, he'd had a much more pleasant morning strolling the cliff path from Polly's house down to the outskirts of Honoré. After all, although Richard had asked him to run a fingertip search of the route the killer might have taken, Dwayne figured that his boss couldn't have been talking literally, so he'd just kept an eye out for anything out of the ordinary. And so far—luckily for him—he'd not been able to find anything out of the ordinary.

Dwayne was therefore in a relaxed mood as he strolled back into Honoré along the beach. It was at times like this that Dwayne found himself overwhelmed by the love he felt for the island. He knew dimly that there was a wider world out there of riches, fast living and fame, but somehow he felt that everyone who strived so hard to better themselves in their lives were somehow missing the point of life, which could never be about money or fame. No, Dwayne mused to himself, life was about knowing who you were, where you were from, and then being comfortable with that. It's why he had some sympathy for Richard's constant confusion and fury. After all, Richard had been ripped from his home where he knew who was who and what was what and been relocated somewhere where he'd had to start all over again.

Dwayne paused a moment, and grunted a laugh to himself. He had *some* sympathy for his boss, but he shouldn't get too carried away.

It was in this spirit of goodwill, then, that Dwayne saw Richard's mother standing on the jetty of the harbour looking at the boats.

'Hey, Jennifer, how's it going?' Dwayne called out, if only because it amused him that he now knew that Richard's mother's name was Jennifer.

Jennifer looked over and waved, and Dwayne soon found himself sauntering over for a chat.

'So how's your day been so far?' Dwayne asked.

Jennifer was enthusiastic as she explained how she'd had a coffee in a beachside bar, and had even been brave enough to try one of the local delicacies, something called a currants roll.

'You had a currants roll?' Dwayne said, impressed. As far as he was concerned, the mixture of currants, pastry and cinnamon in a currants roll was the holy trinity of all known flavours.

'And you know what?' Jennifer said, clearly very proud with herself. 'I even liked it.'

'Of course you liked it!' Dwayne laughed—and he and Jennifer were soon swapping recipes of favourite pastry dishes, with Jennifer simply fascinated by the culinary links they were able to make between the Jamaican pattie and the Cornish pasty, and Dwayne in particular being taken by Jennifer's rhapsodic description of a traditional English plum duff.

In fact, Dwayne and Jennifer were having such a good time that it seemed only natural, now that Dwayne had finished with his boss's immediate task of checking the coastal path, he'd offer to show Jennifer some of the island's sights—although, when Dwayne suggested this to Jennifer, she briefly froze in panic. After all, she was still concerned about the possibility of catching any or all of dengue fever, malaria, chikungunya, rabies, typhoid, yellow fever, and hepatitis A and/or B. But Dwayne's smile was so delightful, Jennifer noticed—and he looked so charming in his police uniform—how could she possibly resist?

'Very well,' she said. 'I'd be delighted to accompany you. Thank you.'

***

Back at Polly's house, it didn't take long for Richard to cut the surveillance bug from its cable using his little pearl-handled pocket knife. Getting his body back out from under the bed proved more of a challenge, but once Richard was finally standing up, he handed Camille the surveillance bug to put in an evidence bag.

'We need to dust it for fingerprints,' he said.

'I think we might be able to do better than that,' Camille said, pulling a large Swiss Army Knife out of her handbag. As she flicked past the array of tools—the magnifying glass, the saw and the hook for carrying parcels of newspaper— Richard couldn't help but make comparisons.

'I didn't know you had such a big penknife,' he said, holding up his own tiny pocket knife.

Camille looked at her boss and laughed.

'It's not how big it is, sir, it's how you use it.'

Richard blushed bright red, which—seeing as he was already bright red from his exertions under the bed— wasn't actually noticeable to Camille as she flicked out a Phillips screwdriver and started on the tiny screws on the surveillance bug.

'I just think,' Richard huffed, 'that seeing as you've been carrying such a useful tool about your person all this time, you might have mentioned it before now.'

'I might have done,' Camille said in agreement. 'Hold on to this, would you?' she said as she popped the back off the device to reveal its electronic innards. 'I want to know, how does the bug broadcast its recordings?'

Using the tip of the screwdriver, she reached into the tiny machine and flicked out the little SIM card that was inside.

'Now that's interesting. If there's a SIM card, then that means someone phones in to get the recordings—or the device phones out—but, either way, this SIM card will be registered to someone's credit card. If we get onto the phone company, they should be able to tell us who owns this.'

Richard looked at Camille, impressed despite himself.

'You can do that, can you?'

There was a knock at the door and Sophie stuck her head into the room.

'Hello,' she said. 'Sorry to interrupt, but Claire's ready for you. She's in the study downstairs.'

'Very good,' Richard said. 'Thanks for letting us know.'

Having instructed Camille to stay behind to contact the phone company, Richard went downstairs to interview Claire on his own.

As he entered the study, he saw Claire was sitting in her wheelchair by the window, her dark hair still wet from her bath, the elegant scoop of her neck and chin in profile to Richard as she looked out at the view outside.

Richard briefly stopped in the doorway. In profile, he could see that Claire resembled her sister far more than she'd ever know. And yet one of them had become a supermodel famous the world over, and the other had never done any modelling work in her life. Richard briefly wondered how that could be, but, looking at Claire, he realised that, irrespective of what Phil had told him about how she hated her sister, his sympathies were naturally tilted in Claire's favour. After all, being first-born must have been a burden to her as well. It had always been her duty to grow up and run the family estate. What was more, Richard found himself musing, although he had no siblings himself, he could well imagine that if he did have any, he'd find them deeply irritating. Just as Claire had found Polly irritating.

'There's something I should tell you,' Claire said without turning around. 'Something about me and my sister.'

Only then did Claire turn and look at Richard. She then pushed her chair towards him—or, at least, she tried to. Richard could see that the little front wheel on the left hand side of her chair seemed to be briefly stuck in position. But then, with a final squeak of protest, it freed itself, started turning normally, and Claire was able to wheel over to him.

'Sorry about that,' she said. 'You spend a fortune on these chairs, and sometimes they're no better than bloody supermarket trolleys.'

Richard smiled despite himself. 'You were saying?'

'Only that you should perhaps know, it was Polly who put me in this wheelchair.'

Richard decided to play the innocent. 'It was?'

'You see,' she continued with sadness in her heart, 'my sister was always different. It was like she was missing the part of her brain that ever thought of consequences.'

And so Claire told the story of the Boxing Day hunt, and Richard noted that it broadly tallied with Phil's version of events, but with one glaring exception. Claire claimed that she'd forgiven her sister for causing her accident.

'You have?' Richard asked, surprised.

Claire looked back at Richard. 'Don't get me wrong. It took me a few years, but, yes, I've forgiven her. I had no choice.'

'How do you mean?'

'When it first happened, I spent six months in hospital, and that was the toughest thing I've had to endure in my life. Because you don't know pain until you're feeling it everywhere, twenty-four hours a day. It gets to the point when you don't remember what it's like *not* to live with pain. You'd accept any compromise, any disability, just for the pain to stop.'

Claire lapsed into silence, and then sighed deeply. It was clear to Richard that even remembering that time in her life was still upsetting for her.

'And when I came out of hospital, I was driven by a rage,' Claire said in a small voice. 'I was still very weak, but it was like this hot fire inside me. This anger at what Polly had done to me. But Polly didn't come back to the UK for years after she'd injured me—she'd run away if you ask me—and I realised, I was using up all this energy keeping this fire of hate alive, but what was it actually achieving? So, after a couple of years, I decided: enough. I got Polly to visit me in Lincolnshire. It was the first time we'd met in person since she'd injured me. I told her I forgave her and we both wept like kids. But if it meant I'd turned a corner, I don't think my forgiveness helped Polly. And I don't think she was in a happy place ever again. I always thought it was why she took heroin. She could forget her life—and who she was—when she was blotto.'

'You knew she was taking drugs?'

'I knew she was a heroin addict, yes. But that was the thing about Polly. She always fell in with the wrong crowd and allowed others to influence her. Whenever I challenged her about her addiction, she just tried to justify it by saying she never injected, she only ever smoked it. It wasn't the same as being a real heroin addict. That's what she believed.

'But yes. Within a few years of my accident, I decided that either I could continue to blame my absent sister for what she'd done to me, or I could accept it and just get on with my life. And I was lucky. I'd inherited the family estate after Father died, I had a lot on my plate, so I decided to keep myself busy. And it worked. I found I was thinking more about the future than I was about the past. More about what I could do rather than what I couldn't.'

'As a matter of interest,' Richard asked, 'if you inherited the family estate, what did Polly inherit?'

Claire had the good grace to look embarrassed.

'Nothing. Unfortunately, Father never forgave her for injuring me, and cut her out of his will.'

'That must have been tough on her,' Richard said.

'It was. Because this is what I began to realise as time passed. I'd got on with my life, and Polly was just doing the same things over and over again. Behaving the same way. Being irresponsible. And I think she'd also begun to notice that she was getting older. She couldn't get by on as little sleep as she used to, she couldn't do photoshoots wasted on drugs. And she wasn't as pretty as she used to be, if that's not a mean thing to say. In the end, I realised I felt sorry for her.'

'I see,' Richard said. 'Although, you know, Phil Adams told us you hated Polly.'

'Him?' Claire said haughtily. 'He's a parasite, that man. A hanger-on. It's people like him who destroyed my sister by getting her into drugs in the first place.'

'He got your sister into drugs?'

'I don't know about that, but I know he and Polly spent most of the nineties together stoned. And if he says I hated Polly, what does he know? I mean, don't get me wrong, I still argued with Polly and found her infuriating as hell—still just as self-absorbed—but I couldn't possibly hate her. Since Mother died, she's all the family I've got left.'

Richard could see the sincerity shine from Claire's eyes. But he still didn't quite buy it.

'No, I'm sorry,' he said. 'I just don't understand. Because what I'm seeing here is two sisters. One inherits everything. The other gets nothing. And the one who inherited everything was almost killed by the one who didn't.'

Claire sighed, understanding Richard's scepticism, but he still wasn't finished.

'And to make matters worse, their father died soon after the accident, cutting the younger twin out of the will entirely.'

'I know,' Claire said, shifting her weight in her wheelchair. 'But Father's death was in no way linked to my accident. He suffered a heart attack while out shooting pheasants. But I agree. Polly was hurt badly when Father cut her out of his will. But if you really want to know, it was how Mother treated her after Father's death that really upset her.'

'And how did your mother treat her?'

'Mother never forgave Polly for injuring me. And, the thing is, Mother could be as pig-headed as Polly. So she stayed in Lincolnshire refusing to communicate with Polly while Polly travelled the world refusing to communicate with Mother.

'When Mother died at the beginning of August last year, they still hadn't reconciled, and when Polly came to the funeral, I could see that Mother's death had hit her hard. So when Polly returned to Saint-Marie, I came out here to make sure she was okay. And I have to say, she was in a bad way when I got here. She was stoned on heroin from morning until night. And I kept telling her she couldn't change the past but she could change the future. She had to get herself into rehab. And then, after a few weeks of being here, something happened that made me think I'd never be able to save her.'

Claire took a deep breath before continuing, and Richard realised that she was preparing herself for the final ascent.

'You see, I don't do drugs. I've always felt it was disgusting that anyone would pollute their body. Especially since my injury. However, Polly insisted I have some marijuana with her one night. She kept insisting, holding this spliff out to me, and, in the end, I took it. I wasn't going to smoke it, I was going to stub it out, but I saw this look in Polly's eyes once it was in my hands. It was a look that was as cold as ice. And then, when I told her that I'd never put any kind of drug in my body, she started to get angry with me. In the end, I ripped the spliff open so that it would be ruined, and that's when I discovered that although it contained a small amount of marijuana, a whole heap of brown powder came out of the spliff as well.'

'Brown powder?'

'It was heroin.'

'Your sister tried to trick you into smoking heroin?'

'She was in a really self-destructive streak at the time, and I think she was lashing out. If she was in that much pain, she wanted everyone else to be in pain as well.'

'Then how can you not hate your sister after she tried to trick you into smoking heroin?'

Claire looked evenly at Richard.

'Because I didn't smoke the heroin. I dodged the bullet. And anyway, I've had a long time to get used to her. She's my sister. Dangerous to know. Damaged. But I don't hate her. I decided long ago that I pitied her.'

Richard realised that his thighs were prickling from the heat that had built up inside his woollen suit, so he went for a little walk around the study, desperate to create any kind of draught that might bring cooler air towards him.

It didn't really work, but he found himself standing by the floor-to-ceiling bookcase that ran down the side of the room. It occurred to him that there was something about the bookcase that was maybe out of place, but he couldn't quite work out what it was. Was it the books themselves?

Now wasn't the time for mulling books and bookcases, Richard told himself, so he turned back to face Claire.

'So what are you doing here this time?' he asked. 'Seeing as Polly tried to hook you on heroin the last time you saw her.'

'After I returned to the UK, Polly really crashed. I mean, *really* crashed. She had a massive overdose. Nearly died.' Richard could see how this was affecting Claire. 'Then, by January of this year she contacted me and said she'd got her strength back enough to finally put herself into rehab. And this time she'd stick it out. And you know what? She did. She completed the full programme.

'But the point is, when Polly left rehab in March of this year, she contacted me again and said she was finally clean, and that she was much more at peace with herself. And what's more, she wanted to make amends with me. Would I come out for a holiday? I didn't know if it was a good idea, but I hadn't seen Polly in nearly a year, so I decided to come out. That was two weeks ago, and I have to say, I've seen no evidence that she was still on drugs while I was out here.'

'And how has Polly been around you on this visit?'

Claire frowned. 'It's hard to say. She was sometimes up—really good fun—and sometimes she seemed down. Worried, almost.'

'And you're sure it wasn't heroin that was affecting her mood?'

'I don't think so. Polly always used to smoke her drugs openly in front of anyone, and none of us have seen her take anything stronger than a cigarette since we've been here.'

Richard remembered what Phil had told him. 'Then, if you're saying she was sometimes worried, could it have been money worries?'

'She didn't mention any money worries to me.'

Richard looked up at the chandelier that hung from the ceiling and it made him think of the identical chandelier in the sitting room next door. This thought made him look back at the bookcase, as it reminded him that the two rooms were ostensibly identical to each other—with the same bay windows, floor layout and chandelier in the centre of both rooms—and the only difference was the bookcase that ran down the side of this room, Polly's study.

But then Richard realised a far more interesting point. Claire's mobile phone had been found inside the chandelier of the sitting room next door, and they'd just found a surveillance bug in Polly's bedroom. Were these two facts perhaps related?

'Can you tell me,' he said, 'have you been bugging your sister?'

'I'm sorry?'

'We've found some kind of surveillance device in Polly's bedroom just now. Did you put it there?'

Claire was at first surprised. And then she was shocked. 'I have no idea what you're talking about. Are you saying someone's been bugging my sister?'

'Then what can you tell me about the threatening letters your sister has been receiving?'

Claire looked at Richard a moment before answering. 'You know about those, do you?'

'Why don't you tell me what you know?'

'Well, I don't know what to say, I've not seen them myself, but Polly told me that someone had been sending her anonymous letters. Hate mail. I guessed it was someone from her world of drugs, so I never enquired too much. As I'm sure you can guess, Polly's hung out with plenty of criminal types in her time.' Claire manoeuvred her wheelchair so that she was now looking directly at Richard. And Richard noticed that her front left wheel stuck again briefly before she could get the wheelchair to move. 'But you're right to ask, because I've been thinking, what if these threatening letters were being sent by the person I saw on the cliff steps just before Polly died. You know, the person I saw going down the steps wearing the yellow raincoat?'

'Yes,' Richard said, 'can I ask about that? Are you sure you didn't see who was wearing the yellow raincoat?'

'I'm sorry. I was dealing with Polly at the time. All I saw was a flash of yellow as whoever it was went down the steps of the cliff just as we arrived at the top of the steps. But it was definitely someone.'

Richard asked a few more questions to try and help Claire unlock her memories, but it was no good. She couldn't remember seeing anything more than she'd already said. So, thanking Claire again for her time, Richard decided he'd go back to the scene of the crime and try to work out for himself what Claire might or might not have seen that morning.

As he arrived at the cliff top, Richard pulled his hankie from his pocket, and, seeing as no one was watching, he wrung the warm sweat out of it onto the grass. *This heat!* he thought to himself as he looked out at the overwhelmingly blue sky and the just-as-overwhelmingly blue sea. But then Richard noticed a tiny cloud far off near the horizon. He felt a fleeting sense of solidarity with that one rain-making device in the whole dazzling firmament. He and the cloud were both of them out of step with the rest of the Caribbean.

Pulling his attention back to the cliff top, Richard tried to imagine what had happened on the day of the murder. Polly had pushed Claire to the top of the cliff—that much was known. But between Polly and Claire disappearing behind the border of shrubs and Polly being thrown to her death, they only had Claire's word for what had happened during the key seconds before the murder.

So what had happened just before Polly was killed?

Richard was interrupted in his musings by the sight of Camille striding around the clump of shrubs towards him holding her notebook in her hand. And, as she came closer, Richard once again noticed how her skin seemed to be burnished bronze in the sunlight. Whereas his skin, he knew, was probably most like an old bar of soap you'd expect to find lurking at the bottom of a washbag: entirely worn out, dull, and not so much white as being absent of colour. Although, Richard realised, in this heat, his skin wasn't so much like a bar of soap, it was more like when you remove the pastry lid to a nice steak and kidney pie, and see that the underside of the pastry is still uncooked and pale, but steaming. That was what his skin felt like to Richard.

Richard shook himself from his reverie as Camille reached him.

'Okay, sir,' she said. 'So I've been putting pressure on the telecoms company to release the name of the person the SIM card from the surveillance bug was registered to, but they didn't want to give me the information without a warrant.'

Richard knew how big companies were reluctant to assist the police unless all the necessary warrants had first been issued.

'But I kept going at them, explaining that this was a murder case, moving up the chain of command, until I spoke to the head of the company on the island. He was able to get up the details for me, and you'll never guess who owns that bug.'

'Why? Who is it?'

'Juliette Moreau.'

'What?' Richard said, puzzled.

'The bug is registered in Juliette Moreau's name.'

Richard was stunned.

Why on earth would Polly's housekeeper have been bugging her bedroom?

Chapter 7

Richard and Camille approached Juliette and Alain's house along the gravel path from Polly's garden. They could see that Alain was outside with the hood up on his old Citroën car and Richard was pleased to see that although Alain had an oily cloth in his hand, he was wearing smart trousers and a clean white short-sleeved shirt. Richard had always admired men who could do messy work without getting messy themselves.

As for Juliette, she was sitting in the shade of the bungalow's verandah looking at her smartphone, which, considering why they were there to see her, Richard thought to himself, was an irony.

'Mrs Moreau, could we have a word?' Richard said as they went through the little gate that led into the front garden.

Juliette looked up from her phone.

'Of course,' she said.

Over by the car, Alain wiped the oil from his hands and came over as well. 'What's this?' he asked.

'We'd just like to ask your wife a few questions.'

'Then, mind if I stick around?' Alain said, putting the cloth down and pulling over a spare chair. Richard and Camille looked at Juliette.

'Mrs Moreau, do you mind us speaking to you in front of your husband?' Camille asked.

Juliette looked at the police as though the question was ridiculous.

'No, of course not.'

'Good,' Richard said, taking over the interview. 'We just wanted to ask you once more where you were at 10am at the time of the murder.'

Juliette was surprised by the question.

'Well, I told you,' she said. 'I was out on a training run. For my triathlon. I explained all this to your colleague.'

'You mean, Police Officer Fidel Best?' Richard asked.

'That's right. He said he'd be checking it out.'

'I see,' Richard said as though he was merely following a dull train of thought through. 'Then can you tell me why you put a surveillance bug under Polly Carter's bed?'

Juliette hadn't seen the question coming, and it was as though someone had slapped her in the face. And, just as gratifyingly for Richard, he could see that Alain was also looking at his wife, startled.

'What?' Juliette eventually managed to say.

'We know the SIM card inside the bug is registered to your credit card. And the bug was taped to the underside of Polly's bed. So, QED, you've been bugging her, the only question is: why?'

'I don't know what you're talking about,' Juliette said, but it was clear she was trying to buy herself time.

'Don't lie to us,' Richard said. 'The telecoms company are sending over the original contract you took out with them for the SIM card. But we already know it has your name and address on it. And your signature.'

Juliette looked from the police to her husband, confusion in her eyes. But there was a moment, Richard saw, where she seemed to come to a decision. He'd seen it often before, and Camille recognised it as well. Against her wishes, Juliette was about to tell them the truth.

'Very well,' she said, drawing herself up straighter in her chair. 'Since you're asking. I don't deny it. I placed that bug there.'

'I see,' Richard said, trying to hide his surprise at Juliette's resolve. 'And may we ask why you did that?'

Juliette's lip curled into a sneer as she said, 'Because my husband had an affair with Polly Carter last Christmas and it's how I managed to catch them at it.'

All the life seemed to drain out of Alain's face as his wife said this, and Richard could see shame flood his cheeks.

'But that's what that woman was like,' Juliette said. 'If she wanted something, she just took it. I hated her.'

Richard was shocked that a witness in a murder case would ever admit to hating the deceased, but he was reminded of how Fidel had said Juliette was a hard woman.

Looking at Juliette now, Richard could see what Fidel meant.

'And the thing is,' Juliette continued, 'I know she'd always wanted my husband. A woman knows these things. But she'd never tried to get him before. She was too busy with her parties. Taking her drugs. And I thought my husband—my good, Christian husband—wouldn't ever have his head turned by such a Jezebel.'

Richard saw Alain's Adam's apple bob as he swallowed, and he almost felt sorry for the man. Almost, of course, but not quite. Infidelity, after all, was infidelity.

Camille turned to Alain. 'Is this true?' she asked.

Alain nodded meekly, ashamed.

'What happened?'

'I'll tell you what happened,' Juliette cut in before her husband could answer. 'That harlot seduced my husband at Christmas—and after all these years of him lecturing me that I wasn't a good enough Catholic!'

'Alain?' Camille asked Alain softly.

Alain looked at Camille like a little boy lost. 'It's true. I had an affair with Polly last Christmas.'

Richard looked at Alain. He seemed so straight-laced with his spotless white shirt and pressed trousers. Like someone out of an advert from the 1950s. He was hardly someone he could imagine Polly having a wild affair with. But then, there was no accounting for tastes, Richard reminded himself.

'So this affair,' Richard said, 'happened before Polly checked herself into rehab in Los Angeles in January?'

'That's right,' Alain said. 'Our...liaison only lasted a few days, and it stopped the moment my wife confronted me with a recording of Polly and me.'

'A recording of you in Polly's bedroom?' Richard offered.

Alain nodded.

'Yes, can I ask about that?' Richard said, turning to Juliette. 'I mean, I know that what your husband did was wrong, but was it really necessary to put a surveillance bug in your employer's bedroom?'

Juliette's eyes narrowed. 'You're not married, are you?'

Richard straightened the tie in his collar as he answered. 'Actually, no.'

'When you think your man's cheating on you...' Juliette left the sentence unfinished, but Richard got the gist. Juliette clearly believed it had been an act of temperance on her part to bug her husband rather than just kill him there and then.

'So what happened when your wife confronted you?' Camille asked Alain.

'I...confessed to everything of course.'

'Only after I played you the recording!' Juliette spat.

'No, that's not true,' Alain said, but with barely any fight in him. 'I denied it at first, I admit that much, but the moment I realised what was at stake—our marriage, Juliette—our life together—I told you everything.'

Richard looked at husband and wife.

'Then I'm curious,' he said. 'How did this surveillance bug work?'

'It was simple,' Juliette said, unable to keep a note of pride out of her voice. 'When I knew my husband had gone up to Polly's house, I could ring into the device and record what it was hearing.'

'Then do you have the recordings you took from it?'

This threw Juliette.

'I'm sorry?' she said.

'If you're the sort of person who bugs bedrooms, I'm sure you're the sort of person who keeps the recordings.'

Juliette looked at Richard, and seemed to be weighing up her options.

'You're right,' she eventually said.

'Then would you get what recordings you have for me?' Richard asked as reasonably as if he was asking a neighbour if he could borrow a cup of sugar.

Juliette had no choice, really, so she got up and went into the house.

Richard noticed that, with his wife gone, Alain seemed to get even more closed-off, even more introverted.

'You okay?' Camille asked him.

'She wasn't a harlot,' Alain said, now that his wife was absent. 'You know. Polly. I mean, she was selfish, she could be wild, but she didn't have a bad bone in her body. She was a good person, you have to believe that.'

Richard remembered how Alain had been gripped by grief when first he'd heard of Polly's death. Of course he had, Richard realised. Only at the beginning of the year, he'd had a passionate affair with her.

'How did it start between you and her?' Camille asked.

'I don't know,' he said. 'It was just after Christmas and it was like her defences were down. She told me she'd ruined her relationships with her sister and both her parents. Her dad had died without forgiving her, she said, there was no way her sister would ever forgive her, either, and now her mum had also died without forgiving her. And as she told me all this, I saw how damaged she was. I got it into my head that she was like a little bird with a broken wing. I felt sorry for her.

'So I tried to talk to her. I thought, at the time, I was motivated by my desire to do the Christian thing. To look out for my neighbour. But I soon realised…well, my interest in her wasn't…' Alain struggled to find the right word. 'Pure,' he eventually conceded. 'But Polly also seemed interested in me. That's what I couldn't understand. And, I don't know how it happened, but I was suddenly in bed with her. I felt so ashamed afterwards, that I'd committed adultery, but the next day…I went to her house again…and this time she was waiting for me. We both knew why I was there. It was like a dream, those few days, but that's the problem with dreams. You wake up.'

Before Alain could say any more, Juliette returned with a USB key drive that she handed to Richard.

'The recordings are on this,' she said.

'Thank you. And don't worry, we'll return it to you once we've copied it.'

'No need,' Juliette said. 'You were right. I already have copies of the sound files.'

'So tell me, Juliette,' Richard said. 'After your husband finished his affair with Polly, was it you who sent her those threatening letters?'

There was the briefest of pauses, and then Juliette looked surprised.

'What threatening letters?' she asked.

'We found anonymous letters in a locked drawer in Polly's study. Threatening her. Was it you who sent them?'

'I don't know what you're talking about,' Juliette said with a hint of challenge in her voice. 'And why would I threaten Polly Carter?'

'Because she had an affair with your husband,' Richard said.

Juliette snorted. 'How on earth could I have threatened her? She was a single woman. And a narcissist. She'd have laughed in my face if I'd tried to tell her what she'd done was wrong. And do you think I'd still be in this job if I'd ever confronted her? So, the fact that I'm still here—all these months later—should prove to you that Polly never had any kind of issues with me. And as for my issues with her, I made sure I shared them only with my husband.'

As Juliette said this, she crossed her arms as though to say that that was all there was to say on the matter. And, on reflection, Richard couldn't help but conclude that she was possibly right.

★★★

Back at the police station, Camille got the sound files from the thumb drive and copied them onto her main computer. Turning the volume up as loud as possible, she played the first file. Initially, it was hard to tell what was going on as all they could hear was a chorus of crickets in the background.

'It must be night-time,' Richard said.

Camille looked at her boss, surprised.

'It's when male crickets rub their legs together to attract a mate.'

'You *have* been reading your book on insects.'

Once again, Richard felt hurt by Camille's tone. Why did it matter to her what he did in his spare time? And what was wrong with his interest in entomology anyway? It was a perfectly valid hobby.

Before Camille could say anything more on the subject, they heard voices speaking from the computer's speakers. The sound was muffled, but it was definitely possible to hear a man—it sounded like Alain—say 'We can't do this'. A woman then replied, 'But that's why we *have* to do this!'

So this was Polly Carter, Richard realised. He and Camille stood in silence as they heard Polly flirtily beg Alain to come to bed with her—goading him on, saying she wanted him, she needed him, and that he was irresistible. Next, Richard and Camille heard Alain beg Polly to put her top back on, that he was married, and that he had to stay faithful to his wife. Polly just laughed, telling Alain that Juliette was off on one of her stupid training runs, it's all she seemed to care about. And then, with a 'Dear God, woman!', there was the sudden sound of bed springs stretching violently—Richard could but presume, because Alain's resistance had finally crumbled and he and Polly had fallen onto the bed together.

Yes, Richard thought to himself, as the sound of the background crickets was finally obliterated by the steady groan of bed springs rhythmically bouncing, Polly and Alain were clearly on the bed now.

And it was only then that Richard realised that he was standing next to Camille while they both listened to an audio recording of two people having sex.

'Chief?!'

Richard whipped his head around and saw Dwayne standing in the doorway. But worse than that, his mother was standing at Dwayne's side.

No one spoke while the sound of rhythmic bouncing filled the room, and then, after a few more moments of shocked silence from Dwayne and Jennifer, Camille threw her head back and laughed raucously while Richard said, 'Dear God, Camille, stop that racket!' as he dived for the mouse on her computer and desperately started clicking at the sound file until he'd managed to silence it.

'What on earth have you two been listening to?' Jennifer asked in wonder.

'What are you doing here?' Richard said, now covering up his embarrassment—as he often did—with rudeness.

'Oh don't worry,' Jennifer said. 'I just wanted you to know, I've had a lovely afternoon with Dwayne here, but I won't be around for dinner tonight. Dwayne's booked me in on a night-time trip to see the hatching turtles.'

Richard looked at his mother. And then he looked at the beaming Dwayne as he stood at her side.

'You've—um—spent the afternoon together?'

'That's right, Chief,' Dwayne said, still grinning. 'We went to the Botanical Gardens. And it turns out your mother knows pretty much all there is to know about flowers.'

'Thank you, Dwayne,' Jennifer said. 'That's very kind of you.'

'And as for police work?' Richard asked sardonically.

'Don't worry,' Dwayne said, still beaming. 'All done.'

'And don't worry about me,' Jennifer said. 'I'm off to Catherine's bar now. According to Dwayne, I haven't visited the island until I've met Catherine and tried a glass of the local rum.'

'You're right there, Jennifer!' Dwayne said, happily.

Jennifer once again thanked Dwayne for her lovely afternoon and left with a smile, which finally allowed Richard to ask Dwayne what clues he'd been able to find on the old smugglers' path. But, even as Dwayne told his boss that he'd unfortunately been unable to find any substantive clues or leads at all, Richard found it hard to concentrate on what he was being told.

His mother had spent the afternoon with Dwayne and was now drinking rum on her own in Catherine's bar? Richard hadn't really known his mother drink much beyond the odd glass of sherry on Christmas morning. Since when did she drink neat spirits in the middle of the afternoon?

Something was up with his mother. But what was it?

Over the next few days, Richard got just as far with his mother as he did with the case, which was to say precisely nowhere.

For starters, just as Dwayne had found no clues on the old smugglers' path, Fidel had also been unable to prove conclusively whether Juliette had been on her 10k run at the time of the murder. The only two witnesses he'd been able to find who remembered seeing her at all, saw her just before 10.30am in Honoré while she'd been waiting to meet up with Alain. This would—theoretically—have still given her enough time to kill Polly on the cliff at 10am and be in Honoré in time to be seen at 10.30.

Fidel also tried to pin down Alain's alibi by talking to the priest who'd officiated at the Sunday service Alain said he'd been attending at the time of the murder. The priest—who Fidel knew well—said he couldn't remember seeing Alain, but then, there were so many people who came to Sunday services that there was every chance Alain had been there and he just hadn't noticed. So, Fidel had started asking around the parishioners he knew had also been at the service, and none of them could remember seeing Alain, either. But seeing as the congregation would have been well over a hundred people and Fidel had so far only spoken to half a dozen of them, he couldn't yet say for sure whether Alain had been there or not. He was just going to have to keep asking.

But Fidel's hard work allowed Richard to write up on the whiteboard that Juliette and Alain still didn't have definitive alibis for the time of the murder.

As for the other suspects, Richard and his team didn't seem to make any more progress.

Richard spoke to Claire's GP back in Lincolnshire who was able to confirm that her accident had indeed left her legs paralysed. Under pressure from Richard, the GP then admitted that it was possible—perhaps—for someone with Claire's injuries to regain limited use in her legs, but he said that it would have been extremely unlikely. What's more, after so many years of inactivity, even if Claire had regained some movement, she'd have been unlikely to have had the strength to walk. When Richard tried to suggest that maybe Claire was suffering from conversion disorder—as Phil had said Polly believed—the GP had just outright laughed. Very few people had conversion disorder, he explained rather patronisingly, it was entirely unlikely that Claire was one of them.

As for Sophie, Dwayne had sprinkled what he insisted on calling his 'love dust' on his contact with her agency back in London, and—primed with what Sophie had already admitted to them—he was able to get the rest of the story out of them. Sophie had indeed been sacked after she'd been caught thieving four fifty pound notes from one of their clients. However, it was the first time that Sophie had ever transgressed, and she'd otherwise had glowing feedback from every single client she'd nursed for the previous fifteen years. And it was partly because they liked Sophie so much that, when Claire asked for her again, they'd been prepared to turn a blind eye and let Sophie accept the booking. In essence, the agency's message was clear: Sophie was a good nurse, she'd committed one terrible lapse of judgement, they didn't want that to tarnish her reputation entirely.

As for Phil Adams, Richard was amazed to learn that, legally, he was indeed Polly's husband. What's more, once they contacted Polly's lawyer, they discovered that Polly had never made a will, so Phil had just inherited her entire estate. Richard went up to the house to tell Phil this news in person, but Phil remained entirely underwhelmed as he continued to insist that Polly died penniless.

As for how wealthy—or otherwise—Polly had been when she died, that had so far been much harder to prove because it turned out that Polly had numerous bank accounts and was in the habit of throwing all letters from the banks straight into the bin unopened. Fidel had tracked down as many of the accounts as he could and had requested her banks send over copy statements of her accounts, but they hadn't arrived yet.

And, while Richard was trying to focus on the case, he still couldn't work out what was up with his mother. Since her first afternoon at Catherine's bar, she'd become firm friends with Catherine and had become something of a fixture in the bar. As he drove home each night, Richard would see his mother and Catherine sitting out on the deck of the bar sharing a drink and a chat. What they talked about, Richard had no idea.

But as Jennifer broke dinner engagement after dinner engagement with her son, Richard realised that he didn't know what he found more baffling: that his mother would come out alone to see him; or that, now she was here, she seemed to have no interest in seeing him.

He was dimly aware that there was a quick solution to his quandary, and that would be if he rang his father and asked him what on earth his mother was up to. However, Richard was pretty sure that he hadn't directly phoned his father since the turn of the century, and he realised—when push came to shove—that he seemed to have lost the belief that he was even capable of speaking to his father on the phone. After all, what would they say to each other?

So, instead of getting to the bottom of what his mother was up to on the island, Richard threw himself into his work, and, in particular, he found himself coming back to the questions at the heart of the case.

How had the killer known to be on the cliff steps at the precise moment that Polly was about to run down them? And how was it possible to explain the coincidence that she'd just said she'd commit suicide as well? And—most baffling of all for Richard—how did the killer then vanish into thin air immediately afterwards? Was it this 'Man in a Yellow Raincoat' that they needed to find? Or someone else? And also, who'd been sending the threatening letters to Polly? And, as much as he tried to focus on the bigger questions, Richard couldn't help but also worry over who it was who'd put Claire's mobile phone in the chandelier of the sitting room before the murder. And why had it been put there? After all, if someone wanted to get rid of a phone, why didn't they just turn it off and put it in a drawer? Or throw it in the sea? Why did it have to be hidden in a chandelier? It had to have some meaning, but what on earth could it be?

On the fifth day of Jennifer's visit, there were significant breakthroughs, both in the case and in Richard's understanding of what his mother was up to.

In the morning, they finally got the reports back from the labs on Guadeloupe.

As for the threatening letters they'd found in Polly's locked drawer, the only fingerprints they'd been able to identify belonged to Polly. What was more, they'd analysed the A4 paper the cut-out letters were glued to—and the glue that had been used—and had only been able to conclude that they were both popular brands that were readily available in the Caribbean and beyond.

As for the autopsy report, that had made for far more interesting reading. Firstly, the pathologist had tested Polly's blood and hair and been able to confirm that she'd not only not had any narcotics in her system when she'd died, but she hadn't taken any narcotics in the previous six months, either.

Polly really had kicked her heroin habit before she'd died—which Richard and his team found surprising to say the least. After all, what were the chances that a long-standing heroin addict would get clean of drugs just in time to be murdered?

But the pathologist was also able to confirm that while it had been the fall from the cliff that had snapped Polly's neck and killed her, she'd sustained a significant injury to her head pre-mortem. There'd been bruising and a deep cut under Polly's hair just behind her left ear. What was more, the pathologist had also been able to recover trace samples of a mossy substance from in and around this wound behind Polly's ear. And the trace samples of moss from her wound matched the moss that was on the branch the police had found at the scene. But then, this was hardly surprising, as the pathologist was also able to prove that the blood on the branch also belonged to Polly.

It all confirmed what Richard had been saying all along. Someone had been waiting on the steps before Polly arrived. This person had then attacked Polly with the branch—hit her in the head and cut her in the forearm as they briefly fought—and then, once Polly had fallen to her death, the killer had hidden the bloody branch in the bush further down the steps.

How the killer then managed to vanish from the steps and get away without either leaving footprints on the sand or being seen by anyone else was still a mystery, though, and one that Richard was mulling as he picked up his lunchtime sandwich from Catherine's bar.

However, before Richard returned to the police station, his attention was drawn by a trilling laugh from the outside seating area. He recognised that laugh.

With a presentiment of disaster, Richard went through to the back of the bar—still holding his banana sandwich neatly wrapped in brown greaseproof paper—and saw his mother sitting at a table overlooking the bay. But what gave Richard pause was the fact that Dwayne was also sitting with his mother—was clearly in mid-anecdote—and he could see his mother trying to stifle a laugh.

'Oh, Dwayne, stop it!' Jennifer said as Richard approached.

Dwayne had the good grace to look awkward as hell the moment he saw his boss.

'Hey, Chief,' Dwayne said. 'I was just passing and Jennifer here called me over. She wanted some advice on the glass-bottomed boat. You know, whether she should go on it or not.'

Richard knew the boat well, if only because he'd always said that a boat with a hull made of glass that operated in shark-infested waters was precisely the last boat he'd ever get on.

'And Dwayne's saying it's a must-see,' Jennifer said.

'But it's a glass-bottomed boat,' Richard said.

'I know, imagine! Apparently you can see all the tropical fish and dolphins through the bottom.'

'Yes,' Richard repeated, unable to comprehend how his mother didn't understand the very simple point he was making. 'But that's because the hull is made of glass. It could break at any moment.'

'Oh I know, but you know what I've decided? You only live once. I'm going to give it a try!'

Richard looked at his mother as though he were looking at a complete stranger.

As the pause grew, Dwayne rose from his chair.

'Anyway, Chief,' he said. 'Glad you've got your lunch. See you around, Jennifer.'

As Dwayne left, Jennifer looked at the confusion in her son's eyes.

'Sit down,' she said. 'I think I owe you an explanation.'

Still clutching his greaseproof package of sandwiches to his chest, Richard sat down, and, as he looked at his mother, he had to acknowledge that he'd rarely seen her look more relaxed. The few days of Caribbean sunshine had given her skin a healthy glow.

'I'm sorry if you think my behaviour is shocking, Richard, but I came out here…' Here, Jennifer sighed sadly, more for herself than for her son. 'I came out here because I wasn't very happy at home.'

Even as Jennifer said the words, Richard realised that his hearing had gone—it was as though there was suddenly a ball of cotton wool engulfing him. His mother *wasn't* happy?

'You see, it's your father.' Here, Jennifer took one of Richard's hands from his packed lunch and cupped it in hers. 'Because we both know he's a very difficult man.' Richard still felt as though he was encased in cotton, he was having difficulty making sense of what his mother was telling him. 'And I have to be honest, it's been tough living with him since he retired.'

Richard's dad had retired three years ago and Richard had presumed that his mother and father had been happy together ever since then. Of course they had. They were his mother and father.

'You see, he just doesn't understand that after all those years of him working all the hours God gave, I've built up a life for myself. And he expects me to drop it all so I can spend time with him. But when I do, he doesn't know what he wants to do. And he's a typical man, he can't do anything on his own. You know, the other day he was having a bath upstairs, I was cooking him his lunch, and then he started calling for me. When I got upstairs and asked him what was wrong, he told me he was bored.

'Well, he's not the only one. I'm bored of not being my own person. So you should know, and there's no easy way to say this, Richard, but you're old enough. I told him we're having a trial separation and then I booked my ticket out here to see you. And I have to say, it's the best thing I've done in years. I was wound up like a spring when I got out here. I think I've been wound up like a spring my whole life. But the Caribbean has relaxed me. Coming here was precisely what I needed.'

Jennifer continued talking about the virtues of Saint-Marie, but Richard realised that he was now so smothered in this feeling of cotton wool pressing down on him from all sides that he'd lost his power of hearing entirely. Eventually, though, he saw that his mother had stopped talking and was now waiting for him to say something.

But what could he say? In truth, this was only partly because what his mother had told him had left him so sideswiped. It was also because he'd spent the last thirty seconds or so inside his cotton wool cocoon reciting the opening lines to Rudyard Kipling's poem 'If' — over and over to himself. Because, it was only now that Richard was truly *in extremis*, that he realised how woefully misjudged Kipling had been. As far as Richard was concerned, 'If you can keep your head when all about you are losing theirs', then it just showed that you clearly hadn't understood the severity of the situation.

'Are you even listening to me?' Jennifer asked, confused by her son's silence.

'No of course I am, it's just…'

Jennifer looked at her troubled son. 'It's a lot to take in.'

'But you and Dad need to be together,' Richard said.

'I know,' Jennifer said. 'And maybe if he could change…? But the thing is, Richard, men don't change. Just look at you. When you came out of the womb, you were frowning.'

'I was?' Richard had had no idea.

Jennifer looked at her son and saw a man in a suit who was still clutching his sandwich to his chest with the one hand she wasn't holding. He'd always been like this, she thought to herself. Concerned, anxious, and always worried that the sky was about to fall on his head.

Jennifer sighed to herself. Was she to blame for the wonderful but limited man she saw sitting in front of her? After all, it had been her who'd obsessively drilled the twin virtues of neatness and precision into him from the moment he could toddle. And it had been her who'd put him in a school uniform when he was four years old. And here he was— forty years later—still basically wearing a school uniform.

But the regret Jennifer had above all others, she thought to herself, was that she'd sent Richard to single-sex boarding schools from the age of eight to eighteen. It hadn't been her idea—it had been Richard's father's—but she wished she'd fought harder to keep her son at home, or at least make sure his boarding school had girls in it. But, back in those days, co-education was seen as a dangerous experiment. You knew where you were with a traditional boarding school. Yes, Jennifer thought to herself, you knew where you were when you sent your only son away from home: you were sewing name tapes onto your eight-year-old child's teddy bear while the tears rolled down your cheeks.

'You're crying,' Richard said, confused.

Jennifer wiped the tears from her eyes.

'I know, darling. Just thinking about the past.'

Richard didn't know what to say.

Luckily for him—or perhaps unluckily, he didn't really know which way round he was facing by this point—Fidel bustled into view, a load of printouts in his hand.

'Sir! Sir!' he said, excitedly, as he approached the table. 'Oh, Jennifer, you look lovely!'

'Thank you, Fidel,' Jennifer said, delighted at the compliment.

'We've finally got hold of Polly Carter's bank statements, sir, and Phil Adams was right, she'd spent all of her money. Sorry,' Fidel added, 'can I say any of this in front of your mother?'

Richard was still trying to realign the world, so found himself giving a strangled grunt of assent.

'Okay,' Fidel said, laying out the bank statements on the table, 'because it's not just that she's got no cash, there's more than that. Firstly, she's not received any income since August of last year, that's over a year without any money coming in.' Fidel was indicating the 'CREDIT' column of the bank statements and Richard was finding his focus finally coming back as he looked at the columns of numbers all arranged in tight lines on the bank statements.

It was true what Fidel was saying. Polly hadn't received any income in the last year, and although in September of the previous year she'd had over one hundred and three thousand dollars in her current account, she was now overdrawn by nearly twelve thousand dollars. And Richard could also see that her three credit card bills had between five and eleven thousand dollars on each of them as well. And, as Richard compared the various statements against each other, he could even spot the 'robbing Peter to pay Paul' technique that the cash-poor often used to handle their debt, with Polly taking out money on one credit card to make the minimum payments on another card.

And then Richard saw it, just as Fidel was about to mention it.

Three days before she died—and the reason why she was now over twelve thousand dollars in debt—Polly had taken ten thousand dollars out of her bank account in cash.

Richard knew very well that nobody takes ten thousand dollars in cash out of their bank unless they're up to something dodgy as hell. But then he realised something even more profound. They'd searched Polly's house from top to bottom after she'd died—looking for the yellow raincoat at first, and then for drugs and for something that the rusty key they found could have opened—and there'd been no cash anywhere, let alone ten thousand dollars. Nor could he think of anything Polly had bought in the last three days before her death that would have cost ten thousand dollars.

'Okay,' Richard said, now fully focused on the case again. 'Why did she need ten thousand dollars? And where is it now?'

'Well that's the thing, sir,' Fidel said. 'Are we even sure she took the money out herself?'

'How do you mean?' Richard asked.

'Well, that's not the only suspicious withdrawal from her bank account. You see, back in February—while Polly was in rehab—there were two massive withdrawals from the same bank account.'

As Fidel was speaking, he turned back through the pages and showed Richard a bank statement from February.

Richard saw what Fidel was referring to at once. Polly had had nearly sixty thousand dollars to her name at the beginning of January, but then there were two different withdrawals the following month. The first took $17,000. The second took $23,000. And both were to the same payee: 'M Brandon'.

And then Richard remembered that Phil Adams had told them that he suspected Max Brandon was a crook who'd been siphoning money from Polly for years. Now here was evidence that Max had cleaned out Polly's bank account back in February. Was that why Max had been so nervous—picking at the skin around his thumbs—the first time he was interviewed by Richard and Camille? Were his nerves shredded because Polly had found out he was a thief?

And had he then killed her before she could tell the police?

Chapter 8

Richard and Camille found Max in Polly's study. He was looking at old magazine covers that featured photos of Polly in various states of dress and undress, Richard could see.

'She was so beautiful,' Max said as Richard picked up one of the magazines and looked at the photo of Polly on the cover. Richard wasn't entirely sure he agreed. He could see that Polly was striking-looking, but beautiful? He felt that beauty was more fresh-faced and optimistic than the dead eyes he saw in the face that were staring out at him.

Putting the magazine down, Richard looked at the bookshelves that ran down the side of the room, and once again had the nagging feeling that there was something about them that was maybe out of place. Or maybe it was just that they were so dusty.

'Anyway, how can I help you?' Max asked.

Looking back at Max, Richard saw a man who was still tense—and the plasters on his two thumbs suggested that he was still struggling with his nerves. So Richard decided to leave Camille to make their case while he went for a wander around the room. What was it about this room that was 'off'?

'Well,' Camille said, recognising with a sigh that Richard had just absented himself from the interview. 'Perhaps you can first tell us why Polly hasn't earned any money in the last year?'

'That's easy enough to explain,' Max said. 'You know she suffered a drugs overdose last year?'

'She was hospitalised in September.'

'That's right, and she wasn't remotely fit to work when she came out, I can tell you. But to be honest, I just presumed she'd take a month or so off to get her strength back and then she'd get back on the horse, as it were. A rather unfortunate metaphor considering what it was that put her in hospital. But she didn't want to do any work when she got out of hospital. I'd ring her, and when she even bothered to answer she'd just say she was too tired to do a shoot. By Christmas, I was seriously beginning to worry for her. She had no interest in taking up any of the jobs I was offering her.'

'So you confronted her?'

'No, that's not my style, but I maybe pointed out how foolhardy she was being. You see, the world of fashion is fickle. It's kind of built into its DNA. And she needed to know that the longer she left it before going back to work, the greater the chance the world would have moved its attention on to the "next big thing" by then.'

'And what did she say to that?'

'That's what I couldn't understand. She didn't seem bothered in the slightest. I rang her a few times over Christmas and she just kept saying "and a Happy New Year to you, too, Max" whenever I tried to tell her she needed to take her career more seriously. And then, at the beginning of January, just as I thought she'd definitely return to work, she checked herself into rehab and vanished from the world for another three months.'

Max was getting more sure of himself as he got further into his story. In fact, Camille saw, he was almost beginning to enjoy himself.

'I have to admit,' Max continued conspiratorially, 'I was frustrated with her. She's my only client. And don't get me wrong, I've earned plenty from her over the years, but she couldn't just walk out on her career. That's the way I saw it. So, when she finally got out of rehab in March, I issued a press release saying she was back on the market, knowing the offers would start to roll in, and you know what? They did. But every time I tried to get Polly to take a job, she just point blank refused to do it. I was appalled. It was like she had a death wish. Again, a rather unfortunate phrase, sorry about that. But it was at this time that she started telling me she had no interest in being a model ever again. It was all pointless, that's what she said. What she really wanted to do was retire to the countryside and have babies. If I'm honest, I thought she was unhinged.'

'Look, sorry to interrupt,' Richard said, 'and maybe it's just me, but is there something wrong with this room?'

Camille threw a warning look at her boss. 'Sir, do you mind?'

'No?' Richard asked again, seemingly unfussed by his *non sequitur.* 'Just me, then. Anyway,' he continued, now turning to look at Max. 'So if Polly hasn't worked since leaving rehab, what are you doing here'

'I beg your pardon?' Max sputtered.

'Only, if she's not working, why does she need to have her agent to hand?'

'But that's the thing. She didn't invite me out here, I came of my own accord. Because...well, she's my only client, so, if you must know, I've been here telling her face-to-face that she has to go back to work. But it didn't matter what I said. She said she'd given up on the modelling.'

'That must have concerned you,' Camille said.

'It did. But I'm a very persuasive person. And I don't give up. I mean, everyone has to earn money, don't they? So, as far as I was concerned, it was just a question of chipping away. She'd have gone back to work eventually. And what was giving me hope that she was about to return to work was how happy she was in herself just before she died.'

This got Richard and Camille's attention.

'You're saying she was *happy* before she died?' Richard said.

'Yes,' Max said, thrown by the question.

'But everyone we've spoken to said Polly was spiky and difficult the whole time.'

Max sighed. 'Sure. She could still be snippy, don't get me wrong, she was all edges that woman, but no one knew Polly as well as I did, and I'm telling you I've never known her happier than she was just before she died.'

'But why was she so happy?'

'I don't know, but I guess it's got to be related to the fact that she'd finally managed to get clean of drugs.'

Richard considered what Max had said. Was he right? It was possible, seeing as the autopsy had shown no drugs in Polly's system—and tests on her hair had shown she'd ingested no drugs for the previous few months as well. Maybe that's what it was? After all, wouldn't kicking a lifelong addiction to heroin be enough to make anyone happy?

And yet, everyone else apart from Max had been so sure that Polly was her usual prickly self in the last few weeks of her life, and there was no doubting that Polly had started an argument with Claire out of thin air just before she died.

As a pause developed in which Richard could see that Max was beginning to believe that the interview was now over, Richard turned and looked at Camille, and they came to a silent understanding. Richard wished for Camille to deliver the *coup de grace*.

'Oh okay,' Camille said, as though the interview was already done and dusted. 'Then one last thing. Perhaps you can tell us why you've been stealing from Polly?'

'I'm sorry?' Max said.

'There's really no point denying it,' Camille said just as easily. 'You see, Phil's already told us that he and Polly had suspicions that you've been taking money from her over the years, and when we got Polly's bank statements we discovered you had. In February of this year you received fifty thousand dollars—in two separate transactions—from her current account.'

'Which is interesting,' Richard said, picking up from his partner, 'seeing as agents are only supposed to get a cut of their client's money when they earn anything. So thank you for telling us that Polly hadn't worked for the previous six months. Now you can tell us, how come you received so much money from her when she wasn't in work?'

'I er…well, we agreed I should have the money,' Max said, rallying. 'It was a loan.'

'It was?' Richard asked, unable to keep the disbelief out of his voice. 'How convenient for you, seeing as Polly's no longer here to gainsay you. Or maybe there's someone else who can corroborate the fact that the money you took from her was a loan?'

Max had no answer to this.

'Okay,' Camille said. 'So what was this loan for?'

Max still didn't have anything to say, and Richard found that this was the perfect moment to shoot the cuffs on his white shirt.

'Very well,' Richard said. 'Then this is how I see it. Either you killed Polly Carter or you didn't. This means that if you *are* the killer, then whatever you're saying to us in this conversation is a lie. Therefore, if you wish to prove your innocence, I'd highly recommend you try to convince me—right now—that you're telling me the truth, the whole truth, and nothing but the truth.'

Max held out for a couple more seconds, but both Richard and Camille knew that silence was their best weapon now.

And when it came, it came as a flood.

'All right, all right!' Max said, suddenly rising from his chair. 'I took the money from her, but it wasn't theft. Okay?'

'Keep talking,' Richard said.

'You see, I wasn't joking when I said Polly's my only client. So if she's not earning, then I'm not earning, and over the last year I've…well, I've developed a bit of a shortfall in my finances. A massive black hole, more like. Not that I'm extravagant. Not really. I mean, I like to travel first class when I can, and I never eat in cheap restaurants, but this is nothing that I'm not owed for the stress I otherwise have to suffer. Running Polly's career was hardly easy at the best of times.

'But the thing is, if I'm being entirely honest…you see, I've always been susceptible to casinos. And roulette in particular. And as long as I've been earning—and you must believe, I *have* been earning—I was on top of my… hobby. And the thing is, I had a system.

'Don't worry, as someone who knows exactly what ten per cent of everything is, I know it's not possible to beat the house when it comes to roulette, but I could just about manage my time so that I could revel in the big wins and walk away when the losses got too damaging. But the thing is, I always lost money in the long run. I knew that. I just had to make sure I had enough cash flow to get me through the losses.

'I only made one mistake after Polly overdosed last September. I carried on playing in the same fashion I'd always done because I guessed my income stream would be starting up again just as soon as she recovered from her overdose.'

Here, Max stopped himself, as though realising something for the first time.

'Actually, who am I kidding?' he said. 'That was just the first of quite a few mistakes. Because it didn't take too long before I owed a grand or so around the gaming tables of London. But that was fine, I had a good line of credit with everyone. I hadn't welched on a debt in my life.

'But, as autumn turned into winter, I still presumed that Polly hadn't given up working for good. It's like I told you. I expected I'd pick up the phone one day and she'd be on the end of it telling me to fix up another photo shoot for her. So I made what I can only say was a reckless decision. I decided that the best way to clear my temporary debts with the gaming houses was by winning at the gaming houses. And, in no time at all, I'd managed to turn a debt of a couple of thousand dollars into a debt of nearly fifteen thousand dollars. And with Polly now in rehab, I knew I had no way of earning the cash to pay any of the money back.'

'So you used your access to Polly's account to take out the cash you needed to cover your debts?' Camille asked.

Max looked so haunted by the question that both Richard and Camille knew the answer before Max had even given it.

'That's right,' he eventually said, his voice hoarse with shame. 'But I was always going to pay her back.'

'But why seventeen?' Richard asked. 'Seeing as you said you only owed fifteen.'

'Because,' Max said, now in the depths of his own personal hell, 'I was convinced that when I'd paid off my debts, I'd be able to turn the two thousand I had left over into enough of a windfall to keep me going in the short term. Remember, Polly was still in rehab, she'd deprived me of my income, I had to live on something!'

'But you lost that as well,' Richard said.

'In one crazy weekend. It's like a type of frenzy when you go rogue like I did that weekend. By Sunday morning, I was up twenty-seven thousand pounds, but by the Monday morning, I'd managed to turn that into a loss of twenty thousand pounds.'

'You racked up a gambling debt again?' Richard was amazed.

'I know,' Max said.

'So, you then stole twenty-three thousand dollars to cover that debt as well.'

Max didn't deny it this time.

'And what have you been living on since then?'

'Thin air. And promises. It's not been easy.'

'But tell me, how long was it before Polly realised you'd cleaned her out? Because we know Polly never opened her bank statements or looked at her financial affairs, so it was probably some time later, wasn't it? Although we know she'd found out before she died, because Phil Adams told us how Polly said she was so skint that she was going to have to put her house up for sale.'

'I...' Max said, before subsiding. 'You're right. A few weeks before she died, Polly rang me. She said she'd finally tried to sort out her financial affairs. She'd discovered she had no money because I'd taken fifty grand from her back in February. I got on a plane the moment she told me she knew. I was so ashamed. And I threw myself at her mercy, saying I'd find a way to pay her back.'

'So what did she say to that?'

'That's the bit I don't understand. Because I wasn't lying when I said Polly was in a good mood before she died. She actually laughed when I told her I'd stolen from her. And better than that, once I'd explained how it had been my gambling addiction that had got me into this mess, she said she'd be happy to wait until I could afford to pay her back.'

'She said that, did she?'

'Yes.'

Richard exchanged a glance with Camille.

'I find that very hard to believe,' he said.

'But you have to believe me! I mean, no one was more surprised than me when she said she was happy to consider the debt a loan, but that's what she said. She was happy.'

Richard looked at Max, sizing him up.

'And once again I find myself asking, did she draw up any papers to formalise this loan?'

'No. That's not how she worked.'

'Which is convenient for you, isn't it? Because I think you've kept your story close to the truth, but it's not the whole truth, is it? For example, I think you were right when you told us you were angry when Polly stopped working after she got out of hospital last year. And I think that anger soon turned into hate, which is why it's been you who's been sending Polly all those anonymous threatening letters.'

Max reeled, and then shook his head in denial, and Richard decided to pounce.

'It *was* you!'

'No!' Max just as quickly shot back. 'I don't know what you're talking about. I'm sorry, I'm just on edge. What letters?'

'Polly's been receiving anonymous letters,' Camille said. 'Saying she deserves to die.'

'Which,' Richard continued, 'rather fits with how you described your feelings towards her when she stopped working. She was all but destroying your career, wasn't she? And that's when I think you decided she deserved to be destroyed. Psychologically, at first. That's why you sent the letters.'

'Look, I don't know what letters you mean.'

'But then,' Richard continued, refusing to be sidetracked by Max's denials, 'by the time Polly checked in to rehab after Christmas, you were so desperate that you had to go beyond psychological bullying, didn't you? Now you felt you should just directly take the money you felt she owed you. And I can almost see the warped logic of it. After all, Polly *should* have been working. She *should* have been giving you that money.'

'No, that's not how it was,' Max stammered. 'And I don't know what you mean about any anonymous letters.

Although, if she's been receiving hate mail, that sometimes happens if you're famous like Polly was. Nutbags out there will send all sorts of rubbish to her.'

'Nice try,' Richard said. 'But what I'd like to know is, how did you get that last ten thousand dollars out of her?'

'What?'

'The ten thousand dollars in cash she gave you three days before she died.'

'She didn't give me any money!' Max said. 'Why would she give me more money? She'd already agreed to let me off my debts!'

'Then can you explain why Polly took ten thousand dollars out of her bank account—in cash—three days before she was murdered?'

Max pulled his hankie from his pocket and mopped his brow.

'No,' he said. 'I don't know anything about any ten thousand dollars in cash.'

'You're lying.'

'I'm not! I'm telling you the truth!'

'She got out that cash for you, but why?'

'She didn't!' Max all but shouted back at Richard, and it was as though Max had finally revealed his true nature. He wasn't a *bon vivant* from the sophisticated world of fashion, he was a street fighter, that's what Richard and Camille could now see in Max's eyes. And Max knew that he'd revealed himself, but was beyond caring.

'Okay. You reckon she gave me a load of cash before she died? Prove it. Because you've searched my room here, and you didn't find any cash, did you? And don't forget,

I was inside this house—upstairs on the landing—when Polly was killed! That's what Sophie said, remember? She saw me go upstairs just before the murder! She then saw me standing at the upstairs window at the precise time of the murder! So even if I admit I had a motive to want Polly dead—and I'll tell you what, I *could* admit it, how would you like that? Polly ruined my life when she stopped working, the stupid cow. But the problem you've got is, I've got a witness who said I was nowhere near at the time of her death, so what are you going to do about that?'

Max looked wild as he finished speaking and Richard leaned back in his chair as though he were considering what Max had said very carefully. Which, of course, he was. After all, Max had just all-but confessed that he wanted Polly dead. But he was right about his alibi as well, because, although Sophie wasn't sure who she saw at the upstairs window at the time of the murder, she said she'd definitely seen Max go up the stairs before she went out into the garden, so how could Max have got past her and Claire and onto the steps of the cliff without being seen?

It was as Richard idly looked up at the chandelier in the ceiling that he realised what had been unsettling him about the room.

The chandelier wasn't precisely in the centre of the ceiling as it was in the other downstairs reception room.

Richard frowned.

That's right. This room was identical in shape to the other sitting room, so how come the chandelier wasn't in the same spot in the middle of the ceiling?

Ignoring Max and Camille entirely, Richard stood up from his chair and slowly turned on the spot. Yes, the room was the same—apart from the floor-to-ceiling bookcase that ran along the side wall. And once again, Richard realised his instinct was making him look at the bookcase.

'Sir?' Camille asked, puzzled.

'One moment,' Richard said.

Richard went over to the bookcase. He pulled down a few books and Camille went over to see what he was doing.

'Sir,' she hissed. 'What are you doing?'

'How deep do you think this bookcase is?'

Richard reached into the shelf and could see that it was about a foot deep. As would be expected with any bookcase.

'Can you clear the way?'

Richard turned so his back was to the bookcase and started to put one polished shoe in front of the other so he could measure the width of the room in Richard-sized feet.

'You see,' he said as though he was making perfect sense. 'I've not been able to settle in this room. And I think it's because it's not the same size as the sitting room next door.'

'It isn't?' Max asked, confused by Richard's behaviour.

'Even though everything else about this room is identical. Look at the chandelier in the ceiling. It's in the centre of the room lengthwise—measured from the door to the bay windows—but it's not central if measured widthways.'

Camille and Max could see that what Richard was saying was true. The dusty old crystal chandelier was much nearer the wall with the bookcase on it than it was to the opposite wall.

'So everyone remember, thirty-eight feet,' Richard finally proclaimed as he finished traversing the width of the room.

And with that, he left the room.

Camille and Max followed Richard only to see him disappearing into the sitting room next door to the study. And when they entered that room, Richard was holding up his finger for silence while repeating his experiment of measuring the width of the room in his footsteps.

While he did this, Camille looked up and saw that Richard was right. The dusty chandelier was much more obviously in the centre of this room than it was in the other.

'Forty-three feet!' Richard called out as he hit the further wall. 'This room is five feet wider than the other room!'

'But that's not surprising,' Max said, still baffled. 'This room doesn't have a floor-to-ceiling bookcase along the side wall.'

'I know, but we just measured the bookcase, didn't we? And it was only about a foot deep. So that still leaves something like four feet of width in that room unaccounted for.'

As Richard said this, he suddenly froze.

Camille realised that Richard was having one of his 'moments'.

'Good grief! You know what this house once was?' Richard said, before striding out of the room again.

Camille turned to Max, an apologetic smile on her face.

'I'm so sorry. He does this.'

Once again, Camille and Max went out of the room together and returned to Polly's study only to find Richard yanking books from the bookshelf in a shimmer of dust.

'Sir…?' Camille asked as carefully as she could.

'Not now, Camille!' Richard called back as he pulled another handful of books from the shelf and dumped them on a nearby armchair.

Camille was doubly puzzled when she realised that it wasn't the books that Richard seemed to be interested in, it was the shelves he was revealing behind them.

It was on the third stack along that Richard finally stopped.

'Got you!'

'Got what, sir?'

'Remember what Juliette said this house used to be? And above all else, remember how I said that any key that itself was kept under lock and key was important?'

As Richard said this, he fished into his pocket and pulled out the old iron key they'd found in Polly's locked filing cabinet.

'Because I reckon I now know what this key opens.'

Richard pointed at the inside of the shelf he'd just cleared.

Camille went over and joined her boss. She could see that on the left hand side of that section of bookcase— where Richard was pointing—there was a little hole that had previously been hidden by the books that were lined up by it.

But it wasn't just any little hole, Camille could see.

It was a keyhole.

'What have you found?' Max asked, desperately wanting to see but also knowing he should keep his distance.

'The reason,' Richard said, 'why this room isn't quite as wide as its twin room next door.'

Richard slipped the key into the keyhole.

It was a perfect fit.

Richard then took hold of the key and turned it carefully to the right. The lock mechanism inside the shelf clicked. It was clearly well oiled from regular use.

'Juliette said this was an old smuggler's house,' Camille said.

Richard looked at Camille.

'Indeed. Shall we?' he asked.

Together they grabbed the empty shelf and pulled.

The whole bookstack swung smoothly open on its hinges just like the secret floor-to-ceiling door it was.

And beyond the section of bookcase they'd just swung open, Richard and Camille saw ancient wooden steps leading down into a subterranean passageway of some sort.

Richard and Camille had just uncovered a secret tunnel.

Chapter 9

'You *knew* that would be there?' Max said, pointing at the passageway behind the bookcase.

'I guessed that something might be behind here, but the real question is, did you know about it?'

Max was shocked by the question. 'I don't even know what it is that you've found.'

'It's a tunnel. An old smugglers' tunnel, I'd imagine, that leads from the house.'

'It is?' Max said. 'Then if it is, it's the first I've heard of it.'

With Max continuing to protest his surprise, Richard ushered him from the room, and Camille went to the police jeep to fetch a couple of torches. It was only during Camille's absence that Richard realised the implications of what he was now obliged to do, which was, to wit, to go down into a secret underground tunnel. A secret underground tunnel that clearly hadn't been signed off as being safe by any kind of structural engineer, and which was no doubt full of poisonous snakes. And poisonous spiders.

By the time Camille returned, Richard had whipped himself up into a frenzy of panic that he was barely able to conceal.

'You okay, sir?' Camille asked.

'Nnnggg,' Richard said.

'Don't worry. I'll go first.'

Camille stepped into the gap behind the open section of bookcase and found herself looking at a set of rickety wooden steps that led almost vertically downwards.

'Hold on, there's got to be a light or something,' she said, jabbing her torch beam around the cobwebby darkness until it illuminated an old Bakelite switch that was attached to the adjacent bookcase. She flicked it on and light flooded up from the tunnel below.

'Okay, we're good to go,' she said.

Richard stepped up to his subordinate and looked over her shoulder at the eight or nine steps that led down into the tunnel.

Camille descended to the bottom and Richard took a deep breath. Well, then. Here goes. He trod down onto the first step and it gave a protesting groan. Richard froze. And then he realised that if the ancient step had groaned as though it were about to snap, then it was probably wise to get off it fast, so he descended quickly to the bottom, each step giving a pantomime groan until he found himself standing in a narrow tunnel hewn directly out of the rock.

Richard could see that the tunnel went off in a roughly straight line, but sloped downwards. There were lightbulbs strung along the wall every ten feet or so, but the slope meant that it was hard to see beyond forty or fifty feet. Richard could smell something in the air and it took him a moment to realise that it was the smell of the sea.

Camille looked back at her boss.

'Shall we see where this leads?' she asked.

Before Richard could answer, Camille strode off—much faster than Richard would have liked. But as much as he was frightened of following Camille, he was far more frightened of being left behind on his own, so he soon caught up with her.

The tunnel was only a few feet taller than him, a foot or so wider, and Richard struggled to keep a lid on his mounting sense of claustrophobia as he imagined the tonnes of rock that were above him and ready—at any moment—to collapse in on his head and crush him to death. To keep a lid on his panic, he counted the lightbulbs as they passed them, and he soon realised that they'd gone a good 150 feet when the tunnel bent to the right and Richard could finally see that there was natural light at the end of the tunnel about a hundred feet away.

'You can speed up now,' Richard said, wiping the sweat from his brow.

At the end of this next section of tunnel, Richard and Camille stepped into a well-lit subterranean cave. The floor, walls and roof of the cave were all rough—it was clearly a natural cave formation—but it was a wide and roomy space, and although there were still lightbulbs shining in a string around the side walls, holes had been punched directly into the rocks high up so shafts of sunlight shone down onto the floor from above.

Richard realised that if there was light coming in through the far wall, then they were almost certainly right up against the cliff edge. And the even stronger smell of sea air in the cave seemed only to confirm this.

Off to one side, Richard saw that there were old boxes, ratty deckchairs and wine and beer bottles piled up in a mess. But as Camille went to check them out, Richard noticed something else. In the far corner of the cave opposite where they'd come in, there was a bright glow of sunlight where a second tunnel led out of the cave.

Richard went up to this second tunnel and could immediately feel the freshness in the air as he stepped into it. In fact, the breeze was now whipping at his hair as he took a few steps around a little jink, and then Richard froze, both hands instinctively shooting out to jam himself firmly into the narrow width of the tunnel.

Richard took a few calming breaths to steady himself, because what he'd just discovered was that immediately around the tight bend, the tunnel opened out onto thin air and a precipitous drop down to the sea a good fifty feet below. All Richard could see—from horizon to horizon—was the sparkling blue Caribbean Sea and bright blue sky. One step further and he'd have fallen fifty feet down into the sea.

Richard steeled himself, even as his arms started to tremble at the effort of keeping himself wedged safely into the tunnel opening. Because if this was a secret smugglers' route—as he guessed it had to be—it didn't make sense that the tunnel would open directly out onto thin air halfway up a cliff face.

Richard knew he had no choice but to go nearer to the edge. And, now he was looking more closely, he could see that the tunnel wall was shorter on the right hand side—which maybe allowed a little path to lead off to the right along the cliff face. Or maybe not. He wouldn't be able to see for sure unless he took another step towards the edge of the tunnel.

Richard scooched his left hand six inches nearer the end of the tunnel, and then he did the same with his left foot. And then he shuffled his right hand six inches nearer, and then his right foot.

After which, he was only six inches nearer the opening and he still couldn't quite see.

So he repeated his crablike progress another few inches towards what he increasingly felt was almost certainly going to be a fall to his death: left hand, left foot, right hand, right foot.

Looking down, Richard gulped to see the sea swelling against the cliff's edge far below. But looking to his right, he could also see that he'd been correct—there was indeed a wide ledge of rock to the side of the entrance. What was more, it was directly behind a far wider outcrop of rock that had a scrappy sort of shrub on it that was at least as tall as Richard was.

Richard realised with a start that if he looked through the leaves of the bush, he could see the staircase that was cut into the cliff face on the other side of it.

The staircase that Polly had been thrown from when she died.

In fact, Richard knew that if he could ignore the absence of any kind of handrail or safety harness—which he most certainly could not—it would only take a couple of steps to get along the ledge and into the safety of the bush, from where it would be easy to step onto the staircase.

In excitement, Richard crab-shuffled back into the relative safety of the tunnel, his mind now awhirl. After all, they'd been trying to work out how the killer had managed to push Polly to her death and then vanish from the steps afterwards—well here was the possible answer! The killer was waiting on the steps before Polly came down them, as they'd been saying all along. He or she then hit Polly with the branch, pushed her to her death and then hid the branch in the bush at the next bend down the steps. Again, as they'd been saying all along. But then the killer carried on down the steps until he or she reached the turn that had the bush on it. It would then have been possible for the killer to push through the bush, take one brave step onto the ledge, and then vanish into the old smugglers' tunnel that led into the chamber.

And from there, it would have been easy to head along the secret tunnel and get back into the house.

'Sir!' Richard heard Camille call from back inside the cave. 'You need to see this.'

Richard returned to the cave. It took him a few moments for his eyes to adjust to the darkness, but he saw that Camille was over by the piles of junk that were on the far side of the chamber.

'Okay, what have you got?' Richard asked her as he approached.

'Well, sir, I reckon this is where Polly came to take her drugs.'

Richard saw that to the side of one of the chairs there was a filthy trunk that had lost its lid long ago. Inside it there were old fashion magazines, glasses still red-rimmed with evaporated wine, an old tin containing cigarette papers, an old cellophane bag of weed, and various bongs, spoons and lighters.

'I see,' Richard said. 'But this must all be historic, seeing as the autopsy found no evidence of any narcotics in her system.'

'Agreed,' Camille said. 'But I bet you won't be able to guess what I've just found stuffed behind the trunk.'

Richard considered how he'd just learnt that it was possible to access the cave directly from the steps on the cliff.

'I don't know, but I imagine that if you're saying that I *can't* guess what it is, then it must be pretty sensational, and if it's stuffed behind the trunk, then I *also* imagine that it's something that can be crushed up into a small space—'

'You don't really have to guess,' Camille interrupted.

'It's not a yellow raincoat of some sort, is it?'

Camille looked at her boss.

'How do you do it?'

'Is that right, though? Have you really found the yellow raincoat?'

'Why don't you tell me?'

Camille nodded her head to indicate the space behind the trunk, and, when Richard looked, he saw it at once. There was something yellow jammed down behind it. Richard pulled out a fresh pair of latex gloves from his inside jacket pocket, put them on, and scraped the trunk away from the rock wall a few inches.

He then picked up the crushed piece of plastic and opened it out.

It was a bright yellow raincoat. Just as Claire had said she'd seen being worn by someone moments before Polly was pushed to her death.

'This almost certainly belongs to the killer,' Richard said.

So who in the house knew about the secret tunnel and had been using it to hide their yellow raincoat?

There was an easy way to find out, and, a few hours later, Richard was back in the police station hovering over the yellow raincoat as Fidel dusted it for prints. A visual inspection hadn't revealed any obvious spots of blood on the raincoat, but Richard knew that didn't mean it *hadn't* been worn by the killer—especially considering how they already knew the killer attacked Polly while holding a long branch so that he or she could keep their distance during the murder.

'I just want to see how it's going,' Richard said for the hundredth time.

'I'm getting there, sir,' Fidel said for the hundred-and-first time.

So far, Fidel had been able to lift seven clean prints from near the front buttons of the raincoat and Dwayne was trying to match these prints against the exclusion prints they'd taken from Sophie, Claire, Max, Phil, Juliette and Alain—and Polly herself, of course.

But none of the seven prints they'd so far been able to lift belonged to anyone from Polly's household. So was the killer, then, someone else entirely? It didn't seem possible, but Camille scanned and uploaded the prints to the central police database that covered the whole of the Caribbean. Maybe there'd be a match somewhere on the system?

However, as the afternoon wore on and Fidel ran out of clean prints to lift from the raincoat, Dwayne confirmed that none of the prints matched anyone from the house, and the main police computer remained just as unforthcoming.

Richard was therefore in a particularly grumpy mood when a courier arrived just as they were about to pack up for the day. And what the courier delivered didn't improve Richard's mood, either, because it turned out that he was returning the threatening letters now they'd been processed by the labs in Guadeloupe.

For want of anything better to do, Richard laid out the six pieces of A4 on his desk and once again tried to work out what sort of warped mind would want to send them to Polly.

y**O**u A**R**e g**O**in**G** t**O** **P**Ay
I K**N**oW w**H**At yo**U** Di**D**
I c**AN** r**UI**n y**OU**
YoU de**S**e**RV**e to die

I hat**E** y**OU**
BEt**T**er **Y**<u>**OU**</u> d**IE**

In particular, Richard tried to imagine who of Polly's house guests might have sent them. He remembered how guilty Max had looked when he was challenged about the letters, but that could have just been his surprise on hearing they existed at all.

Richard packed the letters into his brown leather briefcase, deciding that he'd have another look at them at home that night. Even though the labs had drawn a blank, he wasn't going to give up on the letters just yet.

'Chief?'

Richard looked up to see that Dwayne had sidled over to his desk.

'Yes, Dwayne?'

'Could I have a word?'

'Of course. Any time.'

Dwayne looked at his boss a long moment.

'I mean, now,' Dwayne said in a stage whisper.

'Yes, well, now's a good time for me, too,' Richard said, not remotely understanding why Dwayne was being so clandestine.

Dwayne coughed once, hoping that Richard would understand that he wanted their conversation to be in private.

His hopes were in vain.

'Do you want a glass of water for that cough?' Richard asked.

Dwayne looked at his boss, speechless.

'Really, Dwayne, you come over here and say you want a word and then you won't speak,' Richard said, deeply frustrated.

Camille leaned over from her desk. 'I think Dwayne wants a word in private, sir,' she said.

Richard threw up his hands in exasperation.

'Then why didn't you say so?' he said.

Dwayne's shoulders slumped. 'I'll be in the cells,' he told his boss, before traipsing through the bead curtain that demarcated the 'front' of the station from the 'back'. Richard shook his head in wonder as he followed. Really, there was no understanding his staff sometimes.

The back rooms of the police station contained two iron-barred holding cells, but were otherwise the general dumping ground for the office, so they also contained old fax machines, files, broken crime equipment and any old bits of furniture too decrepit to be of use.

'What is it?' Richard asked, once he'd joined Dwayne.

'You can't blame me, I didn't know it would come to this.'

'What on earth are you talking about?'

'You just have to believe me, Chief. It's not my fault.'

Richard didn't have time for this. 'Just tell me what you've done and we can apportion blame afterwards.'

'It might be easier if I show you,' Dwayne said, fishing out his mobile phone.

Richard was none the wiser as Dwayne showed him a text message that he'd received a few minutes earlier.

It said: *U know any good spots for dinner and a dance? x J*

Richard looked at Dwayne.

'Why are you showing me this message?'

'It's from your mother.'

Richard looked at Dwayne, confused.

'Sorry?' he eventually managed to squeak.

'It's not me, you've got to believe me,' Dwayne said. 'It's just…you know how your mother asked me about the glass-bottomed boat? Well, after that, she asked to meet for a coffee to discuss what she should do next, and so I met her for a coffee and we had a drink and I told her where to go next, and the thing is… I think she's got a thing for me.'

'She's got "a thing" for you?'

'Hey, you can't blame me if women find me attractive.'

'I *can't* blame you?'

'It's animal magnetism. I was born this way.'

'Look, Dwayne, there's only one type of magnetism, it was discovered by an Englishman called William Gilbert in the sixteenth century, and I can tell you right now it has nothing to do with animals.'

'Chief, you're babbling.'

'Of course I'm babbling!' Richard exploded before lowering his voice to a desperate whisper. 'I'm hearing how one of my officers thinks he's inadvertently pulled my mother!'

'Not because I tried to,' Dwayne said. 'that's the point I'm trying to make.'

Richard realised that if he didn't foreclose on the conversation—and fast—he would possibly tip over into insanity. So, thanking Dwayne for the information, he strode out of the police station without another word—and through the life-sapping sunshine without stopping to think—until he'd reached Catherine's bar, where he hoped he might be able to find his mother.

However, as Richard scanned the little tables outside, his mother was nowhere to be seen. Admittedly, there were a couple of tourists sitting at some of the tables, but his mother wasn't one of them. Or rather, that had been Richard's first impression. When he looked a little closer, he saw a male tourist in his fifties—all blue blazer, sailing cap and deck shoes—talking to a laughing woman in a bright orange dress as she knocked back a shot of rum.

The woman was his mother.

Richard strode over to his mother's table, but—at the last moment—he bottled it and found himself hovering merely nearby.

'Richard!' Jennifer said, finally noticing her son before patting the chair next to her. 'Come and join us. This is Major Rupert Fitzgerald. He's on a round-the-world cruise and is currently holed up on Saint-Marie, awaiting repairs.'

'You are, are you?' Richard said with a glint in his eye as he sat down.

'Unfortunately, yes,' Rupert said in a patrician drawl.

'And I suppose,' Richard said, 'you only need a bit more money to finish your repairs.'

Jennifer looked at her son in surprise. 'How did you know that?'

But Richard only had eyes for Rupert.

'And I bet this world cruise means so much to you, Major, doesn't it? But tell me, is it your wife who's died or is it an elderly relative?'

Richard pulled his police warrant and put it down on the table.

'Detective Inspector Richard Poole of the Saint-Marie Police Force, I think you'll find the repairs have been done to your boat and you'll be leaving the island by sunset tonight.'

Rupert cleared his throat, opened his mouth like a landed fish, and then turned to Jennifer, trying to appear as though he hadn't just been busted by the local Old Bill.

'You know what? I'm sure I can get the boat repaired for free and I'll be onto my next port of call. Nice meeting you, Jennifer.' As Rupert said this, he rose and backed a few paces away from his chair before turning to face Richard. 'Detective Inspector.'

'I'm sure we won't meet again,' Richard said.

With a tight nod of agreement, Rupert turned and slipped out of the bar, Jennifer watching him go, a confused look on her face.

'Mother!' Richard hissed at his mother once the coast was clear.

'What?' Jennifer said, now affronted.

'He was a conman! You *have* got to be careful.'

'Did it not occur to you that I already knew that?' Jennifer said. 'I wasn't born yesterday. But, just so you know, I was enjoying talking to him, testing out his background story and seeing how consistent he was. Not that I'm not grateful for you standing up for me, but I am a grown-up. I wish you'd treat me as one.'

'But I don't understand what you're doing here,' Richard said.

Jennifer looked at her son. 'You know what? For the first time in my life, nor do I, and it's liberating. I'm sick of doing as I'm told, being well-behaved, the perfect housewife and mother. That's all I've ever been. While I've been out here, I've realised, no one knows me, I can be who I *want* to be.'

'But this isn't where you want to be,' Richard said before he could stop himself. 'I mean, don't get me wrong, there are lots of people who come here on holiday—God knows why—but this place is a deathtrap! You can't go into the sea without an anemone sticking in your foot, a lion fish poisoning you, or a shark actually eating you alive. And on land, it's even more dangerous. There's sand that gets everywhere, a volcano in the middle of the island that could blow at any moment, and if you're not attacked by creatures that fly and sting you to death, there's always the creepy crawlies that walk and bite you to death to contend with. I mean, just before you got out here I was assaulted in my shower by a lizard.'

'Richard?' Jennifer asked, startled by her son's sudden passion.

'And don't even get me started on the weather! I mean, can you imagine living somewhere where it's hot every day of the year, except for the summer, when it's actually just hotter?'

'It would be lovely.'

'No, you *say* that, Mother, but think about what that actually means. Did you even know, we don't have seasons out here.'

'What do you mean?'

'There aren't seasons in the tropics like there are in the UK. So that's no daffodils coming up in the spring to look forward to—no early season new potatoes, no two-week window for cherries, no harvesting of the wheat fields in September, and no autumn leaves. Ever.'

Jennifer looked suitably taken aback by this news, and Richard pressed home his advantage.

'So for all your excitement with Saint-Marie, don't think for a moment that it's better than what you left behind. Because I know that back home it's grey at times—and rainy—but where we're from is who we are, and this island isn't who you are.'

Jennifer looked at her son, doubt showing in her eyes for the first time. But before she could say anything, Catherine swished over in a blood-red dress, her hair tied up in a purple silk scarf.

'So what did Major Rupert say to you?' she asked conspiratorially as she joined mother and son at the table.

'Well, Catherine,' Jennifer said, 'he was giving me his set-up—just like you said he would—when Richard arrived and got rid of him.'

Catherine looked at Richard, disappointed. 'Oh, Richard.'

'I'm sorry,' Richard said defensively. 'But I didn't realise you both knew he was a conman.'

'Oh well,' Catherine said, already moving on. 'Guess what your mother and I are up to tonight? We're going clubbing!'

'You are?' Richard said, as though he'd just had a stiletto knife stuck into his heart.

'Can you imagine?!' Catherine said, delightedly.

'No, I can't. I really can't.'

Before anyone could say anything more, Fidel headed over from the bar, a printout in his hand.

'Sir! Sir!' he called as he approached, clearly excited.

'What is it, Fidel?'

'We've found a match to the fingerprints on the yellow raincoat!'

'You have?'

'We have!'

'But who is it,' Richard asked, rudely grabbing the printout from Fidel's hands. 'Is it one of the house guests?'

'That's the thing, sir. It isn't. The fingerprints on the coat belong to a man called Luc Pichou.'

Richard could see that Fidel had handed him the police record for a man called Luc Pichou.

He looked back up at Fidel.

'Who the hell is Luc Pichou?'

Chapter 10

There was an area of Honoré just beyond the harbour that it wasn't wise to go to unless you were already known to its residents. It didn't have a name as such, but it was made up of about forty cinder block and corrugated iron dwellings, and, on a sunny day, a tourist might make it halfway down the first road before the general decrepitude and blandly hostile stares from the locals would make them realise the area wasn't even remotely safe. At night, any tourist that made it halfway down a road might not make it out again—and almost certainly not with their wallet, watch or phone.

Dwayne had been born in one of these streets, and—as a one-time resident—the families who lived there accepted him as 'one of their own'. As long as the rest of the police force stayed away, they'd tolerate the odd intervention from Dwayne, if only because, as far as anyone could remember, Dwayne had never intervened. Like any closed-off community, then, the shanty town was most happy when it was left alone to get on with its obscure rules, rituals and observances without undue scrutiny from the outside world. A lot like the British upper classes, Richard had often thought to himself.

'You stay close to my side, and you should be okay,' Dwayne whispered to his boss as he, Richard and Camille walked down the dusty street with Richard trying to put any thoughts of being in a Western movie out of his mind.

'Why don't we just invite this Mr Pichou to the station to help with our inquiries?' Richard asked.

'Don't worry, Chief. It's not far now.'

As Dwayne said this, he turned behind the wreck of an old building with shrubs growing out of the walls and Richard was suddenly plunged into the overpoweringly sweet stench of rotting bins as he followed Dwayne to a cluster of one-storey shacks that were built in the lee of a sheer rock face.

When Dwayne finally indicated the house they were visiting, Richard realised it was the very definition of a lean-to, as it was constructed of what appeared to be driftwood and sheets of ancient corrugated iron, but the whole structure was skewed, as if it had tried to fall over and had only been stopped from doing so by the intervention of the rock face it had fallen against.

Richard couldn't believe this ramshackle shack was inhabited, but he was doubly surprised to see someone inside it sitting on an old armchair and watching television.

This was Luc Pichou, Richard realised. The man was perhaps in his thirties and was wearing old tracksuit trousers and a bright pink string vest. He was wiry—strongly muscled—and he had thick-matted dreadlocks that hung down his back to his waist.

As Dwayne, Richard and Camille approached, Luc looked up at them, suspicion in his eyes.

'No worries,' Dwayne said as an introduction, and then offered up a fist bump for Luc.

Luc reluctantly fist bumped Dwayne. 'What have you brought them for?' he asked, with a nod at Richard and Camille.

Dwayne sat down and explained that they were investigating a murder and he reckoned that maybe Luc could help them. Once Dwayne had made his pitch, Luc sniffed and then looked at Richard and Camille again. He then looked back at Dwayne.

'Who's asking?' Luc said. 'Them? Or you?'

'It's me.'

'On the usual terms?'

Richard didn't quite understand what Luc was referring to, but while Dwayne started having a quiet word with Luc, Richard looked about and couldn't work out if he was horrified by Luc's house or quietly impressed. The cliff face that the structure was leaning against had been painted white, electricity cables and lights had been bolted directly into the rocks, and, among the odds and sods of furniture, Richard could see what looked like a plumbed-in washing machine. Or maybe it was a cooker. It was hard to tell. But the room was colourfully decorated with empty bottles of booze of all types, there were salt-stained wall hangings nailed to bits of wood here and there, and it clearly worked as a functioning home. In fact, Richard found himself realising, his rudimentary shack on the beach that he shared with a lizard he couldn't get rid of, had more in common with this lean-to than was entirely comfortable.

Luc eventually leaned back in his chair and looked at Richard and Camille.

'Okay, so what do you want to know?'

'It's simple,' Richard said. 'We just want to know why we found a yellow raincoat covered in your fingerprints in a tunnel under Polly Carter's house.'

Luc didn't even blink.

'You did?'

'Yes.'

Luc turned to Dwayne. 'And I have your word?'

'Sorry,' Richard said, unable to stop himself. 'And what "word" would this be?'

'Luc's agreed to help us,' Dwayne said, 'with one proviso, Chief. We can't prosecute him if he implicates himself in any kind of illegal activity.'

'Including murder?' Richard asked sarcastically.

'Of course not. But he's talking to us as a confidential informant. That was the deal. If he implicates himself in answering our questions and it's not part of our main investigation, we've got to let it go. That's what I agreed.'

'Or I won't help you,' Luc said.

'That's fine.' Camille quickly jumped in before Richard could complain.

For his part, Richard was dismayed. In what way was it ever acceptable to let anyone off for any kind of misdemeanour? They were the police, after all.

'So why don't you tell us what your coat was doing there?' Camille said, keeping the conversation on track.

'Okay,' Luc said, unfussed. 'My coat's there because I left it there the last time I was there.'

'You admit to being in the tunnel under Polly Carter's house?' Richard asked.

'Yeah.'

'And what were you doing there?'

'Selling Polly drugs.'

Richard and Camille exchanged a sharp glance.

'I'm sorry?'

'I was selling her drugs.'

'But what sort of drugs?'

'What she always ordered from me. Heroin.'

'Hang on, are you saying Polly Carter was still using heroin?'

'Of course, or she wouldn't have ordered any from me.'

'But we've got an autopsy report that says there were no drugs in her system when she died.'

'Then your autopsy report's wrong.'

Richard was reeling.

'When was this?' he asked.

'How do you mean?'

'Can you tell us exactly when it was you sold Polly the heroin?'

Luc had difficulty pinning down the exact day, but with Dwayne's help, they were soon able to work out that it must have been three days before Polly was killed.

'Hang on,' Richard said, unable to get a handle on what Luc was telling them. 'You're saying you went up to Polly's house three days before she was killed?'

'If that's what you're saying.'

Richard remembered that Juliette had said she'd seen a man in a yellow raincoat on the cliff tops a few days before Polly had been killed.

'And were you by any chance wearing your yellow raincoat then?'

'I was, as it happens.'

'And how did you deliver the drugs to Polly?'

'Well,' Luc said, still seemingly entirely unconcerned, 'I've made a tonne of money from that woman over the years, but if you're asking how I got the gear to her, well there's an old path up to her house from here. So I walked. And then, because Polly doesn't like anyone knowing about her habit, she always meets me in this old tunnel under her house.'

'And how do you get to the tunnel?'

'That's easy. You go down the steps in the cliff, but there's this big bush about halfway down, and if you go through it, there's a secret opening in the cliff just behind it. You can step into that tunnel easily enough.'

'I see,' Richard said, not entirely agreeing that it would be easy to get into the tunnel. 'But I have to ask again. Are you really saying that you were delivering heroin to Polly Carter three days before she died?'

'Yeah. And if you're asking, it was Black Tar heroin. The best for smoking. But then that's how she took it, she wouldn't inject. Said her skin was too precious to her.'

'And do you often take her heroin?'

'Used to. But I've not done a deal with her for months.'

'So she's been clean these last few months?'

'I reckon so. Or she's been buying from someone other than me.'

'And how much heroin did you sell her on this occasion?'

Luc paused dramatically before answering.

'Ten thousand dollars.'

'I'm sorry?'

'I know. It was the biggest pay day I've ever had.'

Richard remembered the ten thousand dollars that Polly had taken out of her bank in cash three days before she was killed. If Luc was to be believed, then she'd not taken out the money to give to Max—or anyone else—it had been to buy a vast quantity of heroin. Heroin that wasn't in her system when she died, and, as the tests on her hair proved, she hadn't used in the previous six months, either. So what the hell was going on?

But even as one part of Richard's brain was running through the ramifications of Polly's heroin purchase—if true—there was a far more procedural part of his brain that had fixed on something else.

'So, just to be clear, you're saying you were wearing your yellow raincoat when you took her the heroin three days before she died?'

'That's what I said.'

'And why exactly were you wearing this raincoat?'

Luc looked at Richard as though he were an idiot.

'It was raining.'

'It was?'

'Real hard. But only on the walk up to the house. By the time I got to the cliffs, the sun was out again. That's why I left my coat in the tunnel, I didn't want to wear it on the way back. Which is why I reckon you found it in the tunnel. It's where I left it.'

'And have you been to Polly's house since then?'

'After dropping off that much gear? No way. That's the last time I saw her alive.'

'So you *weren't* there the morning she died?'

'No way. And I wasn't wearing any kind of yellow coat on the day she died. How could I? I've only got one yellow coat and I'd left it in the tunnel three days before.'

'Do you mind if we search your house?' Richard asked.

Luc's eyes narrowed. 'If it's Dwayne who does the searching.'

Richard nodded for Dwayne, and Dwayne got up and started searching the shack.

'Okay,' Richard said. 'So, if you sold Polly ten thousand dollars of heroin, would you mind showing us the cash she gave you?'

'What's that?'

'You must have plenty of the cash still lying around.'

Here, Luc had the good grace to look awkward for the first time.

'That's the thing. You see, Polly's money couldn't have come at a better time for me. I owed a fair bit around the island. For this and that. You know? And it's kind of gone.'

'You had ten thousand dollars' worth of debts on the island?' Richard asked incredulously.

'I know,' Luc said, acknowledging how unlikely this sounded. 'But they'd racked up over the years, and you know how it goes, you borrow money to pay off money.'

'So you admit you've got debts?' Richard asked, sharpening his attention.

Luc made sure he was looking directly at Richard as he answered.

'Not any more,' he said.

Richard looked straight back. He could see that Luc seemed careful around the police—as could be expected of someone with his background—but otherwise he seemed at ease within himself. In which case, Richard decided, it was time to rattle his cage.

'Then let me offer up an alternative theory to the one you've presented us,' Richard said. 'And in this alternate theory, I think Polly did indeed ask you for ten thousand dollars' worth of heroin—like you said—but you didn't deliver it three days before she died. You delivered it on the day she died. Because that was when you killed her.' Richard saw Luc clench his jaw, but he carried on regardless. 'And this is what I think happened. You were heading down the steps of the cliff with the heroin—as arranged with Polly—when you heard a commotion going on back up at the top of the cliff. And that much we know because we've got a witness who places you at the scene of the crime only moments before Polly was killed.'

'*What?*' Luc said, his defences briefly bridged.

'A witness saw someone in a yellow raincoat go down the steps of the cliff just before Polly died.'

'Someone?' Luc said, anger in his voice. 'Or me? Which was it, policeman?'

'Admittedly, it wasn't a positive identification of you, but a person in a yellow raincoat was seen on the steps moments before the murder, a yellow raincoat was found at the scene with only your fingerprints on it, *ergo* the man in the yellow raincoat was you.

'So, there you were on the cliff steps as Polly argued with her sister. Maybe you peeked back around the corner and saw the whole thing. Maybe you even saw the moment when Polly said that she was going to end her life by throwing herself to her death and started running down the stairs. Why she'd threaten to commit suicide first, I don't know. Maybe you'd like to tell me?' Luc didn't move a muscle. 'Very well. It's possible she was just being melodramatic—after all, nearly everyone we meet tells us how histrionic Polly was.

'But, either way, I think you saw a chance to make a fast buck. You waited for her to come around the corner with the ten thousand dollars. And once she'd handed it over to you, you picked up a big stick that was lying around and knocked Polly in the head so she fell to her death. You then hid the murder weapon under a bush, carried on down the cliff steps until you reached the entrance to the secret tunnel, and then vanished into it, knowing you could wait in safety there. Then, later on—that night, maybe—you took off your distinctive yellow coat, slipped back out onto the steps and returned to the safety of the town, entirely unseen. With ten thousand dollars' worth of heroin you could still sell, and a bonus ten grand in cash, because—I'll be honest—people have killed for a lot less.'

There was a long moment while Luc looked at Richard.

'None of that happened,' he eventually said.

Camille stepped in. 'But the problem is, Luc, we've searched Polly's house from top to bottom and we've not found ten thousand dollars' worth of heroin anywhere.'

'I told you!' Luc said, finally lighting the touch paper to his anger. 'I sold her the heroin! What she did with it afterwards isn't my problem! Maybe she's not the only heroin addict in the house? Maybe she bought it for someone else? Have you considered that?'

Richard looked at Luc. He didn't want to admit it, but he hadn't even quite believed his 'proof' of Luc's guilt even as he'd been explaining it to him. After all, it was coincidental in the extreme that Luc would overhear Polly's threat to kill herself at the precise moment that it suited him to kill her. What was more, ten thousand dollars was a bulky amount of cash and, by all accounts, Polly had just been wearing a light summer dress on the morning she was killed—there'd have been nowhere to hide that amount of cash about her person. And, finally, even if Richard could believe that Luc was on the steps at the precise moment he needed to kill Polly, Richard couldn't begin to see how Luc might have got hold of Claire's mobile phone and hidden it in the ceiling chandelier of Polly's sitting room long before then, because Richard was still convinced that understanding why Claire's phone was put in the chandelier was critical to understanding why Polly was killed.

Dwayne reappeared from the recesses of the shack.

'There's no other raincoat here, Chief,' he said. 'Yellow or otherwise.'

'And that's because it's like I told you,' Luc said. 'I left my yellow coat in the tunnel three days before Polly was killed. Because three days before, it was raining—and it never rained the morning she died.'

Richard remembered back to the morning that Polly had been killed and realised that Luc was right. Because, as he'd looked up at the sky to curse a god that had given parrots the ability to crap in cups of tea from a distance, there hadn't been a single cloud to see.

★★★

Back at the police station, Richard found himself unable to control his irritation, and it wasn't just because he found the logic of what Luc had told them increasingly believable. Nor was it entirely because he couldn't stop thinking about his mother and her attempts to live a second youth on the same island that he was trying to solve a murder case—although it was quite a bit to do with that. In fact, it was a lot to do with that. But what Richard tried to focus on was the fact that Polly had apparently bought ten thousand dollars' worth of heroin—if Luc was to be believed—three days before she died. Even though the autopsy report found no evidence of recent drugs use in her body or historic drugs use in her hair.

Looking at the whiteboard, Richard considered the names he could see. Claire, Sophie, Phil, Max, Juliette and Alain. So, if Polly wasn't the heroin addict, then who on that list could she have been buying it for?

It was hard to imagine any of them taking heroin, but there was one person on the list who maybe was a better candidate than the others: Phil Adams. After all, he'd already admitted that when he'd had a week with Polly in Vegas before they got married, they'd spent the whole time getting blasted on drugs together. And Richard remembered that when they'd first interviewed Claire, she'd complained that Phil and Polly had spent most of the nineties stoned on drugs together. And now Richard was thinking about it, he also remembered how he'd felt it was odd when Phil told him that he'd been in rehab for anxiety. Surely, even in Los Angeles, rehab was for greater problems than anxiousness?

But how to find out the truth about whether or not Phil was a user? Going back through Phil's original witness statement, Richard was reminded that Phil had a two-picture deal with a major Hollywood studio, and it occurred to him that they'd be able to help.

A few phone calls later and Richard was talking to the head of personnel at the Hollywood studio Phil was writing his script for. At first the woman-with-the-sing-song-voice was reluctant to help, but once Richard explained that he was heading up a murder case—and they'd both worked out that when he said 'murder' he meant 'homicide'—she said that company guidelines therefore allowed her to share information with the police.

Putting aside Richard's surprise that a company would have H.R. guidelines for one of their employees being involved in a murder inquiry, he was soon able to get the information he needed.

For starters, the head of personnel was able to confirm that the company had been disappointed with the box office for Phil's last film, but he had a two-picture deal with them, so they were trying to make the best of a bad lot.

'But you were disappointed with the performance of his last film?' Richard asked.

'The numbers were terrible,' the woman said breezily. 'It tanked.'

'And did you know that Phil booked himself into rehab after it came out?'

'Did we know?' the woman asked. 'It was our idea he booked himself in.'

'Because of his anxiety?'

'His anxiety?'

'Yes, Phil told us he was in rehab for anxiety.'

There was a pause on the other end of the line.

'It wasn't anxiety, was it?' Richard said.

'Well, I'm sure he was very anxious after the movie came out.'

'But that's not why you suggested he go into rehab, was it?'

'Not exactly.'

'So can you tell me why he did?'

The woman on the end of the line sighed.

'Well, it was never confirmed, but we'd heard rumours from the movie set that Phil had been on drugs for the whole shoot.'

'While he was making the film?'

'That's what the rumours said.'

'Could it have been heroin?'

'As I say, I can't confirm or deny that he was on any one drug for sure. Or we'd have sacked him on the spot. But, after the movie came out, we got Phil's producer to remind him that he had a Moral Turpitude clause to his contract, and maybe now would be a good time to book himself into rehab if he needed to.'

'He has a Moral Turpitude clause in his contract?'

'Everyone who works for us does.'

'And do you think he's been clean of drugs since he got out of rehab?'

'Well…' Here the woman paused briefly, and Richard could tell that she was weighing up her options, so Richard kept silent. 'As it happens, three weeks ago we got an anonymous tip-off that he was using drugs again.'

'You did?'

'We did. So we'll be testing him for drugs when he next returns to the studio lot.'

'And if he fails that drugs test?'

'Oh that's easy. He'll be in breach of his contract and we'll cancel his next movie.'

'Then can you tell me? This tip-off, do you have *any* information on who it was from?'

'I'm sorry, I'm looking at Mr Adams's personnel file here, and all it lists is the cell number of the person who called the tip-off in.'

'But that could be enough. Could you tell me the phone number of the person who tipped you off?'

Richard was amazed to hear the woman read out Polly Carter's mobile phone number to him.

Polly Carter had tried to destroy Phil Adams's movie career just before she'd been murdered.

Chapter 11

Richard rang Phil Adams and learnt that he was already in Honoré that morning, so he asked him to pop into the station when it was convenient.

Phil strolled into the police station fifteen minutes later.

'This is quaint,' he said, looking about himself.

Richard smiled to himself as he offered Phil a chair by his desk. As everyone else already knew—and Phil was about to find out—Camille really didn't like people who patronised her island. And, in fact, as Richard and Camille set up on the other side of the table, Richard decided that there was little point beating around the bush anyway. So he just launched in.

'Thanks for stopping by,' he said, 'as we just want to know why you told us you were in rehab for anxiety, when you were really there for drugs abuse?'

'Who told you that?'

'Is it true, or isn't it?'

Phil looked worried. 'What else do you want to know?'

'Are you refusing to answer the question?'

'What else do you want to know?' Phil repeated.

'Very well. What drugs have you been taking on Saint-Marie while you've been here?'

All Phil's self-confidence crumbled before the police's eyes.

'What...*drugs*?'

Richard leaned forward, as though about to share a secret, which, in a sense, he was.

'Because that's why Polly tipped off your movie studio back in Los Angeles, isn't it? Since you've been on Saint-Marie, she's caught you taking drugs again.'

'How do you know this?'

'Just tell us how Polly found out about your drugs use.'

Phil licked his lips as he tried to find the moisture to speak.

'When she invited me out here, I thought it would be like old times. I'd do my work during the day, but by night we'd party. Only, when I told Polly we should get stoned, she got all holier than thou, saying she'd not gone through all the effort of rehab for me to start using drugs in her house again. I was shocked. This wasn't the Polly I knew. But I needed help with my writing—that's what drugs give me, they help me be creative—so I decided that when I wanted to get a buzz, I'd go to the tunnel under her house.'

'So you knew about that?'

'Sure,' Phil said. 'It's where we used to get caned back in the day. But I think Polly got suspicious. A few days after I got here, I was down in that old cave snorting a line of coke and she found me. She said she'd noticed the key to the bookcase was no longer in her filing cabinet.'

'So you also knew how to get into the locked drawer in Polly's study?'

'What's the big deal? I've known the combination to that filing cabinet for years. The padlock was set to her birthday. She was that vain.'

'So you admit you got the key to the bookcase from there?'

Phil nodded.

'Then you must have also seen the anonymous letters she kept in there?'

'I didn't. I told you, I don't know anything about any anonymous letters.'

'But they were in the same drawer as the key to the bookcase.'

'Well, if they were, I didn't see them.'

'And you expect us to believe that, do you?'

'To be honest, I don't much care what you believe, I'm telling it to you straight. How it happened.'

'Okay. So you got the key without noticing the letters that were also in there, went down into the tunnel and were snorting cocaine when Polly discovered the key was missing and came and found you. Is that right?'

'Yes.'

'And how did she react when she saw you?'

'She was angry. Very angry indeed. She said I'd let myself down, I'd let her down. And if I didn't stop at once, she'd do something drastic to stop me.'

'Like phone up your movie studio and anonymously tip them off that you were still a drug addict.'

'That's right. I didn't believe she would, but then she rang them in front of me so I could see. She said she had to tell them for my own good.'

'Which means that the moment you return to the States, they'll test you for drugs, discover you've been using—you'll be in breach of your contract—and they'll be able to cancel their commitment to make your next feature film.'

Phil frowned. Worried.

'It's why I didn't dare tell you the real reason I was in rehab the first time we talked. If you started investigating me for drugs, I was worried you'd find out that it was Polly who snitched on me to the studio.'

'Because it means you've got a motive to want her dead.'

Phil didn't dare say anything.

'Okay. Then tell us, how did you react after she'd phoned your movie studio?'

'I was angry. I'll admit that much. At first at least. I mean, she's transgressed enough in the past, and we've all had to forgive her—and here she was telling me that this one weakness of mine meant I'd have to lose my career!'

'The shame of it,' Richard said, remembering the original background reports on Phil Adams's family— how they were all diplomats, bankers and academics. He couldn't imagine a more 'establishment' family, and he was sure they'd be appalled to learn that Phil was a drug addict.

Camille looked at Phil carefully. 'When she betrayed you like that, you had to get revenge, didn't you? So you killed her.'

'What? No!' Phil was horrified by the accusation. 'I was only angry to start off with. Because Polly was right—I needed a kick up the arse to get clean, and her telling the studio they had to test me was just what I needed to focus my mind. I stopped taking drugs there and then.'

'So, if we test your hair, it will show you've been clean of drugs for the last few weeks?' Camille asked.

Phil frowned.

'Well, no,' he said. 'I'm just saying I was clean after she told the studio. Since she died…? I've fallen off the waggon a bit, but the point still holds. I'm going to get clean before I go back to the States. And as long as I am clean—which I will be—I'll pass all the tests the studio puts me through, so Polly won't have done anything to affect my career. In fact, the way I see it is, by forcing me to kick my habit, she's maybe saved my career.'

'But you admit you're still using?'

'Here and there. It's been hard.'

'Heroin?'

'No way,' Phil said, recoiling. 'I wasn't lying to you when I said I found Polly's drugs use tough to handle. Cocaine's about my limit. I need it for…well, for confidence.'

Richard looked at Phil with the briefest twinge of sympathy, because he could finally see that he wasn't the super-smooth operator he pretended to be. He was someone with only fragile confidence.

Richard dismissed Phil, reminding him that they could press charges against him for possession of drugs at any time. But Richard knew he had some serious thinking to do. After all, how could Phil's version of Polly—where she was so opposed to his drugs use that she was prepared to jeopardise his career to stop him using—be squared with Luc's statement that he'd sold her ten thousand dollars' worth of heroin three days before she died—a fact that seemed to be corroborated by her withdrawal of ten thousand dollars three days before she died?

It wasn't possible that Luc and Phil's stories could both be true, so which of them was lying?

Richard gathered his team at the whiteboard.

'Okay, everyone,' he said. 'So, what of Phil's testimony can we believe?'

'Well, sir,' Fidel said, 'We searched his room straight after the murder and we found no drugs anywhere, be it cocaine or heroin.'

'But we did find evidence of cocaine use in the tunnel under the house,' Camille said. 'And he's just confessed he's been using, both before and after Polly's death.'

'But why was Polly so opposed to Phil's drugs use when she ordered ten thousand dollars of heroin from Luc three days before she died? Or is Luc lying?'

'I reckon he's telling the truth,' Dwayne said. 'I've been asking around, and everyone's still talking about the big sale Luc made a few weeks back. In fact, he had to call in a lot of favours to get that much heroin together. And since then, he's been settling all his debts and splashing his cash.'

'So he really did sell the heroin to Polly?' Camille asked.

'It's what it looks like to me.'

'And there's something else, sir,' Fidel said. 'Because I've been thinking that if Luc's Polly's dealer, then where's the benefit in killing her? Even if it got him ten thousand dollars. Surely she's worth more to him alive than she is to him dead?'

'Yes, good point,' Richard agreed. 'So, once again we find ourselves back at the beginning. Seeing as Polly had no drugs in her system when she died, then who did she order the ten thousand dollars of heroin for?'

'It has to be Phil Adams,' Camille said. 'He admits to taking Class–A drugs while he's out here, it's got to be him.'

'But why would Polly buy drugs for someone after she'd tipped off his employer that he was still using? It doesn't make sense!'

Richard sighed heavily.

'So what else have we got?' he asked.

'Well, sir,' Fidel said, collecting up his notebook from his desk. 'I've been going around the congregation at my church, and I still can't find anyone who saw Alain at the church service on the Sunday morning that Polly was killed.'

'You can't? How many people have you asked?'

'Well, I've been able to speak to just over fifteen so far.'

'And how many people in total would there have been at that Sunday service do you think?'

'For Sunday services, it would have been well over a hundred.'

'Then is there a quick way of speaking to as many people as possible? It strikes me as odd that no one you've spoken to so far remembers seeing Alain at the Sunday service. I want it categorically proven whether he was there or not.'

'Well, sir,' Fidel said, thinking out loud. 'It's evensong tonight. Maybe the priest would let me stand up at the end and speak to the whole congregation directly?'

'Please do. I want to know if Alain's alibi checks out.'

***

That evening, Richard was in his shack trying not to think about his mother and what she might have been up to while out 'clubbing' with Catherine. To this end, he'd laid out the six anonymous letters on his desk, and had decided that although the labs had been unable to glean anything useful from them, there was still one test that could be carried out on them. And that was to inspect the newsprint on the other side of the cut-out letters that had been glued to the A4 paper. It was something of a long shot, though, and would involve permanently damaging the evidence, but Richard knew that desperate times called for desperate measures. So Richard had got everything he needed: a sharp scalpel, a can of WD-40 solvent, and a head torch.

Bending over his desk, Richard clicked his head torch on to full beam. His plan was to use the scalpel to lift the edge of each glued-down scrap of newspaper and then spray minuscule drops of solvent underneath it to dissolve the glue that held it to the A4. That way, he knew he'd be able to liberate each scrap of newspaper and possibly see what had been printed on the other side.

Richard started on the first letter—the lowercase 'y' from the message that otherwise spelled out 'yOu ARe gOinG tO PAy'.

It was painstaking work, but, after a few minutes, Richard had managed to lift this first intact-but-by-now-very-sodden scrap of newspaper from the sheet of A4 it was glued to. He then, just as carefully, turned the little scrap of newspaper over to see what he could see was printed on the other side of it. Unfortunately, the scrap of newspaper was so drenched with liquid solvent, it was impossible to see. So Richard put it to one side, knowing it would become legible as the solvent evaporated and the scrap of newspaper dried out.

He then looked at the other sheets of A4 paper and counted a further seventy-six newspaper headline letters that had been used to make up the remaining messages. He sighed—but with satisfaction. This was exactly the sort of mind-numbing work he needed to stop the image of his mother in a nightclub from popping into his head.

It was 1am when Richard next got up from his desk. Although he'd failed to get some of the scraps of newspaper from the A4—they'd dissolved to mush when he'd used too much WD-40—he'd been able to liberate forty-three separate scraps of newspaper. They now sat on the table drying.

Richard cricked his neck, went over to his verandah, looked out at the swelling sea, and knew that he still needed to keep himself busy or he'd start thinking about his mother again.

Looking about his crumbling shack for something to do, Richard saw his laptop and remembered that he hadn't yet listened to all of the recordings Juliette had made of her husband being unfaithful with Polly. Fidel had of course— and reported that there'd been nothing else of note on them—but Richard knew that he should listen to them himself. Ignoring the first recording for a moment—after all, he had already listened to most of it in the police station with Camille—Richard decided to start with the second recording Juliette had made. Richard remembered from Fidel's notes, this recording was thirteen minutes long and was mostly filled with the sound of chirping crickets in the background. That seemed innocuous enough to keep him busy.

Richard pressed play on the sound file, sat back in his chair, and the sound of chirping crickets filled the air. In fact, as he listened, Richard realised that the night-time crickets in the recording were chirping a little faster than the real-life crickets that were chirping outside his window. And this nearly-but-not-quite synchronicity reminded Richard of how, when he was growing up, the windscreen wipers on his mother's car moved to a slightly different time interval to the clicks of the car's indicator lights. If both were on at the same time, they'd appear to be going at the same speed for a short while, and then the indicator lights would appear to speed up until it was impossible to imagine two rhythms more opposed to each other. And then they'd start to get closer together in timings until they appeared to be entirely back in sync again.

Richard could well remember being driven to school on rainy Monday mornings, the car steamed up on the inside, the wipers squeaking across the windscreen, and his feet just beginning to thaw from the fan heater while the rest of the car remained ice cold.

And with that thought, Richard's defences collapsed and he let the despair in, not that he really knew how to articulate his feelings beyond a general sense of loss he felt for…well, what? What was it he felt loss for? Richard didn't know, but he was dimly aware that his feelings of absence were for something that maybe he'd never even had.

Richard allowed his confusion to quicken a little into anger. After all, what was his mother doing saying she'd walked out on his father? Didn't their marriage vows mean they had to be together in sickness and health forever and ever amen? That's what marriage was in Richard's mind. An ideal—of course—but also an unbreakable vow. The virtue of the promise was not in its making, but in its observance.

And still the crickets chirped from the computer speakers just out of sync with the crickets outside the window, so that sometimes they seemed to be getting more in time with each other, and then less in time.

And that's when Richard had a stunning realisation.

The chirps in the recording were out of time with the chirps of the crickets outside his window!

Richard dashed over to his bookshelves and scrabbled down his book on the indigenous insects of the Caribbean.

What else would he need? A thermometer—luckily there was one nailed to the outside of the house he could use—and a chart of average temperatures on the island. But first he had to see if his memory was correct. Richard flicked through his book on insects until he found exactly what he was looking for. It was an equation called Dolbear's Law. Richard read it through again to check that he understood it.

$$T_f = 50 + \left(\frac{N_{60} - 40}{4} \right)$$

Yup, he thought to himself, if he could just work through the maths of the equation, there was every chance he'd be able to reveal the identity of Polly Carter's killer!

The following morning, Richard was full of beans as he entered the police station, his laptop and the book on insects wedged firmly under his arm. But before he could unleash any of his findings on his team, Fidel was standing up parade-ground smart behind his desk, his notebook in his hand.

'Good morning, sir!' Fidel said.

'Good morning, Fidel, and how are you this morning?'

'I've made a breakthrough.'

'You have, have you?'

Fidel's instincts twitched as he realised that Richard had made a rival breakthrough.

'Yes I have,' he said with a lot less confidence.

'No, go on, let's hear it,' Richard said, unable to keep the smugness out of his voice.

'Well, sir…it's just, I went to evensong at church last night. As you suggested. And I got up at the end of the service—with the priest's say so, of course—and point blank asked the congregation if they'd seen Alain at the Sunday service the morning Polly was murdered. And the thing is, there was no one there who could remember seeing him!'

'Well well well,' Richard said. 'Good work, Fidel, and that fits with what I was able to work out last night as well.'

'It does, sir?'

'Oh yes,' Richard said as he went to Dwayne's desk and carefully opened his book on insects to reveal that he'd used it to transport all of the individual cut-out newspaper letters that he'd been able to liberate from the sheets of A4. Each one of the scraps was now bone dry and it was possible to read what had been printed on the other side. Although, as the pieces were only a centimetre or so square, there was very little in the way of text on the 'other' side of the letters to be read. Richard quickly instructed Dwayne and Fidel to go through each and every one of them, trying to see if they could at least infer whether the newspaper they'd all been cut from came from Saint-Marie, or the UK—or the US, even, considering that this was where Phil Adams and Polly spent so much of their time.

'As for what I've been up to,' Richard said as he went over to his desk and opened up his laptop, 'all will become clear when I play you this recording that Juliette made of Alain committing adultery with Polly.'

Camille, Dwayne and Fidel all crowded around Richard's laptop as he played the recording of crickets that he'd listened to the night before.

Fidel was the first to speak. 'But there's nothing to hear, sir.'

'Nothing human,' Richard agreed. 'But what's that you can hear in the background?'

'It's just a load of crickets chirping,' Dwayne said.

'Exactly!' Richard said, gleefully. 'Then tell me, what can you hear in *this* recording?'

As he said this, Richard pulled his phone out of his pocket, got up his voice memo application and pressed the play button. Like a magician finally revealing the card that was chosen, Richard then put the phone down on the table while it played out the recording he had made of the crickets chirping outside his window the night before.

Richard's team looked at each other as though Richard had gone mad.

'But that's also just crickets chirping,' Dwayne said.

'Wait!' Camille said, jumping in. 'Don't say anything, it's a trap.'

Richard turned to Camille and raised an eyebrow, a skill he had hitherto been unaware he possessed.

'But don't you want to know how those two recordings prove that Alain's been lying to us?' Richard asked, and then he went over to Dwayne's desk, retrieved his book on the insects of the Caribbean and held it up for all to see.

'You're kidding me,' Camille said. 'The book was useful?'

'*All* knowledge is useful, Camille,' Richard said. 'But, since you're asking, yes, this book on the insects of the Caribbean could well have identified our killer!'

'But how, sir?' Fidel asked, and then he turned to Camille apologetically. 'I'm sorry, but I want to know.'

'Well it's funny you should ask, Fidel,' Richard said, licking his finger and then turning the pages of the old book until he found what he was looking for. 'You see, I remembered reading that there was this chap called Amos Dolbear who, back in the nineteenth century, discovered that the speed of a cricket's chirp was directly proportional to the ambient air temperature outside.'

'Come again?' Dwayne asked.

'In fact,' Richard continued, now in full flow, 'as Dolbear plotted the incidence of cricket chirps against the air temperature, he made a discovery. The relationship between the temperature and the number of chirps was directly correlated such that, if you ever wanted to work out the ambient air temperature—called T_f, let's say—all you had to do was count the number of chirps the cricket made over a minute—N_{60} let's say—subtract forty from that number, divide it by four, and then get your result and add fifty to it.'

There was a very long pause while Richard's team looked at him.

'I'm going to say it again,' Dwayne said to Camille and Fidel before turning back to Richard. 'Come again?'

'Well, Alain told us that he had his affair with Polly over a mad few days at Christmas time. Fair enough. But by counting the number of chirps in the background crickets in the recording his wife made of him and Polly, I was able to work out that there were one hundred and ninety chirps per minute.'

'Wait wait wait wait,' Dwayne said, holding up his hands for everyone's attention. 'You counted the number of chirps in the recording?'

'Of course. And by plugging that number—the one hundred and ninety chirps per minute—into Dolbear's equation, I was able to work out that the ambient temperature outside when Juliette made that recording was eighty-eight degrees Fahrenheit.'

'Which is kind of hot,' Camille said, already realising where Richard was going with this.

'Precisely!' Richard agreed, although he'd have liked to dispute Camille's statement that eighty-eight degrees was only 'kind of' hot. 'And you only get temperatures that high once you get to our summer, which only really kicked in in the last month. In fact, if you look at these printouts, you'll see the significance instantly.'

Here, Richard pulled out pages he'd printed off from the Saint-Marie Department of Meteorology showing daily minimum and maximum temperatures going back to the beginning of the year.

'Because back at Christmas and January—when Alain said the recordings were made—the temperature on the island never reached the dizzy heights of eighty-eight degrees. In fact, the highest it got in both December and January was seventy-five degrees.'

'So you're saying the recordings aren't from then!' Fidel said.

'I am! In fact, if you go through this chart of temperatures for the year, there isn't a single day when the temperature on the island reaches as high as eighty-eight degrees until July, which was only last month.'

Dwayne turned to his boss and very carefully said, 'So you're saying you can use the chirps of crickets to prove in court that the recording of Polly and Alain going to bed together isn't from last Christmas. In fact, it's only a month old.'

'Got it in one,' Richard said.

Chapter 12

Leaving Dwayne and Fidel back at the station to see what they could glean from the scraps of newspaper Richard had prepared the night before, Richard and Camille drove up to Polly's house to speak to Alain and Juliette. On the way, Richard realised that he had a ticklish subject he wanted to broach with his partner.

'Camille?' he asked from the passenger seat, staring directly ahead as though he hadn't just spoken.

Camille gave her boss a glance as she drove. 'Yes, sir?'

Still without moving his head, Richard said, 'I think I want your advice.'

Camille tried not to startle, but in the two years she'd known Richard, he hadn't asked her for her advice even once. But she also knew that Richard was like one of the spiky iguanas that roamed the island. They were best approached from sideways on.

'Oh?' she said, pretending that it wasn't that big a deal.

'Or maybe I don't,' Richard said, immediately losing confidence.

Camille waited. She guessed Richard would come to her if she gave him the space. But Richard continued to sit in silence as Camille drove up the hairpin bends that led to Polly's house. And then he continued to sit in silence as she drove up the dusty driveway. Finally, with a crunch of wheels on gravel, Camille parked outside Polly's house and turned off the thudding diesel engine.

The silence between them grew until Camille could take it no more.

'Then what do you need my advice—' Camille started saying before Richard cut across her with, 'Actually, can we just pretend we never had this conversation?'

'But we've not *had* a conversation, sir,' she said.

'We have. This is a conversation.'

'But it's not. Not if you've not said what you wanted saying, sir.'

'And that's another thing,' Richard blurted, trying to change the subject. 'You never call me Chief like the others do.'

Camille looked at her boss, amazed.

'*What?*'

'The others sometimes call me Chief. Even the Commissioner of Police. But you never do. You only ever call me sir.'

Camille didn't dignify this statement of neurotic neediness with a reply. For his part, Richard realised that he was now feeling pretty stupid, so he went to open the passenger-side door to leave—which was when Camille grabbed his right elbow to stop him.

'But if it's advice you want, it's not me you need to talk to,' Camille said. 'I think you need to talk to my mother.'

'I do?' Richard said. 'Why?'

'Because my mother told me to tell you that if you wanted help sorting your mother out, you needed to talk to her.'

Richard felt shame flood his body.

'She thinks my mother needs sorting out?' he said.

Camille looked at her boss and her heart filled with compassion for this awkward, broken man. 'Your mother's on holiday. On her own. She chats up men she meets in the bar. And your father's nowhere to be seen. You don't have to be a detective to work out something's going on…sir.'

Richard continued looking at his subordinate, unable to say anything. He then looked away from Camille and stared out of the jeep's windscreen for a long moment.

After a fair few further moments of thought, he then said, 'This windscreen's filthy.'

Camille shook her head to herself as she opened the door on her side and climbed out of the jeep. Richard either would go and talk to her mother or he wouldn't. She'd passed on the message. That was all she could do.

They found Alain up by the swimming pool. He was cleaning leaves off the surface with a long pole and net.

'Good morning,' Alain said to Richard and Camille as they approached.

'Good morning,' Richard replied, surprised to see Alain working on the house. 'I see you're still keeping the place spick and span.'

'A photographer's coming round later on to take photos. Mr Adams said he's going to put the house up for sale.'

'Phil Adams is selling the house?' Camille asked.

'That's right. He explained to me how he'd inherited Polly's estate and he was going to sell it all to the highest bidder.'

Richard and Camille looked at each other, surprised. After all, Phil had always claimed that he wasn't interested in Polly's money—indeed, that she didn't have any—but he was acting fast enough to liquidise whatever cash the estate did have, wasn't he? But first things first.

'Could we have a word?'

'Of course,' Alain said.

'Because I think you haven't been entirely truthful with us, have you?'

'I'm sorry?' Alain said.

'For starters, you weren't at church when Polly Carter was killed, were you?'

'I was.'

'Then how come we've not been able to find a single member of the congregation who remembers seeing you?'

'I…I don't know,' Alain said limply.

'But let's park that for the moment, because you've got a far bigger problem to contend with, and that's the fact that we also now know that you didn't finish your affair with Polly at Christmas. It carried on after she returned from rehab, didn't it?'

Alain was stunned. Beyond comprehension.

'But tell me, was it your idea to lie to us that it was over then, or was it your wife's?'

Alain looked from Richard to Camille, and then back from Camille to Richard. He then put down the swimming pool net he was holding and walked away to a bench that was in between two nearby palm trees. Richard and Camille followed and waited for Alain to gather his thoughts—although Richard inched himself over so he was standing in the thin strip of shade that was thrown by the trunk of one of the two palm trees.

Eventually, Alain looked up at the police and there was only pain in his eyes.

'I told Juliette we shouldn't lie to you,' he said.

Camille went and sat down next to Alain on the bench. She didn't say anything, but her presence was enough to make him look at her.

'And you're right,' he said. 'Our affair wasn't over. Juliette made me promise I couldn't tell you. You see, it wasn't just an affair. I fell for Polly. Hard. And she for me. We didn't think we would, but…well, there's no accounting for the affairs of the heart, is there? Because living with Juliette is…well, I believe in the vows we took, but she's a bitter and unkind woman. And with Polly, it just clicked. You know?'

Camille nodded. She wanted Alain to know she understood exactly what he was describing, and her support gave Alain the courage to go on.

'Although I wasn't lying when I said it was a few days over Christmas. Because I discovered that Polly was still secretly smoking heroin. She's got this tunnel under the house she goes to. I know you found it the other day. Anyway, she'd told me she was off the drugs when we started having our affair, but when I realised she'd been lying to me, it made me re-evaluate everything. Because there was something about her keeping this secret from me—and how it made me feel—that made me realise that the whole affair was crazy. I *am* a churchgoer. Whether or not I could be happier with someone else, whether I even like my wife any more—let alone love her—I made my vows before God to stay with Juliette in sickness and in health. So I told Polly it had to end between us.'

'And when was this?'

'The eighteenth of January.'

'And how was Polly when you told her?'

'She was ice calm. You know. She just accepted it. And the next day, she packed her bags and left. I had no idea where she'd gone, or why she'd gone, but I took it as her signal to me that it was over. And I knew what I had to do.' Here, Alain took a deep breath before continuing. 'I had to tell Juliette everything. I had to confess of my sins.'

'She didn't have any recordings of you and Polly at this time?'

'No. But when I told her about affair, I also said that it was all over between me and Polly. Finished.'

'And how did Juliette take the news?'

'She was like a hurricane, throwing mugs and plates and such hurtful words at me, I didn't know what I'd unleashed. But she was the one who was wronged. I had to take it. And what she told you the first time you talked to us was kind of true. Once Polly left the island for rehab, we were up here on our own, and we just had to get on with our lives. After a week or so, it was a bit better, and after that, we seemed to come to an understanding. We'd share the same house. We'd be civil with each other. Up to a point. And maybe we could get our relationship back on track in time.'

'And did you?'

'Not really, but we were at least polite. The only thing that changed was Juliette stopped coming to church with me and instead started training for the island triathlon at the end of this year.'

'And how were you while Polly was gone?'

'I was a mess. Because the more I told myself our affair had been wrong, the more I found myself thinking about Polly. How she'd made me feel. How I felt I could do anything—go anywhere—when I was with her. I was so confused. But as the weeks turned into months, I came to realise that I'd still been in the wrong, and my life with Juliette was my punishment from God for what I'd done.'

'And then, one day, Polly came back.'

'That's right. And then she came back.'

'When exactly was this?' Richard asked.

'The last week of March. And she told me that my words to her had been what she'd finally needed to get her life together. She didn't want to lose me as well, so she'd spent the last two months in rehab, and was now entirely drugs-free. And I'd like to say I resisted her, but I didn't. We restarted our affair the first day she got back.

'And the amazing thing was, Polly really was clean of drugs. I could tell. And I found it humbling. The fact that, after a lifetime of abuse, she'd kicked the habit so she could win me back.'

'But Juliette got suspicious, didn't she?' Richard said.

'From the moment Polly returned,' Alain agreed. 'But I lied to her. Told her nothing was going on. It was like I was the drug addict now, only my drug was Polly, and there were no lies or deceptions I wouldn't do to spend time with her.'

'Including assignations in the secret smugglers' tunnel?' Richard said.

Alain looked at Richard in shame.

'At first,' he said. 'We couldn't *not* see each other. So we'd meet up in the tunnel—but with Juliette off training so hard, we soon found we could meet in Polly's bedroom.'

'Which is where Juliette finally managed to trap you both,' Richard said.

Alain nodded.

'Which was only last month,' Richard added.

Alain nodded.

'You're right. The recordings are only three weeks old. And when Juliette played them to me, it went real bad real quickly. She told me she'd taken me back when any other woman would have kicked me out, and now I was sleeping with the harlot again. That's the word she used to describe Polly. She called her a harlot. And there was something in her anger, in how vindictive she was, that made me realise. Whether or not I'd done what I'd done, I had to leave Juliette. So that's what I told her. It was over between us, I was going to leave. And that's when she went real crazy. Spitting and kicking at me that I couldn't abandon her. To be honest, the more she reacted so mad, the more I knew I *had* to leave her.'

'Did you tell Polly you were leaving your wife?' Camille asked.

Alain nodded once.

'And what did she say?'

'She said she wanted to come with me.'

'She did?'

'She said she'd not worked in nearly a year, her rehab had cost her a fortune, she didn't think she had any money left, but even if she was a pauper, she said she wanted to be with me.' Alain took a sharp breath in, readying himself to finish his story. 'So we made a plan. Polly wanted to mend her relationship with her sister Claire more than anything—that's what she told me—so she said she and I should go and move in to the family farm back in the UK. She couldn't offer me any glamour, she said, but there'd maybe be work for her and me. And we could be together.'

'Did Claire know anything about this?'

'Not as far as I know, but it's why Polly invited Claire out here. She wanted to make amends with her and ask her if we could go and stay with her.'

Alain looked at Richard with such pain that he had to remind himself that whether or not Alain had been through the mill emotionally, he was still a murder suspect.

'Do you know what I see?' Richard said to Alain. 'A man who is religious, that rings true—and a lifelong churchgoer, we know that's also true. But I also see a man who's riven by guilt. Who's conflicted by the fact that he's cheated on his wife. Cheated on his vows. Cheated on God.'

Alain dipped his eyes, unable to deny Richard's words.

'And I also see a man who's been lying to us—lying to his wife. But let's say your affair started with Polly back at Christmas. And that she put herself into rehab soon after. And that your relationship started up again when she returned to the island. We know that much is true. But if you were feeling guilty before, I think that when you rekindled your affair, you were consumed by guilt. And I think you were so eaten up by confusion and shame at your feelings for Polly that you realised there was only one way out, and that's if Polly was put beyond temptation's reach.

'Did you mean to kill her that morning? Maybe not. But you were certainly prepared to wait in hiding and then attack her—the object of your love, the object of your hate. And now she's dead, you're finally able to return to being what you always knew you should have been. A good Christian. A dutiful husband.'

Alain stood up from the bench and looked Richard square in the face.

'Don't you get it? I *loved* Polly.'

'Then where were you on the morning she died?' Richard said, happy to meet fire with fire. 'Because you weren't at church, were you?'

There was a buttoned-up fury to how Alain was holding himself that Richard recognised. It was the anger of someone who felt desperately wronged by life.

'Very well,' Alain said, 'I was at the airport.'

Richard didn't know what to say—he certainly hadn't expected Alain to suddenly reveal another alibi.

'I'm sorry?'

'You're right. I wasn't at church. I was at Saint-Marie airport.'

'So what were you doing at the airport?'

'Buying two single tickets from Saint-Marie to London Stansted. For me and Polly to use. Because I'm not lying when I said we were serious about each other. She and I were going to elope to the UK once she'd cleared it with her sister. To start our new life together.'

'So if we get in touch with Saint-Marie airport,' Richard queried, 'they'll be able to confirm your story?'

'One hundred per cent.'

'But I don't understand. If you've got an alibi for the time of the murder, then why didn't you tell us?'

Alain finally broke Richard's gaze, as he looked back at his bungalow.

'I should have done, but the first time you asked me where I'd been, I didn't know Polly had died, so I told you the cover story—because I didn't want Juliette to know where I'd really been. That I'd been buying the airline tickets that morning. And while I was doing that, that's when Polly was killed. I mean, it's as though God doesn't want me to be happy, isn't it?'

Richard could see how bitter Alain was. But if he was elsewhere at the time of the murder, it didn't much matter how messed up he was, he couldn't be the killer. But did his new alibi check out? That was the question.

Leaving Alain by the pool, Richard and Camille returned to the police jeep with Camille calling the airline desks at the airport. While Camille was on the phone, Richard saw Juliette return to the cottage in her battered Citroën and he went over to talk to her.

'What do you want?' she said irritably, getting bags of shopping out of the car's boot. Richard saw that Juliette was in her tight-fitting Lycra running kit again, with running shoes stained in red dust from the roads nearby.

'We know your husband was still having his affair with Polly when she died.' To her credit, Juliette only paused for the briefest of seconds as she picked up a shopping bag. 'And before you ask, we know this because we've worked out the recordings you gave us were from last month, weren't they? And that means you lied to us when you said their affair was over. Why was that?'

Juliette carefully put her shopping to the ground so she could talk to Richard properly.

'I didn't want to air my laundry in public.'

'I don't buy that,' Richard said. 'You were already airing your laundry by admitting to the affair that your husband had with Polly back at Christmas. So why didn't you want us to know it was still going on?'

'Is it so hard to understand?' she said.

'I'm sorry, I think you'll have to explain it to me.'

'I didn't want *anyone* to know it was still going on.'

'Why not?'

'Don't you get it? I love my husband.'

'Even though he doesn't love you.'

'How dare you say that!' Juliette hissed at Richard. 'He loves me, he just needed to get out from under the spell of that witch!'

'You mean Polly?'

'Of course! I mean, he was a fool, but it wasn't his fault, not the way I saw it. And when she died, I made Alain promise he couldn't tell you that his affair with her was still going on. I didn't want you snooping around our lives, I just wanted to get my husband back to myself.'

'I see,' Richard said, now deciding that while he'd previously known that Juliette was a hard woman, he'd had no idea how close to the edge she was. 'So you think that you and Alain will be together now?'

'Yes,' Juliette said with a sense of desperate finality. 'I've been married before. Twice. But this time, it's going to work out. We're husband and wife. Forever.'

Before Richard could ask Juliette whether she knew about her husband's plans to skip the country with Polly, Camille came over, her notebook in her hand.

'Sir,' Camille said, 'Alain was telling the truth. He was at Saint-Marie airport at 10am.' Here, Camille mentioned the name of a local airline and explained that not only did she manage to speak to someone who remembered Alain buying two tickets to the UK in cash, the computer confirmed that the tickets were bought at 10.06 that morning.

Alain had an alibi for the time of the murder. He was no longer a suspect.

'What are you saying?' Juliette asked, puzzled. 'Alain was at church that morning.'

'I'm sorry,' Camille said, deciding to be tactful. 'But maybe you should ask him where he was yourself.'

'What do you mean? Where was he?'

Richard realised that he didn't have anywhere near his partner's scruples, so he decided to dive in. 'Your husband was buying two one-way tickets to the UK for him and Polly at the time she was killed.'

Juliette recoiled. 'No! It's not possible.'

'Because he *was* leaving you, and I think you knew it.'

'No. He wasn't! He wouldn't leave me.'

'And, as you told us, you do love him—in a warped, possessive and controlling way, if you ask me. Remember, we discovered the surveillance bug you placed to catch your husband cheating. I know how calculating you can be when you want to be. But the thing is, Juliette, now your husband has a watertight alibi, I can't help noticing that you still don't.'

'But I've told you. I was out running that morning.'

'But we can't find a single person who saw you on that run.'

'It was Sunday morning, there weren't many people about.'

'So what I'm wondering is, what if you weren't in fact on your run that morning, but were instead on the cliff steps waiting for Polly?'

'No! And anyway, how could I possibly have known Polly would come down the steps right then?'

'I don't know. Why don't you tell us? Was there another bug we don't know about?'

'No, of course not!'

'But let's see, shall we?' Richard said. 'Because I can well imagine you waiting on the steps to intercept Polly. Maybe you even tricked her into thinking Alain was already in the underground tunnel waiting for her? Because it would be poetic justice to kill her when she thought she was going to meet him, wouldn't it? But whether or not you were planning to do any more than confront her, when Polly announced she was going to commit suicide and ran down the steps, I think it was too much temptation for you. You picked up the branch you found lying on the steps and knocked her off the cliff to her death!'

Juliette was looking at Richard as though he were mad.

'But if I was down the steps, how do you think I got off the beach?'

'You carried on down the steps and hid in the tunnel, didn't you? After all, it was you who first told us that this used to be a smuggler's house.'

'What tunnel?' Juliette asked, wide-eyed.

'Oh come on,' Richard said. 'You've been cleaning the house for years—and for the previous owners before Polly bought the house. You know about the tunnel behind the bookcase.'

Juliette blinked—a moment of indecision—and Richard knew he'd got her. She knew about the secret tunnel.

'I see,' he said. 'Another thing you've lied to us about.'

'I didn't hide in the tunnel! All I did that morning was go on a 10k run and then meet Alain for a coffee in Catherine's bar at 10.30,' she said.

'Which I can't help feeling was rather clever of you—to make sure you were seen in the one bar on the whole island which is run by the mother of a police officer.'

Before Juliette could reply, they all saw a defeated Alain head over from the swimming pool area.

'Tell them!' Juliette squawked as her husband approached. 'You weren't leaving me, were you? You'd not leave me! Tell them!'

Alain looked at his wife with quiet contempt.

'Why are you still lying?' he said to her.

'What?' she said, horrified, as Alain turned to the police.

'I told Juliette I was leaving her the day before Polly died.'

'He didn't! He's lying to you!' Juliette pleaded.

'Enough!' Alain barked at his wife, finally asserting his dominance over her. Very calmly, he turned back to the police. 'I told my wife I was leaving her the day before I went to the airport. On the Saturday. That's the truth.'

Juliette had no answer to this and looked at her husband in despair.

Alain turned to Juliette. 'I'm going inside now. I suggest you do the same, woman.'

Alain left his wife standing among her bags of shopping, and Richard realised that he'd rarely seen anyone look more forlorn than Juliette did at that precise moment.

But if she had known that her husband was leaving her for a new life with Polly, Richard had no doubt now. Juliette could be the killer.

But how to prove it?

Chapter 13

Once Richard and Camille had returned to the police station, Richard discovered that Fidel and Dwayne had been making heavy weather with the scraps of newspaper print he'd left them to process.

'There's tonnes of text on the other sides of these bits of paper, sir,' Fidel said. 'But none of it makes sense. It's just half a word here, half a word there.'

'I see,' Richard said, disappointed that the evidence still hadn't given them any leads. He went to Dwayne's desk where the squares of paper were all laid out, and started to look at the fragments of newspaper for himself. It was just as Fidel had said. On the other side of each cut-out letter was sometimes a scrap of text, sometimes it was blank, and sometimes there was the ink of what had perhaps been a picture or an advert, but it was hard to see what could be gleaned other than the fact that the newspaper was English-language.

As Richard was looking at the newspaper fragments, Dwayne sidled up to him with an ice-cold bottle of water from the fridge.

'Thanks, Dwayne,' Richard said, taking the bottle.

As Richard unscrewed the lid and took a glug of water, Dwayne dipped his head to his ear and quietly said, 'Your mum won't stop texting me, Chief.'

Richard froze—mid-gulp—and then turned to look at Dwayne, who had the good grace to look suitably awkward himself.

'In fact, she keeps saying we should go for a drink.'

Richard coughed in a wild splutter, the water going down the wrong hole in his throat, the liquid dribbling down his chin and onto his shirt and tie.

'Hold on, hold on,' Richard said, heading over to the little kitchen area to the side of the main office and grabbing himself a tea towel to dab at his shirt and tie.

Once he'd re-established a suitable level of sartorial decorum, Richard looked back at the office. Camille and Fidel were both working at their desks—pretending not to have noticed his and Dwayne's exchange—and Dwayne was still standing to the side of his desk looking back at Richard with a desperate look in his eyes that reminded Richard of a rabbit facing a shotgun barrel.

Richard folded the tea towel, placed it by the sink, and remembered how Camille had said that her mother had offered to help him. Richard exhaled, but this wasn't a sigh of defeat. It was the sigh of a man who knew that he was about to strap on his boxing gloves and go into the ring.

'All right, everyone,' Richard said. 'Dwayne, help me get those scraps of newspaper into an envelope. I'm going to look at them down at Catherine's bar.'

Camille looked up from her monitor, guessing why Richard was going to see her mother, but Richard avoided her eye as he helped Dwayne get the bits of paper into an envelope.

A few minutes later, Richard was sitting at the outside seating area of Catherine's bar with the scraps of newspaper spread out on the table in front of him. It was one of those stultifyingly hot days when there wasn't even a hint of a puff of a breeze anywhere on the island and Richard realised he was slowly roasting inside his dark suit.

'Here you are,' Catherine said, bringing over a cup of tea in a china cup.

'Thank you,' Richard said.

'No, thank you,' Catherine lilted, before hovering by Richard's table.

Richard realised he didn't know how to broach the subject of why he was there, so he did what any self-respecting Englishman would do and prevaricated.

'No, thank *you*,' he repeated, before taking a sip from his cup. 'Lovely cup of tea by the way.'

'Camille just rang me,' Catherine said. 'She said you'd not be able to tell me why you were here, but you were here to talk about your mother.'

'Oh. Ah. She said that, did she?'

'That's right.'

'Um. Oh.'

Richard took another quick sip of tea.

'This really is a *lovely* cuppa.'

Catherine dragged over a chair and sat in it.

'All right, I'll speak and you can listen. Because your mother is a wonderful woman. A little highly strung perhaps, but she can also be funny, kind, and she loves you very much. But if she sees that you're happy, she herself is unhappy.'

Richard frowned.

'I know,' Catherine said, misreading Richard's frown. 'She's not happy at all.'

'No, sorry to interrupt, but she thinks I'm *happy* out here?'

'Of course. You are.'

'No I'm not.'

'I don't want to talk about you.'

'But you started it.'

'I didn't.'

'You said I was happy.'

'But you are, aren't you?'

'Look at me, Catherine. Do I look happy to you?'

'It's your mother we're talking about, can you stop being so…male!'

At this, Richard sat up straighter in his chair. Empirical evidence he'd collected over the years had taught him that when a woman accused him of being too male, his only hope was to react in exactly the same way each time, which was to tilt his head to one side as though he was now listening—and continue to remain silent until that person had finished telling him all the different ways that he was in the wrong.

'Thank you,' Catherine said, believing she'd finally got through to Richard. 'Because last night, your mother and I talked. A lot. And I think she's ready to go home. Oh she still says how much she loves it out here—how she's finally living—but I've been running this bar a long time, and I recognise the signs. This is a holiday romance she's having. A holiday romance with the island. I think she still wants to be with your father. I can tell. It's just, he takes her for granted. She's invisible to him. And it kills a woman if she thinks she's invisible.

'And worse than that, your father thinks your mother's job is to shop, cook and clean for him. To get him his meals. To wash his clothes. She told me that since he retired, your father just sits in his chair all day long expecting to be included in whatever your mother's doing. And then, when she does include him in her plans, he just complains that he'd rather be sitting in a chair. This is no way to keep a relationship alive.

'So this is what you've got to do. You've got to get your father to change. To rekindle the romance in their relationship and sweep your mother off her feet.'

Richard tried to imagine his father being romantic and failed. His father was about as romantic as a henge.

'So what do you think?' Catherine asked.

'You're saying you think my father should sweep my mother off her feet?'

'There has to be romance in his soul somewhere.'

'Really, you've not met my father. There isn't,' Richard said.

'Oh but there is,' Catherine said, leaning forward, her eyes twinkling. 'There's romance in *everyone's* heart. Even yours, Richard Poole.'

'But how exactly can I get my father to sweep my mother off her feet seeing as he's currently three thousand miles away?'

'Then you have to get him to come here.'

'Ha!' Richard said. 'My father doesn't go abroad. He always says that there's nothing the world can offer him that he can't do better in the UK.'

'He does?'

'Yes.'

'And that's the person your mother married?'

'Well, in his defence, it *is* true.'

'Then I despair for you! I despair for your mother!'

Catherine was about to get up when a thought occurred to her.

'Although,' she said conspiratorially, 'if your father won't do what you want him to do, why don't you treat him like one of your suspects in a case, and see if you can trick him into revealing himself?'

Richard was interested. 'How do you mean?'

'You could set a trap for him. Like when you wear a secret microphone and trick a criminal into making a confession in front of you. I know you police can be devious when you want to be.'

This gave Richard pause. Was there in fact a way he could trick his father into a grand romantic gesture? It didn't seem possible, and yet there was something about how Catherine had framed the problem that finally seemed to make sense for Richard. What if he viewed his mother's situation as a puzzle that had to be solved? Because the one thing Richard knew about himself was that he was *very* good at solving puzzles.

And with that thought, Richard ducked his eyes back down to the table of cut-out newspaper letters on the table in front of him. And with no idea of how rude he was being, he said, 'Thank you, Catherine, that's very useful, I'll think about what you said.'

For her part, Catherine supposed she'd expected no more from Richard—and she'd certainly been prepared for a lot less. He had at least listened to her.

As for Richard, he was too busy turning the scraps of paper over and looking at them this way and that with a new sense of purpose. And it was as he picked them up and put them down again that he noticed that the letters on two different scraps of paper seemed to be in the same bright red font, and also seemed to be the same point size. Were both letters in fact cut from the same headline?

One of the scraps was the letter 'T', and the other was a 'H'. He turned over the 'T' first and saw that on the other side of the newspaper scrap there was a nonsensical list in tiny type. It said:

castle
beach
ham

Richard was puzzled. What on earth could be the newspaper article that would make a list of such words as 'castle', 'beach', and 'ham'?

Richard then turned over the letter 'H' and saw that there was a similarly sized list of words on the other side, but it made just as little sense.

> Horn
> Hol
> Grant

But Richard was nothing if not diligent, so he turned the scraps of paper back over again to look at the 'H' and 'T' letters on the front. He knew that the most common pair of letters in the English language are 'TH' so he put them back together how he imagined they might have been in the original headline—so they spelled 'Th'—and then he turned the bits of paper over again, only this time keeping them as a pair.

Now that the pieces of paper were aligned properly, on the 'other' side it was possible to see that the scraps of meaningless words weren't meaningless at all. Richard read:

> Horncastle
> Holbeach
> Grantham

Richard knew these were all market towns in Lincolnshire. And that meant that the newspaper that had been used to make the threatening letters had almost certainly come from Lincolnshire.

And only Polly's sister Claire lived in Lincolnshire.

Was it Claire who'd been sending the anonymous letters after all?

***

Once Richard explained to a baffled Camille what he'd been able to deduce from the cut-out letters, they drove up to Polly's house and were soon waiting for Claire in the study. Richard wanted to wait there if only because he was still fascinated by the bookcase that led down into the secret smugglers' tunnel behind.

'It's funny,' he said, 'but once you know that this section of the bookcase swings out, it's obvious. There are even hinges down the right side.'

'So what did my mother say?'

'I'm sorry?'

'When you went to speak to her.'

Richard turned back to look at Camille and flicked some imaginary fluff from the lapel of his suit jacket.

'It has no bearing on the case, so I don't think this is the right forum for a discussion.'

'Of course, sir, and normally I'd agree, but we are actually just waiting for a witness, it can't do any harm to talk about it.'

'But we're not waiting,' Richard said. 'Claire is just coming.'

'She isn't,' Camille said.

'And that's where you're wrong, Camille, because she is.'

Richard held up his finger for silence because he could hear the squeak of a protesting wheel approaching, and, only a few seconds later, the door opened and Sophie pushed Claire into the room—the front left wheel of Claire's wheelchair still squeaking in protest.

'You wanted to see me?' Claire asked.

'We did,' Richard said.

'Then, if that's all, I'll leave,' Sophie said.

'Yes, if you would,' Claire said to Sophie somewhat dismissively.

With Sophie gone, Claire folded her hands into her lap as though she were doing them a favour by her very presence.

'Yes, thank you for meeting us,' Richard said, 'because we wanted to give you the chance to tell us the truth.'

'I don't understand. I've told you the truth.'

'About everything?'

'Of course.'

'Including the fact that you're the person who's been sending the threatening letters to your sister?'

'But I haven't.'

'We've been able to work out that the messages were cut from a newspaper from Lincolnshire. And seeing as you're the only person here who's from Lincolnshire, that means that you're behind the messages. You really shouldn't have used the local newspaper.'

Claire opened her mouth in shock at this news.

Flashing a warning look to her boss to stay well away, Camille pulled up a little wooden chair so she could sit in front of Claire.

'These last ten years must have been so hard for you. Losing your father so soon after your riding accident. And we all know who was to blame for that, don't we? Your sister. Who's caused you pain every day of your life since then. I could understand why you'd want to punish her. Why you'd want her to suffer.'

It was barely perceptible, but Claire nodded.

'It's only natural,' Camille said simply.

Once again, the tiniest of nods from Claire. And when she spoke, her voice was thick with guilt.

'I tried so hard,' she said. 'To move on. To forgive. But it's like there are two me's now. Because what I told you before is true. I get to run a farm, which I love. It even makes me rich. And that version of me counts my blessings almost every day. After all, I know deep down that what Polly did to me was just a stupid accident. She didn't mean to disable me. And that's the me who I am most of the time.

'But then there's the other me. The one who still dreams she can walk and run—and ride my horses—but then wakes up in pain. Who has to suffer the shame of being lifted into and out of a bath. Who can't meet a man who can see beyond the metal frame of my wheelchair.'

'And it was this other version of you that sent those letters?' Camille asked.

'Sort of, but not quite. I made the letters when I was feeling okay about myself. It took a whole weekend.

To find the back copies of the local paper. To think of messages I could make with the letters. And then to cut out and stick the letters on.'

'I don't understand,' Richard said. 'You say that you made the letters when you were feeling…happy?'

'Happy's a bit strong, but definitely in a good place,' Claire said. 'Because, the thing is, I always knew there'd be a day coming up—maybe not that month, or even the next—but I'd wake up at 4am in despair. Without hope. Full of pain. And that version of me needed justice against Polly. The person who'd robbed me of my life. So, whatever state I was in when the despair grabbed me, I'd go to the safe in my study, get out one of these letters, put it in a typed envelope and send it to Polly in the Caribbean. And I know it sounds crazy, but I found that if I had something proactive to do—if I felt I was getting *revenge*—it helped me through the pain.'

Richard noted how Claire had leaned into the word 'revenge' as she said it. Hurting Polly was something that mattered deeply to her—perhaps unsurprisingly, he couldn't help but concede.

'So there were six occasions when you sent the letters?' Camille asked.

'I sent all ten,' Claire said, abashed. 'I think Polly threw the first few away.'

'But she must have known they were from you,' Richard said.

Claire looked at Richard and smiled sadly. 'Not quite. You see, there were a lot of people at the farm and in the village who hated Polly for what she did to me. In fact, pretty much everyone who was out on that Boxing Day hunt that day, for example.'

'But she must have guessed they were from you,' Richard said again.

'I know,' Claire said almost with relish. 'And that's what made the letters such a perfect release for me. Polly would ninety per cent know they were from me, but she wouldn't be able to prove it. You see, I even made sure I was wearing gloves when I touched the paper or the envelope, and I always used pre-gummed stamps. That way I was delivering the message I wanted to deliver when I was in the pit of despair without definitively saying it was me.

'And Polly said she knew the letters were from me the moment I got out here. I denied it of course.' Claire let out a little giggle as she said this, in a seriously misjudged attempt at humour. 'But the strangest thing happened. After I'd told her I'd *not* sent the letters—and explained how it must have been someone else from the estate or village—Polly started crying. I was shocked. I'd never seen her be anything other than dismissive. Even at our mother's funeral last year, she seemed unmoved. And here she was crying and saying how sorry she was she'd screwed my life up. And admitting she'd screwed her life up as well. And she said she wasn't happy. She hadn't been happy for some time, but she was making changes. That's what she said to me when I got out here this time.'

'And what changes were these?' Camille said.

'I don't know. But just before she died, she said she had a gift for me.'

'A gift for you?'

'That's right. It was the night before she died. And she said she had a gift she wanted to give me.'

'Did she tell you what it was?'

'I never found out. She was dead before she could give it to me.'

Richard tried to imagine what that gift could have been. It couldn't have been the heroin, could it? That didn't seem to make sense.

'But the following morning,' Claire continued, 'it was like everything was back to normal, and Polly was her usual arrogant and bullying self. Sitting in the kitchen, being rude and smoking, knowing how much it irritated me. When she asked me to go for a walk with her in the garden, I agreed, if only because I thought she'd explain what was going on—why she was so nice to me the night before, and what had changed overnight to make her suddenly so angry with me again. But the moment we were on our own, she started flipping out at me even more. I didn't know what to think, she was spouting this…hatred at me. Blaming me for her drug addiction, blaming me for making her unhappy—I couldn't work out what I'd done wrong—and then, when we got to the top of the cliffs, she screamed at me that she was going to kill herself, and that's when she ran down the cliff steps.'

As Claire said this, Richard noticed Claire's cheeks briefly pink with embarrassment, and then she looked away.

'What's that?' Richard said, pulling over a chair and sitting down in front of Claire next to Camille.

After a moment, Claire looked back at Richard.

'What's what?' she said.

'What aren't you telling us?'

'I've told you everything,' Claire said, but Richard could see she was flustered.

'No you haven't. When you said your sister ran down the cliff steps, you looked guilty.'

'I did?'

'Why was that?'

'You're mistaken.'

'I'm not.' Richard looked at Claire, and realised something. 'And I can't help noticing that, although you've just recounted the story of your sister's death, you did so without mentioning the man in yellow at all.'

Guilt flashed into Claire's eyes again, and Richard pounced.

'Have you been lying to us about the person in the yellow coat?' he asked, his voice harsh.

Claire looked at Richard, and he could see she was desperate.

'Who was it you saw on the steps before your sister ran down them?'

'Who was it?'

'Yes. Who was it?'

After a moment, Clair said in a small voice, 'No one.'

Silence filled the room, punctuated only by the insistent ticking of the mantelpiece clock.

'You saw…no one?'

'I'm so sorry,' Claire said.

'You saw *no one*?' Richard said again, appalled.

'I'm sure you can explain,' Camille said kindly.

'Well…you see, I was so worried after Polly died. I mean, I was the last person to see her alive, wasn't I? And I soon learnt that no one else apart from me had seen exactly what had happened at the top of the cliff. And the thing is, I knew you'd find out it was Polly who'd disabled me all those years ago. And I also worried you'd find out it was me who'd been sending her those letters. So when you started asking all those questions about where I was when Polly died, I knew I needed to do something to make you look at someone other than me…'

'So you made up seeing someone in a yellow raincoat on the steps to throw us off the scent,' Camille said.

'But I saw a man in yellow on the steps—just not that morning.'

'Hold on,' Richard said, 'did you see *anyone* on the steps immediately before your sister was murdered?'

Claire looked at Richard and shook her head.

'No,' she said. 'But it's like I was saying, a few days beforehand, I *had* seen him. You know, the man in yellow. You see, I'd been out in the garden when I'd seen this person wearing a yellow raincoat head over to the top of the cliff.'

'Was it raining at the time?' Richard asked.

Claire thought for a moment before answering. 'It had been. That's why I went out into the garden. It always smells so nice after a rainfall. But I think that's why I noticed him. I thought it was odd he'd still be wearing his yellow raincoat.'

'And did this happen three days before your sister died by any chance?' Richard asked.

'Yes,' Claire said. 'I suppose it was. But I saw him head down the cliff steps wearing a yellow coat. If it was a man of course. I still can't say for sure if it was a man or a woman. But the point is, later on that morning, when I saw Polly, I mentioned to her that I'd seen this person in a yellow raincoat near the cliff steps, and she looked really panicked and told me that he was a bad man and I was to stay away from him.'

'Really?' Richard asked, sceptically.

'And I'm not joking when I say Polly looked frightened. She had this look on her face that said this person was *really* bad news. I guessed it was someone connected with her drugs somehow. And that's the reason why I mentioned him after Polly died. Seeing as Polly herself was frightened of this man, and he'd been hanging around only a few days before, I wanted you to know about him.'

'Which you did, but in a way which has seriously wasted police time,' Richard said, having difficulty keeping a lid on his anger.

'I know, and I'm sorry. I should have told you the truth from the start.'

Richard went for a wander around the room. He was furious with Claire for having lied to them, but he tucked his personal feelings away so he could concentrate on the one issue that really mattered. Why had Claire said she'd seen someone on the cliff steps beforehand only to change her story? Was she even telling the truth now? What if the fabled 'Man in Yellow' *had* been on the cliff steps just before the murder, but he'd since got to Claire and put pressure on her to change her story?

Mind you, Richard had to concede to himself, it didn't much matter how much Claire changed her story—or how guilty she now looked—she was the only person at the house that day who *couldn't* have killed Polly. Not seeing as Polly had been knocked to her death from partway down a staircase Claire couldn't have possibly got down.

However, even though Claire still couldn't have been the killer, Richard knew that *someone* had killed Polly Carter. But who was it?

Chapter 14

Richard had been standing at the whiteboard without moving for nearly fifteen minutes, and Fidel had come to the conclusion that maybe his boss had fallen asleep standing up like a cow. As for Camille and Dwayne, they were also exchanging worried glances.

Camille scraped her chair back and joined her boss at the board.

'Sir, are you okay?' she asked.

And still Richard didn't move—or acknowledge Camille's presence in any way. He just looked at the dry-erase ink on the rickety whiteboard.

'Sir?'

Richard turned to Camille as though he'd only just realised he was in a police station.

'Who killed Polly Carter, Camille?'

'Well it's not hard,' Dwayne said, as he came over to join his boss and Camille. 'It's one of those people on the board.'

'You're kidding me?' Richard said sarcastically, and Dwayne looked hurt. After all, he'd only been trying to help.

'Although,' Camille said, her brow creasing with thought, 'we've got too many names up there, haven't we?'

Richard turned to Camille. 'How do you mean?'

'Well, for example, it doesn't matter that Alain was having an affair—or lied to us about where he was at the time of the murder. We now know he was at the airport buying airline tickets when Polly was murdered—so he can't be our killer.'

As she said this, Camille picked up the board cloth and wiped out all the information they'd collected on Alain Moreau.

Richard's mouth opened in shock. What had Camille just done?

'And the same is true for both Claire and Sophie,' Camille continued. 'Sophie was in the garden when Polly was pushed from the cliff, so we know she's not the killer, either.'

'Yes,' Richard said hastily, 'but it doesn't mean her name gets wiped from the board.'

Camille ignored her boss and wiped Sophie's name from the board before she then hovered the cloth over Claire's name.

'And as for Claire, just how do you think she got down those steps to commit murder?'

Richard's hand grabbed Camille's wrist to stop her wiping the board any further.

'But she's the victim's sister, we can't possibly remove her from the board.'

'We can.'

'We can't, Camille.'

'But I can,' Dwayne said, as he grabbed the cloth from Camille's hand and wiped Claire's name from the board.

Richard turned to Dwayne, took the cloth from his hand, went over to his desk and slammed the offending item in the desk's top drawer—before very carefully pulling out a bunch of keys from his pocket, choosing a tiny key from the fob and then locking the drawer shut. There, he seemed to be saying to his team as he looked at them. That was the end of that particular madness.

Dwayne licked the palm of his hand and wiped out all the information on the whiteboard they had on Luc Pichou.

'And I don't have Luc down as a killer, either, Chief. I've known him my whole life and he's only ever been a small-time pusher.'

'Dwayne's got a point, sir,' Fidel said from his desk, half rising out of his chair as he did so.

Richard turned very slowly and gave Fidel a hard stare.

'*Et tu*, Fidel?' he said.

Fidel sank back to his seat, suitably chastised.

'Go on, Fidel,' Camille said.

Looking desperately conflicted, Fidel looked from Richard to Camille. And then from Camille back to Richard.

'Oh all right, then!' Richard said in exasperation. 'What were you going to say?'

'Well, it was just, if Luc *is* the killer, then I don't think he'd have left a coat covered in his fingerprints in the smugglers' tunnel.'

'Good point,' Camille said, turning to her boss. 'Don't you think, sir?'

'Yes. All right. I can see that,' Richard said in a tone of voice that made it sound as though there were in fact no areas of agreement between himself and Fidel.

'So that leaves us with only three people who could have been on the cliff steps to kill Polly,' Camille said, pointing at the names that remained on the whiteboard. 'Polly's agent, Max Brandon. The film director, Phil Adams. And Juliette Moreau, the wife of the man Polly was having her affair with. It's one of those three people who killed Polly Carter.'

Despite his team's cavalier attitude to the whiteboard, Richard had to admit that he could see the logic of what Camille was saying. They'd not found a single person who'd seen Juliette out on her run—so she still didn't have a decent alibi—and it wouldn't have been possible for *both* Max and Phil to have been seen standing at an upstairs window, seeing as Sophie only saw one person at the upstairs window. In fact, Richard realised, if they could just work out exactly who it was that Sophie had seen, then maybe it would get their list of remaining suspects from three people down to two. But how to do it, that was the question? Maybe he should get the witnesses to stage a re-enactment?

And with that thought, Richard had a sudden insight about how he could perhaps get his parents back together again. Because Catherine had been right. He should try and trick them—and maybe the best way to do that would be to stage a scene. But how to do it, that was the question?

Richard went over to his desk and for the next two hours got stuck into solving his problem. His team left him alone—presuming he was working hard on the Polly Carter Case.

They were wrong.

And when, later on, Richard announced that he had to go up to Government House to see the Commissioner of Police, his team continued to presume that he was still working on Polly Carter's case.

And they were still wrong.

★★★

The following day, Richard convened his team at Polly's house to re-enact the moments immediately before the murder. Richard was even pleased, for once, to see that it was going to be another day of blistering heat and blue skies. The sunshine and light bouncing off the house would be similar to how it had been at the time of the murder.

Richard sent Camille off with Claire to the top of the cliffs—to the exact spot where Claire said she'd been positioned when Polly had been killed. As for Max, he was inside the house standing by the window of the upstairs landing where he said he'd been standing at the time of the murder—and Fidel stood a few steps behind Max holding a walkie-talkie for when Richard needed to communicate with him. As for Phil, he was in his bedroom in the next door room also standing at the window—again, as he said he'd been on the morning of the murder—with Dwayne standing by for assistance as required.

As for Richard, he was out in the middle of the lawn with Sophie.

'And this was where you were standing?' Richard asked.

'I think so,' Sophie said. 'It was about here.'

'But this is critically important, Sophie. As far as angles go—and the light reflecting on windows, and so on and so forth—it's vital you stand as close to where you think you were when you heard Polly scream.'

'I'm sorry,' she said. 'I was in this general area, but I don't know if I was five feet this way or ten feet that way. But it must have been about here because although I heard Polly scream, I couldn't see Claire on the other side of the shrubs just there.' Here, Sophie pointed at the bank of bushes and shrubs in the large bed that separated the main garden from the cliff top. 'So yes, I suppose I must have been here or hereabouts. I think.'

'Okay,' Richard said. 'Thank you for trying.'

Richard pulled out the police walkie-talkie that was clipped to the belt of his trousers and, as ever when he had to use a walkie-talkie, there was a part of him which reverted to being ten years old—which had been the age he'd been when he received his very first toy walkie-talkie set. It had been his most prized Christmas present that year: two plastic walkie-talkies in deep army green—both with incongruously bright orange buttons on them for tapping out Morse Code—and five metres of white twisted electrical cable joining the two units together. Richard had spent that Christmas holidays in a state of bliss setting up one walkie-talkie in his bedroom with the cable going out of his window and down through the window beneath to the other walkie-talkie unit that he'd placed behind the sofa in the sitting room.

As an only child, Richard didn't of course have anyone to talk to through his walkie-talkie, so half the time he'd sit in his bedroom with the walkie-talkie to his mouth passing on crucial information about the criminals, spies and cutthroats that operated in his parents' cul-de-sac; and, the other half of the time, he hid behind the sofa downstairs with the walkie-talkie clamped to his ear, writing down the descriptions of vice and depravity that he remembered describing when he'd been talking into the other end.

Now, as Richard pressed the push-to-talk button on the police unit, he got his usual frisson of excitement that he was using a walkie-talkie that not only didn't have wire running between the two units, but it also had a real living human being at the other end of it to talk to.

'Romeo Papa to Foxtrot Bravo,' he said. 'Is Mr Brandon in position?'

After a moment, Fidel's voice crackled out of the speaker. 'What's that, sir?'

Richard hadn't really expected any of his team to embrace the NATO-approved phonetic alphabet, but he wasn't going to drop his standards just because they didn't have any.

'Foxtrot Bravo, is Mr Brandon in position?'

'Oh you mean me,' Fidel said. 'Yes. He says he is, sir.'

'Good. Then, Delta Mike, is Mr Adams in position?'

'Sure is, Chief,' Dwayne Myers said over the circuit, unable to hide the smile in his voice.

'Very good, then I'll ask the witness to turn around and start looking back at the house now. Over.' Richard effortlessly slotted the walkie-talkie back onto his belt. 'Okay, Sophie. If you'd turn back to look at the house and let's see which of the two witnesses we can see.'

Standing side by side, Richard and Sophie looked back at the house, and it was instantly apparent why Sophie hadn't quite known what she had seen that morning. There was a glare of reflected sunlight blasting from all of the upstairs windows—especially from the landing window that Richard guessed Max was standing behind. But as Richard looked along the first floor, he reached the last window and was surprised.

There was no glare from that window at all.

And, in fact, as Richard continued to look, he was pretty sure he could see the dim figure of Phil standing behind it.

Richard plucked the walkie-talkie from his belt.

'Delta Mike, this is Romeo Papa. Could you get Phil Adams to wave his arms?' he said into it.

'Sure thing, Chief.'

A moment later, Richard and Sophie both saw the darkened figure in the window lift his arms and wave them from side to side.

'Yes,' Sophie said. 'That must have been the window I saw the person in. I mean, all of the other windows are just sunshine.'

Richard had already come to the same conclusion. So Richard walked another ten paces nearer the house. It was just the same glare. So he walked a few paces off to the left—and to the right—and back and forth—and all Richard ever got was the same reflected sunlight from every window of the house apart from Phil's.

Richard spoke into his walkie-talkie again.

'Foxtrot Bravo, Romeo Papa here. Could you ask Mr Brandon to come closer to his window—and maybe even to wave his arms as well.'

'Yes, sir,' Fidel said.

Richard and Sophie still couldn't make out any sign of Max Brandon standing behind his window. Therefore, Richard realised in mounting excitement, it couldn't have been Max Brandon who Sophie saw at the upstairs window that morning. It could only have been Phil Adams!

Once they'd returned to the police station, Camille wiped Phil Adams's name from the board as she announced, 'So, sir, seeing as it could only have been Phil Adams Sophie saw at the window, we know he's not our killer.'

Camille looked over to see what Richard thought of this sweeping statement, but she could see that he'd gone straight to his desk and was checking his computer.

'I agree,' Fidel said. 'Which means we're left with one of Max Brandon or Juliette Moreau being our killer.'

'And they both have reasons to want Polly Carter dead,' Camille said, still surprised that her boss hadn't tried to stop their theorising.

'My money's on Juliette,' Dwayne said. 'She's been lying to us from the start, she plants surveillance bugs, and—most suspicious of all if you ask me—she's training for a triathlon. I mean, you can't do that level of physical exercise without having deep psychological problems.'

Now it was Dwayne's turn to notice that his boss wasn't listening.

'I'm not sure I agree,' Fidel said. 'Because I know she's been lying to us, but you don't kill the person your husband is having an affair with, do you? You kill your husband. I mean, he's the one who's betrayed Juliette. Not Polly. After all, Polly's a single woman, she's allowed to sleep with whoever she likes, isn't she? So, as I say,' Fidel concluded, only now realising that he'd never been allowed such a long period of air-time to discuss one of his theories before, 'I could imagine Juliette killing Alain, but I don't see why she'd kill Polly Carter.'

And now everyone was looking over and seeing that Richard was apparently oblivious to them all. Camille held up a finger to Fidel and Dwayne to be quiet. She knew how to get her boss's attention.

'And you know what I want to know? How come we found Claire's mobile phone in the chandelier afterwards? That's what keeps bugging me.'

Still nothing from Richard.

'But if you want to know about that,' Dwayne offered, 'what I want to know is, seeing as Polly bought ten thousand dollars of heroin three days before she died, where is it now?'

'Yes, very good, team,' Richard said, standing up from his desk. 'I'm not actually invisible, you know.'

'Just checking you were still with us, sir,' Camille said with a fake smile of support.

'Oh don't worry, you can't get rid of me that easily. But if you must know, I've just received a message that means I'm going to need some help.'

Richard's team shared glances. Their boss was asking for help?

'In particular, I think I'm going to need your help, Dwayne.'

Everyone slowly turned and looked at Dwayne.

'You are?' Dwayne said, uneasily.

'You see,' Richard said before he lost his nerve, 'I understand you have a number of girlfriends on the go at the same time.'

'You *what*?'

'I understand you have a number of girlfriends on the go.'

Dwayne was affronted, and pulled his trousers up as he said, 'I've been dating for many years, Chief, and no one has *ever* been able to prove I've had more than one woman on the go at any one time.'

'But we all know you have more than one woman on the go at any one time.'

'Ah yes, *you* may know that, Chief, but the point is, none of the women do.'

'But tell me, are you currently in a one girlfriend situation, a none girlfriend situation, or perhaps…more than one?'

Dwayne narrowed his eyes. 'Depends who's asking.'

'Because if you've got more than one girlfriend on the go, there's something I'd like to ask of you.'

'What's that? You want…what? A double date?'

'God no!' Richard said, horrified. 'But I would like you to take a bullet for the team. Or rather, for me.'

'How can I take a bullet for the team? I'm not really understanding what you're saying, Chief.'

'Very well, then, first of all I'd like you to text my mother and say you want to meet her for a drink tonight.'

'Woah woah woah,' Dwayne said, holding his hands up for Richard to stop talking right there. 'You want me to have a drink with your mother tonight?'

'And not just a drink, I'd like you to imply that you and her are going on a date.'

'You want me to *date* your mother?'

'In fact, I want you to arrange to meet her in Catherine's bar tonight at 7pm sharp,' Richard said.

'Chief, you're saying words, but they're not making any sense.'

'I don't see what's so hard for you to understand, Dwayne. I need you to arrange a date with my mother at 7pm tonight at Catherine's bar. But don't worry, you won't have to go through with it.'

This threw Dwayne. 'Then why do I have to arrange it?'

Richard suddenly realised he'd shared far more with his team than he'd wanted to, so he started picking up all the case notes for the murder and putting them into his leather briefcase.

'Come on, Chief, what's going on?'

'Tell you what, Dwayne, I'll ring you later to confirm final plans,' Richard said, as he closed the lock on his briefcase with a click. 'But in the meantime, I think you're all right. We're down to one of Juliette Moreau or Max Brandon being our killer, so I'm going to work on the case at home.'

And, making sure he made no further eye contact with his team, Richard scurried out of the police station, leaving his team behind, entirely nonplussed.

What on earth was their boss up to?

★★★

That evening, Richard entered Catherine's bar just before 7pm, not realising that in all of his plans, he'd made one mistake. When he spoke to Dwayne about the timings he wanted him to follow that evening, he'd done so in front of Camille and Fidel. And Richard only realised this was a mistake when he scanned the bar for a quiet corner table and saw Camille and Fidel already waiting for him.

Camille gave a little wave.

Richard went over to them both and hissed, 'What are you doing here?'

'Getting ringside seats for whatever it is you've got going on with Dwayne.'

'I don't have anything planned with Dwayne,' Richard lied.

'But, sir,' Fidel said, 'Dwayne told us you and he have been on the phone all afternoon, and if we wanted to see some fireworks, we should get here by 7pm.'

Richard's shoulders slumped, but he supposed he shouldn't have been surprised if Dwayne had betrayed his confidence. This was Dwayne they were talking about.

'But don't worry, sir,' Fidel said, 'we got you a beer.'

Fidel indicated an ice-cold bottle of beer that was already sitting on the table, and Richard put his briefcase down on the floor, slunk into the spare seat Fidel and Camille had saved for him and took a deep draught from the bottle. Before he'd even finished his first sip, Catherine had sidled over and joined the party with a delighted look already in her eyes.

'Not you as well?' Richard said, before Catherine had even spoken.

'I can't wait to see what you've got planned with Dwayne,' Catherine said excitedly.

Richard knew he had to stop all the excitement at once, so he opened his briefcase and pulled out the piles of case notes he had on Polly Carter's murder.

'Actually, I'm just here to work through the case.'

'Oh,' Catherine said, disappointed. 'Then I'd better go to the bar. I'll watch what happens from there.'

'You do that, Catherine.'

As Catherine returned to the bar, Richard picked up the first witness statement.

'Now, Camille, I've spent the afternoon focusing on our two remaining suspects. Juliette Moreau and Max Brandon.'

As Richard said this, he caught a movement by the main entrance to the bar, and he stopped talking as he, Fidel, Camille and Catherine all saw Dwayne walk into the bar with a young woman on his arm. Dwayne was wearing a garish Hawaiian shirt, old shorts, and a pair of ancient flip-flops that were now a lot more 'flop' than they were 'flip'. In comparison, his date for the night had her shiny blonde hair up in a ponytail, was wearing a strappy white vest top that showed off her golden tan, tight denim shorts that showed off her legs—and, although she wasn't wearing shoes, she was wearing a silver ankle bracelet.

Dwayne didn't give Camille, Richard or Fidel a second glance as he led his date to the bar and ordered some drinks from Catherine.

Back in the corner of the bar, Camille was about to ask Richard what on earth was going on when she became aware that someone else had come in from the street outside and was now standing by their table.

It was Richard's mother.

'Hello, Jennifer,' Camille said, surprised.

As Jennifer pulled over a chair and sat with her son and friends at their table, Richard could see that his mother was wearing a sensible green skirt, flat shoes, a cream cardigan, and her hair was tied up tight in a bun behind her head. She looked like a school ma'am.

'Oh hello, Mother,' Richard said, indicating the case notes on the table. 'We're just working on the case. What are you doing here?'

'Trying to make sure I don't make a terrible mistake, I think.'

'Oh?' Richard said, this time in genuine surprise.

'Because I've been thinking about what you said to me the other day. You remember, how you said that although it was grey at home—and rainy—it's where we're from that makes us who we are?'

'That's right,' Richard said.

'Well, it made me realise how perceptive you were being, using "grey" and "rainy" as metaphors for life back at home.'

Richard didn't quite know what to say. After all, he'd never meant either word to be a metaphor, he'd really just been describing the British climate as being literally both grey and rainy. Luckily for him, though, his mother didn't seem to notice his frown as she carried on talking.

'And although it was bright and sunny here, the Caribbean isn't who I am. And by the evening, I'd realised I definitely didn't want to go dancing in some sweaty nightclub. I don't know where I got that idea from. I didn't even like nightclubs the first time around. All that beer getting sticky on the floor. And the music so loud you can't hear yourself think—let alone talk. And it being so dark that you can't tell if the glass you're drinking from is even clean. And don't even get me started on the state of the loos!

'So, rather than go dancing, I stayed here with your mother, Camille. You really are lucky to have her. She's a wonderfully positive force, isn't she? But the thing is, the more I talked to Catherine, the more I began to realise just how much of a fool I'd made of myself since I got here. Not that I'm apologising—Catherine made that clear to me. I should never apologise—and she's right. I'm *glad* I made a fool of myself. I've loved falling under the spell of the island—but that's all that's happened, isn't it? Since I got to the island I've been under a wonderful, magical spell, but it's not reality. Or rather, it's reality for you, Camille'—Jennifer said this with only kindness in her voice—'but it isn't for me. I mean, it *is* very hot. And I've not been able to go into my bathroom for two days because I think there's a lizard in there.'

'Tell me about it,' Richard said.

But Jennifer still hadn't finished. 'What's more, I asked at the hotel, and you were right, Richard. There really aren't any seasons on the island to speak of. It just goes from hot in the winter to even hotter in the summer. And I can't imagine what life is if you're not looking forward to the next planting season.'

As Jennifer was speaking, a second young blonde woman entered the bar wearing a red dress and black heels, saw Dwayne at the bar with his date and put her hands on her hips.

'Dwayne Myers!' she bellowed in an Australian accent.

As Dwayne and his date looked back at the door, this second woman strode across the bar to where Dwayne was standing and slapped him hard in the face. She then turned and said something short and sharp to the date Dwayne had brought to the bar, at which point this first woman turned to Dwayne and slapped him even harder on the other cheek. And then, without another word, each woman turned on their heels and left the bar by separate exits.

Richard checked his watch. It was 7:05. Dwayne had got his timings to perfection.

Dwayne, for his part, just stood there. He then shook his face a bit, picked an ice cube out of his glass of rum and put it to a cut on his split lip.

Having seen all of this, Jennifer sighed.

'Of course,' Jennifer said, finally understanding—correctly, as it turned out—that Dwayne wasn't exactly the most morally upstanding person on the island to develop a holiday crush on. And there wasn't much more Jennifer needed to say after that.

Dwayne finally noticed his friends in the corner of the bar, and he came over and joined them.

'Hey, Jennifer, glad you could make it,' he said as smoothly as he could while still holding the ice cube to his lip.

'And it's good to see you too, Dwayne,' Jennifer said. 'But tell me, who were those two women?'

'Women?' Dwayne said in wide-eyed innocence. 'What women?'

Jennifer smiled wearily. If Dwayne wanted to pretend he hadn't just been caught cheating—and all while he was supposed to be meeting her for a drink—then she wasn't going to press the point.

In the silence that briefly followed, a man in his sixties walked into the bar wearing an evening jacket, polished black shoes, a crisp white shirt and silk black tie. The man wasn't exactly handsome, but he was tall, broad-shouldered and he had the solidity of an oak tree.

Jennifer saw who it was and slowly rose from her seat as though she were seeing an apparition.

'Graham…?'

The man wearing black tie was Graham Poole—and he looked over and saw his wife standing by the table in a pretty summer dress, her face glowing with health from her time in the tropics.

'Hello, Jennifer,' he said.

As for Richard, he coughed, got out his hankie, wiped his brow, and then wiped his hands of sweat before putting the hankie back in his pocket.

'Hello, Father,' he said, before offering his hand as Graham came over and shook his son's hand firmly.

'Hello, son,' he said. 'Your tie's come loose.'

'No. Sorry. Of course,' Richard said, jamming his tie back up into his neck.

'This is your *father*?' Camille interrupted.

Before Richard could reply, the well-fed Police Commissioner Selwyn Patterson—also in black tie, if a little more shabbily so—ambled into the bar and came over to Richard at his table.

'Ah, good evening, everyone,' the Commissioner said. 'Graham and I were just on our way to dinner at the Ambassador's residence when we decided to pop in for a quick sharpener. How very fortunate that we bumped into you all.'

Just about managing to keep his nerve, Richard introduced his father to his team—and Selwyn in particular was delighted to meet Jennifer, elegantly kissing the back of her hand when they were introduced—but what everyone couldn't help but notice was how Jennifer seemed only to have eyes for her husband, just as he seemed only to have eyes for his wife.

'So tell me,' Richard asked his father, as if he didn't already know the answer, 'what on earth are you doing on Saint-Marie?'

'Well,' Graham said, 'the Commissioner here contacted me yesterday to say that his keynote speaker had dropped out of a special conference the British Ambassador was convening on the island about pan-Caribbean crime.'

'He did?' Camille said, knowing full well that there was no such thing as a pan-Caribbean conference on crime happening on the island.

'A *hastily* convened conference,' Selwyn explained to Camille with a smile. 'But yes, when we were let down, I thought to myself, I know who we should get in to save the day. Our very own Detective Inspector's father, Graham Poole, the one-time Superintendent of the Leicestershire Police Force.'

'So when I got the call from the Commissioner here,' Graham said, 'I agreed to hop on the next plane out. After all, it's always gratifying to pass on one's knowledge to the next generation.'

'And was there another reason you wanted to come out here?' Jennifer asked, her voice tight with emotion.

Graham looked at his wife. His brow creased.

'Yes. Of course.'

Graham wasn't the most communicative of people, and he looked briefly at his son for moral support—but then, Richard was even less communicate than his father was, and he ducked his eyes down to avoid eye contact altogether—so Graham looked back at his wife and, after another long moment, he sighed.

'I wanted to see you.'

Having said this, a silent message seemed to pass between wife and husband that was unreadable to everyone else who was watching. Or rather, it was unreadable to everyone apart from Selwyn, who had been around the block enough times to recognise a rapprochement when he saw one.

'And you see,' Selwyn said, 'it's so fortunate we bumped into you all. Because I know there's a spare space at the welcome dinner we're going to tonight. So, it's just occurred to me, Jennifer, would you like to accompany your husband and me to a black tie dinner at the British Embassy tonight?'

Selwyn's question seemed to unleash a wave of panic in Jennifer.

'But I've got nothing to wear,' she said.

'What you're wearing is perfect,' Graham said.

'But it's not smart enough if it's a black tie do,' Jennifer said again, all of a-twitter.

'Maybe not,' Graham said gruffly, 'but you're wearing it, so it won't matter, will it? Because there won't be another woman at the dinner who'll be as beautiful as you.'

Jennifer looked at her husband, surprise in her eyes. Had he just paid her a compliment? A *romantic* compliment? Jennifer thought for a moment longer—and then her chin lifted imperceptibly as she turned to look at Selwyn.

'Thank you very much for asking. I'd love to come to the dinner.'

And then a wondrous thing happened.

Graham smiled.

He then lifted his right arm and offered it for his wife.

With a smile, Jennifer took her husband's arm, and without either of them exchanging another word, Graham strode manfully out of the bar, Jennifer floating on his arm at his side.

Richard realised he'd been holding his breath for a very long time and he let it out in relief.

'Thanks for everything, sir,' he said to Selwyn.

Selwyn inclined his head in acknowledgement. 'Always happy to help,' he said, clearly delighted by the evening's turn of events. And then, Selwyn followed Graham and Jennifer out of the bar.

Although Fidel, Dwayne and Camille all looked in wonder at Richard, it was Catherine—beetling over from the other side of the bar—who got the first word in.

'Oh, bravo, Richard! Bravo!'

'What just happened?' Fidel asked.

'Yes, sir. Did you just do that?' Camille asked.

'Me? You saw me, Camille, I didn't do a thing. But I think I'd like to buy everyone a drink, and—in honour of our illustrious hostess—I think we should have one of your reasonably priced bottles of French champagne, Catherine.'

'Of course!'

'And do you maybe also have one of those large bags of locally produced crisps that are five per cent potato and ninety-five per cent cooking oil? I think we need to have a couple of kilograms of those as well.'

Catherine was beaming as she stepped up to Richard and kissed him once on each cheek.

'You did it. I knew you would, you clever boy!' she said.

'You knew about this?' Camille asked her mother, but Catherine didn't want to steal any of Richard's thunder, so she just smiled enigmatically and returned to the bar to get the drinks together.

'You orchestrated that whole encounter, didn't you?' Camille said, before looking at Dwayne. 'Come on, Dwayne, admit it, the Inspector made you come to the bar with one girlfriend, and then get caught by another girlfriend—and all so that Jennifer would arrive and see you apparently cheating on her!'

'Hey!' Dwayne said in mock outrage. 'Those women weren't my girlfriends, they're just two Australians I met on the beach half an hour ago.'

Now it was Richard's turn to be surprised. 'Hang on, you're saying you'd never met either of those two women before?'

Dwayne's grin just got wider, and he held up the palm of his hand which had a mobile phone number written across it in biro.

'I may not have met them before, but I'm meeting them both later on tonight. We're going on a double date.'

'Who with?'

'Well, me and them—that's what a double date is: when two women get to date me.'

'But hold on,' Camille said to her boss before Dwayne sidetracked the whole conversation. 'If you lined up Dwayne to be in here being caught cheating on a woman, how did you get the Commissioner to walk into the bar with your father only a few minutes later?'

'Ah, well, Camille,' Richard said, 'I'm sure the Commissioner couldn't possibly be involved in anything so underhand as abusing his official position on the island.'

'But that's *all* the Commissioner ever does,' Dwayne said.

'In your opinion, Dwayne. I couldn't possibly comment.'

'But are you saying,' Camille said, as impressed as she was amused, 'that we're supposed to believe it's a complete coincidence that your mother should see Dwayne two-timing on a woman just seconds before your father just happens to walk into the same bar wearing evening dress and looking all smart and romantic?'

Richard realised that this would be a good time to see if he could still raise one eyebrow independently of the other—and he was gratified to discover that, in fact, he could.

'I think you'll find, Camille, it's just that. A happy coincidence.'

'But you don't believe in coincidences!'

'Well, I must be wrong on this occasion,' Richard said.

'But come on, sir!' Fidel said. 'You stage-managed the whole thing, you must have done.'

Richard looked at Fidel. He'd just set off half a thought for him about Polly Carter's murder, because his team were correct—it of course hadn't been a coincidence that Selwyn had walked into the bar with Graham at that precise moment. The whole thing had been previously planned over a *very* awkward cup of tea in the Commissioner's office. And what Richard had had to promise to the Commissioner in return for his help didn't bear thinking about as far as Richard was concerned.

But knowing that a huge amount of effort had gone into making his father's encounter with his mother look entirely coincidental, Richard found himself wondering: in what way might Polly Carter's arrival on the cliff steps at the precise moment that the killer needed her to be there have been similarly stage-managed? It didn't seem in any way possible, and yet, if Richard had managed to get his father to walk into a bar on the other side of the world at a specific time, why couldn't the killer have similarly manoeuvred Polly Carter?

With a rush of excitement, Richard realised he needed to go back to the case notes at once. So, without saying another word, he grabbed up the notes from the table and started stuffing them back into his leather briefcase.

'Sir?' Camille asked.

'I think I'm onto something, Camille.'

'What?'

'I'll let you know when I know.'

'You'll let us know what when you know what?' Dwayne asked.

Without another word, Richard strode from the bar, leaving his friends behind, baffled and infuriated. But Richard didn't care, he knew this was important, and as he strode down the starlit road to his shack on the beach, he felt a surging and entirely atypical sense of optimism. It was as if, having finally given his parents the chance to get back together, he had finally freed his brain to think about the case with clarity. So, back in his shack, he lay out the initial statements from the witnesses on his bed and looked at all the names.

Claire Carter, Sophie Wessel, Phil Adams, Max Brandon, Juliette Moreau, Alain Moreau and Luc Pichou. One of those seven people killed Polly Carter, and Richard decided that he wasn't going to go to bed until he'd worked out who it was.

After a quick once-round with his handy dustbuster to remove the worst of the sand from the floorboards, Richard got into his M&S pyjamas and slippers and sat down in his one tatty armchair to read through the whole case from start to finish.

But this time he'd know that Claire could have been lying to them from the start. And that Alain's affair had been still ongoing when Polly died. And that Polly had ordered ten thousand dollars' worth of heroin three days before she died—even though she, herself, hadn't taken any of it. And that there'd been no 'Man in a Yellow Raincoat' on the steps beforehand—although he'd been there three days beforehand. And, above all, Richard now knew that there was a secret tunnel that led from the house to the cliffs.

It was just before dawn when it happened.

At the time, Richard was outside on his verandah watching the sky lighten from darkness into day. He was supposed to be on a five-minute break, but he was instead considering how the killer had managed to be on the cliff steps before the murder—and had also managed to hide Claire's phone in the chandelier before the murder as well—and he was wondering how these two apparently unrelated facts could perhaps be connected. And it was as he thought back to the mobile phone in the chandelier that Richard made the key breakthrough—because he suddenly realised that there was one very clear way that Claire's mobile phone could be said to be connected to Polly's arrival on the cliff steps.

In fact, as Richard continued to work through the logic of his realisation, a feeling of excitement filled him like a cork about to pop from a bottle of champagne. The phone was indeed the key to solving the whole case!

And then, as Richard looked out over the cloudless dawn sky with the knowledge that it was going to be another boiling hot day in the Caribbean, he finally worked it out.

He knew who had killed Polly Carter.

Chapter 15

Later that morning, Richard gathered Claire, Sophie, Juliette, Alain, Max, Phil, and Luc in the sitting room of Polly's house. Luc in particular had not taken kindly to being woken up so early and being brought to Polly's house, and he was now sitting off to one side looking edgy. As for Camille, Fidel and Dwayne, they stood around the perimeter of the room in case the killer tried to make a run for it.

'Thank you all for joining us,' Richard said.

'But what do you want?' Alain asked, worried.

'With six of you? Very little. But with the remaining seventh person, I want to arrest them for the murder of Polly Carter!'

The witnesses all looked at each other, suddenly worried.

'But before I reveal who the killer is, I want to spend a moment discussing our victim, because—all along—it's been almost impossible to work out exactly who Polly Carter was. After all, she was a world-famous model who had apparently turned her back on being a world-famous model. Or had she? She was the wild party animal who, according to Alain here, wanted to go back to the UK and live on a farm. But can he be believed? What's more, she was a longtime heroin addict who'd finally kicked her addiction—and yet, according to Luc, she'd recently bought ten thousand dollars' worth of heroin. Assuming, of course, he's telling us the truth. And if Max said that he'd never seen Polly happier over the last few weeks of her life, then why was she so furious with Claire on the morning of her death? You see, it's so hard to work out exactly who someone is when all you've got is the hearsay of those who survive her. And it's especially hard when one of those people is the murderer and has been manipulating us from the start.

'So was Polly selfish or kind? Forgiving or cynical? And, at the simplest of levels, was she happy with her life—as both Max and Alain told us—or was she actually so unhappy that she wanted to commit suicide—as Claire insists? Because that's what Claire said happened that morning, didn't she? She claims that Polly said she was going to end her life just seconds before she ran down the cliff steps and was brutally murdered. Which, as coincidences go, is pretty colossal, don't you think? But let's unpack that a bit, shall we?

'You see, it's interesting we found no suicide note back at the house, isn't it? Just as it's interesting that Polly never mentioned any suicidal thoughts to anyone else before that morning. And, it's also interesting that although Sophie was in the garden nearby at the time, she didn't hear exactly what Polly was saying to you, Claire. So there's no independent witness to confirm that Polly was telling you she was about to end her own life.'

'It's not my fault Sophie was too far away to hear,' Claire said.

'That's right,' Richard agreed. 'But she wasn't just too far away to hear what was going on, was she? She was also too far away to *see* what was going on as well, what with there being a great big bed of shrubs in between you and her at the time. In fact, when we get down to it, it was only you, Claire, who witnessed Polly's apparent suicide attempt in any meaningful way. Is that a coincidence? I don't think so. Because when it comes to murder, I don't believe in coincidences.'

Richard said this directly at Claire, and the colour drained from her face.

'Especially when we look at the relationship you had with your sister, the woman who ten years ago pulled a Boxing Day prank on you so catastrophic that you've spent every day of your life since then in a wheelchair. As you finally admitted to us, it's not something you've ever been able to forgive her for, is it? And the string of threatening letters you've been sending her only proves to me just how messed up your relationship with your sister really was.

'And then we come to your lie to us that you saw a "Man in a Yellow Raincoat" on the cliff steps just before your sister was murdered. In fact, when I think about it, I can't imagine anyone who's done more to hinder this case than you, Claire.'

'I thought you'd think I'd killed her!'

'I bet you did, especially when we discovered that Polly believed you suffered a condition called conversion disorder—where you are capable of walking and yet, for one psychological reason or another, choose not to. So did you get out of your wheelchair that morning and push your sister to her death?

'Well, here's the thing: even though you had a motive to want your sister dead, we spoke to your GP back in the UK.' Here, Richard looked up at the others in the room. 'He told us in no uncertain terms that Claire wasn't suffering from conversion disorder. In fact, he said her injuries are real—she really can't walk—and, seeing as Polly was pushed to her death from partway down a flight of steps Claire couldn't possibly have got down, we can only conclude that Claire Carter didn't kill her sister.'

Richard let this hang in the air a moment before he turned to Sophie.

'Which brings me to you, Sophie. You were the second person to the scene, and so, with Claire out of the frame, I had to consider, could you be our killer? Well, seeing as everyone else says you were on the lawn outside the house at the time of the murder, it's hard to see how you could also have been on the cliff steps at the same time—but your presence in front of the house did allow us to confirm one other significant fact. And that's that although both Max and Phil claimed to be standing at an upstairs window at the time of the murder, you only saw one person looking out at the garden.

'Now, the re-enactment we staged suggested that the person you saw must have been Phil Adams—standing at his bedroom window—which is interesting because there's no doubting that Phil had a motive to want Polly dead: the day Polly tipped off his movie studio that he was still taking drugs, she effectively ended his career.

'And yet, I can't help feeling that Phil hadn't reached crisis point with his studio just yet. After all, I believed him when he said he was going to try and get clean before he returned to the States. So what I found myself realising was that I'd perhaps believe Phil killing Polly if he'd *already* failed his drugs test because of her tip-off, but he hadn't failed it yet. And what's more, Polly had even told Phil what she'd done so he'd have plenty of time to get clean before he returned to the States.'

'And I told you,' Phil said insistently, 'I am going to get clean!'

'Yes,' Richard said. 'And as long as you believed you had a chance of getting clean—and seeing as we've got a witness who saw you at your window at the time of the murder—I don't see how you could be our killer, either.'

'Thank you!' Phil said before nervously running his hand through his hair in relief.

'Which brings me to the secret underground tunnel that runs from Polly's house to the cliff steps. Because although Claire was lying to us when she said there was a "Man in

Yellow" on the steps just before the murder, there had to have been *someone* on the steps who attacked Polly. And yet, until we uncovered the old smugglers' tunnel, it was difficult to see how this person could have got to and from the murder site unseen.

'So who was it who'd used the tunnel to kill Polly? It couldn't have been Claire or Sophie—they were both above ground the whole time. And if Phil was at the upstairs window, it couldn't have been him, either. Which leaves only four people who might have been able to use the tunnel to get to and from the cliffs to commit the murder. Max, Juliette, Alain and Luc.'

As Richard said this, he looked at each of the four remaining suspects in turn.

'But even that list is too long, isn't it? Because Alain couldn't have been the killer, could he? I mean, it's true that he lied to us that his affair with Polly was over when it was nothing of the sort—and he even lied to us about where he was at the time of the murder—but that's the point, isn't it? He was *elsewhere* at the time of the murder. Buying aeroplane tickets. He didn't kill Polly Carter.'

Alain looked at Richard as though he didn't quite understand that he'd just been ruled out of the murder inquiry.

'And then there were three,' Richard said holding up three fingers. 'Luc Pichou, Max Brandon, and Juliette Moreau. All three of you arguably benefited from Polly's death, and not one of you has a proven alibi for the time of murder. But let's interrogate that statement a bit.'

'Damned right you should,' Max interrupted. 'Because I'm telling you, I didn't kill her!'

'And I'm inclined to believe you. Because, even though Polly found out you'd been stealing from her, it's interesting that she hadn't told the police yet, isn't it? Even though we know she found out about your theft some time ago. And you've been in Polly's house for weeks yourself, Max. If your theft had been a big issue for Polly, I think she'd have thrown you out by now—or gone to the police—and the truth of the matter is that she'd done neither of those things. Which rather suggests that maybe you were right. She *had* forgiven you for the theft. Or had at least told you you could pay the money you stole back as and when you were able to.'

'Finally!' Max said. 'But you're also forgetting the fact that I was standing at the upstairs landing looking at Sophie in the garden when Polly was killed.'

'But were you?'

'Look, I don't much care what you think, I'm just telling you that that's where I was standing when Polly was killed, whether or not Sophie or anyone else saw me!'

'And that's very much the point, isn't it?' Richard agreed. 'Because although you couldn't be seen at the window at the time, it didn't mean you *weren't* standing there. But we'll come back to this in a moment, if that's okay. Because next I want to look at you, Luc.

Here, Richard turned to face Luc.'

'And to be honest, it's never really made much sense that you'd be our killer, Luc. After all, as one of my officers pointed out to me, if it was you who killed Polly, you'd hardly leave a plastic raincoat covered in your fingerprints in a secret hideout right by the scene of the crime.' As Richard said this, a grin of pride lit up Fidel's face. 'And as long as you believed Polly would continue to order her heroin from you, she was worth considerably more to you alive than she was to you dead.

'Which means—through a process of deduction—that there's only one person left who could be our killer,' Richard said, turning with a cold smile to face Juliette. 'Juliette Moreau.'

Juliette, for her part, was studiously looking at the floor in front of her feet—she was refusing to meet Richard's gaze.

'Because there's no doubting that Polly's murder—being pushed to her death from a cliff—has always felt like a *crime passionel*. And, of all the people gathered here, I can't imagine anyone who hated Polly more than you did. After all, Polly seduced your husband last Christmas. And then, when she came back from rehab in Los Angeles, she seduced him again—or that's how you viewed it. And let's be honest, setting a surveillance bug in your employer's bedroom is hardly the behaviour of a rational person. I can well imagine that killing Polly would be the next logical step for you, once you'd proven to your satisfaction that she and your husband were still carrying on their affair.

'But here's what I kept coming up against. Even if you wanted to kill Polly—and I bet you've wished her dead often enough in the past—just how did you know that Polly would be on the cliff steps *at that precise moment*? And I don't see how you could have got hold of Claire's

THE KILLING OF POLLY CARTER

mobile phone beforehand to hide it in the chandelier up there, either.' As Richard said this, he indicated the dusty chandelier directly above their heads. 'Because, the fact that Claire's phone ended up hidden in this room that morning has always made it clear to me that, at some level, this murder was pre-meditated. And yet I couldn't for the life of me work out how you, Juliette, could have possibly known that Polly was even going to go to the cliff top that morning—let alone have known to hide Claire's mobile in this room beforehand.'

'Hang on,' Phil Adams said. 'Are you saying that Juliette didn't kill Polly, either?'

'Yes,' Richard said, really very pleased with himself. 'That's precisely what I'm saying.'

'You are?' Juliette asked, finally daring to look at Richard.

'I am,' Richard said. 'You didn't kill Polly Carter.'

'Then who did?' Phil asked.

'How do you mean?'

'Well,' Phil continued, not sure if he was about to make a fool of himself or not, 'you've gone around this room and ruled each one of us out one by one, so who killed Polly?'

Richard held up a finger to get Phil's attention.

'Oh don't worry,' he said. 'The killer's in this room, you have my word, but I needed to explain the logic of how I finally came to work it out. You see, I couldn't see how *any* of you could have been on the cliff steps beforehand, until I identified the one key fact of the whole case. When we pulled Claire's mobile phone out of the chandelier, it had two sets of fingerprints on it. Claire's, of course—it was her phone. But it also had fingerprints on it from one other person. Polly herself.

'I dismissed this fact at the time. After all, it's hardly surprising to learn that a phone has been handled by the phone owner's sibling, is it? And instead I continued to presume that the phone had been put in the chandelier by the *real* killer, who'd had the good sense to be wearing gloves at the time so that his or her fingerprints didn't get on the phone. But that was to forget Occam's Razor.'

'What's that?' Alain asked.

'Well, William of Occam was a Franciscan monk from the thirteenth century, and he came up with the idea that if you ever have a group of competing theories—for example, who put a phone inside a chandelier—and you want to know which of the theories is correct, then, in the absence of any one theory being better than another, you should always choose the one that's simplest to explain.

'And when I applied Occam's Razor to the problem of who put Claire's phone in the chandelier—seeing as only Claire and Polly's fingerprints were ever found on it—I realised that I should consider that it was one of Claire or Polly who had hidden the phone in the chandelier on the morning of the murder. And—once again using Occam's Razor—seeing as it would have been nigh-on impossible for Claire to get the phone into the chandelier—seeing as she's confined to a wheelchair—it must therefore have been Polly who put it there. And it was when I realised this fact that I decided to apply Occam's Razor to the whole case. And finally, it started to make sense to me.

'After all, who was the only person that morning who could have known in advance that Polly was about to invite Claire for a walk? Well—logically—the only person who knew for sure that Polly was about to ask Claire to go for a walk that morning was Polly herself. And the only person in the house that day who could have known for sure that Polly was about to commit suicide—before running down the steps of the cliff to do just that—was Polly as well.'

'Then it *was* suicide?' Alain said, confused.

'Oh no, it was murder,' Richard said, warming to his theme. 'But I'm just pointing out that it was Polly who took Claire into the garden. Just as it was Polly who started up an argument with her once they were in the garden. Just as it was Polly who announced out of the blue that she was about to commit suicide. And it was Polly who put Claire's phone in the chandelier.'

'Listen,' Max interrupted. 'Could you just tell us who killed her?'

'You want answers?' Richard replied. 'Very well, then, Claire, can I ask you something?'

Claire looked at Richard, but the look was guarded, as though she were holding something back.

'As we all know, you lost the power of your legs in your riding accident ten years ago. Didn't you?'

'That's right,' Claire said, worried.

'And your GP's made it clear to us that you don't suffer from conversion disorder.'

'As you've already said once,' Claire said, tartly.

'Then, I'm sorry for the inconvenience, but could I ask if you could get from your wheelchair and onto this sofa here?'

As Richard said this, he pointed at a battered old sofa that was near to Claire's side.

Claire looked affronted. 'I beg your pardon?'

'I just wondered if you'd be able to vacate your wheelchair and get onto the sofa here?'

'Why?'

'If you could just do as I ask and all will become clear.'

Claire still looked affronted, but Sophie half rose from her chair.

'I can help,' she said.

'There's no need, Sophie,' Richard said. 'I'm sure Claire can manage.'

Claire looked from Sophie to Richard. She then manoeuvred her wheelchair so that it was at ninety degrees to one of the armrests of the sofa and then clicked on the brake. She then—rather expertly, Richard had to note— put both hands on the corner of the sofa's armrest, and used it as a pivot so she could quickly swing herself onto the tatty cushions.

Once there, she looked up at Richard defiantly. 'Okay?'

Richard seemed entirely unbothered as he went over to inspect the wheelchair.

'You see,' he said. 'All along there's been a paradox at the heart of this case that I've not been able to solve. And that's the question of why Polly, a woman who was found with no drugs in her system, ordered ten thousand dollars of heroin three days before she was killed. I mean, it doesn't even begin to make sense, does it? But then, nor does it seem likely that a heroin addict would manage to kick her addiction only to be murdered a few months later. I mean, talk about bad luck! Common sense says that—somehow—her drugs use has to be related to her murder, doesn't it? And you know what? That's exactly right. Polly's heroin use was at the very heart of why she was murdered, as I think I'm about to prove.'

As Richard said this he picked the wheelchair up by its back wheels and turned it upside down so that its four wheels were now pointing up in the air. Before anyone could say anything, he then reached into his trouser pocket and pulled out a brand new Leatherman Wingman Multi-Tool, and looked dead-eyed at Camille as he expertly flipped it open like a butterfly knife to reveal a rather natty set of pliers. Camille raised an eyebrow, pretending to be impressed with Richard's penknife *savoir faire*, but Richard had already turned his attention to the front left wheel of the wheelchair that he'd noticed hadn't been turning properly the last few times he'd seen Claire. And, as he used the pliers to unscrew the little wheel's restraining bolt, he carried on speaking.

'Because we know Polly bought ten thousand dollars' worth of heroin three days before she died, so another puzzle we've been trying to solve is, where on earth is it? After all, that's a lot of heroin to suddenly vanish—and we've searched this house without finding it or any trace of it. And yet, although we've searched high and low for it, I finally realised that there was one place we'd never looked. And I'm sure I'm not the only person here who's noticed that the front left wheel of Claire's wheelchair has, of late, developed a surprising tendency to get stuck.'

With a final grunt of effort, Richard managed to unscrew the little wheel from the wheelchair. He then he held it up to inspect the threads of the bolt that had affixed it to the chair.

'Ah yes, well that would explain it. I think this wheel's recently been removed and screwed back on—but it looks like it's been cross-threaded. That would explain why it's been out of kilter.'

Putting the wheel to one side, Richard looked down into the hollow tube of the wheelchair frame. He then flipped his Leatherman around until he'd got up another tool with a hook on the end of a prong. As he reached into the hollow tube with it, he said, 'You see, Luc here blew the case wide open—had we but known it at the time—when he pointed out that if Polly had been clean when she'd died, then who else might she have been buying the heroin for? And this is the important point, because—if it wasn't for Juliette or Alain—then, considering how bulky that much heroin would have been, the person who Polly bought it for must have had a plan for smuggling the heroin off the island when they finally left Saint-Marie. And what better method for smuggling ten thousand dollars' worth of heroin through customs than inside the hollow frame of a wheelchair?'

As Richard said this, he withdrew the hook out of the metal tube—and pulled a cellophane-wrapped tube of brown paste out of the metal tubing. When he'd got it free, it was possible to see that the tube of brown paste was about two feet long.

'So, Claire,' Richard said, 'perhaps you'd like to tell us why there's ten thousand dollars' worth of heroin hidden inside the frame of your wheelchair?'

Chapter 16

Claire looked at Richard, horrified. 'I don't know how that got there!'

'Is that so? Because once I'd realised that Polly's fingerprints were on the phone in the chandelier—and only Polly could have known that she was going to say she wanted to end her life that morning—I came to realise that there was one last aspect of the case I had yet to consider. And that was the fact that while Claire almost certainly had a motive to want Polly dead, Polly also had a motive to want her sister Claire dead.

'I mean, look at it from Polly's point of view. She was second born. She'd always known she wouldn't inherit the family estate. Or the family money. It's no wonder she spent her life trying and failing to find happiness. First through fame and notoriety, and, latterly, through her heroin addiction. And it couldn't have helped her mental equilibrium when she then caused her older sister to lose the use of her legs—especially when her father died so soon afterwards after without having ever forgiven her for what she'd done. But then, nor had her mother forgiven her by the time she died last year, either. And we know how badly her mother's death affected Polly, because it was soon after that she took an all-but fatal overdose of heroin.

'And through all this time, I think Polly saw her older sister Claire get the love from her parents that she herself craved but, because of one silly mistake in the past—as she saw it—she was never going to get. In fact, as the years passed, it would only have been natural if Polly's despair at ever being loved turned into hate—particularly when she started receiving anonymous death threats from her sister.

'If that had been all Polly had been coping with at the time, I think she perhaps might have been able to manage, but it wasn't long after the letters started to arrive that Polly also discovered that her agent Max had stolen pretty much the last fifty thousand dollars she had from her. As she admitted to Phil just before she died—and we've been able to prove since her death—Polly had no money, even after all her years of hard work. No pension. No savings. She'd spent it all. The future looked bleak for her.

'And finally this brings us to the body that we found on the beach on the morning of the murder, because it just doesn't seem likely that a heroin addict of many years' standing—especially when she'd recently been buying heroin—would have no heroin in her system when she died, does it? So this is what I began to wonder. If there was no heroin in the body on the beach, then maybe the body on the beach didn't belong to Polly Carter? And then, what I found myself remembering was, when I first met you, Claire, how much like your twin sister you looked.'

There was general consternation in the room as Richard said this, with all of the witnesses trying to talk at once.

'Wait wait wait,' Phil finally said the loudest, his hands held up to silence everyone. 'Are you suggesting that Polly swapped places with Claire before pushing Claire to her death and taking her place herself?'

Richard looked at the room. 'It would explain why Claire's trying to smuggle ten thousand dollars' worth of heroin out of the country. Claire isn't Claire. She's Polly— and, now she's lost everything out here in the Caribbean, she wants to go back to Lincolnshire to claim the family farm and the family money that would always have been hers if only she'd been born a few seconds before her twin sister, rather than a few seconds afterwards.'

'But we'd have recognised the swap!' Max said.

'I know you would, and that means that all of you must have been in on this from the start.'

Juliette rose from her seat.

'But why would we help her do that? I hated Polly Carter!'

'And there you have me, Juliette!' Richard replied. 'Because I could perhaps imagine Phil or Alain maybe going through with the plan of pretending that the dead body of Claire belonged to Polly, but I can't for the life of me work out why the rest of you would. It's just asking too much of too disparate a group of people with so little in common.

'And to show how ludicrous the idea of the two sisters swapping places really is, if they *had* swapped places—with all of you now covering up for the swap—the pathologist would surely have noticed that the body we sent him for analysis would have had evidence of serious historical fractures in the legs, pelvis and back—seeing as the body would have actually belonged to Claire and not Polly. But the pathologist found no historical damage to any of the bones, and so it couldn't possibly have been Claire who fell to her death that day. It was indeed Polly.

'And I tell you all this because you have to understand just how desperate I was before I got to the final answer!'

Here, Richard turned back to Claire.

'Now, don't worry, Claire, I know that you are Claire and not Polly, but you said that the night before your sister was killed, she "had a gift" for you. Is that right?'

'Yes. That's what she told me.'

'That's right. It didn't seem to ring true when you told us, because the next day Polly was back to being her usual sniping self with you, but I made myself consider, what if what she told you the night before was true? There *was* a gift she was planning to give you the following day.'

'But how will we ever know what that gift was?' Claire asked.

'Well, I know, of course. And so does the killer. Isn't that right, Sophie?'

'What's that?' Sophie said.

'It was you who killed Polly Carter.'

Everyone realised what Richard had just said, and they all slowly turned and looked in horror at Sophie.

'What?' Sophie eventually stammered.

'You heard me. You killed Polly Carter.'

'But that's not possible,' Phil said. 'I was looking at Sophie when Polly was killed. She was on the lawn.'

'I know,' Richard said. 'Clever, wasn't she? Managing to be in two places at once. Although I should perhaps have known something was up when I first interviewed you all and Sophie said that while she inspected Polly's body after she fell, she didn't notice the deep gash on the inside of her right arm. After all, as a trained nurse, you'd expect her to notice that, don't you think?'

'But how did she kill her?' Max asked, still trying to make sense of Richard's announcement. 'Seeing as she was on the lawn at the time?'

'Oh that was easy to fathom once I'd worked out she had an accomplice.'

This got everyone's attention.

'You don't think it was me, do you?' Claire eventually asked.

'Don't worry,' Richard said. 'I know you're entirely innocent and had nothing to do with your sister's murder, Claire. In fact, Sophie's accomplice isn't in this room.'

'Then who was it?' Alain asked.

'The last person you could possibly expect to be Sophie's accomplice.'

'And who was that?'

'It was Polly herself.'

'*What?*'

'That's right. Polly colluded in her own murder. Unwittingly, of course. But remember what a terrible decision-maker everyone said Polly was,' Richard said, pulling his little notebook out of his inside pocket as he spoke. 'In fact, when we first interviewed you, Phil, you told us Polly "was a terrible judge of character and one of the easiest people in the world to manipulate. She was like a child when it came to money, so she'd give it away to any and every sob story that came along." And, Claire, you yourself said your twin sister was "missing the part of her brain that ever thought of consequences", and "she always fell in with the wrong crowd and allowed others to influence her".' As Richard flipped his notebook shut again, he said, 'In this instance, the person who she allowed to influence her was you, Sophie.'

Sophie was looking wired, panicked, and as though she could bolt at any moment. Dwayne and Fidel discreetly moved into position behind her.

'And this is the tragedy of the case,' Richard said, turning back to the room. 'Because all along we've been trying to work out whether Polly had kicked her drugs—or if she was happy when she died—and I think that both these statements were true. As I think the state of her bedroom showed us, if only we'd thought it through properly at the time. Because someone who took pride in having a spotless bedroom was—I think—all the proof we needed that Polly was beginning to take back control in her life. Polly *was* happy when she died. She *was* clean of drugs.

'And that was because of you, Alain. Because it's like you've been saying all along. At Christmas last year, you fell for Polly. And she fell for you. And it was because of her love for you that she made herself go through with rehab and finally kick her drug habit. After all, you'd said she couldn't have you unless she was clean.

'But I think your effect on her runs even deeper than that. I think Polly spent her time in Rehab realising how badly she'd led her life up until she met you. And when she finally returned to Saint-Marie, she'd decided that changes had to be made. For starters, she wanted to make it up with you, Claire. After all, she'd already seen a mother and father die with their relationships with her in tatters, she didn't want the same to happen to you. And I think that while she knew you'd been sending her the anonymous letters, she wanted to show you that she forgave you and that she'd changed.

'And she really had changed. Max was right when he told us that Polly was happy before she died and wanted to retire to the countryside and have babies. That was her new plan. To lead a simpler life with Alain. To start a family with him. And to be reconciled with her sister. And, being the terrible judge of character we know her to be, I think she told Sophie all her plans, didn't she?'

'Why on earth would she tell my nurse any of this?' Claire said imperiously. 'She never told me!'

'Oh, I think we'll discover that Sophie and Polly knew each other far more than Sophie would ever want us to know. Isn't that right, Sophie?'

As Richard said this directly to Sophie, her gaze slipped away. She wasn't saying.

'But to go back to Polly's state of mind just before she died, that's why she was prepared to forgive you for stealing all that money from her bank account, Max. And even agree to let you take the money as a loan that you paid back when you could. You see, she'd learnt. Finally learnt. She didn't need money to be happy.

'And, I'm sorry to say, Phil, but it was also why she came down so hard on you when she discovered you were still using drugs yourself. She'd embraced her new drugs-free life with the passion of the recently converted, and she expected you to do the same. And we may agree that telling your movie company about your drugs use was naive at best—and a betrayal at worst—but I think she honestly thought she was helping you. After all, she might have had a new set of priorities in life, but she was still terrible at understanding the consequences of her actions. Which brings me rather neatly, though I say so myself, to why Sophie killed Polly.

'And to understand that, we have to go back to last year, just after Polly and Claire's mother had died, when Polly was at her most self-destructive—just before she took a near-fatal overdose of heroin. Claire, you told a story from that time of how Polly tried to get you to smoke a spliff that she'd secretly laced with heroin, but here's what I should have noticed sooner: if she tried that trick on you, who else did she try the trick on?

'Because, if Claire was here last year, we know her nurse came with her as well. Her agency nurse, Sophie Wessel.

So, if Polly was so messed up last year that she'd offer a heroin spliff to her sister, I think she tried the exact same trick on Sophie as well. And although Claire didn't fall for it, Sophie wasn't so lucky. Were you?'

As Richard said this, he looked at Sophie, and everyone could see that although she was trying not to give anything away, her eyes were glistening with tears. What Richard was saying was hitting home.

'I can well imagine how exciting it must have been, hanging out with a world-famous supermodel. Smoking drugs together. But you had no idea how destructive Polly was at that time—and you *definitely* had no idea that the spliffs she was offering you were laced with heroin, did you?

'And by the time you found out the truth, it was too late. You had heroin in your system. You wanted more. And I bet Polly was delighted to give it to you. After all, as Claire told us, Polly was trying to destroy herself following her mother's death, and she wanted as many people to go down with her as possible.

'We can only guess how Sophie felt when she returned to the UK. A heroin addict. That's why she ended up stealing from her clients. She needed the extra money to fund her addiction. And although she was forced into admitting that her client left out bait money to catch a member of staff who'd been stealing cash, what Sophie didn't tell us was that the member of staff they needed to catch was her. After all,' Richard said, turning to the room, 'seeing as Claire isn't a heroin addict—but we just found the missing heroin packed in her wheelchair—who else would have hidden it there knowing they could get it out again once they were back in the UK if not Sophie?'

Richard turned back to face Sophie. 'And we'll know you're a heroin addict—and that Claire is clean—when we test samples of hair from you both. It's really going to be very easy to prove that it was you who put the heroin in Claire's wheelchair.'

A sob caught in Sophie's throat as Richard said this, but he didn't drop eye contact with her.

'The anger you've felt for Polly over this last year has grown like a cancer inside you, hasn't it? Because, although you told us you were glad to end your job as a private nurse to the wealthy, I think the opposite is true. After all, you'd been doing your job for over a decade and a half, and there'd never been a single complaint against your name in all that time. I think that was because you took pride in your job. In fact, you loved it, didn't you? And who wouldn't? Living in fine houses, eating only the best food—and travelling the world first class. It's been the high life for you these last fifteen years, but, because of what Polly did to you, you lost access to it all.

'And then, when you got a call from your old agency saying Claire wanted you to accompany her to Saint-Marie again, you jumped at the chance. Did you come to the island specifically to murder Polly Carter? We'll never know, but I imagine that nothing prepared you for the fact that when you finally met up with Polly after a year in which you'd become a thieving addict who'd lost your dream job, you found a woman who was now at peace, in love, and clean of the very drugs she'd blighted your life with. Because when you asked to score some heroin from her, she didn't have any, did she? Of course she didn't. She'd been clean of drugs since she returned from rehab in Los Angeles.

'And I reckon it was then that she told you her story. Of how she'd fallen in love with Alain. How she'd finally stopped using. And how she wanted to make amends to her sister, Claire. But none of this helped you. You needed heroin and you knew who had to get it for you. The woman who'd made you an addict in the first place.

'And I bet Polly didn't want to help you. After all, we know she'd already tipped off Phil's studio about his drugs use. But then, Polly hadn't caused Phil's drug addiction, had she? Whereas she was squarely to blame for yours, as I'm sure you made very clear to her. And I bet you were able to make her feel truly terrible about what she'd done to you. You maybe even blackmailed her, threatening to tell Alain about how she'd destroyed your life with heroin if she didn't get you the drugs you needed. But either way, you bullied and cajoled Polly until she accepted that it was her responsibility to sort you out with your next fix. And foolish, trusting, Polly, she got you the heroin you wanted.

'That's right,' Richard said to the room. 'Polly really was trying to make amends before she started her new life back in the UK with Alain. And although she hoped that this grand gesture—buying a vast quantity of heroin—went some way to clearing her debt with Sophie, she had no idea that it didn't even come close as far as Sophie was concerned. Because, by now, Sophie had murder in her heart. In fact, the way I think Sophie saw it was, Polly had tricked her into destroying her life, so now she was going to trick Polly into destroying her life.'

'But you don't understand,' Max said, unable to keep quiet any longer. 'Whether or not what you're saying is true, there's no way Sophie could have been on the steps to push Polly to her death. I was looking at her from the upstairs window of the house with my own eyes.'

'That's right, Max. And I'm sorry I ever doubted you.'

'And I could see Sophie as well when Polly was killed,' Phil agreed.

'And how clever Sophie's been,' Richard said, 'making sure we never quite managed to pin down who she was looking at at the time of the murder. Because, as long as we continued to question who she was looking at, we would always be presuming she couldn't be the killer because she was so clearly on the lawn at the time of the murder.'

'But she was!' Max said.

'But she wasn't,' Richard said, 'because that's not when Polly Carter was killed,' Richard said. 'Isn't that right, Sophie?'

Richard said this directly at Sophie. And, as though on cue, a fat tear rolled down her cheek.

'Because, when Polly told you about how she wanted to make amends with Claire, I think she mentioned to you that she believed that Claire suffered from conversion disorder, didn't she? And, as Claire's nurse, you realised that you were in a unique position to fan the flames of this mistaken belief. So you told Polly that, in your professional opinion—as a trained nurse—you also had your suspicions that Claire was faking her injuries. And I bet Polly lapped it up. After all, if Claire could walk again, then Polly could stop feeling so guilty about causing her disability. In fact, I bet she clung to the lies you told her like a survivor from a shipwreck clinging to a life raft.'

Richard turned to Claire.

'That's what Polly was referring to when she told you she had a gift for you. She thought she was about to return the power of walking to you. By giving you a shock so great that it would breach your psychological defences and force you to get out of your wheelchair. That's why she took you off to the cliff tops that morning—and started an argument out of thin air—and then threatened to commit suicide—it was because she wanted to get you into a fever pitch of emotion where you'd step out of your wheelchair to save her.'

Richard turned and looked at all of Polly's friends in the room.

'It's like you've all been saying all along. Polly really was very easy to manipulate, and she was a *terrible* judge of character. The reason why she died was because she allowed herself to trust Sophie here.

'But it finally explains why we found Claire's mobile phone in the chandelier up there with Polly's fingerprints on it,' Richard said, indicating the chandelier above their heads. 'She couldn't have Claire phoning for an ambulance when she pulled off her trick. There couldn't be any safety net. And that's also why she chose to put it in a chandelier of all places. It was Polly's little joke. Because as far as Polly was concerned, once Claire had got down the cliff steps and discovered that she wasn't dead after all, she thought that she and Claire would walk back to the house together and Claire would be able to reach up to the chandelier and get the phone back for herself.

'But that's not what happened, because she didn't know that although Polly was trying to trick her sister, Sophie had plans to double-cross Polly. And this is how she did it.

'After Polly ran down the steps of the cliff and disappeared around the first bend, she let out an ear-piercing scream as though she were plummeting to her death. This was all part of the plan Sophie had got her to agree to. Polly then ran down the remainder of the steps and threw herself to the sand to make it look as though she had indeed just fallen to her death from the cliff. I'm sure that Sophie impressed on Polly the need to make the illusion of death look flawless if they were going to smash down Claire's psychological barriers to walking.

'But this explains why, when I first asked Sophie about the gash in Polly's arm, she didn't know about it. After all, when Sophie first got down to the beach and turned Polly's body over, Polly wasn't in any way hurt, she was only play-acting dead.

'But it meant that Polly played straight into your hands, Sophie. Didn't she? Because now you had at least one witness—Claire—who would swear blind in a court of law that Polly jumped to her death *before* you'd even arrived on the scene.

'But what you knew—and Polly didn't—was, Claire didn't suffer from conversion disorder. Did she? So she *couldn't* run after her sister to stop her even if she'd wanted to. Or go down the steps of the cliff to investigate.

'So, once you were down on the beach with Polly's apparently dead body, you then called up to Claire and told her to get an ambulance, knowing that, because she didn't have her mobile on her, she'd have to wheel herself back to the house to make the call. At which point, I imagine Polly finally opened her eyes. Maybe she was even disappointed that you had told Claire to go off to phone for an ambulance. After all, Polly was in no way injured, it would surely be taking the trick too far to have an ambulance arrive at the house.

'And so, I imagine the pair of you returned back up the cliff steps together. To stop Claire from making the call, perhaps—or to confess to Claire that it had all been a prank that hadn't worked—we won't know exactly, but this is when the murder actually happened.'

Richard turned to Sophie before continuing.

'I wonder what mood Polly was in on her final ascent back up the cliff stairs. Upset, I'd imagine, that her trick hadn't worked on her sister as you'd said it would. But as Polly approached the last bend in the staircase before she got to the top, she still had no idea that rather than her having manipulated her sister, it had been you who'd been manipulating her into making it look like she'd committed suicide while you had an alibi elsewhere in the garden.

'And the final genius of your plan was, although it had required a number of key events to go your way up to this point, you hadn't actually committed any kind of a crime yet. Although that was about to change. And for the murder itself you needed no real planning or finesse at all. You just needed a big stick and an unsuspecting victim.

'So, just before Polly turned for the last flight of steps at the top of the cliff, you picked up the piece of driftwood you'd placed there earlier and smashed it into Polly's head, trying to knock her over the edge of the steps so that this time she'd fall to her death for real.

'But Polly fought back, didn't she? Even if only briefly, she was able to grab at the branch with her hands. There was a tussle—which you won—and about the only mistake you made was to not notice that Polly had gashed her inner forearm as she finally lost her grip on the branch. But you did it. You got your revenge. You killed the woman who'd made you an addict. Who'd ruined your life.

'And, with Polly now dead for real, you then rushed down the steps and hid the branch in a bush—although you didn't have enough time to notice that the branch now had a smear of Polly's blood on it—before you carried on down to the beach and made sure you were found waiting by the body of Polly when Claire and Max returned to the scene having called for an ambulance a few minutes later.'

Richard turned to look directly at Sophie.

'And how clever you were, because what did Claire see when she got back to the scene? She saw her sister Polly lying dead on the beach—just as she expected to see. And she saw her nurse standing at her sister's side—just as she expected to see. But this time, Polly really was dead.'

As Richard finished his story, Sophie's body bent over in her chair and great racking sobs of grief and remorse heaved through her.

'Dwayne,' Richard said calmly. 'If you would?'

Wails of pain emitted from Sophie as Dwayne fastened the handcuffs to her wrists and led her from the room, but all the other witnesses watched on, stony-faced.

With Sophie gone, the remaining witnesses turned, one by one, and looked at Richard in wonder.

'Thank you,' Claire said, speaking on behalf of all of them.

Richard didn't need to say anything in reply. He'd avenged Polly Carter's death, and the witnesses' looks of gratitude were all the thanks he needed.

***

Later on that afternoon, Sophie was in the cells, having made a teary, confused, but—most importantly of all—admissible confession of murder, Camille was at her desk scanning the confession into the main police computer, Dwayne was finishing writing out the log sheets for the arrest and Fidel was bagging the heroin for sending off-island for analysis by the labs on Guadeloupe. And while they were all doing this, Richard stood in front of the whiteboard with the cloth in his hand. He'd rubbed off all the remaining names and information they'd had up there—and now all that was left was the name of the victim, Polly Carter.

Richard realised that when he'd started investigating the case, he'd presumed that Polly Carter was going to be a vacuous and air-headed idiot. But he'd been wrong. There was something about her desperate and ultimately doomed lifelong attempt to find peace for herself, and love from her family, that had touched him deeply.

Richard wiped the name 'Polly Carter' from the board, and she was gone.

He put the cloth down.

'Well, I hear congratulations are in order,' a voice said from the doorway of the police station.

Richard turned and saw that his father had entered wearing khaki slacks and a bright red polo shirt. Jennifer stepped into the station just to her husband's side, a shy smile on her face.

'Selwyn just phoned to say you caught Polly Carter's killer,' Graham said, easing himself down proprietorially on the corner of Dwayne's desk. 'And he also said it was one of the most brilliant pieces of detecting he's ever seen.'

'He said that?' Richard said, thrilled.

'But I'm sorry to say I had to disagree with him.'

There was a sharp intake of breath from Camille, but Richard somehow wasn't surprised. Of course his father disagreed. He disagreed with everything he did.

'You see,' Graham said, 'I had to disagree with him because, as far as I can see, *every* time my son does any detecting, it's brilliant.'

After a moment of startled incomprehension, Richard found fireworks of joy exploding in front of his eyes. Had his father just paid him a compliment? After all these years, had Graham Poole, one-time Superintendent of the Leicestershire Police Force, current President of the Oadby Rotary Club, Secretary of the Newton Harcourt golf club, and senior Sidesman at St James-The-Less, just paid him an actual, real, spoken-out-loud-in-front-of-witnesses compliment?

As Dwayne, Camille and Fidel's faces all warmed into wide smiles, Richard—now suddenly panicked that his father would realise he'd made a mistake and retract what he'd just said—broke in with, 'So what about last night? How was the dinner at the British Embassy?'

Jennifer's eyes sparkled as she said, 'Well! I sat next to the Ambassador himself. And then, afterwards, there was a recital from a local band who are apparently *very* popular—and the whole thing finished with coffee and rum on the roof of the residence watching shooting stars in the night sky. It was magical!'

Richard's team could see how happy Jennifer was, and their smiles widened.

'Anyway,' Graham said, 'we don't want to interrupt your well-earned celebrations, but could I have a quick word with you, Richard? Perhaps outside on the verandah?'

Richard straightened his tie and pretended he wasn't instantly nervous.

'Okay,' he said.

Graham led out to the verandah and Richard followed his father, unable to catch his mother's eye as he went. What had he done wrong now?

Stepping out into the heat of the late afternoon sun, Richard's suit immediately started to prickle on his body, but he didn't want his father to know how uncomfortable he felt—either physically or emotionally.

For his part, Graham seemed content to lean on the balustrade and look out at the view.

'So, how's the conference going?' Richard said, in lieu of understanding what was going on.

'There's no conference,' Graham said without even turning around to look at his son.

'But there must be,' Richard said, unable to keep the note of desperation out of his voice. 'You know, if the Commissioner invited you over to speak at a conference. Or why would he have invited you?'

Graham turned to look at his son, and Richard was puzzled to see only tiredness in his father's eyes.

'The whole conference was a con trick to get me out here so I could hook up again with your mother. As I told the Commissioner after the evening finished last night. Don't worry, though, I thanked him for the invite, but I said that now I was out here, there was no need to go on with the charade.'

'You told the Commissioner you knew there was no conference?'

'I did.'

'And what did he say to that?'

'I'm glad to say he respected me enough to admit I was right. And he even told me that he only invited me out here because you asked him to.'

Richard's heart sank, and he felt a trickle of sweat slip down his forehead onto his cheek that he didn't dare wipe off.

'It's true,' Richard said, ashamed—of course—but also knowing that he couldn't lie to his father.

Graham let out a throaty chuckle.

'No need to beat yourself up about it. I'm glad you did.'

Richard frowned, sure that his ears must have deceived him.

'What's that?' he said.

Richard's father turned from his son and went back to staring out at the view of the Caribbean sea sparkling in the harbour. Richard could see that his father was mentally geeing himself up.

'You see, when your mother just upped and left like that, I decided I wouldn't chase after her. God knows why. I'm too stubborn. I'm sure you'd agree with that. But I decided I'd just stick my head in the sand and do nothing. I don't suppose you can imagine reacting to a situation in your life like that?'

Richard, of course, knew that he basically reacted to *every* situation in his life precisely like that, but he kept his counsel, and his father continued.

'And then I got a phone call from your Commissioner. I guessed it was a fit-up from the start, but it also made me realise. I wanted to be on the next plane out here. I wanted to get your mother back. So thank you, son. For what you did for me. For what you did for your mother.'

Richard was stunned. Had his father just paid him *another* compliment? What was going on?

After a few more moments of silent wonder, Richard decided that maybe he'd give the balustrade a go as well, and so he tentatively leant his forearms on it and took up position at his father's side to look out at the view. Admittedly, he found that he had to squint against the reflected sunlight on the water of the harbour, but he also found this silent side-by-side communion strangely peaceful.

In fact, as Richard screwed up his eyes against the headache-inducing brightness, he realised that this was the closest he'd ever come to any kind of accord with his father. And, as he threw a glance sideways, he noticed for the first time how his father's neck didn't quite fill the eighteen-inch shirt collar he knew he wore, and the skin of his neck had fluted in wrinkles as well. His father was getting old, Richard realised.

Richard decided that this was the moment that he should say something meaningful, but he was at a loss. You don't spend over four decades petrified of someone, he realised, and then have something nice lined up to say after one sideways glance.

Jennifer beetled out of the police station and was delighted to see father and son leaning against the balustrade, side by side.

'Graham, our plane will be leaving soon,' she said. 'And you know how we have to be there at least two hours before the desk opens—in case of any last-minute problems.'

'Oh?' Richard said, surprised. 'Are you going back to the UK?'

'Oh no,' Jennifer said, delight in her eyes. 'Actually, we've decided to go on to Cuba. I've always wanted to go there.'

'You are?' Richard said, amazed. And then he realised what his mother had actually said. 'Sorry, you've always wanted to go to *Cuba*?'

Jennifer beamed and Graham stood up from the balustrade. He looked at Richard.

'Sure. It was something we used to talk about. Going to Cuba. Hiring a classic 1950s Chevrolet, touring the island, and learning to dance the Salsa.'

Richard was sure that his ears were deceiving him this time.

'Your tie's come loose, son,' Graham said with a smile.

'It has?' Richard said, his hand instinctively going to the knot in reflexive panic.

'No it's all right,' his mother said. 'It looks nice a little loose.'

Richard no longer knew which way was up and which way was down, because if his father had recently paid him at least two compliments, his mother had now quite clearly said that she was prepared to accept less-than-perfect sartorial standards in him.

He tightened the knot on his tie anyway.

You had to have some standards in life.

And then, with a few more parting words that they should all stay in touch more—and with the promise that they'd send their son a postcard from Cuba—Graham shook Richard's hand, Jennifer kissed him on both cheeks, and then husband and wife left down the steps together.

As Richard watched his parents head down into the street together and hail a taxi, Camille, Fidel and Dwayne came out of the police station and joined Richard on the verandah.

Dwayne turned to his boss. 'I don't know how you did it, but you did it.'

Richard was just as surprised as Dwayne. 'I did, didn't I?'

'Nice one, Chief.'

'Thank you, Dwayne.'

'And I can second that,' Fidel said. 'Nice one, Chief.'

'Thank you, Fidel.'

Richard turned to Camille, knowing that now—finally!—she'd do the decent thing and call him 'Chief'. And, as he looked into his Detective Sergeant's eyes, he could see the knowing twinkle that showed him that she knew perfectly well what he was expecting her to say.

'Nice one,' she said, before pausing dramatically. 'Sir,' she then finished.

Richard blinked.

She hadn't called him Chief. The wilful, insolent, pig-headed—and frankly insubordinate—Camille still hadn't called him Chief! And as he saw smirks begin to play around Dwayne and Fidel's mouths, he realised that they'd realised the same thing, too.

'Don't you all have some work to do?' he barked.

'Not really, Chief,' Dwayne said. 'You see, we've already caught the killer. She's in the cells.'

'Then what about processing the evidence and writing up the reports? Have we done all that?' Richard asked, refusing to back down.

'All processed and written up, sir,' Fidel said, also deeply amused by his boss's grump.

'Then there must be some on-going training you all need to be getting on with?' Richard finally said.

Dwayne just laughed.

'The amount of overtime we've clocked over the last few weeks, I'm not even on shift any more, Chief. So I'm suggesting we all go to Catherine's bar for a celebratory drink.'

And with that, Dwayne tripped down the steps and started to head off to Catherine's bar.

With a guilty smile and quick bob of his head—'Me too, sir'—Fidel turned and followed Dwayne before Richard could call him back.

Now it was just Camille and Richard left on the verandah.

Camille smiled for her boss, happy now that she'd scored her point to put their usual bickering to one side.

'Dwayne's right, sir. You should come for a drink. Tell you what, seeing as we're celebrating, if you come to the bar, I'll even promise to buy you a drink.'

As Richard looked at Camille, an odd feeling began to seep through him. Maybe, for once, perhaps he *did* want to have a drink with Camille and the rest of the team.

But Camille's recent refusal to call him Chief still smarted, and he knew that if she was too stubborn to accommodate his wishes—well then, two could play at that game, couldn't they?

So—rather cleverly, he thought to himself—Richard refused even to give an answer to Camille's question, and instead he just stood there, knowing that his lack of answer would be all the answer he need give.

Richard saw the hope in Camille's eyes fade. He then knew he'd 'won' when she sighed to herself, turned, and headed away from the police station without another word, shaking her head to herself.

Yes, he thought to himself, that showed her who was boss.

And anyway, he now realised, he didn't want to spend the evening in a rowdy bar toasting their success with endless bottles of beer—or, heaven forbid, having to drink one of Catherine's near-lethal cocktails. No, Richard instinctively knew what he'd much rather be doing.

He was going to have a quiet evening at home with a nice cup of tea and finish reading his book on the indigenous insects of the Caribbean. Now *that* was how to spend an evening.

And with that thought, Richard almost smiled to himself.

Almost.

But not quite.

★ ★ ★ ★ ★

ACKNOWLEDGEMENTS

I'd like to thank Tony Jordan, Belinda Campbell, Alex Jones, Tim Key and James Hall for all the work they do on the TV series. It's mostly because of them that it remains so succesful. As for the *Death in Paradise* books, I am blessed in having a phenomenal team at Mira/Harlequin: Alison Lindsay, Nick Bates, Darren Shoffren and Taryn Sachs in particular have all worked their socks off promoting the first book, and I'm extremely grateful for their good cheer and support over the last year. And, of course, an even bigger thanks has to go to my editor, Sally Williamson. Her continued enthusiasm has kept me sane through the long months of writing, her incisive notes have kept the story on track, and her ability to escort me from the annual office party before I embarrassed myself any further has kept my reputation (just about) intact.

I would also like to thank the fabulously-talented Louise McGrory, the designer of both this book's cover and the cover for *A Meditation on Murder*. There's no point writing a novel if no-one picks it up in a shop, and I'm thrilled with how brilliantly she's represented Richard, Saint-Marie and the world of each book in her cover designs.

I'd like to thank my literary agent, Ed Wilson, for his support during the writing process; my TV and film agent Charlotte Knight, for her support at all other times; and also a special thanks—as ever— to Molly Ker Hawn, who has always given fabulous advice, and always at the drop of a hat. You need champions cheering you on when you start writing a novel— it really is a lot of words to put one in front of another—and so I'd also like to thank Richard Westcott and Georgie Bevan, who both read an early draft of the book, and their notes and enthusiasm helped me get through these last few months of writing and re-writing.

Finally, I would also like to thank my wife, Katie Breathwick, and our children, Charlie and James. Katie's notes on the early drafts of the novel proved critically important (as ever), and her tolerance of my neurotic self-absorption during the writing process is nothing short of heroic. As for Charlie and James, I'd like to thank them for putting up with a father who is sometimes grouchy and nearly always absent-minded during the writing process. And not just then, now I think about it. But everything I write—one way or another—is for you. Love you.

Robert Thorogood
Marlow, October, 2015

Can't wait for another
Death in Paradise mystery?

Keep reading for an extract from

A Meditation on Murder

available now!

Prologue

Aslan Kennedy had no need of an alarm clock. Instead, he found he woke every morning quite naturally as the sun began to peek over the horizon.

In fact, he'd been waking with the sun ever since he'd decided a few years back that he no longer believed in alarm clocks. Any more than he believed in money, the internet, or any kind of 'one cup' tea bag. For Aslan—hotel-owner, yoga instructor and self-styled Spiritual Guru—the wristwatch, with its arbitrary division of seconds, minutes and hours, was a potent symbol of enslavement. A manacle mankind wore while they worshipped at the false idol they called progress.

It made making appointments with him a little trying, of course. But that wasn't Aslan's problem. Not the way he saw it.

On this particular morning, Aslan lay quietly in bed (mahogany, Belle Epoque) until he felt his chakras align. He then swung his legs out onto the teak floorboards (Thai, imported) and padded over to a floor-length mirror (gilt-framed, Regency) where he inspected his reflection. The man who stared back at him looked much older than his fifty-six years—if only because his flowing white hair, beard and white cotton nightshirt gave him a Jesus/Gandalf vibe. But, as Aslan would be the first to admit, the miracle was that he was alive at all. And, as far as he was concerned, the reason why he'd been able to turn his life around was entirely down to his wonderful wife, Rianka.

Aslan turned back to look at Rianka as she slept twisted in the cotton sheets of their bed. She looked so at peace, Aslan thought to himself. Like a beautiful angel. And, as he'd told himself a thousand times over the last decade and a half, he owed everything that was now good in his life to this woman. It was that simple. And debts like that could never be repaid.

Once Aslan had got dressed, he swept down the mahogany staircase of The Retreat, careful his white cotton robes didn't knock over any of the artfully arranged ethnic icons or trinkets that variously stood on pedestals or hung from the wall. At the bottom of the stairs, he turned into the hotel's ultra-modern kitchen and was pleased to see that someone had already laid out a willow pattern teapot and porcelain cups on a tray for him.

Aslan started the kettle boiling and looked out of the window. Manicured lawns stretched down through an avenue of tall palm trees to the hotel's beach, where the Caribbean sea sparkled emerald green as it lapped against the white sand. With a smile, Aslan saw that the guests for the Sunrise Healing were already on the beach, stretching and taking the air following their early-morning swim.

Mind you, his eyesight wasn't what it once was, and, as he looked more closely at the five people in their swim things, he found himself frowning. Was that really who was going to be in the Sunrise Healing session with him? In fact, Aslan realised, if that's who was attending the session, then something had gone seriously wrong.

Aslan's attention was brought back to the room as the kettle came to the boil with a click. He poured the water into the pot and let the familiar smell of green tea calm him. After all, he had much more in his life to worry about than who was or wasn't attending one of his therapy sessions. Perhaps this was no more than karma realigning itself?

He couldn't hide from his past forever, could he?

By the time Aslan took the tray of tea outside, he'd decided that he'd just carry on as normal. He'd lead the guests to the Meditation Space. Just as normal. He'd lock the room down. Just as normal. He'd then share a cup of tea with them all and start the Healing. Just as normal.

'Good morning!' Aslan called out to get the attention of the five guests down on the beach. They all turned and looked up at him. A few of them even waved.

Yes, he decided to himself, it was all going to be just fine.

★

It was half an hour later when the screaming started.

At the time, most of the hotel guests were finishing their breakfast in the outdoor dining area, or were already wearing white cotton robes and heading off to their first treatment of the day. As for Rianka Kennedy, Aslan's wife, she was sitting out on the hotel's verandah, a wicker basket of sewing at her feet as she darned one of her husband's socks.

The scream seemed to be coming from one of the treatment rooms that sat in the middle of The Retreat's largest lawn: a timber and paper Japanese tea house that Aslan and Rianka had christened the 'Meditation Space'.

When a second scream joined the first, Rianka found herself running across the grass towards the Meditation Space. It was a good hundred yards away and, when Rianka had covered about half the distance, Dominic De Vere, The Retreat's tanned and taut handyman, appeared as if by magic from around the side of a clump of bougainvillea. As usual he was wearing only cut-off jeans, flip-flops and a utility belt full of various tools.

'What's that racket?' he asked somewhat redundantly as Rianka flashed past him. After a moment, he turned and trotted after her.

Rianka got to the door of the Meditation Space, and, as there was no handle on the outside of it, tried to jam her fingers into the gap between the door and the frame with no success. It wouldn't budge—it was locked from the inside.

'What's going on?' she called out over the sound of screams.

Dominic finally flapped over on his flip–flops and caught up with Rianka, if not the situation.

'What's happening?' he asked.

'Dominic, get that door open!'

'I can't. There's no door handle.'

'Use your knife! Just cut through the paper!'

'Oh! Of course!'

Dominic grabbed the Stanley knife from the pouch at his belt and clicked the triangular blade out. He was about to slash through the paper of the tea house's wall when they both saw it: a bloody hand pressed up against the inside.

They then heard a man's voice, thick with fear: 'Help!'

And then a different female voice: 'Oh god! Oh god!'

There was a scrabbling while someone wrestled with the lock on the inside of the door. A few moments later, the door was yanked inwards by Ben Jenkins, who then just stood there in lumpen horror.

Ignoring Ben, Rianka stepped into the Meditation Space and saw that Paul Sellars was lying on his back on a prayer mat, having difficulty waking up. Ann, his wife, was kneeling at his side shaking his shoulders. Rianka could see that both of them had spots of blood on their white cotton robes. As for Saskia Filbee, she was standing off to one side, her hands over her mouth, stifling another scream. There was blood on her sleeve as well.

But it was the woman standing in the centre of the room that drew Rianka's attention. Her name was Julia Higgins. She was in her early twenties, she'd been working at The Retreat for the last six months, and in her left hand she was holding a bloody carving knife.

At Julia's feet a man was lying quite still, his once white robes, beard and hair now drenched in blood, a number of vicious knife wounds in his back.

Aslan Kennedy—hotel-owner, yoga instructor and self-styled Spiritual Guru—had clearly just been viciously stabbed to death.

'I killed him,' Julia said.

And now it was Rianka's turn to scream.

Chapter One

A few hours before the murder of Aslan Kennedy, Detective Inspector Richard Poole was also awake. This wasn't because he'd trained himself to turn delicately to each day's sunrise like a flower; it was because he was hot, bothered, and he'd been awake since a frog had started croaking outside his window—inexplicably—just before 4am.

But then, Richard thought to himself, this was entirely typical, because if he wasn't being assaulted by frog choruses in the middle of the night, it was torrential downpours like a troupe of Gene Kellys tap-dancing on his tin roof; or it was whole dunes of sand being blown across his floorboards by the hot Caribbean wind. In fact, Richard considered, in all ways and at all times, life on the tropical island of Saint-Marie was a misery.

Admittedly, he'd collected empirical evidence that suggested that Saint-Marie was a popular holiday destination for tens of thousands of other people, but what did other people know? This was an island where it was sunny every second of every single day apart from the ten minutes each morning and night when a tropical storm would appear out of nowhere and rain hard enough to flatten cows. And that wasn't even counting the three months of the year when it was no longer the hot season because it was now the hurricane season—which, in truth, was just as hot as the hot season, but altogether more hurricaney.

And none of this even included the constant and unrelenting humidity, which—Richard often found himself claiming—was well over one hundred per cent. (Of course, Richard knew that this was scientifically impossible, but he also knew that the one time he'd received a precious box of Walker's crisps in the post from his mother, the crisps had gone soggy within minutes of him opening any of the packets. It was like some exquisite punishment that had been specifically designed to torture him. The insides of each packet contained perfect crisps right up to but not including the precise moment he opened the packet and tried to eat one, at which point they immediately went stale in the sultry tropical air.)

This and other wild roller coasters of despair looped through Richard's mind as he lay in bed, wide awake, his bedside alarm clock clicking from 04:18 to 04:19, surely the most miserable minute in the twenty-four hour clock, Richard found himself musing.

A slick of sweat slipped down his neck and into the collar of his Marks and Spencer pyjamas, and before he could stop himself, Richard became a kicking machine, scissoring his legs in a frenzied attack on his sheets until they'd been balled up and dashed to the floor.

He slumped back onto the old mattress and exhaled in exasperation. Why did everything have to be so hard?

There was nothing for it, he might as well get up.

He turned on the lights and padded into the tiny kitchenette and washroom that had somehow been crammed into the inside porch of his shack as if by someone who no doubt felt that the galley kitchens on sailboats were altogether too roomy. Surely there was a way of packing even more cooking and cleaning equipment into even less space?

He went to the metal sink that was squashed in between his fridge and his front door, and discovered that he wasn't the only person looking for a drink. A bright green lizard was already in the sink catching drops of water as they fell from the tap above.

The lizard was called Harry. Or, rather, Richard had named the lizard Harry when he'd discovered that the shack he'd been assigned to live in already came with a reptilian sitting tenant. And, like every flat-share Richard had ever been involved in, it had been a disaster from the start.

As Harry turned his attention back to catching drops of water with his pink-flashing tongue, Richard found himself thinking—not for the first time—that he should just get rid of the bloody creature.

But how to do it, that was the question.

A few hours later, Richard was sitting behind his desk in Honoré Police Station using the internet to research legal and possibly not-so-legal methods of household pest con-

trol when Detective Sergeant Camille Bordey swished over
to his desk, a gleam in her eye.

'So tell me…what do you want for lunch?'

Camille was bright, lithe, and one of the most naturally
attractive women on the island, but as Richard looked up
from his reverie—irked at the interruption—he frowned
like a barn owl who'd just received some bad news.

'Camille, don't interrupt me when I'm working.'

'Oh, sorry,' Camille said, not sorry at all. 'What are you
working on?'

'Oh, you know. Work,' he said, suspiciously. 'What do you
want?'

'Me? I just wanted to take your lunch order.'

Richard finally looked at his partner. She was young,
fresh-faced, and threw herself at life with a wondrous abandon that Richard didn't even remotely understand. In fact,
as Richard considered Camille, he found himself once again
marvelling at how much his partner was a complete mystery to him. In truth, he knew that he was limited in his understanding of women by the fact that he'd been educated
at a single-sex boarding school and hadn't had any kind of
meaningful conversation with a woman who wasn't either
his mother or his House Matron before the age of eighteen,
but Camille seemed even more impossible to comprehend
than most women.

To begin with, she was French. To end with, she was
French. And in between all that, she was French. This
meant—to Richard's mind at least—that she was unreliable,
incapable of following orders, and was, all in all, a wild card
and loose cannon. In truth, Richard was scared witless of

her. Not that he'd ever admitted as much. Even to himself.

'You know what I want for lunch, Camille,' he said imperiously, trying to take back control of the conversation. 'Because I've had the same lunch every single day I've been on this godforsaken island.'

'But *Maman* says she's got some spiced yams and rice she can plate up for us all. Or there's curried goat left over from—'

'Thank you, Camille, but I'd much rather just have my usual.'

Camille looked at her boss, her eyes sparkling as she got out her police notebook and made a big show of writing down his lunch order. 'One…banana…sandwich.'

'Thank you, Camille,' Richard said, somehow aware that he'd been made to look stupid, but not knowing quite how it had happened.

Camille grabbed up her handbag, sashayed out of the room, and Richard waited to see who of Dwayne or Fidel would appear first from behind their computer monitors.

It was Ordinary Police Officer Dwayne Myers. But then, as the elder statesman of the station, this was no real surprise.

Richard tolerated Dwayne—liked him, even—but it was always against his better judgement. Dwayne was in his fifties but looked like he was no older than thirty and, while he wore non-regulation trainers and a bead necklace with his uniform, he was always immaculately turned out. In fact, it was something Richard had always felt he and Dwayne had in common, their sartorial precision. And while Richard knew that Dwayne wasn't really very interested in being thorough, punctual or following any kind of orders, he was a marvel at digging up information through 'unofficial' channels. And on a small tropical island like Saint-Marie, there were a lot of unofficial channels.

'Seriously, Chief,' Dwayne said. 'You can't have the same lunch day after day.'

'I went to boarding school for ten years. Watch me.'

And now Sergeant Fidel Best's head appeared to the side of his monitor, his young and trusting face puzzled. Fidel was a proper copper, Richard felt. He was meticulous, keen, utterly tireless, and, above all else, he knew correct procedure. The only downside to Fidel was that he was overly keen, so he'd sometimes continue with a line of inquiry long after it was sensible to drop it. Like now, Richard found himself thinking, as Fidel said, 'But, sir, don't you get bored eating the same meal every day of your life?'

'Yes. Extremely. But what can I do?'

'Well, sir, order a different lunch?'

'No, I think I'll stick to my banana sandwich, if you don't mind. You know where you are with a banana sandwich.'

'I know,' Dwayne said, almost awestruck by his boss's dogged determination never to embrace change. 'Eating a banana sandwich.'

The office phone rang and Richard huffed. 'No, it's alright, you two stay where you are, I'll get it.'

Richard went to the sun-bleached counter and plucked up the ancient phone's handset.

'Honoré Police Station, this is Detective Inspector Richard Poole speaking. How can I be of assistance?'

Richard listened a moment before cupping the phone and turning back to his team.

'Fidel. Phone Camille. Cancel the banana sandwich. There's been a murder.'

★

Rianka had set up The Retreat eighteen years ago when she'd bought a derelict sugar plantation for a knock-down price. The main house had been abandoned for nearly fifty years by this time, but it wasn't its outside that Rianka found herself responding to, it was the inside. Admittedly, the interior wasn't much less damaged, but what Rianka noticed was how the rooms were still as beautifully proportioned and airy as they'd always been; the rotten ceilings were just as high; the main staircase, while leaf-swept and missing many of its boards, was just as grand. To Rianka, the house was no less than a metaphor for the island itself— shabby on the outside, but full of soul on the inside—and, within the year, she'd restored the main house and grounds to their former glory and opened for business as a luxury hotel called 'The Plantation'.

When Rianka then got together with Aslan, they'd increasingly started to market the hotel as a high-end health farm, and it wasn't long before they'd relaunched the whole venture as a luxury spa that was now called 'The Plantation Spa'.

The business went from strength to strength.

Then, as Aslan got more involved in exploring the spiritual side of life, he started offering holistic treatments and therapies to hotel guests—either led by him, or by other instructors he hired especially—and it wasn't long before they'd relaunched the hotel for a third and final time as 'The Retreat'.

For a good few years now, the hotel had been specifically tailored to the internationally wealthy who wanted to heal their minds just as much as they wanted to heal their bodies. Guests could sign up for sessions in healing, be it Crystal, Reiki or Sunrise; or yoga, be it Bikram or Hatha; or meditation, be it Zazen or Transcendental.

Now, as the police drove up the gravel driveway in convoy, their blue lights flashing dimly in the bright Caribbean sunshine, they could see that the main hotel building was the old plantation owner's house; manicured lawns swept down to a private beach, and there were incongruous quasi-religious buildings dotted here and there around the grounds with hotel guests coming and going from them.

Richard, Camille and Fidel climbed out of the police Land Rover and Dwayne dismounted from the Force's only other vehicle, a 1950s Harley-Davidson motorbike that had an entirely illegal sidecar attached to it. No one quite knew where this bike-with-sidecar had come from, or how it had got tricked up in the livery of the Saint-Marie Police Force, but legend had it—and records seemed to confirm—that it had joined the Saint-Marie Police Force just after Dwayne did. Not that Dwayne was saying.

Dominic came out of the house—still wearing flip-flops and cut-off shorts, but the gravity of the situation was such that he'd deigned to slip on a vest.

'Man, I'm glad to see you,' he said, running a hand

through his lustrous hair before shaking his head a little so his mane would settle.

'Yes,' Richard said. 'And who are you?'

'Dominic De Vere. The Retreat's handyman.'

Dominic was British and Richard could tell from his drawling accent that he was from a moneyed background. In fact, Richard knew the type well. Posh, dim, wealthy, entitled—and therefore able to waft through life exploring the counter-culture as a hobby. No doubt, if Dominic's money ever ran out, he'd make a phone call to one of his old school chums, land a high-paid job in the City and then, for the rest of his life, complain that 'the youth of to-day' were feckless layabouts.

It was fair to say that Richard disliked Dominic on sight.

'If you could just take us to the body,' he said.

'Sure thing.'

Richard had no interest in continuing the conversation with someone who wore a shark tooth on a string around his neck, so they all walked on in silence until they reached the corner of the house, which is when Dominic stopped and frowned. Richard looked at him.

'Sorry, is there a problem?' Richard asked.

It was clear that there was, but Dominic didn't know where to start.

'Go on,' Camille said altogether more tolerantly.

'Okay,' Dominic said. 'Well, it's just…'

As Dominic stopped speaking, he started to waft his hands near Richard's body.

'What on earth are you doing?' Richard asked.

'I've never seen this before.'

'I'm a police officer, would you stop stroking my arms?'

'But this isn't possible.'

This got Richard's attention. 'What's not possible?'

Dominic exhaled as if he was about to deliver some very bad news.

'You don't have an aura.'

Richard looked at Dominic a long moment.

'I know I don't. Auras don't exist. Now, if you don't mind, I'd like you to stay exactly where you are while we go and inspect the body.'

'But your team all have auras.'

'We do?' Camille said eagerly, holding up her hand for her boss to wait. She wanted to hear this out.

'Of course you do,' Dominic continued, smiling easily for Camille's benefit. 'Yours is yellow, golden...it's like sunlight. Warm. Impetuous. Open. Sexually adventurous.'

Camille seemed delighted by this analysis as Dominic held her gaze much longer than he needed to, and Richard found himself noticing that Dominic wasn't just tanned, muscly and heroically square-jawed, he was also extremely good-looking. In a slightly obvious way of course, Richard found himself adding as an afterthought in his head.

Dominic next turned his attention to Fidel and considered the air that encompassed him.

'As for you, you're blues and greens...of kindness...valour. Hard work. Hey, you're one of the good guys.'

Fidel blushed. He was clearly just as thrilled with his 'reading' as Camille had been with hers.

'Oh for heaven's sakes!' Richard said. 'Thank you, Mr De Vere, but I can see that people are congregated over there'—Richard pointed at the Meditation Space as it sat some way away on the lawn—'and I want to make this clear: my colleagues and I are going over to the crime scene right now, and you're going to stay right here.'

'But what about me?' Dwayne said, eager as a puppy dog. 'What's my aura?'

Richard huffed in indignation as Dominic turned to Dwayne and took his time to consider. But then a knowing smile slipped onto Dominic's lips.

'You're like me. A shape-shifter.'

Dwayne beamed at what he perceived to be the highest of compliments.

'I knew it.'

Dominic turned back to Richard. 'But I'm telling you, when I look at you, I don't see…anything.'

'Whereas I see a murder scene over there, so thank you very much for your help. Team, you're with me, but if you try to move even an inch'—Richard said this to Dominic—'I'm going to arrest you for wasting police time.'

Richard strode off across the lawn, his team trying not to catch each other's eyes as they got into their boss's slip-stream. After all, it wouldn't do to turn up at a murder scene giggling.

But then, there was no chance of Richard or his team laughing by the time they arrived at the Meditation Space, where they found six shell-shocked Brits sitting or stand-ing on the grass. Five of them were wearing white cotton robes that were variously spattered in drying blood. The sixth of them—Rianka—was sitting on the grass on her own. She was wearing a long Indian-style skirt with little mirrors sewn into the hemline, a light summer blouse, and leather sandals.

'Okay, my name's Detective Inspector Richard Poole,' Richard said. 'And this is Detective Sergeant Camille Bordey. Can any of you tell me what happened?'

'That's simple,' said a well-tanned man in his fifties with a Yorkshire accent, a thick gold chain just visible around his neck. Richard also had time to notice a chunky gold watch on the man's wrist. Clearly he was seriously wealthy.

'The name's Ben Jenkins,' the man said. 'And you should know, that woman over there, she says her name's Julia Higgins. And she's admitted it all. She killed Aslan Kennedy.'

Richard could see that Ben was pointing at a young woman in a bloodied white robe who was standing on her own on the grass. She was in her early twenties, had long blonde hair that was tied up in a ponytail, and she was looking back at Richard with doe eyes, seemingly as dismayed by the accusation as everyone else. But she wasn't denying it, either, Richard noted.

With a quick nod of his head, Richard indicated that Dwayne should ghost over to Julia and make sure she didn't make a run for it. As Dwayne started to move, Richard turned back to Ben.

'And where's the body?'

'In there.' Ben pointed at the Meditation Space.

Richard turned to the group. 'Then if you'd all just wait here, please. The Detective Sergeant and I will only be a moment. Camille?'

Richard headed over to the Meditation Space, Camille

coming over to join him, but Richard found himself stopping at the threshold to the building.

'One moment,' Richard said as he held his hand up for Camille to pause, because it was only now as Richard approached that he saw that the walls to the building were made of paper. In fact, as he looked closer, he could see that the paper was waxy, clearly very strong, and was even somewhat translucent. Richard put his hand on the other side of the door and noticed that he could still dimly see his hand's shape through the paper.

'What are you doing?' Camille asked.

Richard ignored Camille as he took a moment to inspect the door to the building. He saw that there was no handle on the outside, but there was a Yale-style latch lock on the inside of the door that was screwed deep into the wooden frame—and that there was a corresponding housing on the door frame that it slotted into when the room was locked.

But without a keyhole on the outside, it appeared as though the door could only be locked and unlocked from the inside. Richard filed this information away for later consideration.

Stepping into the room, Richard immediately understood why the walls and roof were made of translucent paper, because every inch of the walls glowed with brilliant sunshine. And not only was it brighter inside the room than it was outside, it was significantly hotter too, like being at the heart of a supernova. Which was just bloody typical, Richard thought to himself.

Camille joined Richard inside and looked at her boss as he prickled in his suit.

'Hot, isn't it?' she said, helpfully.

Richard decided to ignore his partner and instead, squinting against the light, saw that the body of a man lay sticky with blood in the middle of the floor. His hair, beard and white robes were now thick with blood. And there was a bloody knife on the floor by the body.

Richard gave the room a quick once-over, but there wasn't much to see. The floor was polished hardwood planks; there were six woven prayer mats arranged in a circle around a tray of tea things. Six pairs of fabric eye masks and six wireless headphones were also lying here and there, but other than that the room was empty. No furniture— no cupboards, tables, chairs, statues or other ornaments—to hide behind or conceal murder weapons in.

To all intents and purposes the room was entirely bare.

Richard bent down and picked up one of the wireless headsets. He put it to his ear and frowned.

'What is it?' Camille asked.

'I don't know,' Richard said, listening, but unable to work out what the noise was.

It was a strange keening.

He listened a bit longer, but, as far as he could tell, it was just more of the same yawling noise. And then dread filled his heart as he realised what it was.

With a shudder, he said, 'It's whales singing.'

Richard lowered the headphones, sharpish, and put them back down on the floor, before he joined Camille at the centre of the room to inspect the victim.

Crouching down, Richard could see that the murder weapon to the side of the body was a carving knife of some sort. Utterly vicious. The blade was covered in blood, although the handle seemed to be clean.

'We're going to need to get this bagged and tested for prints,' Richard said.

Camille was inspecting the body.

'There are no signs of a struggle...no fabric or skin caught under the victim's fingernails...and no cuts to the hands, wrists or arms. It doesn't look like he tried to defend himself from the attack.'

Richard looked at the tray of tea things on the floor by the pool of blood that had spread from the body. The teapot was willow pattern and there were six bone china cups that had all been turned upside down on the floor, one cup in front of each prayer mat. Richard tried to work out what had happened.

If the mats and cups were to be believed, there'd been six people in here. They'd all been sitting on the prayer mats around the tray of tea things. They'd all then had a cup of tea and turned their cup over and placed it down on the floor in front of them to show that they'd finished their drink.

But how did the eye masks and headphones fit into this? And how exactly had the victim been killed?

Camille inspected the stab wounds in the victim's back.

'There appear to be five separate sharp force injuries in the victim's neck, shoulder and back,' she said. 'Two wounds on the right side of the neck, and three wounds on the right side of his shoulder and back. I'd say the assailant was standing behind the victim—and was almost certainly right-handed.'

Richard came over and could see the sense of what

Camille was saying. The pattern of wounds suggested that the victim could only have been killed by someone who was standing behind him and striking into his neck and back holding a knife right-handed.

Richard made himself look at the face of Aslan as it lay in a pool of blood on the floor. Who was this man? What had he done to warrant such a violent death?

Richard exhaled. This was his job. To start with the end of the story: the body; the murder. And then he had to uncover the evidence that would allow him to wind time back until he could prove—categorically prove—who'd been standing above the body when the victim was killed; who it was that had wielded the knife.

Richard always made a silent promise to the victims of murder, and he made it once again now: he'd catch their killer. Whatever it took. He wouldn't rest until the killer was behind bars.

A flash of light caught Richard's eye in the far corner of the room. He turned back to look, but the little flash of light had gone as soon as it appeared. So he moved his head a fraction. No, still nothing. He moved his head back. There it was again.

There was something shiny on the floorboards he hadn't noticed before.

'What are you doing?' Camille asked as Richard went over to the wall at the end of the room and got down on his hands and knees to inspect the floor.

'What's this doing here?' he asked.

'What is it?' Camille asked as she came over to join her boss.

Richard found himself looking at a shiny drawing pin. It was just sitting there loose on the floorboards.

'It's a drawing pin.'

'And why's that of interest?'

'Didn't you see all of the witnesses out there?' Richard said.

'Of course. What about them?'

Richard turned to his partner as though he was a magician about to reveal the end of a particularly impressive trick. 'Because, I'm sure you noticed, Camille, that most of the witnesses were barefoot.'

Camille was utterly unimpressed. 'So?'

'So who would leave a drawing pin like this loose in a room where people were going about barefoot?'

Camille waited a moment before answering. 'That's it?'

'What do you mean, "that's it"?' Richard asked, irritated.

'Your big revelation? That there's a drawing pin at the scene of crime?'

'No, Camille, that's not what I said.'

'But it is. I just heard you.'

'No you didn't. You heard me say that it's *loose* on the floor. That's what's interesting. For example,' he said, standing up and indicating the rough-hewn wooden pillars and beams that made up the internal structure of the paper house, 'if I found a drawing pin in one of these wooden pillars, that would be less interesting. It would just mean that someone had pinned something to a pillar. But here?' Richard pointed at the drawing pin as it sat blamelessly on the polished hardwood floor. 'How did it get there? Who dropped it?'

'You're right,' Camille said, deadpan. 'We've got a dead body over there that's covered in knife wounds, so let's concentrate on a tiny piece of metal we've found on the floor over here. In fact, I think you're right! What if the carving knife we found by the body is a double bluff and the killer used this tiny drawing pin to stab the victim to death?'

Richard decided to ignore his subordinate entirely. Without another word, he went outside again, pulling his hankie as he went and mopping his brow. Really, he thought to himself, his life on Saint-Marie was blighted by bloody sunshine. His shirt collar chafed at his neck; the dark wool of his suit trousers stretched hot and tight across his thighs; and his suit jacket pressed heavy and scorching against his shoulders and back. Wearing a suit in the Caribbean was like living inside a bloody Corby trouser press. But what could he do? He had to wear a woollen suit. He was a Detective Inspector. And Detective Inspectors wore dark woollen suits, that's just how it was.

Richard saw that an ambulance had arrived over by the main house and paramedics were getting out a gurney.

'Very well, Camille,' he said. 'While I talk to our apparent murderer, I want you to take the remaining witnesses off. And I want you to get the paramedics to take samples of the witnesses' blood and urine.'

'You think the tea they were all drinking was maybe drugged?'

'I don't know, but that was a pretty frenzied attack, I'd be interested to know if anyone was under the influence of anything.'

Richard next turned to the youngest member of the

team. 'Fidel, I want you working the scene—but be sure to bag the drawing pin that's loose on the floor by the far wall.'

Fidel looked at his boss. 'You want me to bag a drawing pin, sir?'

'Yes.'

'That's on the floor by the far wall?'

'That's right,' Richard said again.

Before Fidel could ask why his boss wanted a drawing pin bagged for analysis, Richard turned and started heading for Julia, who was still being guarded by Dwayne.

As he approached, Richard pulled a little notebook and silver retractable pencil from an inside pocket. He clicked the lead out and said, 'Hello. My name's Detective Inspector Richard Poole. I'm investigating the murder of the man we've just found in that paper and wood structure just there.'

Richard indicated the tea house and Julia nodded slowly. She understood. Richard looked at Dwayne and he shrugged as if to say that Richard was right, the witness was indeed this slow.

Richard was at his most gentle and coaxing as he tried to find out who the woman was and what had happened. In truth, Richard didn't really have a 'gentle' or 'coaxing' side—his idea of doing either was to leave slightly longer pauses in between each of his questions—but he found his manner softened anyway as Julia was so naturally beautiful. It brought out Richard's paternal side. Or that's what he told himself. As she talked, he was able to notice how sparkling and blue her eyes were; and how her skin was bronzed by a golden tan; and how her blonde hair seemed to capture the Caribbean sunlight and radiate it back out in golden strands of light.

It turned out that the young woman's name was Julia Higgins. She was twenty-three years old and had graduated from Bournemouth University the year before having completed a degree in alternative medicine. Since then, she'd been working and travelling, but at the beginning of the year she'd come out to The Retreat for a holiday. She'd loved the experience so much—and had got on so well with the owners, Rianka and Aslan—that she'd asked if she could stay on.

Julia was surprised when they said yes, but, apparently, her timing couldn't have been better. Rianka and Aslan had been looking for help in the office for some time, so they offered Julia free lodging, a small wage—but, most importantly, free access to all of the treatments and therapies—and in return all Julia had to do was a few hours of secretarial support each day. It was an arrangement that had suited both parties and Julia had been happily working at The Retreat for the last six months.

As Julia told her story, Richard tried to work out what he found so puzzling about her. After a while, he realised what it was. Julia was clearly still numbed from the shock of what she'd done—of course she was—but she was also acting as though she was just as keen as Richard to identify the murderer. Which was odd, considering that she was the apparent murderer.

'Then tell me,' Richard finally asked, knowing it couldn't be put off any longer, 'did you kill the man we found in there?'

Julia blinked back tears as she looked deep into Richard's eyes and said, 'His name's Aslan Kennedy. And I think so.'

'You *think* so?'

Julia gulped. She then decided that maybe Richard was right to want this point clarified. 'I know so.'

'You know so?'

Julia nodded slowly, frowning.

'Then can you tell me what happened?'

'That's what I don't get. I don't know.'

'You don't know how you killed him?' Richard exchanged a quick glance with Dwayne. What was this?

Julia explained how she'd been looking forward to the Sunrise Healing, it was the only therapy Aslan still had time to lead himself.

'So we all went into the Meditation Space,' she continued.

'Meditation Space?' Richard asked.

Julia indicated the Japanese tea house. 'It's what Aslan and Rianka call that building there.'

'And who went inside with you?'

Julia thought for a moment. 'Well, Aslan…and four other hotel guests. Their names are Saskia, Paul, Ann and Ben.'

'So there were only six people in total in there?'

'That's right,' Julia said. 'The five of us plus Aslan when he locked us inside.'

Richard caught Dwayne's eye, both thinking the same thing.

'I'm sorry,' Richard said. 'He locked you in?'

'That's right,' Julia said, puzzled. 'It's a Yale lock. You know, one of those latches that closes itself. And Aslan locked it before we all sat down. He said he didn't want us to be disturbed.'

'I see,' Richard said making a note in his book. 'And then what happened?'

'Well,' Julia said, 'we then all sat on our prayer mats and shared a cup of tea. It's a way of relaxing before the session starts. And then we put on our eyemasks and headphones and lay down on our prayer mats. Although Aslan tends to stay sitting up, cross-legged. He's far more advanced in reaching an autogenic state than the rest of us.'

'I see,' Richard said, not really seeing anything at all. 'And what's an autogenic state?'

'It's a state of perfect relaxation, and it's what the Sunrise Healing's all about. You lie down, put on some headphones and an eye mask and the idea is to let your mind wander as the sounds of nature and the rays of sunlight overwhelm you. It's like being plugged into a recharging station. You wake up half an hour later full of energy. But this time, the next thing I knew, I was standing over Aslan's body holding a knife…I killed him.'

As Julia was saying this, she lifted her bloodied hand and looked at it as if she couldn't understand how it was attached to her body.

Richard noticed that Julia was holding up her left hand.

'Tell me,' he said, as though it wasn't of much consequence, 'are you left-handed?'

'That's right,' Julia said, puzzled by the question. 'Why?'

Richard smiled blandly. 'No reason.'

'It was like an out of body experience. I could see myself with the knife…but if I'm honest, I don't actually remember the moment. You know…I was just standing there, the knife in my hand. And that poor man was at my feet…not moving…!'

Julia was overwhelmed by her memories and started to weep. Richard flashed a panicked look at Dwayne. What was he supposed to do now?

Dwayne stepped in.

'Hey. We don't have to do this now. We can take you in, get you a lawyer. Take your statement later.'

Julia turned to Dwayne with a look of gratitude, and she wiped her tears from her cheek.

'No,' Julia said, after a moment's thought. 'You have to know what happened. I owe that to Aslan.'

Richard was frankly baffled. Since when did self-confessed killers feel they owed anything to the corpse they'd just created? Dwayne looked over at his boss and shrugged that maybe they should carry on.

'Okay,' Richard said. 'But don't worry. Only a couple of questions, then we'll be done.'

In short order, Richard got the remaining details. Julia was able to explain how she had no particular grudge against Aslan. In fact she liked him. Which was why she was stunned to discover that she'd just killed him. What's more, she not only hated knives, she had no idea where the knife came from that she'd just used to kill Aslan, or how she'd managed to smuggle it into the Meditation Space.

In fact, Richard had to conclude, Julia seemed no less baffled by the murder than he was.

'So, to sum up,' Richard said checking over the notes he'd taken. 'You say you have no motive—you have no idea where the knife came from—you don't know how you got it into the Meditation Space with you—you have no clear memory of actually killing the victim—but you'd nonethless like to confess to his murder?'

Julia looked at Richard.

'But I have to. It was me. I killed him.'

Richard looked at Dwayne. Dwayne looked at Richard. Oh well, a confession was a confession. Dwayne got out his handcuffs and started to bind them to Julia's wrists. As he did this, he cautioned her.

'Julia Higgins, I'm arresting you on suspicion of murder. You do not have to say anything, but it may harm your defence if you do not mention, when questioned, something which you later rely on in court. Anything you do say may be given in evidence.'

'But before you go, can I ask you one last question?' Richard said.

'Of course.'

'Do you know why there's a drawing pin on the floor of the Meditation Space?'

Julia didn't really understand the question.

'What drawing pin?'

So that was the end of that.

As Dwayne led Julia off, Richard took a moment to look about himself. The old plantation owner's house that was now the main hotel building sat in a sea of manicured lawns, and wouldn't have looked out of place in the French Quarter of New Orleans. It was all wrought-iron balconies and horizontal planks of white-painted wood. But Richard also noted the other structures that were dotted around the hotel's grounds. There was what looked like a red and gold Shinto shrine off in one clearing; a colonnade of vine-entwined Corinthian pillars straight out of Ancient Greece in another; and, up on a bluff that overlooked the sparkling sea, there appeared to be a Thai temple, with sharply sloped roofs in copper green.

It was all very strange and incongruous to Richard's mind. As for the hotel's guests, Richard could see that they'd apparently all vanished into thin air, although—now he was looking—he could see a clump of them down on the beach looking back at him.

Camille came over from the house and Richard went to meet her.

'Okay,' Camille said. 'I've sent Rianka—the wife—to her room and I've said I'll go to her as soon as I can. As for the other witnesses, they're off getting changed into their normal clothes. I've then told them to meet by the ambulance so we can take samples.'

'Good work. Thank you.'

'But what did Julia say? Is she the murderer?'

'Oh yes. She's made a full confession.'

Camille looked at Richard and shifted her weight onto one hip, a suspicious look slipping into her eyes.

'And yet…?'

'I don't know, it's just she didn't really make a very good fist at explaining the murder.'

'She didn't?'

'No. For example, she didn't say she had any reason to want to kill the deceased. In fact, she said how much she liked him. And she claimed she not only hadn't seen the knife before that she used to kill him, but she had no idea where it even came from.'

'But she's the murderer, of course she'd say that. She's lying.'

'I know. But seeing as she's already confessed to killing him, why bother to lie that she doesn't know what her motive was, what her means were or what her opportunity was?'

Camille could see the logic of what Richard was saying.

'And she's also left-handed,' Richard said.

'She is?'

'Or so she says.'

'Maybe she's trying to trick you.'

'Maybe.'

Camille knew her boss well. 'You don't think she did it, do you?'

'I don't know what I think—but it's definitely not stacking up. Not yet. Not if she can't provide us with a decent means, motive and opportunity. And there's something else as well.' Richard paused a moment, and then turned back to face the Japanese tea house. 'It's this tea house. Because Julia also said Aslan locked her and the others inside it before they started their meditation.'

'So?'

Richard looked at his partner. 'Well, it's obvious, isn't it?'

Camille refused to be drawn, so Richard explained for her.

'Because who in their right mind would allow themselves to be locked inside a room with four other potential witnesses before committing murder?'

Camille considered this a moment and then said, 'Oh. I see what you mean.'

'Precisely. Why not kill him in the dead of night? Or when he's on his own?'

Richard looked over at the Meditation Space again.

'If you ask me, there's something about that tea house that's important. Something we haven't realised yet. Either because of how it's made—or where it's located—but the victim had to be killed inside it in broad daylight in front of a load of other potential witnesses. Why?'